LET'S KILL THE TEACHER

ALAN DENT

By the same author

IS THAT YOU MR CLOONEY? 2008

GOD'S LABORATORIES 2012

LET'S KILL THE TEACHER

ALAN DENT

First published October 2012
As by S. Kadison ISBN 978-1-291-01483-9
This reprint as by Alan Dent March 2021

© Alan Dent

ISBN 978-1-913144-25-8

Cover : susslich – Ruth Murray

PENNILESS PRESS PUBLICATIONS
Website : www.pennilesspress.co.uk/books

CONTENTS

KATIE JAMESON

Every Friday and Saturday the streets of the little town filled with drinkers. The young women wore flimsy tops and pelmet skirts, even in the most biting weather. The young men, in a display of macho resilience, strode around in shirt sleeves, barking and laughing joylessly; failing to reason that if the women could expose their flesh to the chill, it could hardly be proof of masculinity. The pubs were crammed and noisy with musak. In the cheap curry houses and low-grade pizzerias the waiters didn't have time to blink. As evening declined into night the atmosphere gained a hint of threat. The dark police vans waited on the corners. Inevitably the sirens wailed, there was a scuffle, people were yanked and bundled to the cells. So it went , week after week, like a lathe set to run at a regular rate.

Matterface seldom went into town. It was too young, raucous and threatening. He liked his local where he could lean against the corner bar , slowly pour five pints into his rotund belly and hold forth, confident his education and quick temper would prevent contradiction. Everybody knew not to cross him. When John Vernon told him his views on economics were tosh, he threatened to break his teeth. He was one of those men who quickly flip into irrational, exaggerated reactions to the merest perceived slight. A challenge to his opinions was fended off with the violence of man fighting for his life. One Saturday, however, at a loose end, he went early to the *Dog* where, years ago, a group of bikers used to gather. He was still a motorcyclist; in good weather he would head for the hills and could take a bend at reckless speed or rev up to a hundred and twenty on a long stretch; but since he lost control on a left-hander, smashed through a hedge and ended in a shallow river his hip broken and his bike demolished, he'd become more cautious. It was a nostalgic visit. He was sentimental. The old days. The camaraderie, hard drinking and fights. But the pub was no longer a rendez-vous. It was quiet and served a small, polite constituency. He swigged a quick, whetting pint and going out into the yet sparsely peopled street saw ahead a figure he recognised at once. Guilty about following, he slinked close to the buildings, hurrying to catch up. It was Watt all right, hand in hand with a blonde on tottering heels, twenty years his junior. He followed till they slipped into a little trattoria, then caught a taxi home thinking all the while of the advantage he might gain.

7

On Monday he was up early and in that near-frantic rush which was his way of dealing with the demands of work, panted and sweated around the house before dropping heavily into the seat and driving to school. In the corridor he came across the despised Katie Jameson. A somewhat nervous but ambitious young woman he loathed her as he did all subordinates.

"You haven't shown me those lesson plans yet," he said abruptly.

"I told you, Mick, the union says I don't have to."

"And I say you do. Today or I'll flatten you."

He wagged his stubby finger in her face and waddled away as fast as his bulk would allow. He was pleased with himself for having threatened her and he liked the shock and fear on her face. In his classroom he met Lou Wiper, pale, sullen, defensive she looked as though she'd passed a depressing weekend.

"I just gave it to Katie," he said.

"What did you say?"

"I said I'd lay her out if I didn't get those plans."

"She'll go to the boss."

He stared at his accomplice.

"No need to worry about him."

"We should take a grievance."

"For what?"

"The meeting. She said we were incompetent."

"Did she?"

"I heard her."

"Okay. We'll take a grievance."

Later, Matterface knocked on Watt's door. The muffled call made his heart leap. He hated being summoned. Having to wait enraged him. He wanted to barge in. Why should he give way to a younger, lesser man?

Watt was at his desk, his flimsy, gold glasses halfway down his nose, the usual wad of papers in front of him.

"Morning, Mick. Sit down."

Matterface had an impulse to respond:

"Do you think I'm going to stand to talk to a runt like you?"

Watt finished reading his page.

"Sorry, Mick. What can I do for you?"

"Katie Jameson."

"Sorry?"

"We need rid."

"Why's that, Mick?"

"Useless."

"Brent seems to think she's done well since we promoted her."

"He's a wimp."

"Mick, I have to object to you talking about a colleague in those terms."

"You're wasting your breath."

"I have to stop you there, Mick."

"I was in town on Saturday."

Sweat ran slowly down Matterface's temples like rain descending a window. His face was flushed. Watt blinked, unhooked his glasses and took his chin in his hands.

"What are you saying?"

"I was in town. I saw you nipping into that little Italian on Brunswick Square. Good was it?"

"Very good. You should try it."

"I don't eat out. Not much fun on your own."

"No."

"Wife enjoy it?"

"Sorry?"

"Mrs Watt. Is she partial to Italian?"

"She wasn't with me. She was unwell."

"No, I didn't think it was her."

"Who's that, Mick?"

"The woman on your arm."

"Oh, you mean my daughter!"

"I've met your daughter."

"Have you?"

"I've met her. More than once. She's a brunette."

"She is. Naturally. She dyes it. They all do these days. She dyes it peroxide."

"She's tall."

"Sorry?"

"Your daughter. She's a tall girl. She's taller than you. She must be over six feet."

"That's right. She's tall. She's a big lass."

"I'd know her anywhere."

"It must be a year since you've seen her."

"I've a mind for faces, for demeanours. I'd know her. I'd pick her out in a thousand."

"That's amazing."

"Mrs Watt better?"

"Sarah? Call her Sarah. She doesn't stand on ceremony. Yes, just a tummy bug. She's fine."

"That's good. I'm pleased to hear that. I must mention it to her next time we meet."

"That's kind."

"Anyway. Katie. I'm taking a grievance."

"Why's that?"

"She called me incompetent."

"Did she?"

"In a meeting."

"Is it minuted?"

"No. It was informal."

"That may be a problem."

"I doubt it."

"You have to give it me in writing, Mick. We have to stick to procedure. Everything above board."

"Of course. All proper and as it should be."

"It can be an unpleasant business."

"That doesn't bother me."

"Well, I'll wait for your letter then."

"I'll do it today."

"Good. That's good. No time like the present."

Matterface went to the gents and swilled cold water over his cheeks. His heart was racing in spite of his beta-blockers. His breathing was short and rapid. He rested his palms on the edge of the basin. Once, he'd been quick and strong. He was school champion at wrist-wrestling. In a fight, he used his head and knees as well as his fists. He'd never imagined he would become slow, his thighs would tighten and he'd pant climbing stairs. He'd never imagined either being abandoned. For twenty-three years he'd believed his wife was too weak to go, but one day he came home to find a note and her wardrobes empty. If he'd known where to find her he'd have given her a thump. His face in the mirror scared him. Swollen, florid, marked by all the signs of age, it was the face of a man who has failed. He was subject leader for English. He earned almost forty thousand. The mortgage on his big house in a village four miles from town was paid. He'd bought his wife out and struggled with the repayments. He had plenty to congratulate himself for, but the knowledge of failure ran through his veins like sap through a stem. He should have been a headteacher. He was unfairly overlooked. Men like Watt, weak men, had overtaken him. And now the profession was feminised. Young women who couldn't control a class were rising like drain-water in a flood. He was fifty-eight. How much longer would he live? Maybe he should pack it in. The stress couldn't be good for him. But as he'd done a thousand times he ran through the quick calculations: a pension of about eighteen grand and a lump sum of fifty-four. He'd be okay. He could manage. He could cut back. But his pride rebelled. His income would be lower than teachers thirty-five years younger! It was the first step to an old age of scrimping neglect. He had to go on. He would keep going to sixty-five if he had to. He would fight to his final breath to be as good as the next man and what did that mean if not earning as much and having the same status?

Despite the cooling water, the sweat was trickling again. Under his arms, his shirt was soaked. He yanked a paper towel, dabbed his face and went to find Lou Wiper.

"I've told Watt we're taking a grievance."

"Is he on our side?"

"He has to be."

"I don't get it."

Matterface stared hard at her. Her frightened look made him want to seize her throat. Such a poor accomplice! Yet he admired her vindictiveness almost as much as her subordination. He pushed his face close.

"I saw him in town. On Saturday. With his floozie. He gets in my way, I go to his wife."

"Shit!"

"We can do what we like. Let's get Jameson in a meeting this afternoon. We're all free last thing. Go and tell her to be in the office."

"What if she says no?"

"Nobody says no to me," and his face came closer, his eyes bulged, he glanced down at her cleavage, met her gaze, looked again at her exposed flesh , turned and left.

Lou Wiper knew Katie Jameson was teaching year 7. She went straight to her room, walked in without knocking and held out a paper.

"Mick wants you in a meeting in the English office at half two. Don't be late."

"What's it about?"

"What does that matter?"

"I need to know what it's about," said Jameson looking at the paper.

"Whatever it's about, you have to be there."

Jameson turned to look at the unusually silent and attentive class.

"There should be an agenda."

"It's informal."

"But what is it about, Lou? I don't understand why you can't tell me."

"Mick's called it."

"Then why didn't he come to see me?"

"He sent me."

"I'm not coming unless I know what it's about."

"You have to come."

"No I don't."

"It's non-contact time. If you don't come, Mick will have you disciplined."

"Disciplined? For what?"

"Do what you're told."

"Who's going to be at the meeting?"

"Ask Mick."

"I'm not coming."

"That's up to you, but watch out."

Wiper left. Striding the corridor, she was glad the pupils had heard. It would spread like 'flu in October. The thought of Jameson's nervous face, the little tremble of her hands as she took the paper, the sorry plea in her voice, made Wiper glad. She wanted to see her prostrate, just like Connie Egger who had to be dragged out screaming, whose nervous collapse was complete and who never came back. She and Mick had done a good job. Drip by drip they'd poisoned the cup of her confidence till she couldn't face a class. But that was nothing to what they'd do to Jameson.

"I told her," she said to him at lunch.

"What did she say?"

"She says she's not coming."

"I'll have her on a disciplinary."

"She wants an agenda."

"My arse!"

At two thirty, Matterface and Wiper were sitting in the little English

13

office with their mugs of coffee. It had once been a simple store-room but Matterface, feeling an office was in keeping with his status, threw out hundreds of books, had more shelving put up, bought a new desk and computer for himself and treated the place as his *sanctum sanctorum*. Gloomy, ill-ventilated and with a heavy oak door, a relic of the long gone days when the place was a grammar school, the room was chilly on the hottest days in August.

"She's not coming," said Wiper.

"I'll have her in the Head's office in the morning if she doesn't."

"Shall I go and look for her?"

"No."

"What's our plan?"

"Hit her with the grievance."

"First off?"

"Get the best punch in at the beginning."

"She might flounce out."

"She won't flounce while I'm around."

There came a timid knock.

"Come in!"

Jameson entered as if her presence brought with it an insupportable odour. Matterface and Wiper looked down at their papers.

"What's this about, Mick?"

"What's what about?"

"Why have you asked me to a meeting?"

"It's just a meeting."

"What about?"

"Sit down."

"Is there an agenda?"

"No."

"There should be."

"Who says?"

"It's good practice."

"Who says?"

"Union advice is…."

"I'm in a union."

"I know. But I'm not staying unless…"

"Sit down."

"I will if you tell me what the meeting's…"

"Sit down, for god's sake."

He'd pulled off his glasses and thumped the table.

"I don't have to put up with that kind of behaviour."

" Who's running this department?"

"I'm not questioning your position."

"No, you're not. We're taking a grievance against you."

"What?"

"I've told Tom Watt today."

"A grievance."

"You said we were incompetent," said Wiper.

"When?"

"In the meeting."

"What meeting?"

"Departmental," said Matterface.

"I didn't."

"You did. We both heard you," said Wiper.

"I didn't say that."

"We both heard you," said Matterface. "We're taking a grievance."

"You're questioning our professionalism," said Wiper.

"It's slander," said Matterface.

"You're slandering us. That's a legal matter," said Wiper.

"I'm not staying."

"You can go now," said Matterface putting on his glasses.

"What about the meeting."

"The meeting's over."

"You've got the information," said Wiper.

When Jameson had left, she turned to Matterface. Sweat was dripping from his chin.

"Well, what do you think?"

"What's to think?"

"She'll bring in the union."

"Screw the union."

"We'll have to synchronise our stories."

"There's nothing to fear. We'll have her."

They submitted their letters and a few days later Watt called them in one by one. The union's local official had written asking to see minutes of the meeting.

"I told you, it was informal."

"We need evidence, Mick."

"We heard it."

"That's not enough."

"Isn't it?"

"It might not be."

"It should be."

"Why?"

"You wouldn't question my word would you?"

"Not me, Mick. Her union."

"They don't decide."

"In a grievance, the governors decide, Mick"

"You appoint them."

"Not all of them."

"They're in your pocket."

"I don't think I like that, Mick."

"It's true."

"The union will fight hard. If there's no evidence…"

"I told you, we heard her."

The union officer requested a meeting. They gathered in Watt's office at the end of a rainy afternoon. She was a big, bulky woman in her fifties, one of those radicals who had known the swirling expectations of the sixties and been battered by the eddying waves of reaction in her thirties, but who had stayed true to her vision of a sunny democracy whose beneficent light reached even into the workplace. A hard-working maths teacher, running a department and leading a year as pastoral head, she was overwhelmed and had elaborated a slow, diligent, unflustered manner which allowed her to keep going seventeen hours a day; though the black moons beneath her eyes and the greyness of her complexion spoke of lack of sleep and fresh air. For Jameson, who sat beside her, the meeting might have been an appearance before a hanging judge, but for Martha Franklin, it was routine. She knew the school and had once caught Watt out badly: he'd changed comments on performance management documents to justify blocking promotions.

Matterface sat opposite her. He despised her instantly. Overweight, frumpy, she reminded him of his disappeared wife, except she exuded confidence, even nonchalance. He wanted her to fear him. He would have liked to have seen on her features the sparrow's twitchiness he saw in Jameson. He suspected she would be competent and articulate which goaded him to insult her. After all, what could anybody do to him? What he knew kept him safe.

"There seems some doubt," she said, "over the accusation."

"Both Mick and Lou heard the comment," said Watt.

"But they're hardly independent."

"It's a matter of perception," said Watt. "Perhaps Katie didn't quite mean it the way it was taken."

"How else could it be taken?" said Matterface.

"What exactly is she alleged to have said?" asked Franklin.

"There's no alleged about it," said Matterface.

"We heard her," said Wiper.

"The precise form of words is important," said Franklin.

"She said we are incompetent," said Wiper.

"So, in speech marks, she said: "You are incompetent"."

"Yes."

"How do you know she was talking about both of you?"

"She was," said Matterface.

"As the meeting wasn't minuted, we've no way of getting the context. It just seems odd someone should pipe up in a meeting, a propos of not very much, "you're incompetent"."

"She did," said Wiper.

"It's slander," said Matterface.

"It's the way it's taken," said Watt.

"We can't get agreement," said Franklin. "Ms Jameson doesn't believe she said it. She certainly doesn't remember. It would be unfortunate for this to proceed to grievance. I've spoken to Ms Jameson, and though we're not prepared to admit to the form of words Mr Matterface and Ms Wiper claim, we're willing to accept they feel something was said which offended them. Ms Jameson apologizes for that. She is willing to say that anything she said which caused offence is withdrawn. Are you willing to accept that so we can find a *modus vivendi* and everyone can get on with their job?"

"I want it in writing," said Matterface.

"That's fine," said Franklin.

"I want my own apology," said Wiper.

"We'll do that. A letter to each of you and that will be the end of the matter?"

"That seems a good way forward," said Watt.

Matterface and Wiper went to his classroom. She sat on the edge of the table as he stomped about, shoving papers in his filing cabinet and generally tidying an already impeccable order.

"What do we do now?"

"That bitch!" said Matterface.

"We've agreed not to pursue it."

"We've agreed nothing."

"We turn down the letters?"

"I'll have her sacked and nothing less."

"The union woman will object."

"She's an impotent bitch. We're having our grievance."

The following day Matterface took a small, white envelope inscribed Mick, in a neat, tight hand, from his pigeon-hole. The letter read:

Dear Mick,

I am sorry if during the last departmental meeting I said anything which offended you. I didn't mean to. I hope we can now put the misunderstanding behind us and get on with teaching.

Sincerely, Katie.

He found Wiper and discovered the wording of the letter to her was identical.

"Silly cow!" he said.

He went at once to Watt.

"This is no good."

"What's the matter, Mick."

"I'm not having it."

"But she's apologised, Mick."

"She has to apologise for calling me incompetent."

"She doesn't recall that."

"I do."

"This is a way forward."

"Not for me."

"You're making me think you don't want a resolution."

"She needs to be sacked."

"People have rights. We can't just sack her willy-nilly."

"I'm taking the grievance."

"I can't stop you."

"No-one can stop me."

He recounted the interview to Wiper and she in turn went to Watt who summoned Katie Jameson. He explained to her. Pale and tense she twisted her hands in her lap.

"It would be easier if you write an apology for having called them

19

incompetent."

"But I didn't."

"Well, you don't remember."

"No, I didn't. I never said it. They're making it up."

"Why would they do that?"

"They want me sacked."

"Oh, that's getting things out of perspective!"

"Look what they did to Connie."

"Sorry?"

At Watt's bridling, she felt her confidence subside. His face took on the alertness of a stalking cat. The tight suggestion of threat sat on his shoulders, arms and hands. She was afraid to speak but she knew clearly enough what needed to be said. It was no secret. The whole school was *au courant*. Poor Connie had been driven half insane, tranquillized and referred to a psychiatrist; it had taken her two years to start to function normally. Everyone knew she was a perfectly good teacher. Mick and Lou's strategy wasn't subtle or concealed. And Watt himself was a bully. Hadn't he hunted down Aidan Richardson, put him on competency, destroyed him so his niece could apply for his job? And wasn't she now Subject Leader after only one year in the school? The corruption was blatant, yet her tongue froze. To say what everyone knew was forbidden. All speech had become a form of deception and collusion. Watt stared at her.

"She was forced out," she said, her voice cracking.

"I don't think so, Katie. I think she left on health grounds."

"But they destroyed her!" she cried.

"You'd better be careful what you say. Nobody gets destroyed here. That's not how this school works."

"Why won't they accept my apology?"

"You haven't apologised for the offence."

"I can't apologise for something I didn't do."

"Why not?"

Jameson sent long, rambling, emotionally-charged e-mails to Franklin. At every hurtful recollection, she turned on her lap-top. She had little capacity for objectivity and even less for discipline of style. The sense of the self-evident rightness of her position robbed her of the will to restraint and she fell into one of those outpourings of justified complaint which seem exaggerated and strained to those who hear them but utterly understated to those who make them. Martha Franklin sifted them and did what she could but her efforts to settle came to nothing, Jameson crumpled under the stress, was signed off and prescribed heavy doses of anti-depressants which robbed her of the ability to read or express subtle communication, and the grievance went ahead.

The Chair of the three-strong committee was Mrs Clatworthy, a small, dark, neat woman in a natty navy-blue suit. She smiled broadly at the tableful and welcomed them as if they were together to celebrate a christening. Beside Watt was his *chétive* secretary, a quick vole of a woman whose nose twitched like a hamster's and whose scrawny hand transcribed the proceedings like a machine. She looked over her flimsy glasses only when something shocked or delighted her, otherwise she might have been a recalcitrant learner on Ritalin. In addition to Franklin and Jameson were Dick Pullen, the County's HR man and the two wing committee members: Mr Greencut, a rotund, be-suited local butcher, florid in complexion and dull in speech, whose daughters were in the school and Mrs Sander, another parent-governor, over-dressed like the poor invited to society events, who met no-one's eyes and said nothing.

Wiper was first to be questioned by Franklin.

"Can you tell us exactly what Ms Jameson said in the meeting on 24th November?"

"She said I was incompetent."

"In what context?"

"No particular context."

"Everything has a context, Mrs Wiper. Nothing happens without a context. There must have been some subject under discussion."

"I don't remember."

"You don't remember what the meeting was about?"

"Not in detail. It was informal."

"How informal?"

"What do you mean?"

"Well, was it just a chat? Was there an agenda?"

"No there wasn't an agenda."

"Were the date and time decided in advance."

"I suppose so."

"And there were just the three of you?"

"Yes."

"But there are six in the department?"

"Yes."

"Why weren't the other three invited."

"I don't know."

"But you're Second in Department, Mrs Wiper. A meeting is arranged, a time and venue decided, yet three members of the department aren't invited. Isn't that a bit odd?"

"I think Mick just wanted a word with Katie."

"About what?"

"I don't know."

"Wanted a word. That sometimes means something negative, doesn't it."

"It can do."

"Was it on this occasion?"

"I can't remember."

"But you can remember that Ms Jameson called you incompetent."

"Yes, you don't forget something like that."

"Was she speaking to just you?"

"I don't think so."

"Why not?"

"The way she said it."

"What way?"

"As if she meant both of us."

"So let's try to get clear just how this alleged remark was made.

What were you talking about."

"I can't remember."

"You must remember something that was discussed."

"We talked about levels."

"What about them?"

"Making sure the sublevels were accurate."

"Is that when Ms Jameson made the alleged remark."

"It could have been."

"Mrs Wiper, you're as vague as a melting mist except over one detail. Given your recollection of the meeting is so inadequate, how can we set any store by your conviction?"

"I just remember it because it was so hurtful."

"Did Ms Jameson simply blurt out, you're incompetent!"

"More or less."

"That seems extraordinary behaviour, doesn't it."

"Her behaviour is extraordinary."

Franklin had dug out a witness. Judy Nicol had been a supply teacher in the department at the time Connie Egger suffered her breakdown. She'd submitted a written statement about systematic bullying and hearing Mick Matterface tell Connie to "go and fuck herself". No longer teaching, relaxed and pleasant, dressed in a dark green skirt and jacket she looked appropriately formal but exuded friendliness. Mrs Clatworthy questioned her. Matter-of-fact and brief she confirmed what she'd written. When Franklin got her turn she said:

"Would it be true to say, during your time here, there was a culture of bullying in the English department?"

"Yes."

"And can you be sure you heard Mr Matterface tell Mrs Egger to go and fuck herself?"

"Oh yes! I was there. I heard him."

When Wiper was asked what she thought she said:

"She was only a supply teacher. She wasn't here very long. She's not reliable."

Matterface put up a much more aggressive defence. To every question he replied, you're wasting your breath or I refuse to answer that or this isn't relevant or I heard what I heard. When Mrs Clatworthy suggested he might be a little more forthcoming he said:

"If the questions were more intelligent, Chair, I would be willing to answer them in kind."

It took three weeks for the judgement to appear. They recommended Ms Jameson should apologise for the inappropriate remark. Also, she should attend a course designed to improve her "communication skills". External mediation to improve relationships in the department should be tried and Mr Matterface and Mrs Wiper should accept the intervention of a member of the Senior Leadership Team in their department until working relationships were restored.

Franklin advised Jameson to write the apologies: it would be worth it to get the mediation. Once Matterface and Wiper received their letters, they went to Watt and refused all intervention. Franklin made angry calls to Watt and Dick Pullen, but the protocol was voluntary. They were within their rights. When Jameson returned to work they ignored her. She lasted a fortnight. The doctor prescribed more Prozac.

Recently, the school has undergone an Ofsted. It was deemed outstanding, and in the paragraph on senior management is written: *under the leadership of a very able Headteacher, the school is exceptionally well managed.* Its anti-bullying policy was also singled out for praise. Tom Watt has been awarded a CBE, Mrs Wiper promoted to Advanced Skills Teacher, and Matterface temporarily made Assistant Head.

Katie Jameson spent six weeks in a psychiatric unit. Her first suicide attempt was unsuccessful.

MOZZARELLA PASTA PENNE

Eddie Windle had no interest in horse racing, but Neville Delafield, one of his fellow commercial travellers, was in the bookies every day. Sometimes he had spectacular wins, three hundred or five hundred pounds, and when Eddie thought of his thousand a year salary, he was tempted to join in. But he was influenced by his wife who considered gambling the work of the Devil and the desire to gain something for nothing a sign of lack of character. He didn't agree with her. If he'd imagined for a minute he could make regular money in the bookies he'd've been by Neville's side like his shadow. He tried a little experiment: every morning he turned to the racing page and picked a horse. In his diary he kept a record of what he'd've won or lost if he'd staked a shilling. After three weeks he was eleven shillings down. He was pleased with himself. It was scientific. Eddie put great faith in science though he knew nothing about it having left school at thirteen to take a job as a flour boy in the Co-op. He conveyed his results to Neville.

"An unlucky run," he said.

"You can't argue with that," said Eddie. "It's proof."

"Proof of what?" said Neville, lifting his pint.

"That if I'd put a shilling on a horse a day I'd be ten bob worse off."

Eddie stirred the milk into his coffee. He didn't drink, partly because his wife thought alcohol the work of the Devil but mainly because he'd read scientific evidence of the damage it could do.

"Or proof you picked the wrong horses."

"I did what you said. I studied form."

"Yes, but there's a secret to it, Eddie. Call it gambler's intuition."

"I don't believe in intuition," said Eddie. "I believe in science."

"Really? Take a look at that brunette by the window. Does your science tell you she's game?"

Eddie glanced at the young woman. She was one of those girls who convey potential availability in every gesture. Slender, well groomed and very pretty Eddie felt a pang of jealousy in seeing her; he would like to be married to a girl like that. He admitted to himself Avril was

25

a let down. She was a diligent housewife. She washed, cooked, scrubbed, cleaned, but she wasn't exciting. She had no wish to excite him as a man. He felt she made love to him perfunctorily. A girl like that would be different. Of course, she was fifteen years younger than Avril but he wondered if a fling with such a girl might not be worth the gamble.

"Very nice," he said.

"Yes. Anyone can see that. But is she game?"

"I'd say so."

"How?"

"I don't know. Just something about her."

"You're right Eddie. She'd drop 'em for tuppence. Intuition. That's what you need when you're chasing women or backing horses."

"Intuition can let you down."

"Let's see."

Neville quaffed his pint and went over to the girl. He offered her a Peter Stuyvesant which he lit with the silver lighter his wife had given him for their tenth anniversary. He sat down opposite her and within minutes they were laughing and Eddie noticed how she was giving little signals of willingness: touching her heavy thigh with her fingertips, adjusting her thin, white blouse to draw attention to her rich breasts. He drank his tepid coffee feeling demoralised. Not that Neville was any better with women than him. He could have gone over to the girl just as confidently, though he wouldn't have offered her a cigarette: Avril thought them the work of the Devil and he'd read an article about what they can do to your lungs. But he could have seduced her just as well as Neville. When they got up to leave Neville, with his arm around her slim waist, turned and winked. Eddie smiled and nodded. It was a pleasant afternoon in early April. Where would he take her? Maybe they'd do it in the back of his car. He pictured the girl, her light grey skirt pulled up round her tiny waist, her tights and knickers on the floor, her blouse wide open and her bra awry, her head thrown back as Neville humped away. He had three calls to make. How he wished he was with a girl like that, sinking his hard cock in her as she made helpless little cries of pleasure. But where would he take her? Maybe somewhere quiet by the river where he'd do it in the open air. Neville certainly knew how to make a gamble pay off. Eddie left a shilling for his coffee and walked to his car. A girl of eighteen or so in a mini skirt passed him. He smiled but she ignored him. Anyway, he only had three calls.

It was not long after that Neville asked him if he wanted to go to Catterick races the following Saturday.

"I've got a mate who works in the stables. Tipped me off. We go for a yankee we could clean up."

"What's a yankee?" said Eddie.

"Six doubles four trebles and an accumulator, but don't worry about that. The point is the horses. They're certs, Eddie. Certs."

"You can't be certain about race horses, Nev. That's not scientific."

"Was I scientific about Myra?"

"You were lucky."

"Not kiddin' I was lucky, Eddie. Goes like a bunny. Cunt like a mouse's ear-hole."

Eddie wondered if she'd be coming to Catterick but he didn't like to ask. Maybe she was one of those girls who do it with two men. Or maybe he could grab her backside when Neville wasn't looking and get his share.

"I'll have to square it with Avril."

"Tell her it's a football match."

"I'll tell her it's the races. I'll persuade her."

"Make it easy on yourself. Never tell the truth to women. They don't like it."

Avril exploded.

"Waste of good money."

"It's a day out."

"For you."

"You can come."

He thought at once of the girl in the grey skirt. Surely at Catterick races there'd be plenty of girls looking for a bit of fun.

"What would I want with gambling? Anyway, who'd take care of the children?"

"Your dad'd have 'em."

"Think I'm asking my dad to look after the children while you go throwing our money away on horses. You're a damn fool."

That was strong language for Avril who thought swearing the work of the Devil. Eddie had read an article that said swearing could be good for you by releasing tension. But he never swore in front of his wife.

"You could come. You could go round the shops for a few hours."

"Go. Go and be done with it."

And she stormed out.

Eddie drove so that Neville could have a drink, but he didn't have one, he had seven pints and three whiskies. Their first horse came in at three to one. The second won at evens. The third, a six to one shot, beat the field by two lengths. Eddie was amazed.

"How much will we get if the last one wins?"

Neville was scribbling figures in the margins of *The Sporting Life* and mumbling drunkenly.

"Two thousand six hundred. No. Hang on, hang on. Three thousand…"

"That can't be right, Neville."

But it was. The last horse, *Amber Eyes*, was third till the final stretch.

"Don't bother," said Neville, "we've won anyway. We've done okay. Look at that. Could you shag the arse off it."

Eddie turned and saw a little blonde girl, about nineteen, with a skirt so short as she bent to pick up her bag, her white knickers covering her neat little backside were on show. Surely it was a come on. Surely she'd spotted him and thought he looked her type. When she looked over he smiled. She turned away with a disdainful toss of her head.

"Come on, you bugger!" Neville was shouting as he whacked the fence with his rolled paper.

Amber Eyes was neck and neck with *Mercury's Orbit*. There were four furlongs to go. Eddie felt his heart pounding heavily. The riders were working their whips and the horses looked as if they were running from a mushroom cloud. Eddie couldn't tell which one was

28

winning.

"Oh fuck it!" said Neville.

Eddie heard over the Tannoy that is was a photo finish.

"We might have done it, Nev."

"Fuck it! That fucking jockey. Why didn't he whip the bastard harder?"

"Let's wait for the result. Don't get worked up."

"Photo fucking finish," said Neville. "I need a drink."

He pulled a flask in a leather case from his pocket and swigged.

"Hey. She's giving me the icy eye-ball that randy bitch."

"Who?" said Eddie, looking round.

"Blonde. Look at the tits on that. School milk for you."

Eddie stared at the blonde girl who didn't look their way at all.

"You're imagining it, Nev."

"Imaginin'? Wait till she's sucking my cock in the back of your car."

The result of the photo was announced. *Amber Eyes* had won at eight to one. Neville threw his paper in the air.

"We've fuckin' done it, Eddie. How much did I say?"

"Three thousand. Three thousand odd."

"I'm gonna have a word with angel tits over here."

Eddie was left on his own amongst the crowd. He watched Neville who approached, on his unsteady legs, the girl and her friend, a tall, rather gawky lass with short, black hair, a big nose and spots. He was obviously telling her about the win. Why hadn't he thought of doing that? Within seconds he had his arm round the blonde's shoulder. He looked round at Eddie and gave a little jerk of his head in the direction of the bar. Eddie followed them noticing how thin the legs of the tall girl were.

"This is my mate, Eddie. We work together. We've just won five grand between us, girls. You're in for a good time."

The little blonde laughed, showing her horsey teeth, while her pal lowered her eyes bashfully as Eddie acknowledged her.

"Five?" said Eddie.

29

"Ah, what the hell. Thousands. Enough to look after these two lovely ladies for the afternoon in grand style."

The girls drank vodka and lime. Neville was on double whiskies and Eddie had a Britvic orange. It turned out they were secretaries in a warehousing and transport company. The blonde, June, was engaged to a fireman who was on shift. Dot didn't have a boyfriend. According to June she was shy. When Eddie and Neville stood next to one another at the urinal, Neville said:

"Let's get a hotel."

"What?"

"Two double rooms. Shag the arses off 'em while they're pissed, buy 'em a meal and fuck off."

"If we're back too late Avril'll smell a rat."

"Give her a ring. Tell the her the car won't start."

Neville collected the winnings from the crestfallen bookie: three thousand eight hundred and seventy two pounds, four shillings and threepence. He counted out the notes into two piles as the girls looked on, making ooo-er faces.

"Here, buy yourself a nice dress," and Neville shoved a fiver inside June's bra as she made a mouth as round as a doughnut and let out a whoop.

Eddie had to drive till they found a nice hotel. They booked in as Mr and Mrs Collins and Mr and Mrs Sinclair, names that Eddie asserted would arouse no suspicion. Neville paid in cash from the great wad of limp notes he drew from his pocket.

"Good day at the races," he said to the receptionist. "I'll buy you a drink later."

Eddie and Dot's room was big with a window looking out over fields. Dot sat on the end of the double bed covered with a yellow eiderdown, her knees together and her shoulders hunched.

"I've just got to make a phone call," he said, "won't be a minute."

He told Avril the car wouldn't start but she didn't believe him. It was only a year old. The company kept it in tip-top condition. Did he think she was stupid? She knew what he was up to. He was drunk. She knew Neville all right. They were both drunk. That was what he was doing. Waiting to sober up.

"Yes," he said to her, "you're right. You're quite right."

She told him he should be ashamed of himself. She was at home looking after the children and he was throwing money away and getting drunk. He was no better than a spiv. And how much had he lost?

"No, Avril, we've won."

"What do you mean won? How much?"

"Thousands."

"Don't be stupid. You're drunk."

She banged the phone down.

As he went back up stairs (he never took a lift because he'd read somewhere that using your thigh muscles sent the blood back to your heart and kept it healthy) he was thinking how nice it would be to be married to a woman who responded sunnily. Why couldn't Avril ease up? Why was she always as taut as a corset and spiky as a chestnut's husk? She could have listened to him and he could have explained that he had one thousand nine hundred and thirty six pounds in his pocket. They'd be able to buy a house. No more rent. Somewhere with a garden, a bathroom and some space for the kids. It could have been a conversation as sweet as lavender. But their conversations were never like that. If he laughed at Al Read on the radio, she said it was stupid. If he bought a new tie she said he had no taste. If he said the pork was particularly good at Sunday dinner she said it was tough and tasteless. If he bought a new record by Frank Sinatra she said he couldn't sing and she preferred Paul Robeson. Sometimes he would say the opposite of what he thought:

"These apples are mealy? Where'd you get 'em?"

"Mealy? They're as crisp as new notes " she'd snap, and he was glad that, for once, they agreed.

The truth was, if he'd had anywhere else to go, he would never have gone home. Not even the children were enough. Then the thought came to him that he did have somewhere else to go. He had nearly two thousand quid. It was his. You could buy a three-bedroom semi in Hardleton for that. He could put his foot down: either she changed her ways or he'd live alone. But there was no taming this shrew. He knew well enough she couldn't change. That was the source of his despair. She could no more be straightened out than a tree on a promontory battered by the wind and bent nearly double as it grew.

Avril was happy when she was miserable. She enjoyed disagreeing with people. She liked to be unpleasant. That was the horrible truth and he had to live with it or use the money in his pockets to escape.

Dot was in exactly the same position on the edge of the bed. Eddie envied Neville the long blonde hair, lovely breasts, full lips, strong thighs, flat stomach, tight bum and flirty disposition of June. He almost thought it would be better giving up all idea of getting into bed with the morose and unresponsive Dot.

"Cup o' tea?" he said.

"No thanks." She smiled.

He sat next to her and put his hand on her knee. She didn't move. He twisted his neck to bring his lips up against hers. They were thin and immobile but warm. That was something. He tried to press his mouth on hers so she'd have to reciprocate but she simply let him. He pushed her back gently and climbed on top of her. She was skinny. Her breasts were like those of a twelve year-old. He went on kissing her as if there was a passion between them but soon he thought it was hopeless. The only thing was to get her clothes off. He rolled her on her side to unzip her black dress which he pulled down over her bony shoulders. Her bra was white with a lace pattern. One of those trite items of underwear the big stores sell. As he took it off it seemed to him it didn't belong to her. It was as if it were still on sale in the shop. Anyone's bra if they handed over the money. He threw it on the floor and started sucking her breast. She lay back as passive as if the doctor were listening to her chest. Her nipple had grown hard in his mouth. Well, that was excitement. So he carried on. He pulled her dress off over her legs. She was wearing black frilly knickers. He thought it odd. Avril always wore matching colours. He tugged them off. She had a thick copse of black pubic hair. Its dark profusion excited him. It was reminiscent of undergrowth and made him think of his days in the woods as a boy when a group of them would idle hours away blissfully, and the calm they found among the trees and bushes, the odour of decay in autumn and of renewal in spring; odours so specific to place they were different in the woods by the church where the bluebells huddled thickly in every clearing and the bigger woods by the derelict farm where the dry scent of the clayey earth mingled with the smell of the cows in the neighbouring field, wrapped themselves round the excitements of unexpected encounters with girls whose cheeks were burned by the wind and whose bodies were as slender and lissom as saplings. It made him think she should be a passionate, sexy, writhing, sweating woman; but she lay, her head turned towards the window and didn't make a sound, as he slipped his finger inside her. She didn't look at him.

"Do you want me to carry on?" he said.

"If you like."

"If you like. It's your choice."

He felt suddenly utterly ludicrous. He was fully dressed in a hotel room in Yorkshire on a Saturday afternoon with a young woman he knew only as Dot and who he'd met not much more than a couple of hours earlier, his finger inserted between her legs with all the intimacy of a gynaecological examination, trying to convince himself it was an exciting seduction of the kind he imagined taking place between Neville and June.

"I don't mind," she said.

"Perhaps we should forget it."

"Carry on. If you like."

He stood up and took off his clothes. When he lay on top of her he tried to kiss her mouth but she turned her head away. He kissed and bit her neck, sucked her nipples and worked his fingers inside her. She was warm and wet enough. It was real in that sense.

" I haven't got a johnny," he said.

"You'll have to pull out."

He slipped inside her and it was good to feel her tight, lubricated flesh against his cock. It was very nice. Really very nice. So he started to pump vigorously.

"Don't forget to pull out," she said.

Her arms were splayed across the bed, her face turned aside, but after a few minutes she turned to look at him, straight in the eyes. She was biting her lip like a little child unsure of her ground or seeking forgiveness; she raised her eyebrows inquisitively. Was she deliberately humiliating him? He felt terribly alone, even more alone than making love to the brittle Avril. But the pleasure kept him going. It was an odd little contest between the intense sensations focused on his cock and a powerful desire to escape, to be as far as possible from the demeaning experience of looking into the face of a thoroughly disinterested and detached woman while he was naked and inside her. But he said to himself he just wanted to come. He just wanted to work off his hard-on. He was raised on his arms, thrusting away, looking into her pale, impassive face whose forehead was dotted with pustular acne . When he felt himself on the verge, he lost the will to withdraw; but she pushed against his chest and twisted her hips violently to the right so his dick sprang free and his spunk shot out in two long arcs to land on her white flank.

"Have you got a handkerchief?" she said.

He went to his suit and took from his trouser pocket the handkerchief Avril had carefully ironed into a thick little square. He told her there was no need to iron them; he could fold them himself and they'd be neat enough; but she insisted and on Sunday evenings would stand at the board for three hours flattening towels, sheets, underpants and knickers. It was a good quality handkerchief his mother had bought him one Christmas with his initial embroidered in the corner in a red flourish. He handed it to the girl who flicked it open and wiped herself, then screwed it up and wiped some more.

"Thank you."

He took it from her feeling stupid and exposed. His half erect cock was throbbing and giving tiny jerks. He noticed her looking at it and he tried to read her expression but all he could see was blankness, as if her emotions had been wiped out. She pulled her legs round and sat on the edge of the bed, her thin back with the spots across her shoulders all too visible. He found her unattractive. She was an odd creature both physically and mentally. He felt the sticky handkerchief in his hand and wondered if he should throw it away; but if he did, Avril would be sure to miss it and there'd be awkward questions, so he put it back in his trouser pocket and reminded himself to wash it before Avril got to it. Without speaking to her, which he felt was rude and sorry but inevitable as he had nothing to say, he went into the little bathroom and washed himself. There was no doubt he was satisfied, to an extent. That post-ejaculation release had come over him and he felt better for it, but at the same time it was awful. There was a girl on the bed he felt might be some kind of psychiatric case and he didn't want to see her or speak to her again. He'd have to be polite. They'd go and meet up with Neville and June. But it was truly terrible and he felt more isolated even than after sex with Avril when she always accused him of messing the bed, tore off the sheets and put on new ones, even if it was after midnight, and slept with her back to him. He wished he'd had nothing to do with the girl. He could have stayed in the bar. He might have met some friendly, chatty girl who he could have got on with.

He went back into the bedroom. Dot was dressed, sitting in the chair by the bed, smoking. All he had to hide himself was his towel. He gathered his clothes and was about to go into the bathroom to get dressed.

"What you going in there for?"

"Get dressed."

"Might as well do it here. I've seen everything."

He looked at her and he saw that hard stare she'd fixed on him while they were on the bed. He tried to dress without letting her see his cock and balls.

"Can you do me a favour?" she said.

"What's that?" he said, as he pulled on his trousers.

"Can you lend me two hundred quid?"

He went on getting dressed and didn't look at her.

"Two hundred quid," he said, "what for?"

"Medical expenses."

"Are you ill?"

He stood facing her, trying to pull himself to his full height and appear authoritative and responsible like a headmaster dressing down a wayward pupil, but it was difficult given he'd just rubbed himself off in her cunt and he felt his shoulders hunching and his stomach muscles giving way.

"I might be."

"Two hundred quid is a lot of money."

"You've just won two thousand."

"Not quite."

"I won't bother you any more."

He was about to accuse her of blackmail, to call her a vicious, low creature, but he was in no position. She was staring at him with her impassive, dull expression. Her grey face and her narcotic eyes

35

scared him. She didn't have the usual feelings and responses. She was a cold, machine of a creature. He wished he'd never seen her. Was this just the beginning? Was she going to come after him and take money off him week after week? He imagined himself being cleaned out.

"I can give you fifty quid," he said.

"Is that all I'm worth," she replied, drawing on her Number Six.

"You don't need to pay it back. Fifty quid and were quits."

"That won't go far. Make it two hundred and you'll hear no more from me."

He had no doubt she was capable of something monstrous. She might turn up at the house and introduce herself to Avril. She was demented enough. Hadn't she just let him shag her, after all, when there was not a ripple of pleasure or passion in it for her? But the thought came to him that he'd just shagged her even though she'd been as absent as a neglectful father. Was he as demented as her? He quickly smothered the thought with the downy pillow of self-justification: it was different for a man. Hadn't he asked her and hadn't she agreed? A man could do no more than ask. If she'd said no he would have stopped. She was worse than a whore, at least they asked for the money first, or so he'd heard. She tricked him. Like Avril. She too was all willingness until they were married and the children were born, even if she enjoyed intimacy no more than she enjoyed jazz, which he was allowed to listen to only when she was out. Then one day she said to him: "You can keep your hands off me if you don't mind." There was a long dry spell, a desert of misery and humiliation he trudged through under the torturing sun of young women whose breasts bounced enticingly and whose knickers flashed like a blade at midday when they uncrossed their legs, till at last he lay he his hand on her belly as she was about to go to sleep and she said: "Be quick about it. I want to be up early." They fell into a routine: once a fortnight or so he put his arm round her in bed, she stroked his cock for a few minutes, he pulled on a condom, climbed on her and worked up a quick rhythm while she lay as still as anaesthetised and he came as fast as he could. She pulled down her nightie, turned over and went to sleep. He'd been badly gulled. Two hundred pounds after all, wasn't so bad compared to what living with Avril cost him: not the money, but the injury, the constant consciousness that he'd let himself walk into her trap and that for no more than a few months of relatively pleasant sex, he had a sinner's portion of penance as she snapped at him, mocked him and made him crawl as a supplicant for entrance to her cunt.

He knotted his tie and pulled it into position in front of the mirror.

"Okay," he said.

He counted out two hundred pounds in fivers. She took it, put it in her bag, got up and opened the door.

"Aren't you going to wait?"

"For what?"

"For me. We'll go and meet Neville and June."

Her eyes looked into his for five seconds. Her face showed no expression. She closed the door.

Eddie found Neville alone in the bar, a pint and a double whiskey in front of him.

"Where's June?"

"Gone."

"Gone where?"

Neville shrugged his shoulders.

"Good shag?"

"Eh?"

"Yours. Dot. Go a bit?"

"Oh yeah." He paused. "Did June ask you for money?"

"Money?"

"Yeah. Did she?"

"I gave her a tip."

"Did she ask?"

"Not in so many words."

"How much?"

"Not much. Worth every penny. Mouse's earhole, Eddie."

"How much?"

"Hundred quid."

"Is that what she asked for?"

"She didn't ask. I rewarded her. She was a good girl."

"Dot asked for two hundred."

"Give it her?"

"Yeah."

"Worth it, eh?"

"Yeah."

Neville fell asleep in the front seat five minutes after they set off, his snoring and farting providing a farcical accompaniment to Eddie's gloomy thoughts. They'd been led by the nose. Had Neville given her only a hundred? He pulled up in a lay-by, slipped his mate's wallet from his inside pocket and counted the notes. Just short of sixteen hundred . He must have given her three. As he drove on, Eddie wondered what had gone on between them. Neville was so drunk it wouldn't have surprised him if he couldn't get a hard on. He imagined them, Neville flat out on his back his trousers round his ankles, his shoes and socks on his feet, the lovely June tugging away at his floppy cock which stayed as spongy as a cushion while he fell asleep, snoring and farting and she went through his wallet. It made him laugh out loud. Mouse's earhole! She swindled him all right, just like Dot. Only it wasn't so bad for Neville: he hadn't actually done it. He hadn't come inside a living corpse. Eddie hadn't only given away two hundred quid of the biggest windfall he'd ever have in his life, he'd have to worry that she might turn up, that she might spill the beans, that the phone might ring and it might be her, that Avril might answer.

She didn't speak to him for a week apart from spitting insults, crackling orders and asking him what he'd been doing to get his handkerchief in such a mess. He said he'd had to wipe up some glue and when she pressed him explained that Neville cut up the racing page and glued bits together as a way of picking winners and the glue had got all over the table in the bar and he'd used his handkerchief to wipe it. He didn't think for a minute she'd believe it. He imagined her pulling the dried little scrunch into a square and realising what had made it sticky and dried hard, but she said no more about it and he twigged that it was because she was sure of herself, so supremely confident that she had him browbeaten, the truth could never enter her mind. Then he was glad of what he'd done, even though it was as unsatisfying as chewing on grass. On Saturday night, thinking she might have softened a little he sneaked his fingers under the hem of her nightie.

"What do you think you're doing?" she said

He didn't reply but moved his hand to between her legs and began to caress her lips. She shoved it away.

"None of that," she said as if it were all one word. "Put a condom on if you must but for god's sake hurry up."

When he shoved his cock in her he thought how much nicer it was inside Dot: she was younger, more moist and he didn't have a condom making his cock feel as if it was a thousand miles from contact with what it needed. He wondered if Avril would let him do it bareback, so he pull out, whipped off the johnny and tried to get back in. She crossed her legs as if she was about to wet the bed, shoved him by the shoulders and switched on the bedside lamp. She had an expression on her face like a Mother Superior who has just found a priest fingering through her discarded underwear.

"What's got into you!" she said.

"It's so much nicer," he pleaded.

"Nicer? It's not nice for me, I can tell you. There's nothing nice about it. You stink. Do you know that? When did you last have a bath? You stink of sweat. Do you think that's nice? And these sheets are clean on. Do you think I want your wet sperm all over them. I think you've gone mad, Eddie Windle. I really do."

The failed attempt haunted him all week. The world was populated by pretty, handsome, cute, gorgeous, bright, kissable, curvaceous, sublime, bonny, fair, statuesque, adorable, dazzling, radiant, buxom, dainty, petite, tall, winsome, charming, raving beauties, dream girls, bathing belles, dazzlers, smashers, scorchers, lulus, Aphrodites, peaches, beauties, pin-up girls, who existed solely to remind him he was married to a peevish fishwife, a bad livered vixen, a prickly crosspatch, a choleric spitfire, a ratty Xanthippe, a thin skinned fury, a querulous scold, a bilious battle-axe, a waspish virago, a fractious hornet, a snarling mad-dog, a cross-grained bear; and he was at a loss to understand why. The simple happiness which he assumed was the bread and butter of everyone he saw around him, in the street, during

39

his weekly visit to the office, in shops, cafes, pubs, the Post Office, had evaded him utterly. His life was a simple misery. At every turn Avril peeved him. She could envenom the most innocent exchange. If he said:

"Would you like a cup of tea?"

She'd respond:

"Do I ever have a cup of tea at this time of day?" or "Not if you're making it. I'll make my own. Yours is either like tar or cat's urine."

She had a genius for annoyance and took pleasure in goading and riling him. She stirred his bile so expertly and frequently he was always trying to get out of her way and find some means of calming his pounding heart. She taunted and maddened him to the point of violence. If a man had done the same, he would have turned on him with his fists raised. Yes, he knew, she did it deliberately to humiliate him. To strip him of his manhood. Only a coward would raise his fist to a woman or a child. But when a man was affronted, insulted, when his blood was a burning fuse, he would react physically. Anything else left his dignity in tatters. And Avril used it against him over and over. He was alone. Terribly alone. How could he talk about this to his mates or colleagues? Who would want to listen to such a pathetic tale? And she turned the children against him. The thought brought him to a jarring halt. He was being robbed even of that, of the right to be a good father. He went and sat in the *Kardomah*. He ordered a scone with jam and cream and a coffee. The taste of the confectionery was a kind of home. In truth, he had nowhere to live. He was never at ease in his own living-room and the bedroom was an arena of anxiety. He had to make do with these little moments of belonging. But he was thinking about his children. Never mind Avril. He would do the best for them. He planned what he would say when he got home. He would assert his rights. He would change the way things worked. For once, he would get his own way.

"Look," he said to Avril pushing the property page of the Evening Echo under her nose as she peeled potatoes.

"I'm busy. Take it away," she said swiping at the paper.

But Eddie pulled it deftly away from her blow, grabbed the potato peeler and held the page in front of her face.

"No, no. You'll look. Never mind you're too busy. Look at this.

Look at this house. We can afford this."

She looked in his face and then at the page. For a second she seemed discomfited, but quickly her features assumed their characteristic disdain.

"Don't talk soft. Eighteen hundred pounds. We'd have to borrow every penny."

"We wouldn't have to borrow anything."

"You've gone mad. I always said there was lunacy in your family. It's your mother. She's……"

"Never mind my mother. I won seventeen hundred pounds at Catterick."

She stared at him then looked at the page.

"Where is it?"

"Upstairs."

"I don't believe you."

He went to the bedroom and opened the wardrobe where he'd hidden the money inside the shoes he kept for best. Already he knew he'd won. They might be living in the house her grandmother left to her mother. They might be paying her mother only five shilling a week rent, but he knew Avril; a three bedroom semi in Hardleton would be too much to resist. They'd be living among doctors, teachers, solicitors, professional and educated people. He knew her ingrained snobbery would be impotent to say no. He went down to the kitchen and counted out the notes in front of her with studied slowness. She took the money in her hands and made it neat.

"I'll keep this," she said.

"No you won't. I won it."

"You can't handle money like me. I'll talk to my mother about what we should do."

"Your mother can go to Hell."

"Eddie Windle, you'll regret that."

He tried to take the notes but she pulled them away so he grabbed her wrist and forced them from her.

"You great bully," she said and lashed out at his face with her fists.

He dodged away.

"We'll buy that house, or one like it. For the children. A good place for them to grow up. I don't give a tinker's cuss for what your mother says. That's what we'll do because this is my money and I make the decision."

She was crying and panting with anger. He knew she would have liked to kill him. She would have pulled a carving knife from the drawer and driven it into his heart if she thought she could get away with it. Cowardice held her back, nothing more. He folded the notes, put them in his pocket and went into the living room where he turned on the radio and sat on the sofa. At length she came through.

"It's a nice house," she said.

"It is."

"When shall we go and look at it?"

"I'll make an appointment tomorrow."

The house they were renting was worth about eight hundred. Eddie was amazed at the difference a thousand made. There was a garden front and rear, a garage, two big bedrooms and a box-room, a bathroom big enough to hold a dance in, a separate toilet, a lounge with a lovely bay window whose leaded lights had Avril in raptures, a back room whose fireplace and wooden surround were truly posh and whose big square bay looked out on the garden contained by tall privets. Avril walked round as if she had a million in the bank and might buy this to store her valuables. The children ran up and down stairs and chased about the garden. Eddie felt he could make a new beginning. Things would be different when they moved here, oh yes, very different.

As the place was empty, the previous owners having emigrated to Venezuela, they were able to move in quickly. The night before the removal, Eddie climbed into bed and lay on his back. To his surprise, Avril turned over and began stroking his cock. She pulled off her nightie and lay on her front. He climbed on top of her and she pulled her knees up so her backside was in the air and he slipped in without a condom his hands on her breasts and as he pumped madly in this newness of abandon she even let out one or two tiny, barely audible sounds of something reminiscent of pleasure.

"Now I might have a baby," she said when he was done.

"We'll have a big enough house."

After they'd been in their new home a month, Eddie decided he was going to do something he'd never done before: cook for his family. The idea came to him because one of his colleagues was Italian and told him about the beautiful food his mother made in Calabria: the evocation of tomatoes in olive oil, aubergines lightly grilled, pasta in creamy sauce with delicately fried bacon made him feel deprived: all they ever ate at home was meat and two veg, hot pot, stewing steak, bacon and eggs, sausage and mash, liver and onions, corned beef hash, white bread and butter, fish and chips, toad in the hole. It was a constraining tradition which he felt an urgent need to dismiss. Why should they eat such restricted fare just because that's what Avril's mother used to make? Why should they worry if the neighbours would raise an eyebrow at hearing they'd headed off into the dangerous, bohemian territory of foreign food? Avril had spoken derisively of the curry house which she'd heard had opened in Elmwick, where the Indian and Pakistani immigrants had started to arrive. Eddie had noticed some of the women in their bright blue, orange or yellow clothes walking the grey pavements in front of the dismal shops and pale or grubby houses and it had cheered him up: it was like a blaze of exotic sunshine striking across the milky, northern sky, or the sudden arrival of an unknown odour of cooking from some distant land. He'd been abroad during the war and his time in Egypt had released his senses, like steam dislodging nasal congestion. There was a world beyond the blackened bricks of industrial Lancashire and not only because there were no cold canals where people tossed their old prams and bikes and lads sat fishing and freezing in February, or because blokes didn't pull up the collars of their threadbare overcoats and tug down their flat caps as they left the factory nor roll up their trouser legs and read the racing pages of *The Daily Mirror* in the beach at Blackpool on bank holidays; people didn't think the same; they didn't act the same; it was a big world and there were many possibilities of being and thinking, so why should he stick to the narrow one which seemed absolutely right to Avril and her mother who considered Warrington an alien country?

"What's wrong with a curry house?" he said to Avril. "We could try it."

"Heaven knows what they serve. They're not civilized. They eat dogs."

"Don't be ridiculous. We should broaden our horizons."

"There's nothing wrong with my horizons. I'm not interested in your fancy notions."

Fancy notions. That was Avril all right. That was Avril's mother. She went to Mass twice a day, voted Tory and read *The News of the World*. Her life was a tiny triangle whose geometry was that the scandal on the hypotenuse was equal to the sum of the piety and snobbery of the other two sides. Well, he was going to cook for his family, for his children; he was going to open the door of their little northern cage and let them fly; his children had wings and their lives could be so much bigger than his. He was thirty-five and if not for the war he would never have spent more than a few weeks outside the north-west, and certainly would never have left the country. It was a bitter irony he should have that madman Hitler to thank for his opportunity; but life was odd and things never happened as you expected.

"I'll cook lunch on Sunday," he said.

"You will not."

Avril looked genuinely shocked, as if he'd said he'd just strangled the woman next door or robbed the *Trustee Savings Bank*.

"No. I want to. It's my treat for you and the children."

"Treat? What kind of treat is it to eat the rubbish you cook?"

He laughed and his laughter was genuine. Avril seemed truly funny. She was ridiculous. He was married to an absurd woman who thought that a man cooking the Sunday lunch was a subversion of the natural order. What a poor pathetic creature she was, wedded to this petty bit of power she could exert over him in the home. Her mother was the same. For a lifetime she'd taken her husband's wage and given him back a few pence for pocket money. She'd treated him like a child and he'd accepted it because of the perverse northern idea that women rule the home like a Caliph his tribe. But a new world was on the way. The old order in which the man was a heartbeat with a wage packet was giving way. The home as the tiny dictatorship of women where they behaved more high-handedly than Stalin because it was the only realm in which they had any influence was crumbling like old bricks. And he was glad. His marriage to Avril was a constant degradation. He wanted a free, open, happy relation with a woman and to hell with marriage if it couldn't provide it. He had to change things and cooking Sunday lunch was a small beginning.

"What are you laughing at?"

"Let me cook rubbish and see what the children think."

"I'm not having them go hungry. They'll never eat what you cook. They have to go to school on Monday."

"Well, if they won't eat it, you can cook them something for tea. Don't be so stick-in-the-mud. Open up."

"I'm not stick-in-the-mud. I know what's right. It's my place to do the cooking."

"Why?"

"What do you mean why?"

"Aren't many chefs men?"

"That's not the same."

"Why not?"

"If you want to be a chef be a chef but not in my kitchen."

All the same, on Sunday morning he assembled his ingredients. Gino, his colleague, had given him a recipe for Mozzarella Pasta Penne and had told him under no circumstances to used tinned tomatoes: he must buy fresh and peel them.

"What are you boiling tomatoes for?" said Avril.

"I'm not boiling them, I'm breaking the skins so I can peel them."

"What d'you want to peel tomatoes for? There's a tin in the cupboard."

"Ah, but Avril, they won't taste anything like these. The key is freshness. Everything fresh, just like Calabria."

"You've got a slate loose," she said.

She followed his every move, told him the children wouldn't like Mozzarella or Parmesan, tutted at his excessive use of black pepper which she claimed would make the children cough and said it wasn't a balanced meal, just stodge in a sauce.

"I'm making a salad too," he said, refusing to be provoked.

45

"A salad. For Sunday lunch," and she rolled her eyes to heaven as if he'd said the Bible wasn't the word of God.

It was a simple dish, easy and quick to prepare, which was one of the things Eddie liked. He loathed the way Avril would take to the kitchen at half past eight, immediately after Mass, and work solidly till two to put on the table the dry beef and soggy cabbage and cauliflower that were as depressing as the rain that lashed at the windows in October. He knew her hours in the kitchen weren't necessary but a mark of power: she was in her laboratory and must be left alone; everyone must wait till dinner was ready; no-one dared not be at the table when she announced the arrival of food. So he relished the idea of a dish that was nourishing, wholesome and tasty which could be ready in forty minutes.

The table was laid. The children sat waiting. Eddie brought the dish through.

"There's salad too." he said, smiling at his girl and boy as he turned to fetch it.

When he returned he served them with a big spoon. The steaming pasta sat on their plates like a rejection of everything they'd ever eaten. He put a little island of salad on the edge of each.

"Well, give it a try," he said.

The children lifted their forks to their mouths. Eddie stood by the table. He wanted to see them eating delightedly before he sat down.

"Is it good?"

The children shot glances at Avril who was standing behind him. He didn't know, nor did he suspect that she was vigorously shaking her head and indicating to the children they should put down their knives and forks. They stopped chewing.

"Don't you like it?"

They both put down their cutlery.

"Try a bit more. You'll get used to it. You've never had Italian food."

But Avril, a fierce look on her face was still shaking her head as if they risked death by taking another bite. The children sat still, looked at one another and said nothing. Eddie was about to sit down and help himself but Avril grabbed the dish.

"Never mind, children," she said. "I'll make some proper food."

She rushed from the dining-room.

"Hey, Avril, bring that back."

He smiled at the children as he got up but when he arrived in the kitchen she'd already tipped the pasta in the dustbin.

"For Christ's sake."

"Don't add blasphemy to your sins. I told you they wouldn't like it."

"They just needed to get used to it."

"Used to it? This is England. We don't eat that stuff."

"Lots of people eat it."

"Not in this house. Now I've got to start and cook a proper meal. And look at the time. You make me sick, Eddie. You really do."

He went to the dining-room and told the children they could go and play for a while; their mother would make them something to eat. It was okay. They didn't need to worry. He'd made the wrong choice. He smiled at them and then went into the living-room and put a Sinatra record on the gramophone. His heart was beating heavily. He thought of the girl at Catterick, the paltry sex and the loss of his two hundred quid. He remembered the sex with Avril the night before they moved. His thoughts suddenly skipped to Egypt, to the heat, the desert, the teeming streets of Cairo, the dark eyes of the African women, the sensuality of their slow movement beneath their robes. What sort of life was this? He heard the children running upstairs shouting in the fantasy of their game. They at least were grappling healthily with life. What but the love of his children kept him in this chair? Without that he would walk out now and never come back. He'd rather sleep alone on a park bench than share his bed with Avril. He sat for a sad hour listening to the crooning voice and regretting his life. If only he'd known it would come to this. If only he'd known.

The door swung swiftly open, Avril came in and switched off the gramophone.

"There's no hot water," she announced.

"What?"

"No hot water. Must be something wrong with the immersion."

47

"Probably the thermostat," he said. "I'll take it out and get a new one tomorrow."

"And there's something else," she said. "I'm expecting."

She marched out slamming the door behind her.

ADIOS ZAPATA

Every morning for the past five years Dave Zapata had walked the two and a half miles to school and every evening he had walked home; sometimes at three-thirty, sometimes at four, sometimes at five or six if he had marking or there was a meeting. He retraced his steps to the dormer bungalow where he'd lived with Angela for thirty-two years. Their children were grown: Melanie a GP in Suffolk where she shared a thatch-roofed, gentrified cottage with William. He took the train to his London chambers most mornings; Andrew site manager for a merchant bank, supervising a staff of forty and married to Kerrie whose research into muscle ageing kept her busy three days a week. The others she spent with their ten-month old daughter, Jade. Tonight, Dave Zapata had to write a letter of application for the position of Temporary Director of Sixth Form. He'd been Assistant Head for twenty-seven years, before they changed his title to Assistant Director. Now the Headteacher had left under a cloud after a collective complaint from the staff, the Director of Sixth Form was to take charge of the school till an appointment was made and the request for applications had been pinned to the notice board.

It was one of those April afternoons when the sky clears, the sun threatens to warm everything but a pleasant nip remains and you have to pull on your coat to walk down the street. Angela wasn't yet home from her Indian head massage class: she ran three sessions a week which brought in a bit of pocket money and he indulged her, though it was pitiful compared to his salary. He put a chair on the patio which he'd laid himself when they'd had the conservatory built and poured a glass of Beaujolais. On his A4 pad, he began to draft his letter but it seemed barely worth the trouble. Who else could they give the post to? As far as he knew, the only other applicant was Aaron Beard. It was true, he was earmarked for progression. Roy Sail, the existing Director, had taken him under his wing. They shared a passion for motorbikes, rode out together along the open roads of the Yorkshire Dales most weekends, were constantly in one another's homes and, most importantly, Sail's vainglory was flattered by the sycophantic attentions of the younger man. Beard was one of those people, intelligent but lacking in social subtlety, who rising from the working-class and finding the mores of the middle-classes baffling, make an unconditional agreement with them as the surest means of

49

survival. Sail, scion of a an upper-middle class, Home Counties family, educated at a minor public school, recognised an acolyte and made clear, without ever saying so, that submissive complaisance would see doors open. Zapata smiled to himself thinking of this. Beard was sure to rise. His day would dawn. He would be an Assistant Head or maybe Headteacher if things fell right, but twenty-seven years experience was unarguable. The job was in the bag. It was almost an embarrassment to apply.

It was chillier than he thought. He took the chair inside, slid closed the patio door, poured another glass and sat at the kitchen table. He had so much experience, it was difficult to condense . Into his head came the thought of playing tennis against a weak opponent. He always restrained his shots. He would win, two and two, or one and two, something comfortable; but it was unseemly to turn on all his power and athleticism against someone who struggled to return even a moderately fast serve. This wasn't like applying for his first job when he had to brim with enthusiasm and willingness to please. It was more akin to being presented with an award and having to make a speech marinated in modesty, to smile, to nod, to thank fulsomely, and yet to know it could have been given to no-one else.

When he'd filled one side, he replenished his glass. He wondered if he should end it there or add some simple line like: I feel anything additional should wait till the interview. He had nothing to prove and writing paragraph after paragraph about his work in the sixth form, the sporting achievements, the hundreds of references written, the thousands of interviews with potential students, his diplomacy over staff disputes, his instigation of the Community Involvement Scheme, struck him as telling the school what they already knew. He was one of the five most senior pastoral staff. His record was exemplary. He hadn't had a day off in fifteen years. The staff and students alike respected him. He played a key role in the PTA. It was like enumerating your attractions to a woman who was besotted with you.

Angela arrived as he was filling his fourth glass.

"What shall I make for tea?" she said before he'd looked up.

"Anything will do ."

"Give us a clue, Dave," and she was already on her knees grabbing at packets in the freezer. "What about salmon fish-cakes, new potatoes and a nice salad?"

"Fine."

She paused for a few seconds looking intently at the two frozen rounds, covered in breadcrumbs in the blue polystyrene tray.

"No, I don't fancy that at all. What about pepperoni pizza? I could add some spring onions, mushrooms.......Mmm? What do you think?"

"Yeah, great."

She put the ice-covered box on the work-surface and shut the freezer door with her knee.

"What should we have with it?"

"Bit of salad would do me."

"Baked potato?"

"If you fancy."

Holding the box gingerly she slipped on her glasses and read the ingredients and cooking time.

"No, I've gone off that idea."

"What about lamb curry? I froze this two weeks ago."

"Perfect."

"No, I don't fancy lamb at all. I could eat a nice prawn curry. Yes. We don't have any prawns do we?"

She was rooting in the fridge trying to remember if she bought any on her Sunday visit to Sainsbury's.

"Did I buy any, Dave? I was sure I did."

"Beats me."

"What about a take-away? They do a lovely prawn dhansak at the Little India. Shall I ring?"

"If you like."

"What do you want?"

"I'll share whatever you have."

So she rang and he heard her poshing up her voice on the phone, then she was tripping up the stairs and calling:

"I'm going to get in the shower before the food arrives. We've got half an hour. You can come and scrub my back if you like."

He put down the pad and waited till he heard the water running. He almost couldn't be bothered. The soporific effect of the wine together with the cockiness about his application made him sink into the lethargic pleasure of the moment, like a constrictor digesting its prey. Wasn't he a man whose life had everything? A still trim and obliging little wife; a nice home in the suburbs worth a hundred grand more than the national average; two successful children; a senior position in one of the most prestigious schools in the county; the respect and admiration of the local community; an inheritance of quarter of a million or more to come on his father's death (and at eighty-three and two heart attacks behind him it couldn't be long), and even more when Angela's parents popped their clogs. The only dark cloud was his sister who married young, divorced early and turned to drink. He stayed away from her. Failure gave him the creeps. The last time he visited her cramped and smelly terrace he came home feeling sick. The rotting frames, the front door patched with odd strips of unpainted timber, the bare stairs, the dirty bath, the sink piled with unwashed pots, the clutter of accumulated debris in the yard, all spoke of decline, of that want of desire for persistent betterment which was the abiding tenor of his life. He felt contaminated and wanted to burn his clothes and scrub himself. But she was expelled from his consciousness. His horizons ended with the unmeritorious. The clear sun of success shone on his existence, and if he wasn't a millionaire, if they hadn't been able to afford to send their children to private schools as they would have liked, if he didn't drive a Mercedes or have shares in merchant banks, there were many below him. He'd read in the *Sunday Times* that people on his salary were in the top ten percent of the workforce. Ten percent. Pretty good. Of course, the top one percent had the private jets and more wealth between them than entire nations, but his position was secure. Good luck to them, he thought. They'd made it by their own efforts. Like him. He'd risen into the top ten percent and that was something. Yes, not everyone could say that and it was something.

He finished what was in his glass and went upstairs listening to the music of the splashing water. Outside the bathroom he called "I'm here!" and began to unbutton his shirt.

They opened another bottle with the meal and when it was done, he was too far gone to finish his letter.

"You write it," he said to Angela.

"Don't be daft!"

"Wouldn't make any difference."

He needed two paracetamol before he set off in the morning. It went through his head during his brisk walk that his headaches were more frequent and he'd had a persistent ache, of the kind he got if he'd slept with his head in an awkward position, for months. Young, he'd been able to drink with virtually no detriment. He assumed age was the problem.

During his free two hours, he shut himself away in his cubby-hole office and worked on the letter. The school dated back to the mid sixteenth century, though none of the original buildings still existed, and he was up in the rafters in the old block where the ceiling sloped precipitately and a tiny window of four square panes looked out over the Headmaster's garden and the playing fields which stretched away to the woods and the farm before the steep decline to the river. The flowering cherries were full of light, pink blossom and the thin branches swayed like the arms of an entranced dancer in the breeze. How lucky he had been. In three years time he'd turn sixty and take his pension. Part of him wanted to stay on. He could see himself still walking in each day at the age of seventy and as he taught almost exclusively sixth-form, he could cope in the classroom for years yet. But Angela insisted and he knew she was right. Thirty-six years was long enough. For the thousandth time he ran through the quick pension calculation in his head: twenty-three thousand a year plus a lump sum of sixty-nine. With his savings that'd come to more than two hundred grand and in a long-term bond he'd get six or seven percent. Then it couldn't be long before.....Yes, he was a lucky man and now, when he might have expected nothing more, he was going to get this small promotion and in retirement when people asked him what he'd done he'd be able to say: "Teacher. Director of Sixth Form at Larkgate School." He added another sentence and lifted his head. Aaron Beard was following the path between the rugby fields dressed in his tracksuit, a thunderer round his neck and a ball under his arm. He was brisk and moved as if he was being watched or filmed, a hint of self-consciousness never leaving him. Zapata recalled when he'd started in the school and come in for some ribbing from the old stagers for his naivety. He tried too hard to behave as if Larkgate was in his blood and it came across as empty and made them chuckle. But his exorbitant effort to adjust had been rewarded.

He was one of those people who lean on institutions and sensing from his first day that the staff thought themselves a cut above, that an urbane disdain informed their attitude to the neighbouring comprehensives which had been upgraded from secondary moderns while they were the ancient, revered, quasi-public-school grammar forced to take a downward step, he began to introduce a note of snobbery into his conversation which clashed with his working-class accent and demeanour. Zapata smiled at the memory of it. He was fond of Beard. He was clubbable, enjoyed a drink and a dirty joke. He'd even toyed with asking him if he wanted to join the Masons. Out of nowhere, Roy Sail was on the path. The two of them stopped. Sail was holding a paper in front of Beard and pointing things out. For a few seconds, Zapata read nothing into it, then all at once the idea came to him they were talking about the job. Was Sail coaching him? Was he giving him tips? Did he favour him? But why? Because they were mates? He watched them intently. Sail was nodding as Beard spoke into his face. Zapata got up and went down the stairs but when he got to path, they'd gone. He went back to his room, read through his draft , tore it up and began to scribble fiercely.

By the time Angela arrived home that evening, he'd finished the first bottle.

"There was probably nothing in it, Dave. It's just the application playing on your mind. More salad?"

"Yeah, yeah."

He put another forkful of salmon frittata in his mouth and picked up his glass.

"They wouldn't pass you over after all these years."

"Things have changed," he said and she noticed a sad, faraway cast in his look.

"How? There's plenty of salad left."

"They like to promote the young folk. Roy's very keen on it. It's everywhere. You know, the old idea that you have to win your spurs and experience counts; it's gone. They made Katie Inkster Director of Learning for Key Stage 4 when she was still an NQT."

"Oh, but there was no-one with your record going after it! Was there?"

"Tony Burton."

"He's not as senior as you."

"He's a Subject Leader. He's fifty-four. She's twenty-two."

"Are you going to finish the salad. Be a shame to waste it."

"I've had enough."

"Why not talk to Roy. You're old friends."

"What would he say?"

"He'd tell you straight I hope."

"How could he, if that's what they're thinking of?"

"Well exactly, they can't decide it beforehand. You're bound to do better than him in interview."

He emptied his glass.

"Is there another bottle of that Sauvignon?"

He woke at four o'clock. Angela was curled in her usual way with her chin raised and the duvet gripped in her right fist. It was true Roy was an old friend. They'd been on holiday together four or five times. Their children used to go to one another's birthday parties. How many evenings had he and Pauline been for dinner? He was William's godfather after all! All that counted for nothing. What would he do in Roy's place? Favour an old mate? But was it so bad? He was well-respected. They'd give him a good send-off when he retired. How much did they collect for Len Spillman? £350? He'd do better than that. Maybe £500. Deputy Director of sixth-form at Larkgate was good going. Back in bed his heart pounded unpleasantly. His headache was getting worse. He got up again and took two paracetamol. When he closed his eyes and pulled the duvet up he saw himself being told by Roy that unfortunately……

"What the fuck do you mean, unfortunately….."

He tried to picture himself being gracious and accepting; the elder statesman, magnanimous in defeat, smiling, relaxed, too successful, wise and experienced to pay attention to pettiness. But thoughts of violence kept appearing. His last glance at the clock showed five fifty-seven.

The walk to school was twice as long. He spent his free hours working on his letter and at lunch-time noticed Beard wasn't in the staff-room. He usually sat in the sportsman's corner. The P.E. staff and blokes who ran teams liked to get together over the sports pages. They made a loud little group who occupied the far end near the notice board and read avidly the reports of their favourite teams' matches, shaking their heads over managers and referees and becoming morose when their confident predictions came to nothing. Beard was always amongst them and his bray could be heard in the corridor. His absence made Zapata fret and though he told himself there was no reason to believe he was with Roy Sail, he couldn't put the thought of conspiracy out of his mind. He was sitting next to Vic Addison, an unfortunate music teacher who'd been passed over for five or six promotions. There were only two staff in his department and when Harry Harmonica, as the pupils called him, retired after thirty-eight years, Addison imagined he'd have a good chance. But they refused him an interview and everyone gave him a wide berth. Larkgate wasn't the sort of place where anyone wanted to be too close to failure. Though Addison was reputed to be intellectually sharp (he'd published a book on Stravinsky and composed pieces that had been performed by professional orchestras), the word went round that he wasn't up to the job. He applied for pastoral roles to raise his status but was never taken seriously and soon became a marginal figure who people spoke about as a waste of space and someone the school would be better off without. But Zapata's daughter had taken music at A Level and thought he was terrific. Listening to her tell him how inspired the lessons were, how he made them laugh and work hard at the same time and how he could clearly explain the most complex parts of musical theory so they suddenly seemed obvious, he'd slowly come to view him as a wronged figure. But that was life. As his father had always said: "Life isn't fair, son. Never forget that." He'd never thought Addison was the victim of any concerted campaign, he was just a bit of an odd character: his suits were scruffy, he never polished his shoes, his wife was known to drink like a Pole, and he'd once said to Zapata: "I'll never be accepted by the middle-classes no matter how hard I try." He just wasn't a Larkgate person. Zapata had always treated him with a little condescending kindness and tolerance. Melanie had got an A after all and her clarinet playing became confident and mature under Addison's tuition. But today he thought of him differently.

"When are the interviews?" Addison asked between mouthfuls of lamb samosa.

"Twenty fifth."

"Just you and Aaron I believe."

"Yeah."

Zapata experienced a moment of dread, as if death itself had spoken to him. Did Addison assume the job was his? Or did he know something? Was the whole school aware? Were the rumours circulating and was he the lonely fool who didn't know what everyone else had twigged? Was he now a sad figure like Addison? But the idea was ridiculous! Addison had worked for twenty-seven years and achieved no promotion at all. He was a reject. There was no comparison. All the same, the heavy thought that he was about to be turned down, that a younger, much less experienced man was about to get the job he'd thought was his by right brought the edifice of his status crashing like a house long secretly undermined in its foundations whose gable end suddenly falls in a chaos of bricks and dust. Still, he felt closer to Beard. He began to realize the heavy burden of failure. He'd always gone along with the idea that the higher you rose, the greater your stress, and like the rest of the management had exaggerated, without knowing it, how much he had to do and how burdensome it was. Yet now he understood that no amount of responsibility can bear down on you with the inexorable force of being slighted. It hadn't yet happened but he felt impotent, empty and angry. How must Addison feel? All those years of hard work. All those lessons none of his colleagues knew about. They knew the visible repudiation and no-one was willing to believe the hierarchy was irrational; not if they had or might have a place in it; the only conclusion was he was hopeless. It was true: in spite of knowing how good his lessons could be, Zapata had always thought of him as a slightly pathetic figure. Now he was filled with the horrible anticipation that in his last years he was going to become a nobody, a kind of vagrant, someone who had over-stayed his welcome, a man who reached for elevation everyone knew he wouldn't attain and in failing fell flat on his face in the mud.

"You should be pretty safe," said Addison.

"Think so?"

At the end of the afternoon he finished his application and put it in Roy Sail's pigeon-hole. He had included every achievement, every team he'd run, every extra-curricular contribution, every course he'd been on, every trip organized; but above all he had underlined his long contribution to the sixth-form, his innovations in the curriculum, his supervision of the prefect system and his outstanding record of exam results. He hoped Roy would read between the lines: he was going to fight every inch of the way in interview. He wouldn't let them shoulder him aside. He would insist on a de-briefing. How could Beard possibly compare?

Angela was late home. She'd told him she was going for a drink with her sister but he'd forgotten. He didn't bother making any food and by the time she arrived had finished two bottles.

"Where've you been?"

"For a drink with Debbie. I told you."

"Did you?"

"Don't you remember?"

"No."

"Is there any food?"

"I was waiting for you."

"Oh, David!"

She was on her knees, yanking packets from the freezer. They opened another bottle of white and Dave drank three glasses then sprawled on the sofa in front of the plasma tv watching football. She sat beside him with a copy of *Cosmopolitan*. He was in one of those moods when drink took over making him uncommunicative and oddly self-satisfied. She went to make herself a coffee and tried to find something to clean or tidy in the immaculate kitchen. That was one of the drawbacks of having a cleaner. The two chocolate topped oat biscuits she ate didn't satisfy her. The rich sweet butteriness in her mouth made her want more, but she told herself it was a foolish indulgence and at eleven o'clock sure to give her indigestion. By the time she'd drunk her coffee Dave was snoring so she switched off the set and enjoyed the quiet. Oh, it was so nice to live in a place like this! Behind the bungalow were fields which half a mile further nudged a little wood and beyond that more rough fields with little hillocks and petty dales then the copse with the stream and the rickety little bridge. Being at the end of the lane there was no traffic. The town was five miles away. They'd worked hard and spent money to get the bungalow just so and the gardener kept things neat and pretty all year round. She would have liked to move out to the country, right out to where each house had acres of its own and neighbours nipped round to one another in their four by fours. But Dave wouldn't put up with a long drive to work. As she sat alone, her husband lost to the booze, she ran each detail of each room of the house through her mind. A jolt hit her when she realised she'd left a pair of shoes in the middle of the floor in the small bedroom. She jumped up and went to put them away in the wardrobe. For a second she regretted her children moving away. There had been such pleasure when they were here, when this had been William's room. Her sudden collapse of feeling brought the thought of nothing but decline for them now. She closed the door, went briskly to the kitchen and wiped down all the surfaces.

"Dave!" she shook him till he roused. "Come on, it's midnight."

When his head fell into the pillow he said:

"Got the application in. Fuckin' good I tell you. Fuckin' good."

"Well, will you stop fretting now?"

"I'll stop fretting when I've got the job."

The interview panel was Roy and the two Assistant Heads, who sat at either side of him like bodyguards attending a President. He'd always thought of them as like-minded colleagues, conscientious and ambitious, but now they seemed ludicrously sycophantic. Were they going to display any independence? Why were they here if only to nod in agreement? He found himself thinking of Addison and the uncomfortable idea made him wriggle in his chair. Roy asked him how he envisaged the future of the sixth-form, how he would attract more students, what he would do to compete with the local colleges, how he would change the culture of the place to fit the assumptions of today's youngsters, what new qualifications could be offered, how the school could overcome the public perception of old-fashionedness. They gave him no chance to plead his record. When they asked him if he had any questions he couldn't think of anything.

He went straight to his room. The desperate thought of writing his letter of resignation came to him but pacing around he realised it would make him appear more ridiculous than ever. The only thing to do was be cool, to appear as if he was batting away this disappointment like a wasp in summer. Yet the thought of locking himself away was overwhelming. He wanted to walk out and never return, but how could he not return to a place which had been his life for so long? Then a countervailing voice said to him that maybe they were right: he was the old guard, he'd had his day, it needed a younger mind to take the place forward. The generosity of the idea calmed him, but as he sat by the window hoping he'd found a simple answer to his torment, anger surged in him as he overthrew the pusillanimous excuse: they'd done him over, they'd screwed him, they'd humiliated him in a way he could never repair. It was a temporary post, for fuck's sake! He was the obvious candidate. Six months, twelve months at the outside and a new Head would be in post and Sail restored to his role. They were getting Beard ready for senior responsibility and he was the fall guy. They'd dumped on him. They'd pissed all over him. Try as he might, the thought of all his years of success couldn't ease the profound sense of injury.

And his headache was becoming unbearable.

At ten past three Sail called him in. The announcement was posted on the notice-board. He avoided the staff-room, went home on the bell, took two paracetamol and opened a bottle of Sauvignon.

"It's disgraceful!" said Angela pulling a trout from the freezer.

"The old ways of doing things are gone," said Dave. "I was a fool to apply."

"Oh no! You had to apply. They'll look silly if he messes up. Do you want sauté potatoes with this?"

"No, applying was my mistake. I should've seen it coming. I was acting according to the old rules. But the gentlemanly culture is no more. It's cut-throat now. They promote them younger and younger because they're cheap and compliant."

"Bur Aaron isn't that young, is he? And he won't be cheap."

"Cheaper than me. And when they give him a permanent position in the SLT, he'll be earning about what I get now. But the point is the message it sends."

"Shall I do salad or veg?"

"Salad."

"What message."

"Experience counts for nothing. The young need show no respect for their elders. Anyone who'll do what they're told will get promotion even if they're wet behind the ears."

"Have you eaten the spring onions?"

"No."

"It'll backfire on them. All those youngsters running things. There'll be some terrible mistakes. Are you sure you haven't eaten them?"

"But they'll save a lot of money," he scoffed. "If I hadn't applied I'd be sitting pretty . I could say I didn't want it. I've done my bit. I'm winding down. I could've risen above it all. But I'm a laughing stock. The pillock who applied for a tiny temporary promotion after twenty-seven years. I should've been the natural successor. I thought I was. Now I'm like Vic Addison and every day I'll have to go in and be reminded of my humiliation."

"It's not a humiliation. With your record. He'll be Director for six months and then what? You've all those years behind you. They can't take that away from you, Dave."

"They just have."

No-one said a word. Beard went at everything with extra zest: his stride was stronger, his laugh louder, his shoulders straighter, his chin higher. Zapata carried on as if nothing had happened. He tried to wear a complaisant expression. But he was like a man bereaved making small-talk to strangers and the churning in his organs, the heavy pounding of his heart and the overwhelming desire to hide away, sapped his energy and dragged him down. The only relief was wine. After two bottles, he began not to care and after the third he dismissed Sail as a sly cunt, Beard was a worthless little arsehole and the school itself a cross between a gulag and Bedlam. When the drink had done all it could, he staggered around the house cursing and laughing while Angela sat on the white leather sofa daintily sipping her second glass. Then he fell into bed, groaning and farting, got up in the early hours to swig water and take painkillers, and every morning woke with a worse headache than the morning before.

Six months later he walked to school one morning, hung his coat in the gents, went into the staffroom and collapsed. Eileen Westmorland, the busy little bursar and first-aider buzzed around him like a bee after pollen, took his pulse, loosened his collar and was convinced it was a heart attack. The ambulancemen lifted him into a wheelchair and the ambulance drew slowly out of the playground as dozens of eager young faces pressed against the windows to savour the best of this moment of high excitement. The rumours went round amongst them that Mr Zapata was dead, he'd had a heart attack, there been a fight in the staffroom, and one of the toughs from Year 11 had headbutted him. But the next day he was there, early as ever, determined not to be kept off school by a minor bit of dizziness. A week later he collapsed in the middle of a lesson and two frantic Year 9s came running to the school office shouting that Mr Zapata was cold stone dead on the floor of room 52. Another ambulance arrived and this time he was stretchered down the stairs while a dozen staff tried to disperse the kids who pressed around hoping to see something gruesome, to catch their first glimpse of a corpse, to be able to tell all their mates of the gallons of blood that poured from his ears or how his brains were dripping from his wide open skull.

Zapata was off school for two days and came back with a monitor wired to his chest and a discernible tremor in his hands. He made a joke of it, saying he felt like the bionic man but he had to go to the hospital for blood tests, to be wired up to machines which beeped and buzzed and whose screens showed jagged peaks in response to his pulse; but the weeks went by and they were no nearer understanding what was wrong with him. Then Angela read a piece in a Sunday supplement about how to spot the signs of an impending or minor stroke and one of the things to look for was facial distortion. Her heart raced and she jumped up from the sofa. For two years and more she'd noticed that Dave's right eyelid was badly tugged downwards, especially first thing in the morning. She'd assumed it was a just age.

"You should have a brain scan," she said.

"If they think I need a brain scan they'll give me one."

"Perhaps they just haven't thought of it."

"Why shouldn't they? They're doctors. Let them make the decisions."

"Are you sure you should have another glass, Dave?"

"It's only my third."

"I know, but till they've worked out what's wrong...."

"They haven't told me not to drink."

"You should ask about a brain scan though. It said in this article.."

"That's just women's magazine stuff."

"Well ask!"

"Okay. I'll ask."

But the cardiac specialist didn't feel there was any need. He was convinced there was an underlying heart problem and in due course he'd be able to tease it out. So Zapata stayed wired up, his blood pressure was checked, he was put on a treadmill, his headaches made him take painkillers every four hours, and he collapsed in the living-room, the bedroom, the kitchen, the garden, the street and a restaurant. Finally Angela went with him to see his GP who said they could get a brain scan but there'd be a long wait.

"We'll pay," said Angela.

"It's expensive."

"How much?"

"Perhaps a thousand maybe fifteen hundred."

"We can manage that. How quickly can it be done?"

"Oh, probably within a week."

In the car, Zapata was sullen.

"It's probably money down the drain."

"Well, at least we'll know."

"It's a lot of money to find nothing."

"Let's hope they do find nothing. It'll be the best thousand quid I've ever spent."

What was a thousand quid after all? In the long run, they'd be worth more than a million. It was something for a lad who'd started out in a two-up, two-down terrace. What a great country he lived in? Of course, it wasn't quite America. He sometimes wished they'd moved over there. He would've had a fair chance of finding teaching work and Angela could have run a nice business in yoga, massage, reflexology; they might've bought a ranch and lived the great, free life of Americans. He might even have left teaching himself and tried educational publishing or consultancy. Yes, consultancy! That was the thing to bring in the money. All the same, they'd done well. It was a great system which allowed people to get on and make something of themselves. So what was a thousand quid when they had seventy grand in the bank and two big inheritances coming their way? All the same, it bothered him. Spending money bothered him, unless it was on a new car which everyone would see, or an exotic holiday beyond the pocket of most people. But to spend money on a brain scan that would probably reveal nothing went against the grain. Why couldn't the NHS provide? He paid his taxes like the next man. Wasn't that the idea: you pay your taxes and when you're ill the system looks after you? He'd paid into a private scheme too, but when they looked at the small print, it turned out brain scans weren't covered; and though he resented that, he felt the private way was right. If he'd lived in America he would have paid into a proper scheme and his scan would have been provided in a gleaming, state-of-the-art facility open only to those with money. He wouldn't have to mix with the riff-raff. That was the problem with this country: those who worked hard and did the right thing were dragged down by the feckless, the chavs, the council estate crew living on generous benefits provided by folk who got up in the morning. He'd read somewhere about gated developments and he thought it was a great idea; maybe they'd move to one when he was better. A place where you drive up to huge, black, iron gates which open as slowly as a canal lock when you swipe your card and close behind you as you roll over the private tarmac to your exclusive house in an enclave where the lower classes never come. That was the way forward, so that people like them could enjoy the benefits of their hard work away from the unpleasantness of those types you see in town; pale, harassed looking characters in cheap clothes, the women with orange skins, dyed hair and eyelashes like tarantula's legs, the brats screaming in their flimsy pushchairs and the blokes swigging Carling from cans, strutting like they own the place. So the thousand quid could be spent to please Angela. It was a small percentage of the fortune they'd ultimately have and invested it'd bring in good dividends. Yes, this truly was a great country where people like him, starting out very modestly in life could end up millionaires! He laughed to himself: if anyone had told him as a kid he'd ever be a millionaire, he'd've scoffed. These days of course it was the billionaires who mattered. He'd never make that. Too late. But maybe the kids? You never know, work hard and get a lucky break....They were turning into the drive and his headache was becoming fierce. When he got out of the car, he staggered over the flower bed and fell on his face on the manicured lawn.

The brain scan discovered a tumour as big as an orange.

It turned out to be a brain stem glioma. Ms Rasaratnam, the young, beautiful and softly-spoken consultant, explained they were more common in children, this one was almost certainly inoperable. They would do a needle biopsy to get a proper diagnosis but the treatment would very likely be radiation and chemotherapy. When Angela asked what the prognosis might be, she knew at once from Ms Rasaratnam's face it was gloomy.

"Let's do the biopsy and then I'll be able to give you a better answer."

"Will he live?"

"It's too early to say."

"But you must know. If it's inoperable, that's much worse isn't it? If you were a gambling woman, would you put money on him surviving?"

Ms Rasaratnam was one of those people whose high-mindedness is as clear from their features as viciousness on the face of a snarling dog; as she turned and looked straight at Angela, in her big, brown eyes and the set of her mouth the pleading distraught wife saw something that calmed and lifted her.

"I wouldn't," said the doctor.

"How long?"

"I could only guess."

"Give me your best."

"A few weeks."

All the way home, trying to hold back her tears in the traffic, those words rang through her consciousness. That was it. A few weeks and his life would be wiped out and with it all she relied on and their shared plans for a happy retirement. Like everyone who has suffered a terrible, fundamental shock, whose life has just been knocked sideways, she was amazed and bewildered by the way existence went on as if nothing had changed. That was life. The great wrecking boulder of death came cascading down on some poor soul, and everyone else went about their affairs as if their routines were eternal. She wanted to wind down the window and shout at passers-by:

"You're going to die, you know! You might only have a few weeks!"

Within a month he was moved to the beautiful, clean hospice whose grounds were full of old oaks and horse chestnuts. From his window he could see huge rhododendrons in bloom and the purple flowers swaying in the least breeze reminded him of the uncontrollable tremor in his hands. Visitors arrived every day and while he was grateful, he found having to talk about something other than his impending death a strain. It was all he could think of and there was nothing to feel but grief. Most people would begin by saying: "How are you, Dave?" and he always wanted to reply: "Dying. How are you?" But politeness made him put on a brave face. People talked about football or what was in the news and everyone said what a lovely place the hospice was and how wonderful the staff. He wanted to say: "Yes, I couldn't wish for a nicer place to die but I'd rather be in a hovel and have twenty years ahead of me." When he was alone, he kept running the facts of his life through his mind and it was true what they said: they flashed before him, his whole life resuméed in a few images which scuttled through his mind in seconds. He began to think that life was impossibly cruel. He realised he'd believed that such things didn't happen to people like him. He was fit. He walked every day. He'd always been sporty. He didn't smoke. The statistics were in his favour. He wasn't yet sixty. He was going to die before his own father, before Angela's mother. And he would never be a millionaire. The thought that kept him from the despair which stalked all his hours, was that his life amounted to something: he'd brought up two children; he'd been married for more than thirty years; and he'd worked at Larkgate. His contribution couldn't be forgotten. Surely his name would live on? He'd taught thousands who would remember him. But then the dark recollection of his humiliation returned. Would he be remembered as a failure? Would history judge him as the man who leapt and missed the ledge, falling into the bottomless pit of shame? His agitation made him want to get up and do something, but he was confined. He could no longer even get out of his chair without help.

One afternoon, Aaron Beard arrived. He strode in with that strong gait which gave the impression of a man who meant business and his broad smile had a slightly strained look, as if it never came from what was most essential in him, as if it was hard work and had to cover a grimmer, more clenched disposition.

"Hello Dave, how are you, mate? Good to see you!"

Zapata held out his frail hand to be shaken and the younger, powerful grip   almost brought him to tears. Beard bent from the waist to look out of the window.

"What a fantastic view, eh? This is a lovely room , Dave. Smashing place."

"Yeah, it is. Very nice."

He wanted to say: "You can have it if you want. Take my place, we'll get the coffin lengthened." It was impossible to make small talk in the face of death and yet impossible to do anything else. It struck him how strange it was that no-one who came to visit said: "Well, I'm sorry you're dying mate and I hope you don't suffer." But no-one dared go anywhere near death. As for himself, he wanted to say: "I'm dying. I'm bloody well dying and it's terrible. I had so much life left to live. It's terrible, terrible, terrible!"

"I brought you some grapes," said Beard. "Red. Do you prefer red. They're seedless so you won't have to spit the pips all over the carpet."

He rocked back and guffawed at his own levity.

"How's the treatment going then, Dave?"

"Treatment?"

"Chemo is it?"

"They've stopped the treatment."

"Well that might be a good sign, eh?"

Zapata looked him in the eyes. He despised him. Hate would have been ridiculous, but he looked down on him for behaving shabbily. Yet had he really done anything wrong? An opportunity had arisen and he'd gone after it. Was there anything to object to in that? All his life Zapata had believed in opportunity. He'd thought it marvellous that society was organised around it and people could work and fight and push to get on; but now the alien thought seized his mind that opportunity was a form of cruelty. It was a trick. It had humiliated him after half a lifetime of loyalty. He'd never imagined it could be used against him, that a quiet conspiracy could unseat him and install a much younger, less experienced colleague. He despised Beard like he despised his old friend Sail and in his moment's anguish as he looked into his rival's healthy face he sensed the world had turned against him; what he had put his trust in had turned out to be a corruption, a mockery. He was rejected, demeaned, cast off and now death was taking him; his hands shook; he began to sob and his features contorted like those of a frightened child.

"Eh, what's up? You okay, Dave? Hang on mate I'll get someone. Hang on."

The nurse thought it best if Beard left. As she tended to Zapata she heard him mumble: "Bastard! Slimy little bastard!"

Angela came as usual in the evening. He ate a little grilled fish and new potatoes. When she left he was sleeping. At six in the morning the nurse found him dead.

Two hundred packed St Mary's On The Hill for his funeral. Sail suggested to the governors naming the new library after the dead man and three months later an opening ceremony for the Dave Zapata Library was held at which the chair of governors unveiled a plaque and a portrait of Zapata painted by an ex-pupil, now an RA. Because he died in service, Angela got £90,000. She donated half of it to the school; the place, she said, he'd always loved.

A VICTIM

When she kicked her husband out the last thing Mrs Wiswell wanted was to appear independent. She was forty, an intelligent woman who'd missed out on education being born too early to benefit from the 1944 reform; she could have got herself some training and found relatively remunerative work; but victims weren't supposed to be resourceful. Had she pulled herself up, stared hard at her new reality like a child who wakes in a strange bedroom and needs seconds to orient herself, had she let the steel that was in her intestines glint for a moment in the sunshine of public interest, no-one would have pitied her. In her mind, that was the choice things resolved themselves into; either she drew on her resources and showed everyone she was capable, could shift for herself and would sweep away the ruins of her jerry built marriage to construct in its place a sturdy residence of independence and happiness; or she sank into helplessness and called on Christian pity to come to her aid. The latter appealed to her ingrained Methodism. Religion, like every other influence, plays on the individual sensibility and imagination, and as we are as unique in our brains as our fingerprints, everyone's religion is their own. For Ginny Wiswell, the overwhelming truth of Christianity was that help must come to those who suffer; God was good and would not turn away from a soul in need; the Devil, on the other hand, took the side of those who pushed, who knew where their interest lay and how to pursue it, who provoked fear rather than compassion. These crude ideas had been fed into her mind when she was no more than a child of three and rooting in the fresh soil of innocence had grown into thick shrubs of ignorance, fear and certainty which kept all rational enlightenment hidden. It might be 1962, the rebellion of youth might be sweeping aside decades of deference, but that prevailed little on a mentality formed in the grim backstreets of a poor northern town in the twenties and thirties. She made a choice to let depression, hopelessness and despair flood the plain of her humiliated being and she waited in vain for Christian succour, as Christ himself found only abandonment on the cross.

She had three children. So did her husband but she was determined he shouldn't. Shoving him out of the door for being unable to keep his fly zipped was also expelling him from her life and everything to do with it. She had virtue on her side and virtue knows little of the pity she sought for herself. Had anyone suggested to her that depriving her children of their father might not be the best for them, she would have been as shocked as when she discovered the apparently nice young couple in the next room at the Norbreck Hydro, Blackpool, the last time they had a week there in the summer, weren't married but were living as man and wife. When she told this in outrage to her fourteen year-old, Kath realised it was a real agony for her. The daughter had absorbed the more liberal attitudes of the time. Oh, she believed in marriage, but she didn't see why a girl shouldn't find out beforehand. And though she thought her mother's idea absurd, she couldn't but feel inordinately sorry for her. Her pain, though the result of a distorted view of things, was real. Kath looked at her mother's contorted features and her huddled posture; she wasn't one of those vulgar women who puff up their chests and loudly denounce their neighbours over the fence for their slovenly or immoral habits while leaving the sheets on the bed for six months and not telling the shopkeeper if they got too much change; in her poor little mind, formed in primitive religion in the reduced mean streets of a town where the vicious lived well and lorded, it was a given truth that a man and woman should make their vows before god prior to getting familiar. The thought of the immorality of sex before marriage almost made her physically sick.

"Well, never mind," said Kath, "never mind. Leave them to their business."

In spite of herself, there were moments when Ginny was glad Stan had left. The marriage was never any good. She put up with it. They got by. They got along, more or less, that was the best that could be said; but now she didn't have him making her stomach turn with his selfish ways or forcing her to wrap herself in the bedclothes so as not to touch him during the night; she had the big bed to herself and some mornings she would wake as the sunshine was making the flowery curtains transparent and she would feel content; the bed was warm; she could lie there quietly for half an hour; it was a nice room with a large, semi-circular bay and the grove was quiet; the Stag furniture was very high quality; she felt herself lucky. She heard Paul getting himself ready for school and Kath running a bath. Pippa was still asleep. For a few minutes she was able to believe life had been good to her; but her mood was soon subverted. She found herself thinking of her status. She was a woman abandoned. The respectability of marriage, which had always meant so much to her, had been torn from her like a hand caught in a loom and ripped off at the wrist. What did people think of her? A woman on her own was always suspect. Did the neighbours connive at her satisfactions? She knew how people speculated and talked and she knew how they loved nothing more than finding fault in others. She had to turn herself into such a pillar of virtue no-one would be able to say a word. The idea of another man was anathema. She'd fallen for Stan's charm, his good-looks, his easy smile, embracing chat and suave clothes; what sort of world was it where your feelings could lead you astray so badly? A fallen world. Henceforth it was the purity of Heaven she would cleave to.

By the time she got out of bed, Paul had left the house and Kath was pulling on her gaberdine. They were independent children who never gave her a moment's trouble. Paul was always out early because he wanted to kick a football in the playground. He would make himself toast and tea, clear any mess, wash his mug, shove his arms into his wind-jammer, grab his Frido and run off to meet his mates. Kath was already capable of running a household: she took two pounds from her mother, went to the Co-op, the fishmonger, the butcher and the ironmonger and came back with stewing steak, bread, flour, apples, oranges, bananas, a nice piece of cod, washing powder and change. Ginny never needed to plug in the vacuum, nor lift the iron except for her own clothes, the sheets and the underwear and towels she insisted on smoothing before they went in the drawers. The children always washed up after themselves, Paul pushed the stiff Qualcast up and down the oblong lawn and jabbed the hoe at the weeds; he even sanded the loose paint off the downstairs frames and repainted, but she wouldn't let him climb a ladder. Once a week Kath stripped the sheets from the beds and put them in the tub. Ginny almost resented that: she liked to spend all Sunday morning, from seven till twelve, filling and emptying the machine whose agitator rocked backwards and forwards with a terrible, industrial churn, dragging the heavy clothes out with her wooden pincers and feeding them through the tight rollers, pegging them out on the line for the neighbours to see. It was hard sweaty work but it made her feel good, once it was over. Kath said to her one day:

"Sue's mum has one of the new twin-tubs. They're much less work."

"Won't have one," snapped Ginny.

There was an association in her mind between too-efficient house-hold machines and laziness; and idleness was the work of the Devil. He wanted us to have leisure, for when we aren't working we are prey to His foul temptations. Mrs Hothersall had an automatic and a cleaner, but what did she spend her time doing? Going from one cof-fee morning to another and playing whist. No, Ginny was sure that to be burdened with work was to avoid sin. She was so obsessed with finding things to do (climbing the step-ladders every day to wipe the lampshades, getting down on her knees to scrub the vestibule and the front step for the fifth time in a week) she barely noticed how good her children were.

Pippa sat up in her little bed in the alcove.

"Is it morning time?"

"It is. Come on. Downstairs."

The child played with her posh-frocked dolls and building bricks in the living-room while Ginny went to the kitchen to make breakfast. Everything was neat. She took the mug Paul had washed and left upturned on the drainer and washed it once more, dried it and put it in the wooden cupboard. In a few days time her mornings would no longer be so relaxed: she'd made a deal with Stan – he could stop paying maintenance if he signed the house over to her. Her mind had been plagued by thoughts of being made homeless. This gave her the guarantee of a home for her and her children. Had she known the law kept her safe, that Stan could do nothing until Pippa was eighteen, that what the courts called the matrimonial home was hers for anoth-er fifteen years, she might have acted differently; but she didn't seek legal advice. The barrister who represented her in her divorce had the stench of alcohol on his breath. Nor was he willing to listen to her story of the unhappiness she'd suffered in marriage. The legal pro-fession was full of clever Devils. She made the decision for herself. But without maintenance she had to bring in money. She took a job as a school cleaner: split shifts, six thirty till eight and four till six. She was to start the following Monday. Mrs Buzzington, a pillar of the Railway Mission, had agreed to look after Pippa for the few minutes each day needed to allow Paul and Kath to get off to school and come home. That morning, Ginny called on her.

"Sorry to disturb you, Mrs Buzzington. Are you washing?"

"No, come in Mrs Wiswell. Hello, Pippa. Sit down, love. I was just cleaning the kitchen windows. "

"Oh, I know. Don't they get a mess. I'm at mine every day."

"You have it to do."

"Always better to be busy, Mrs Buzzington. The Devil makes work."

"He does. Will you have a cup of tea?"

"No. I'm not stoppin'. I just wanted to be sure everything's all right for next week."

"Champion," said Mrs Buzzington, wiping down the kitchen table. "Kath'll bring her twenty past eight."

"Kath or Paul."

"You've got good children, Mrs Wiswell."

"They're not bad, in spite of their father."

Mrs Buzzington speeded up her wiping. The child sat quietly on a stool at the table chewing the sleeve of her coat.

"It'll be fine. It's only a few minutes every day. I'm glad to help."

"It's very Christian of you, Mrs Buzzington. That was Stan's problem. He had no religion."

Mrs Buzzington went to the sink and turned on the noisy tap to rinse her cloth.

"He caused me a lot of unhappiness, Mrs Buzzington. A lot of unhappiness."

"Are you sure you wouldn't like a cup of tea?"

"No. This child. I don't know. I don't know what's to become of her."

"We must just do our best, Mrs Wiswell."

"I'd never've imagined it. To think of the grand lads I could've married. And him. He couldn't resist any young thing who batted her eyelids at him."

"Well, if she's here at twenty past on Monday, I'll be ready."

Mrs Buzzington wrung her cloth and began to take off her apron.

"He's caused me some grief. I've been near to sticking my head in't gas oven before today, I'll tell you."

The child was chewing diligently on her sleeve.

"Would you like a biscuit, love?" said Mrs Buzzington.

"She's had her breakfast. The doctor said to me, he said, "You're a very disturbed woman." That's what he said. Who wouldn't be with what I've been through?"

"What about a rusk?" said Mrs Buzzington and she grabbed a small pair of wooden steps and climbed the two rungs to reach the packet from the top shelf. She was no more than five feet one, a stubby, energetic little woman who in her day had been fierce with a hockey stick. Now all her energy went into keeping her house as clean as a surgeon's hands. She passed the round, dry, biscuit to the child who took it without smiling and began to soften it in her mouth.

"I'm off the tranquilizers. I couldn't put up with those. That's what he did to me, my husband, put me on tranquilizers. God'll punish him. But I've got this child to bring up. It's no picnic on your own, Mrs Buzzington."

"Well, I'd better be getting on. I've the bathroom to see to now."

"The milkman said to me, "I don't know where he's lookin'." He's seen her. Nineteen she is. Her eyes meet in the middle."

"Is that nice?" said Mrs Buzzington to the girl who nodded but whose face showed no response.

"I said to him, "I don't want you round here, Stan. You're not giving me a chance." "Chance of what?" he said. Talk about thick. Thick as that wall. Well, he wasn't brought up right. His mother was no better than she should be. I said to her, I said, "Somebody neglected him when he was young." "Well, it wasn't me," she said. And her who left him as a kiddie and ran off with her fancy man. You wouldn't believe it, Mrs Buzzington."

"I'd better be going upstairs now or I'll never get done."

"Look at her. Three years old and no father. What's to become of you, Pippa? Eh? I'm sure I don't know. I'm sure I don't."

"Goodbye then, Mrs Wiswell. I'll see you on Monday, Pippa. Goodbye now." And she held the kitchen door open so Mrs Wiswell had no choice but to take her child's hand and leave.

"It's not a life, Mrs Buzzington, I'll tell you," she said as she went. "It's no more than an existence. That's what it is. An existence."

"Thanks for calling," said Mrs Buzzington and closed the door.

Once she began work, Ginny felt very virtuous. She earned four pounds a week. That and the family allowance was all she had. Paul and Kath got the idea. They both took paper rounds and saved the money to pay for their own clothes. They never asked their mother for a penny. When there was a school trip to Paris which cost forty pounds, Kath put up twenty.

"I'll ask my dad if he can pay the rest."

"You'll do no such thing!"

And Ginny took the money from her savings account where there was two hundred pounds she'd accumulated before the divorce.

Nothing new was ever bought for the house. Every week was a struggle to avoid disaster. But the months went by. Kath, who passed five O Levels left school at sixteen and took a job in an insurance office. She handed over half her money. Paul would buy bread, milk and eggs from his paper round. Ginny expected to feel good. She was doing the right thing. She was exerting strenuous control. She never went out. She had no friends. She worked. She scrimped. She kept the house as best she could. She went to church every Sunday. Yet the well-being that was supposed to accompany virtue never arrived. Nor did the Christians of the suburbs come running to her aid. She was alone. She toiled. She lived a more restricted life than a nun. She told herself she was doing the best for her children. Their father was a selfish reprobate who deserved their hatred, but she was virtue itself. Nevertheless, all the muscular self-discipline brought no comfort: her mood was almost permanently low; she found herself expecting some change to come over her each day but nothing happened. Where was it then, the reward for being good the Bible said was inevitable? She began to think she would have to wait till she got to Heaven. Perhaps these awful days of unrelieved work and pennypinching were the mere, short prelude to an eternity of bliss? When she thought of that she felt better. The weight of negative fate lifted from her. For a few hours or even a few days she experienced that lightness of feeling we call happiness when nothing seems burdensome and even the most banal and simple tasks bring well-being. In these moods even cleaning the toilet seemed pleasant because it was making things bright and clean. But the clear sky of untroubled life soon darkened; most of the women around her had husbands who behaved decently; she lived in a nice suburb where the houses were spacious and the gardens well-kept; but she, her life was crumbling like a Victorian sewer and the voracious rat of misery gnawed endlessly behind the closed doors of her mind.

It was at the end of the day she felt most desperate. As she walked home from the angular, squat Secondary Modern, along the lane where cows grazed in the fields and at the end of the farm road the house stood, solid, ancient and independent, she asked herself why she didn't live there; why wasn't she the wife of a hard-working farmer who owned acres? Why hadn't a good life fallen to her? Why had she made a bad marriage and why were even her children a burden? She would think of her girlhood, the happy days in the little house in the back streets; the gas lights and cobbles were symbols of a lost world; even the outside toilet, so cold in winter, was a locale of delight compared to the emptiness of her comfortable bathroom; her taciturn father who smoked his pipe, read his paper and came and went to his work in the mill, and her big-framed, ever-active mother who dominated the house and her four children with her endless scrubbing, washing, tidying and admonitions, had provided a security as reliable as the Lord Himself. How carefree she'd been running to and from her school where Mr Lloyd could instil terror with a glance; how full of promise life had been as she played whip and top with her brothers on the big flagstones of the pavement; how charming the world was even in this poor corner of the town without trees, grass or flowers so long as you had a pal to laugh with and you could spark your clogs on the kerb stone and skip a turning rope till bedtime in summer. Now she had to drag home and make tea. She was tired from her cleaning but more from her humiliation. The teachers in their suits walked by her on the corridors and she felt demeaned. The place she had in the world was hardly worth occupying. She wanted to cry with her Saviour, "Oh Lord, why hast thou forsaken me?" In the evening she read the local paper, watched *Coronation St* or *The Wednesday Play*. Sometimes she would try to talk to Kath as if they were friends rather than mother and daughter, but the girl became uncomfortable and went up to her room. The sound of her door closing formed ice in Ginny's heart. At ten, weary and with nothing to look forward to but another day of pride-stripping work and stomach-sinking scrimping, she went to bed with a mug of cocoa.

One May afternoon when her thoughts had become as heavy as the shopping bags of potatoes and flour she carried home from town, Paul came running to meet her as she turned into the grove. What did he want? What was he looking so pleased with himself about? He was dressed in the tennis kit he'd bought for himself and carrying the racquet Stan left behind. Ginny disliked his playing tennis. She refused to watch him or take any interest. Hadn't Stan wasted his time at the club a few doors away? And what had he got up to with Eileen Savage and Wendy Holmes? He couldn't play for toffee either. Nor could Paul, she was sure. And here he was, running to her after she'd spent two hours cleaning toilets and polishing floors. The little fool! He was like his father. Tennis! What good was that to anyone? She didn't want to talk to him. She didn't want to be pestered. She wanted to go into the house, cook the tea and bang their plates down in front of them. But the boy was coming towards her. Her boy. She felt strangely unattached. In the way he ran, she spotted something of Stan; he had the same wobbly stride. It almost embarrassed her to see him run, as it had to see Stan play football. She'd stood on the touchline only a few times. He was energetic and keen but she couldn't bear to watch. He made a few good passes and tackles and had a shot at goal but she felt he was pretentious; he wasn't any good. He should give it up. She didn't like to be associated with his puffing, sweaty effort. Had he been Stanley Matthews, she would have liked it. That would have been something to be proud of; but this amateur enthusiasm was far from Heavenly perfection. She believed you should do only what God had destined you for; she could cook and clean, knit, sew and she'd always been a good walker. Her father's brother was a dedicated rambler and sometimes he'd taken her out on a Sunday, over the hills, across muddy farmyards where tethered sheep dogs barked madly, slipping on the stones in singing streams where the water from the tops ran clear, gurgling with the purity of Nature. If only Paul were coming towards her in his hiking boots. His racquet was tucked under his left arm. The collar of his Fred Perry shirt was raised and its three buttons unfastened. Vanity. Just like Stan. He checked himself in the mirror before going to the court, tugged the wings of his collar, ran his little black comb through his quiff. He was a handsome young lad but she could take no delight in his attractiveness. She almost wished him ugly. He had his looks from her as well as his father for as a young woman she'd been exceptionally pretty and even now that time, neglect and unhappiness had carved their thoughtless signatures onto the polished surface of her beauty, her eyes sometimes flashed with charm and her smile was that of a young girl full of promise; but she hated to see Stan's

77

features in him. She would have preferred him to be like her brothers who took after their mother and were ugly-boned and heavy featured. Had he been walking towards her in black, the tight, white dog-collar round his slim neck, a Bible in his hand, she would've been glad to meet him. As everything she relied on collapsed like a rotten fence against which you lean your weight, the one source of certainty was the word of God. Yet he advanced. His very youth was a slight to her. The bright afternoon whose warm air was a balm affronted her. She kept her eyes fixed on the ground. She hoped he would turn back.

"Mum!"

The excitement in his voice made her wince.

"I've beaten Nick Heywood. I'm through to the semi-final."

"Don't bother me," she said, "can't you see I'm tired?"

The boy went immediately quiet. He walked beside her. From moment to moment he looked at her face but she refused to turn her eyes to him. When they entered the house, she went straight to the kitchen. She heard him go upstairs. She peeled potatoes for chips and set the gas under the frying pan where the thick lard had solidified. She knew she'd wounded him and she was glad. Running to her like that. As if tennis was of any importance. And she with the tea to cook. The chips sizzled in the fat. She cracked eggs into the melted lard and buttered a stack of white bread. Pippa, who Kath had been entertaining in the lounge, came through with her doll in her arms.

"Go and wash your hands in the bathroom then sit at the table."

She set the plate of bread in the middle of the cloth, took the vinegar and tomato ketchup from the cupboard. When she lifted the metal basket from the pan the chips were browned to a turn. She felt pleased with herself. It was basic fare but did she have time to do more? Before Stan left she would spend all day cooking a splendid meal. They were fed. They should be grateful. She tipped the chips onto plates. Pippa climbed onto a chair. Going into the hallway, Ginny called:

"Katherine! Paul! Come and get your tea before it goes cold."

She sat down and began to eat and at once she realised how hungry she was, how tasty even these simple chips were and she wished she'd taken the time to make something she could really relish.

"Where's our Paul?" said Kath as she came in.

"In his bedroom. Shout him."

Kath went to the foot of the stairs.

"Paul! Paul! Come down. Your tea's going cold."

She heard his door as she turned away, as did her mother, then his step on the stair. Ginny took a slice of bread. When he came in, without looking at him she said:

"Have you washed your hands?"

He went through to the kitchen and they heard the water drumming against the steel. When he came to the table Ginny glanced at him. He was no longer wearing his tennis kit.

NYE BEVAN IS DEAD, DAD.

When Pam's elder brother was elected President of the Student's Union in 1972 as an International Socialist, his parents laughed about it at the table.

"Enjoy it while you can, he'll probably end up a Liberal," said her father.

"Give him some credit. He'll fall into the Labour Party," her mother retorted

"Yeah, he'll probably be a junior minister talking crap on the telly."

Pam wasn't sure what to make of it. She followed her parents' political line: they voted Labour, belonged to unions, boycotted Barclays and wouldn't buy South African oranges. Tom, her brother, was much more steeped in politics than her. She wanted to do well. He wanted to change the world. Tom had breezed through school; a bright scientist he was reading Physics which she found impossibly hard. She had to struggle to get through; but she was top in English and determined to make something of it. She was a little bit disturbed by his election. She felt something of an outsider in her family because they were all so politically attuned. Still, her mother was very attentive and praised her for her good marks and encouraged her to do well, and her dad put his arm round her as he read her reports and said, "I'm proud of you, lass. I'm proud of you."

When she went to university in 1979, there were no International Socialists on the executive. The mood was much more to her liking; students were less concerned with the state of the world and more interested in their career prospects. She harboured a secret admiration for Mrs Thatcher, though her parents despised her. She would never have voted Tory but the sense that life was a struggle for scarce rewards, everyone against everyone and the spoils to the winner was something she liked. She quickly found herself outclassed by some of her fellow students, especially James Kirkwood who was one of those fearsome intellectuals who could ruthlessly tear ideas apart or examine a text in the most minute detail and produce interpretation as easily as breathing. She made it her business to get to know him.

"Jim," he said.

"Sorry?"

"Don't call me James. Only my mother calls me that."

"Oh, okay."

She sat in the armchair at the foot of his bed while he sat on the chair by the alcove desk. He'd made her a coffee, a real coffee, not the Nescafe her dad drank all the time. It was an aromatic, lovely drink. She was delighted to sit in his room on a cold Wednesday afternoon sipping and chatting.

"Well," he said, "he's rehearsing the same conflicts over and over. His real subject, and his only subject, is his parents' marriage. He was ruined. They destroyed him. His mother especially. She bound him to her when her love for her husband collapsed. Think how that must have felt for him as a kid. He was taking his father's place. But it's not the classic oedipal thing. I don't take Freud at face value anyway. No, it's power. His mother was a bitterly disappointed woman. She married a man to complement her but she found his easygoing ways, his drinking and his unabashed pleasures vulgar. She was, in fact, a snob. Lawrence was trapped. His mother exploited him but Lawrence loved his father. I'd say he loved him more than her. But she stopped him. That's a horrible thing, to stop your child loving his father. Her emotional greed was almost boundless. This was the great tragedy of Lawrence's life, that his parents' marriage failed. It hurt him inordinately. He wanted to mend it. He wanted men and women to love one another so little Bert Lawrence wouldn't be hurt anymore. And the truth is he never understood. He never grasped why his mother and father couldn't get on. So he brought it all down to sex. If only they could have had orgasms together everything would have been right. But it wasn't that. His mother married the wrong man. She was too prissy. She should have married someone middle-class. A Methodist. Someone stern who loved a Sunday sermon. Lawrence's father loved the flowers of Nottinghamshire. He had a real feel for life. That's where Lawrence got it from. He was like his father in lots of ways and his mother hated his father. You see how bad that would make you feel?"

"But surely he wrote about other things," she said.

"Such as?"

She was unnerved by the way he looked directly at her when he said these things.

"Well, all that stuff about industrial civilisation and how it's anti-life. He's always using the word life in a special way. It doesn't just mean biology. But I think there's a big part of his work that's about rejecting modern industry and society and looking for a simpler way of life that's in touch with nature."

"Ruskin."

"What?" she sipped her coffee looked askance at him with wide eyes.

"He inherited all that from Ruskin. And Thoreau. Probably Thoreau more than Ruskin. If I do a Phd I'm going to write about Thoreau's influence on Lawrence. HDT and DHL. Lawrence was deeply influenced by Walden Pond, all that return to nature stuff. Building your own little cabin and living frugally. And Thoreau had this amazing capacity to just contemplate nature. His mother complained about him being impractical and spending hours gazing at flowers or something. Yeah. Lawrence just grabbed that wholesale. It reminded him of his dad. But it's not his real theme. It's an addition. His theme was his parents' marriage and how it cut him to pieces emotionally as a boy."

Pam didn't really take to Lawrence. She thought he was unfair to women and she found his work always on the side of men. Her favourite writer was Wilkie Collins. She liked a good story and a ghost or detective story above all. She had to hang on by her fingernails as she climbed the cliff face of *Middlemarch* or *Under The Volcano*. She wished she was like Kirkwood: immersed in literary and intellectual life. He read Proust for fun. But then she thought she wouldn't want to be like him because he was obviously going to spend his life writing books about Lawrence or Chaucer or Zola. She didn't want to do that. It was a life apart. Who would read such books? He was going to be part of an intellectual world hardly anyone paid attention to. She wanted to be in the middle of the crowd on the pavement. She wanted to move with the mass. That would give her the chance to push her way to the front. James might become a big intellectual. He'd probably be a professor by the time he was thirty, but who cares about professors? He'd deliver his lectures, teach his seminars, publish his books, attend conferences and be highly thought of among a few hundred people who take all that stuff seriously. The thought of it made her almost nauseous. She saw herself as a Headteacher or Advisor. Someone who could be busy and efficient and tell other people how to get on with their jobs. James was all questions. Everything he said was a kind of question. Even when he produced some clever ideas about Lawrence it was as if he was asking if they might be right. He was always thinking at that point at which certainty dissolved. Talking to him was like walking on the deck of a ten-foot pleasure boat in a storm round Cape Horn. She always felt as if everything reliable was being put in question. She wanted something solid. Above all she wanted to feel she was important and in control. In truth, she'd rather read Ngaio Marsh than Mrs Gaskell. A good thriller was just the kind of thing she liked to go to bed with. It put reading in its proper place: a leisure activity, something to pass the time. But she worked hard because she wanted a good degree and to get on.

For a short time she thought she might entice James into a relationship. She liked the idea of a man who wouldn't be a competitor. He was so lost in his books he wouldn't fight her for dominance. A go-getting man might want her to stay at home, or work part-time. But she could imagine imposing the domestic burdens on James without him having the guile to see what was happening. And in any case, what would it matter to him? He could stay at home and read and write. No. She was the one who needed a career. And wasn't that the way the world was going? Women were taking their place. She wanted hers. James had no ambition in the common way: he didn't want to be in charge or to have money. His ambition was to write good books and to get his interpretation of literature right. She thought it was touchingly naïve. But though she flirted and provoked, swaying her knees apart as she sat in his armchair or wearing a tantalizingly short skirt with black stocking and knee-length boots, he never so much as touched her. When he took up with Pauline Redman, who was dumpy, dowdy, wore glasses and chain smoked, she realized it was because, like him, she had a mind permanently on the edge of doubt. She was articulate and brimmed with ideas in seminars. All the same, Pam couldn't but feel slighted that James could prefer Pauline's unprepossessing body to hers.

Her friendship with him dwindled. She started going out with Colin Niven. Like her he was keen to get on.

"There are some great jobs in the Labour Party," he would say.

When she took him home one weekend and he expressed that very idea while they were having Nescafe in the kitchen, her dad said:

83

"The Labour Party is supposed to be about changing the world, not getting on in it."

"It's an old-fashioned view," she said to Colin. "He's sentimental about Clem Attlee and Nye Bevan. He thinks it's still 1945."

"No reason you can't be a socialist and be rich," said Colin.

"Of course not," said Pam.

"We want a society where people can get on."

"Of course we do."

They both got upper seconds and went on to do PGCEs. They got along pleasantly but there was always a little grit in the gears: Colin had his career mapped out – a Scale One post, move on after a year, two at the most, a Scale Two to get some experience then leap to Scale Three and Head of Department; keep your nose clean, get on all the right courses, keep well in with the Head and Advisors and go for Deputy Headships as soon as possible; he would be a Head by thirty-five at the latest, and after that, well who could say. Pam listened and shifted in her chair.

"What if I get promoted before you?" she said.

"That's fine. No problem with that."

"Whoever earns more gets to follow their career."

"We both can."

"But if we get married, Colin….."

"Let's not dig the grave before the coffin's ordered."

"I'm talking about marriage!"

"I was being metaphorical."

"Someone will have to look after the children."

"There are nurseries."

"I know. But someone has to do the chores. Drop them off. Pick them up."

"We can share."

"That's what I'm saying, Colin. If I'm too busy in my career, I won't have time. We'll have to decide whose career comes first."

"We can both have careers. It'll work out."

But it didn't. The matter of careers and precedence became the fishbone in their throats. It was the sandpaper on the tips of their fingers when they touched one another. The thought Colin might overtake her began to obsess Pam. When he found his first teaching post before her, she was furious.

"Rotherham?"

"It's a good school. And remember, I'll only be there for a year or two."

"I'm looking for jobs all over the country."

"Fine."

She got an interview in Cambridge. It was a big primary in a very middle-class area.

"It's an excellent place to start," she said.

"I'll enjoy coming down. And we can nip to London for shows and stuff."

She was appointed, found herself a tiny flat on the third floor of a big house, worked till ten every night, all Sunday afternoon and did everything she could think of to make a good impression. When Colin suggested visiting for the weekend she found she resented his presumption and the idea of him being in her flat irritated her. She told him she was far too busy. She liked to close the door and sit marking books or preparing wall displays. Always in her mind was the idea of the advancement it would bring. She knew Mr Marchant, the Headteacher, was pleased with her. She was determined to be his favourite. She found herself flirting with him. She noticed him once casting a glance at her cleavage so when she had to go and speak to him about her idea for an Innovations Day, she wore a low-cut blouse and made sure she leant forward to pull some papers from her bag. Not that she would have dreamed of any kind of relationship. Had he made a move towards her she would have protested and reported him to the governors; but every weapon was useful in the fight to get on. It was a little bit of innocent flirting after all and if it unnerved him somewhat and put him on the defensive, all the better for her. Women couldn't be too scrupulous about their methods. They had a lot of catching up to do. Men were in charge and women faced the glass ceiling. Wasn't it true that if your path to success was strewn with nails, if you were blindfolded and left to stumble in the dark, you could be forgiven a little rule-breaking? Nobody ever got anywhere by being modest, honest and fair. That was obvious. Of course, it was important always to proclaim the value of modesty, honesty and fairness. Appearances must be maintained.

"I've got funding from the Institute for Innovations in Arts and Sciences," she said, handing him a file.

"Yes," he said. "That's good. Very good."

She could see he was merely looking over the papers and wouldn't read them.

"The idea would be to have a whole school assembly to start the day where I'd give a presentation and explain to the children…."

She'd thought of everything. She wasn't going to leave any corner of curtain awry where a light she disapproved of might filter in. She wanted her plan accepted as a *fait accompli* without possibility of the slightest revision. She would be in charge for the day. The Head himself would have to comply. She would carry out an evaluation and ensure the event was classed an extraordinary success. She would use it to bid for promotion.

"There's one thing," said the Head.

"Yes."

"Don't you think this is perhaps stepping on Janet Michelson's toes?"

"I don't think so," and she leaned forward to scratch her ankle looking him in the eyes all the while.

He looked away and fiddled with the papers.

"It's just that she does have a remit for curricular innovation and she might see this as encroaching."

"Has she complained?"

"Complained? No. She's mentioned the programme but not complained as such."

The next day Pam caught Mrs Michelson alone in the staffroom.

"Janet. Oh, I'm glad you're here. I just wanted to ask you about the Innovations Day. The Head is very keen, of course. And the governors think it's excellent. Do you think it fits in well with what you're doing for curriculum innovation?"

"I think it's fine, Pam. Only curriculum is my responsibility so I think you should stay away from that."

"Of course. Though it's too late to change the programme now, isn't it?"

She smiled, turned and walked away before Janet could reply, and later in the day, knocked on the Head's door, went in and told him she'd spoken to Mrs Michelson and she was quite happy with what was planned.

Pam's dislike of Mrs Michelson was visceral. She was one of those women who'd made her way in the sixties and seventies and was now settled into her position as Deputy Head. Pam saw her as a blockage, a barrier to be swept away. The old idea of working for twenty years, proving your worth, being promoted because of your experience was anathema to her. Why should she wait? There was nothing Janet could do she couldn't. She belonged to a disappearing world. People waited politely for promotion in those days. But Pam was too impatient to be polite. Thinking about other people's feelings was silly. You had to look after yourself and get ahead. If you didn't understand that, you were lost. The government was talking about city technology colleges and breaking up the old, paternalistic State provision; you had to be where the action was; you couldn't live in the 1980s as if they were the 1960s. That would be like her dad who imagined the world stopped in 1945, or maybe 1964, or perhaps 1974 when Labour won twice on the promise of the fundamental shift of wealth and power to working people he was always banging on about. She had a vague sense of betrayal: she would never actually vote Tory, but this was the way the world was going; what would happen to you if you resisted? When she went home for a visit, her dad ranted against the government and her mother said Mrs Thatcher understood nothing about the women's movement. It was all well and good for them, they didn't have to make their way in the new order. Her dad was in his mid-fifties. He'd soon be retiring. He could sit in his chair by the fire, read the *New Internationalist* and elaborate his theories of a world based on the best in human nature; but she had to contend, every day, with the worst. People weren't nice. Not when it came to money and status. Oh, she could go to the pub with her colleagues on a Friday evening and everyone got along like a rocket. They could arrange a Christmas meal, put on silly hats, get tipsy and be the best of friends. But friendship was as weak as twice brewed tea compared to the force of ambition. She valued her friends, but not one of them was worth sacrificing her career for. Come to that, she couldn't think of toning down her ambition for the sake of a man she loved. No, her desire to get on came first. That's what she sensed in Mrs Thatcher: an unflinching willingness to dismiss whatever stood in the way of success. And what was success? It was money, status, power. It was the admiring gaze of others. It was being able to read in the paper that you were among the top ten percent of earners in the country. What was love compared to that? Yet love had to be important. The last thing she wanted was to be left on the shelf. It was a question of having it all, as she'd heard someone say on the radio. Why shouldn't women have it all? The idea inspired her and made her stride more purposeful. It struck her that the kind of relationship her parents had was a thing of the past: it contained a kind of resistance; it was a way of fending off the harshness of the realm of career and ambition. Hadn't her dad always said work finishes at five and doesn't come over my doorstep? Her mother and father had a gentle, tender way of being in each others' company; they were always making jokes about money and the rich and politicians and laughing till their ribs rattled. It was odd. No-one could be like that any more, not if they were going to get on; and if they didn't, they'd be so crushed by failure they'd never sustain a relationship. No, this was a new world and she had to get along in it. A job wasn't something you started in the morning and finished in the evening and went home and forgot; it was the way you defined yourself. You couldn't take the risk that someone else would work harder and gain a centimetre. No, a career was vital for a woman. She must take her place in the world, she must shine, she must be a superwoman. That's what her mother didn't understand; she was just a woman who'd done a job to make a bit of money, pin money. How demeaning. Pam didn't want pin money she wanted to be among the best paid women in the country; she wanted a big house and a nice car and the self-esteem that went with them. That was how things were. Without money and status you were nobody, despite all her parents' talk of equality.

The Innovations Day was a great success. The Head loved it. The Chair of Governors loved it. The children enjoyed themselves and learned a lot. All the same, whispers filtered to Pam about staff dissatisfaction: they felt it was a box-ticking exercise; she was promot-

ing herself more than looking after the children. No-one said anything to her face but it made her aware of how important it was to
have the right people on your side.

It was at this time she met John Dudley. Like her he was from the
north. He was a journalist who made much of his hard-bitten attitude: the media was a tough world to survive in; you got nowhere
without using your claws. He should know. He came from the back
streets of a small northern town and now he wrote a column for an
important daily, but more interestingly, was getting to know the right
people in the Labour Party.

"It's all about manipulation," he said pouring another glass of Pinot
Grigio. "Honesty, principle. All that stuff. Forget it. They trample
you in the mud. Where are the votes? That's my question. Sniff out
the votes that win elections and do what you have to do to get them.
That's how you get power and it's the only way."

She liked this because it bolstered her sense that her parents no longer understood, but at the same time allowed to her to stay true to
what she'd been brought up with. This was Labour, but it wasn't the
romantic, left-wing Labour of Nye Bevan and Michael Foot. It
chimed with her own need to get on. It was cynical, aggressive and it
required never quite telling the truth to anyone, including yourself.
Dudley had a big flat in London, ate at *The Ivy*, knew the politicians
on the rise, was friendly with important people at the BBC. Lifted
into this atmosphere of power and plentiful money (Dudley jumped
into taxis without a thought for the fare, bought at least two bottles of
wine a day, paid for expensive seats at the theatre or the opera,
notched up debt on his credit card as if it would never need to paid
off and constantly complained that you couldn't live in London on
less that five hundred thousand a year) Pam felt the future opening
up for her. She found a job in the capital. She took on more responsibility. It was a big school in a poor borough and the children
shocked her. On the first day she asked a boy to move desks:

"Fuck off. I'm not sitting there."

She had to adjust her thinking, her teaching, her way of dealing with
the pupils and she had to work much harder. She'd thought she was
pushing herself as far as she could in Cambridge, but here the ex-
haustion was terrible. At first she thought she'd get used to it and it
would fade, but soon she realized it was going to be her life. It was a

matter of keeping going. There was no space for ease. Nothing was a joy. It was a test. Either you kept up or you were a failure. When, in passing she mentioned to John how it felt he said:

"That's how things are when you start to get near the top. No release. You want to get anywhere you've got to take the pressure. Imagine what it's like being PM. That's a bone-crusher of a job. Keeps the wrong people out. To get to the top you've got to have all the qualities. You've got to be clever but you've got to be ruthless. And you've got to fuck off everything in your life except work. What keeps you going is ambition. You see, I can say to myself I'm John Dudley. I have a column in a national paper. People read me. I change people's minds. I make a difference. I am somebody. You know what that is? It's a drug."

He took another swig of Bordeaux.

"It's better than sex. It's better than anything. Nothing in the world can compare to the thrill of power. That's what life is about. Think. Isn't that what Darwin was saying? You've got to pass on your genes. Your genes. No other fucker's genes. They're competition. Your genes. And what's the best way to do that? Power. Simple. Biology impels us to have power. That's why it's such a drug."

"But I'm exhausted," she said, "and I don't have any power."

"You will. Keep pushing. Keep alert. Fuck off the opposition. You'll get your position. What's the alternative, not being tired and having no control? Just being some fuckwit in the system? Who wants to live like that? Might as well be dead."

"Isn't this supposed to be democracy?" she said. "Aren't those people supposed to matter."

But this last effort to hang onto the lifebelt of principle was as hopeless as her attempts to get John to drink less.

"Know what democracy is? Like herding sheep. What do people know? The economy is complex. Most people don't know what a gilt is. How do markets work? Most people have no idea. Democracy is a way of persuading the majority to hand over power to those of us who understand."

John knew what he was talking about. People who mattered in the Labour Party wanted to listen to him. He was making the right contacts, positioning himself for an important post. The more time she

spent with him and the more politicians she met, the more she realised how naïve her parents were. They genuinely put their faith in
democracy. They believed the votes of millions like them could
change the world; but she met those who had power and their view
of the people oscillated between indifference and contempt. The
electorate was an inconvenience. At first she was shocked, but little
by little their views became hers and their contempt began to seem
natural. There was no connection between the world of power in
which John moved and the world of her parents. All the politicians
she got to know wanted to be important on the world stage. They
wanted a place in history and would do almost anything to get it.
Whenever they talked about what they wanted to enact, the final fi-
nesse was how they could sell it. They were no better than double
glazing salesmen in their mentality. One thing they all agreed on was
the importance of ambiguity, of holding back, of never saying clearly
what you meant. They discussed endlessly how a message could be
framed to put together a majority but they never talked like her parents: they never discussed what was right. She realised that somehow
she'd accepted her parents' perspective, even as she'd embraced the
go-getting they reviled. But they were on the other side of a barrier
few would ever cross. There was a power divide much more potent
than the class divide her dad railed against. Crossing the class divide
was getting easier; more people were going to university; you could
start life in the back streets, qualify as a barrister and earn a hundred
thousand a year; but the power divide was much harder to cross because the opportunities were far fewer. It wasn't a matter of being
Head of some quango or executive of some public body or other; that
was mere influence. Power lay with a palmful of people. As John
said, most people elected to parliament weren't bright enough to run
a bike shop. Their purpose was to go into the lobbies when they were
told. Of course, they had to look after their constituents, but that was
easy. There was so much advice available, and in any case, most
MPs simply referred people on to some expert agency. No, the real
power was with no more than a dozen ministers and civil servants.
They could get their own way over anything. It shocked and excited
her. She wanted to turn away from it but she was fascinated. Imagine
being within that tiny ring. People like her parents just didn't matter.
However they voted the same kind of people would end up in power.
It wasn't possible anymore for a self-educated Nye Bevan to come
from the valleys to establish a National Health Service. He would be

stopped. The press would crucify him. His own party would turn against him. He would wail impotently from the backbenches. What a fool her dad was. All that stuff about her granddad coming back from the war and voting for a new world. All gone. The new world was a fight for money and power and few would come through. She felt as though she'd been initiated into a secret society. She'd been handed special knowledge, and though part of her wanted to tell everyone what they believed was illusory, there was a stronger impulse to take advantage, to stick close to John and spend her life among the only people who mattered.

By the time Ofsted was established she was married with two young children, was Headteacher of a school where most of the pupils were poor, many didn't have English as their first language and where the outcomes were disappointing.

"How am I supposed to look good in an inspection?" she said to John. "Look at our intake. That's the problem."

"No," said John filling his glass with Chianti, "that's old thinking. Poverty is no excuse. If the school lets the kids down, it must be punished."

"We don't let them down, we're facing impossible odds."

"I don't believe that."

"Well, you're wrong, John. I do the job."

"No I'm not. What you've got to focus on is results. See those kids as results machines. Everything that can't be measured, kick it out. Focus and measure. Focus and measure. Then you can turn it round."

At first it struck Pam these were wild ideas generated by people far from classrooms with no real understanding. She put up a little, fleeting resistance; but then the defeating thought came to her that John was right: power was in the hands of people like him and however remote from reality their ideas, they would carry the day. Little by little she found herself thinking like him and changing what went on in school to fit his ideas. It was true: if you put the required outcomes first, it was possible to make things look much better. She'd always begun with the child, with his or her inclinations, strengths, weaknesses and needs; how the child fitted the system was another matter. Now she realised how the child fitted the system was all that mattered. The children had to be trained to provide the results the system needed. The thought of doing badly in an OFSTED filled her with such rank fear she would have shaved the pupils' heads and put them in straightjackets if the inspectors had demanded it. The old days were gone. The pretence that the children came first had to be maintained, but the truth was the system was expected to make the politicians look good. She listened to John. She understood how it worked: results must improve so the Party could go to the country and say it was turning things round. There was too much failure in the system, too many schools where children left with few or no qualifications. That's how the system was measured. That was the meaning of success. The clue was to push up the results, to batter the public with outcomes. John viewed the comprehensive system as a failure. Pam knew this was unfair, but the need to pull in votes overcame everything. They had to be seen to be doing something. They were like pregnant fathers pacing before the birthing room. They had to look busy and purposeful. Elections were won from the middleground. It was vital to appeal to the middle-classes and they didn't believe in socialised provision; they wanted choice; they wanted public services to be like supermarkets; they wanted to choose a school like they chose a car. That was what mattered: the system must be broken up, opened out and made to look like a market. Then the middle-classes could be persuaded to vote Labour and John could have a job in government.

Pam found it all extraordinarily confusing and deeply troubling but one thing sustained her: the idea of her own success. If she could come through in this new world, if she could make money, be congratulated by OFSTED, if she could be one of the few who made it to the top, she could put all her doubts, anxieties and principles aside. What, after all, was the alternative? To stand up against the system. To tell the truth when power was on the march? That was to face being crushed. She would be sidelined, she would be demoted. She would be a no-one. She would earn a poor salary and face pressure from those above her. She would be sacked. No. She would be the one to put on pressure. She would say yes to whatever those with power asked. Wasn't she doing the best for the pupils? Wasn't she working to ensure they got the best results? Weren't good results the way to good jobs and a better life? She was conscientious to a fault. She did everything required of her. She could hold her head high. The first task was to come through the inspection with flying colours. She told her staff things would have to change.

There was a little revolt. Teachers said they didn't want to spend their time putting numbers in boxes. It didn't help the children. They complained music and drama were being sacrificed. They said making children jump through hoops to get the results OFSTED wanted wasn't educating them. They argued that the standard lesson Pam insisted they deliver was constraining, dull and diminished variety. Pam listened, thanked them for their contribution then made it clear that anyone who didn't conform would face competency procedures. The few weeks before the inspectors arrived were ghastly. The atmosphere in the school was frozen with fear and cloddish conformism. The children became anxious. Pam told them in assembly the school was on trial. If they let themselves down it might be closed. They must be on their best behaviour and work very hard.

The inspectors weren't without criticisms, but they liked what they saw: diligent children, standard lessons, punctilious paperwork, an obvious strenuous attempt to please. There was a long way to go but they judged the school good and improving. In particular they praised Pam and their description of her as a very able Headteacher who sets exacting standards for her staff and pupils lodged in her brain. She ensured it was one of the quotations she had printed, framed and displayed in the foyer. She could almost have had it carved in stone. All her doubts disappeared. She was right. She was on her way. Henceforth she was ever more conformist and compliant. She had come to believe whatever she was told to do must be right.

In 2010, Pam was asked to take over a failing school. She knew what she had to do. She made it clear she would accept the post only if money was available to improve the place physically. It had been left to decline for years. The roof leaked. The windows were draughty. Rats roamed the bins at night. It was one of those schools which serve the very poor. The parents had no idea how to fight for improvements. They had no contacts. They couldn't write letters to the paper. The authority wasn't afraid of them. With difficult decisions to make, Nelson Rd had been overlooked. The children were ashamed of their school. They knew no more than a mile away, was Portland Primary, a beautiful school in sweet grounds, full of pupils whose parents were doctors, lawyers, accountants, professors, bank managers. They knew the Portland kids called their school smelly Nelson. So over the summer holiday the builders moved in and when the term began it was in a bright, fresh, clean school which smelt of paint and new furniture.

But that was cosmetic.

From the first, she imposed herself on the staff. They had to hand over their lesson plans for the week by eight o'clock on Monday morning. They had to mark to her scheme. They had to teach in the way she told them. She was frequently in school till midnight and she expected them to stay late. When they complained they had lives outside school, she told them they must conform or get on the bus. Slowly and reluctantly they began to bend to her will but one held out. Anna Pollitt had worked in the school for nearly thirty years and was a year from retirement. Pam thought she would simply ignore her for a year and she would go on her way, but when it became clear she didn't intend to retire her mind changed.

"I don't have your lessons plans, Anna."

"I'm not spending my weekend doing lessons plans I don't need."

"We all need to do lesson plans."

"I've been teaching nearly three decades. A detailed plan of every lesson? I can make a Christmas cake without a recipe."

"That's facetious, Anna."

"I apologise."

"Can you let me have your plans by eight every Monday, please?"

"No."

"I have to warn you that if you refuse I will be forced to invoke the school's disciplinary procedures."

"Why can't we have a debate?"

"There's no need for debate. I'm the Headteacher."

"We can still discuss how useful and necessary lesson plans are. The staff would like to have their say."

"There's no point. Whatever the staff think I'm in charge. I have to do what OFSTED require. If you teach in this school you'll produce lesson plans. That's that."

"Yes. It's about control."

"I beg your pardon?"

"Whether I need to do plans or not, you want control. It's power. I'm not submitting to that. I can teach without plans and putting numbers in boxes. I'll use my time and energy to do what's best for the children. And I don't see why I shouldn't decide that."

Pam suddenly felt as if her dad was sitting before her. It was just the kind of thing he'd say. He believed in the right of the people at the bottom to make their own decisions. He thought democracy was about power resting with the majority. But she knew that was silly. The world had to be run by experts. What did the majority know? What did the people at the bottom understand? How could they make decisions? John was right: democracy was a way of manipulating the many so they fell in line with the ideas of the few. As for equality, that was a mere abstraction. Yes, we were all equals in so far as racism had been driven out of public life and homophobia was becoming unacceptable; yes, women must not be discriminated against and the disabled must have access to supermarkets and theatres; but equality of wealth or power? That was a sick idea. There had to be a few people making the important decisions. That was how the world worked. Her dad might laugh at hierarchy and claim it was founded on the belief in god, but it was true: you couldn't trust people to make decisions for themselves. And if a few had to make the decisions, they must have the rewards. That's why she earned sixty thousand and Anna thirty-five. In that monetary difference lay the symbol of important distinction. It was outrageous Anna could question her authority. She was doing what was demanded by the government and the government was elected by the people. She was entirely justified in telling Anna what to do. The system had to be run from the top and everyone in it must do what they were asked. She had a small duty. A petty authority. But it must be obeyed just as she must obey those above her. She had taken over this school to prove herself. She was going to succeed. She had to please her superiors. What did people like Anna matter? She would force her to agree. She would make her comply or she would sack her.

But when she invoked the disciplinary procedures, Anna submitted spatchcock plans. Pam accused her of not doing them properly, Anna replied she had done them; there were no grounds for disciplinary action; if the plans weren't up to scratch, that wasn't a disciplinary matter. Pam began competency procedures. She observed Anna's lessons and judged them wanting. She checked her marking and claimed it didn't follow the school's format. A compromise agreement was settled and Anna disappeared. Her victory made Pam intent on finding more shortcomings. It became almost an obsession. She was sure the staff were against her. They were plotting. They were lazy and would bring her and the school down. She needed a younger, more compliant staff. She needed people she'd appointed who would understand from the first they must follow her instructions to the letter. One by one she picked off her staff. It was as easy as buttering toast to go into a classroom and find a teacher unsatisfactory. She began to relish it. When she had first done it she felt awkward and a little guilty. But now she felt justified. She agreed with the view that teachers were not up to scratch. She and a few like her were the saviours of the system. There was a need to squeeze out all the second-rate staff. Little by little she began to see almost everyone as second-rate. It was only the odd teacher who was like herself in attitude, demeanour and practice she could believe in. Even when she'd cleaned out all the pre-existing staff but one, she felt the new appointees were letting her down. She had to watch them more closely, impose tighter rules. It was a simple fact: too many teachers were feckless shirkers and it was the task of people like her to save the children from them.

She spent more and more time at work. Her children got used to communicating with her by text message and e-mail. They were lucky if they saw her for two hours a week.

"I have an important job to do," she told them. "You're teenagers now. You must take responsibility for yourselves."

John reinforced the message. He was hardly at home. Even though his exciting time at the heart of government had come to an end in May 2010, he was catching trains and planes from city to city, town to town and country to country making speeches and attending meetings in a manic flurry of activity and booze-fuddled nights in hotels. His drinking was diligent. If they were in the house together at the weekend, he would start with a glass of wine in the early afternoon. By five the first bottle was empty. By eight the third was opened and by midnight he was finishing the scotch. Being in the house was a torment to him. He went out whenever he could. An evening at home made him as jumpy as a hungry flea. Pam turned from her disappointment in her marriage to her success in her job. She took a week during the summer holidays. At Christmas she was back in school on the 27th. She worked every half-term holiday. If her staff left before six she would ask them why they needed to go early. She told them six weeks was far too long to be away from school and they should make an effort to come in during the summer.

The first inspection declared the school outstanding. She was awarded Primary Headteacher of the year. The government invited her to join a working party on school improvement. She was recruited to train future Heads. A long article about her appeared in the national press. There was a photo of her surrounded by smiling children. They loved her. She'd given them a school to be proud of. They were getting good results. She was a success. The governors admired and supported her. The parents thought she was wonderful.

A few weeks after the newspaper article, her mother died. It was a horrible shock. Though she'd often thought of her parents' demise once they'd become slow and weak, the fact of death was still hard. She and John went to stay with her father so they could arrange the funeral but Pam wouldn't miss work. She drove two hundred miles back and forth. Her father was shrunken and grey and the loss had shattered his usual cheerfulness. Once the burial was over, her brother had flown back to America, and things were becoming quiet, John went off to a conference in Paris and Pam stayed on her own for the weekend. She realised it was the first time in her life she'd been alone with her father in his house. It was strange. She felt no real connection to him any more. He was her father. She had to do her duty as a daughter. But she had no desire to be with him. His presence spoke of a past she'd rejected and his future was death. He was a stranger. This man who had loved her, who had cuddled and comforted her as a child, who had done all the trite and wonderful things fathers do for their children-carried her on his shoulders, fished for shrimps and crabs in rock pools on holiday - was now someone she found it hard to talk to. It upset her and to calm herself she went about cleaning the house, pulling on rubber gloves and scrubbing the skirting boards or climbing a step-ladder to wipe the light shades. When they sat opposite one another at the table on Sunday evening she felt almost like an intruder.

"Your mother was very proud of you when she read that article," he said.

"Good. "

"So am I."

"Thanks, dad."

"Don't thank me. You did it yourself."

"I'm glad it makes you happy."

He looked up from his plate. In his blue eyes she saw the old sparkle of defiance and mischief.

"It doesn't make me happy. In fact it pisses me off."

She laughed.

"I thought you were proud of me."

"I am. It's a common fault in parents. I'm proud that you've achieved something and I'm glad you live well materially. But all the same."

She was determined not to argue with him. He was an old man. He reminded her of the Michael Foot he so admired, living beyond ninety, frail but still trying to burn with the old fire.

"All the same?"

"You're going to convert your school to an Academy?"

"We are."

"Why?"

"Because it's best for the children."

"Which children?"

"The children in the school."

"You know what's best for those children?" he said, pointing his fork at her.

"What?"

"What's best for all children."

"But I run one school, dad. I have to do what's best for my pupils."

"God bless me and my wife, my son John and his wife, us four, no more."

"It's not like that. All schools should become Academies."

"What's the point of that?"

"Equality."

He rocked back in his chair and laughed like in the old days. For a second she saw him as he was when she was young. Always laughing, always full of vim, always raging against the latest injustice, always with a kind word and gentle hand.

"Pam, you can't see what's on the end of your nose. What's the point of a Rolls-Royce if everyone has one? To want to own a Rolls-Royce is an ugly impulse. So ugly a strenuous propaganda has to work night and day to convince people of the opposite. We are egotists by nature but our egotism is vile. It's what we must fight against."

Pam had heard this kind of thing so often it was as unmoving as the arrival of the milkman. It had always been a little bit beyond her. Tom understood it and her mother and father lived within the caressive circle of their shared radicalism; but she had always felt a little left out. If she tried to imitate her parents' socialism, it came out wrong. Her sincere feeling was that she had to get on with life in the existing circumstances.

"Are you saying I'm an egotist, dad?"

She saw a flicker of pain in his face.

"I'm not insulting you personally, Pam. But an Academy. Why?"

"It's the way things are moving. It gets money for the school."

"And for you."

"Of course."

He put down his knife and fork.

"Is that your motivation?"

"It's part of it. What's wrong with that? What's wrong with doing well and getting on?"

"Purely this." He curled the thumb and forefinger of his right hand into a little circle. "What matters is not that you get on but how. There are right and wrong ways of making money, right and wrong ways of being successful. And you have to choose."

"I can't choose, dad. I'm part of a system. There isn't enough flexibility to choose. Either you do what the system requires or you fail."

"Maybe failing is the right thing to do."

"And be at the bottom? Earn poor money? Live in a crappy place? What's the good of that?"

"Of course," he began eating again, "there is no good in that."

She hoped the discussion was over and that too old and tired to revive his customary Herculean mental fight against the forces of injustice and reaction he would accept times had changed. She hoped especially he would congratulate her, then she could treat him kindly, in a way that befits a man for whom life is a few rooms, a walk to the corner shop for the paper, a snooze in the chair, an hour listening to the radio; a man already nursed in the arms of death. There was silence for a minute.

"You know what the problem is, Pam?" he raised his head and his eyes were wide. She saw in them an energy and passion a man of his age shouldn't be capable of. She shook her head.

"I'm sure you'll tell me."

"You're right. Being at the bottom is bad. Poor pay is bad. Poor living conditions are bad. Everybody tries to look after themselves in the system. I did that. No-one can be expected not to. But it's not the answer. The point isn't to lift yourself out of what is bad, but to lift society. To lift everybody. The point is not to be full of ambition for yourself but for the society that makes you. Everything we are is social. Everything. Outside society we are mindless. We evolved to be social. We have to make the best in the human mind define the way we live. The Tories do the opposite. They raise greed and mean-spiritedness to the level of principle. That's what Academies are for. To set people against one another. To break up the education system and let private interests in. To make education a business. And that's a lie, Pam. It's a big lie. They have to use public money because the free market won't provide education. The drive for personal gain is mean and selfish. Adam Smith himself says the pursuit of private wealth is a delusion. In every way it's the wealth we share that make us. Don't do it, Pam. Walk away. Keep your school in the public sector."

"It's too late, dad."

"You have one life. I tell you posterity sees with different eyes and its judgements are harsh. All these attacks on the public sector will be seen for what they are: cheap, mendacious, bullying, destructive. Does the thought of that make you happy?"

"The future is the future. I have to live in the present. What does it matter to me what people think when I'm dead?"

" It matters enormously. More than anything."

She was astonished. What could he mean? She stared at him as if he were a madman. He was looking at her in that way she recalled from the days when she was a teenager and he would provoke her with ideas and when she floundered, laugh, put his arm around her and kiss her cheek. She almost believed he was going to get up and do exactly that. She almost believed he was forty again. There was something indestructible about him. In spite of his frailty, his stiff, slow movements, there was a quick shrew still alive in his mind, scurrying, collecting, nibbling. It disappointed her because she felt in spite of her age and achievements, he was still ahead of her. It was as if she would never surpass him. But what could he mean? How could posterity matter more than anything? What did she care for what the world thought once she was eaten by worms? It threw her into confusion and anger.

"That's a silly idea."

"No. We belong to the future. To know the future will judge us well is a present pleasure and to know it will judge us badly is a present misery. Do you think people like Hitler or Stalin could be happy? They were miserable. People like that live with the misery of know-ing how they will be judged. It's what drives their need for control. The present is defined by the future. If you don't understand that, you're lost."

"The future is defined by the present," she said feeling at once that her ideas were running away with her, that it was not really her speaking. Was the future defined by the present? She'd just said so. Was it true? It seemed to her it must be though it was an idea she'd never formulated.

"You're right. What sort of future do Academies point to?"

She felt unable and threatened. It was unfair of him to expect her to have thought it through. She wasn't like him. She didn't spend her life thinking about everything. She wanted to be able to accept. She wanted someone else to do the thinking.

"Better schools for everyone," she said.

"Then why not improve the ones we've got?"

"Academies are free to make their own choices. There'll be more variety. That can't be a bad thing."

"Variety is disastrous unless it's real. Five hundred different tooth-pastes all with the same ingredients isn't variety, it's marketing. False choice. That's what commercialism is about because real choice is hard. It means thinking and being responsible. And how will you be free in your Academy?"

"I'll no longer be told what to do by the local authority."

"You'll be told what to do by the Secretary of State."

"I don't think so."

"How can it be otherwise? That's where responsibility lies."

She was confused and disappointed. Was it true she was a dupe? Was she falling for a nasty, political trick? It all seemed so clear and easy in her own mind: she did what she had to, she did it well, she pleased the inspectors and she was rewarded. It seemed as natural as sleeping. It was true, she would be told what to do. She would have to follow the rules or she'd be in trouble. But how could she stand against the fierce wind of conformity? What was the point? He could see it but she couldn't. To her it was a blank. It was defeat and diffi-culty. The world that might be wasn't enough to motivate her. It was the world that was she needed. The future was the future's business. Trying to follow her dad's thinking was like trying to find her way in the fog in an unknown landscape.

He was eating in his slow, slightly obscene old man's way. She was saddened by the memory of him as young and vigorous. It almost made her glad that he argued with her because it meant he was still strongly in touch with life although everything about him looked weak and withdrawn. She'd cleaned her plate and was waiting for him.

"Want some apple pie?" she said.

He shook his head.

"Gives me indigestion."

"Cup of tea."

He finished his last mouthful.

"Cup of tea. I'll go and sit on the sofa. I hate these straight-backed chairs."

She laughed.

"You know what, Pam," he said smiling at her in the way he always used to. "I'm proud of you. You've done well."

The following week she was in her office when she spotted Sally Hyde driving out of the car park at three thirty. She made one of her stern mental notes to keep an eye on her. She noticed her leaving at the same time almost every day then one Friday she heard an engine start, took off her reading glasses went to the window and looking through the blinds, saw Sally's car reversing. She looked at the clock: three eighteen. Before going home at nine, early because it was the weekend, she put a note in her colleague's pigeon-hole and on Monday morning Sally was in her office. Pam liked her. She would have been happy to have a friendship with her; but this was a different context. Whether you liked your staff as people was irrelevant. Whether a member of staff was a good person made no difference. What mattered was whether they obeyed the rules. Pam found she enjoyed the little thrill it gave her to set aside her liking for someone in order to deal with them as an employee. It was strange, the little lift of power; being able to set aside the normal subtleties of human conversation, to simplify the unfathomable complexity of reading and responding to another person's inner life and to merely impose and insist. It gave her a queer sense of security. It was not at all like the shifting, uncertain waters of personal relationships. Nothing like the troubled connection between her and John. It was more like controlling a puppet. She enjoyed making small insistences her staff had to conform to. It was intensely exciting to feel another human being forced to act according to her command. It left her with a sense of peace, an illusion of invulnerability.

"Did you leave school premises early on Friday?"

"No, three twenty."

"Three eighteen."

"Eighteen?"

"I checked the clock."

"My phone said three twenty."

"You must use the school clocks."

"I thought it was three twenty."

"It wasn't. The best thing is to stay well after the end of the school day then you can't make the mistake."

"I had to get away."

"Why?"

"Personal reasons."

"We all have personal lives."

"I'm sorry. I thought it was three twenty."

"I've noticed you leave early most days."

"No, I leave after three twenty."

"Yes, but when I say early I mean three thirty or four o'clock."

"That's not early."

"What I mean, Sally, is early compared to other staff."

"The school day ends at three twenty."

"But our work doesn't end with the school day."

"I do plenty of work at home."

"We have to do what's best for the children. That's not negotiable."

"I do."

"Leaving early gives the wrong impression."

"I'm not trying to create an impression."

Pam felt a short stab of insult.

" You know I'm often here till eleven or midnight…"

"That's your choice."

"It's what has to be done."

Sally said nothing. Perhaps this was the time to stop the interview; but Pam didn't want her to go away thinking it was fine to leave at three thirty every day. She couldn't get out of her head the picture of Sally enjoying herself. Maybe she was shopping or meeting a friend for coffee or sitting on the sofa at home with a magazine or a book. She could be sure she wasn't enjoying herself only if she kept her in school. It was true the school day ended at three twenty and she was free to leave, except on Mondays and Thursdays when there were meetings; but Pam despised the idea of staff being able to stick to their contract. It was a minimum. Everyone was expected to exceed it by far, by a hundred per cent. What would happen if people worked to their contract? It was a legal agreement but beyond that was the demand to prove yourself. It was the real demand. A moral demand. The insight struck her with the force of an epoch-changing scientific discovery; Sally wasn't simply a lax employee, she was morally reprehensible.

She took off her reading glasses.

"You are, of course, free to leave at three twenty."

"I know."

"But it's not fair to the other staff, let alone the children."

"Not fair?"

"Everyone stays late."

"Because you force them to."

Pam was outraged and could have lost her temper but she pushed her anger behind her coldly professional demeanour.

"I don't force anyone, Sally."

"People are frightened to leave at the end of the day."

"Frightened?"

"Yes."

"I'm astonished you can say that. It's ridiculous."

"It's the truth."

"No-one is frightened of me. People want to do the best for the children."

"That's not what they say in the staff-room."

Staff-room whingeing was something Pam joked about when she met other Heads. It was one of those aspects of school life which gave her a sense of superiority and security. Of course staff moaned. That was something management took for granted. Staff were supposed to moan; they didn't come to work to be happy. It had become part of her *Weltanschauung* that if staff didn't complain, she wasn't doing her job properly. A good manager kept staff on their toes and as there was a natural tendency for staff to be lazy, to cut corners, to make life pleasant for themselves, a good manager expected staff to be disgruntled; but she'd always flattered herself with the thought her school was harmonious because the staff respected her, because she knew how to deal with them.

106

"Are you saying I'm a bully?"

"People are frightened of what will happen if they don't do what you want and they know you want them to stay late."

"I want them to work hard for the children."

"A lot of time after school is wasted."

"Wasted."

"People clock watch. They stay late to please you but they don't always get much done. Sometimes people just have a chat in the staffroom for most of the time."

"This is ridiculous, Sally."

"I don't think so."

"You know my position. I've always made it plain. If you work here you do the best for the children or you can get on the bus."

"Is there anything wrong with my work?"

Pam put her reading glasses on and pretended to be intent on something in front of her. She knew if she accepted that Sally's work was good, she was undermining her own argument. On the other hand, she knew there was no criticism she could make off the top of her head. She felt she was being challenged; her regime was under threat. What puzzled her was why this previously obedient teacher had changed.

"Everyone can improve."

"I'm improving all the time."

What Sally had said niggled away at Pam for days. She wasn't having anything to do with the accusation she was a bully; she did her job well; it was necessary to keep staff in line. But she wanted to find out why Sally's attitude had changed. A few discreet conversations and she discovered her marriage had broken down and she was alone with the children. At first it softened her feeling, but immediately there came a reaction: was she using personal difficulties as an excuse?; did she imagine it was legitimate to leave school at three thirty every day just because she had two children to look after?; didn't she know everyone had personal difficulties of some kind? The thought of her vulnerability made Pam think she would be easy to defeat. The way to do it was obvious.

She announced a new round of observations: she would be visiting everyone's class two or three times over the next fortnight; everyone would get a grade for their lesson in line with OFSTED criteria.

Sally was one of those quick, neat, highly organised teachers children find it easy to follow. From the moment she entered the classroom she was talking and her energy drove the lessons forward; the children launched into activity and she went from table to table correcting and encouraging. She had the ability to keep going at the same high level of positive input and the absence of slackening in her lessons kept the children interested and keen. But she had two very troublesome boys to deal with: Callum was the child of a hero-in-addict mother and a drug dealer father serving a long prison sentence and Josh's single-parent mother had been sectioned as a schizophrenic. Both were very difficult to settle. They liked one another's company because they shared a wild refusal of norms; they lived in the isolation of their grief and disappointment and it made them impulsive and oppositional. Sally didn't punish them but admonished, brought them back to their work again and again, talked gently and patiently and felt if she'd kept them in the room all day and they hadn't thrown chairs, she'd done well.

When Pam called her in to discuss the lessons, she began by saying Callum and Josh were off-task sixty per cent of the time.

"They're statemented," said Sally.

"We can't allow our standards to drop for statemented children."

"I'm not dropping standards. No-one could keep those two focused for an entire lesson."

"We have to keep them focused."

"I do my best for them."

"You were trying hard, but they're not getting what they deserve."

"I really need an assistant."

"I can't afford to provide an assistant for only two pupils."

"Then those boys are bound to be difficult."

"We can't blame the pupils."

"I'm not blaming them. They're troubled."

"We educate everybody. Our standards are the same for all pupils."

"Callum and Josh are disturbed boys. You just can't expect them to behave like well-balanced children."

"Teachers have to be competent whatever the circumstances."

Sally was looking hard at her.

"Are you saying I'm not competent?"

"Those lessons were unsatisfactory, Sally."

"Why?"

"Nearly ten per cent of the pupils were off-task for more than half the lesson."

"Ten per cent?"

"Two out of twenty-nine is nearly ten per cent."

"It's nearer five."

"I'm not quibbling."

"Those lessons were perfectly satisfactory, apart from those two boys."

"Exactly. We can't have lessons which are satisfactory apart from this or that. And as you know, I don't accept lessons which are satisfactory. In my school all lessons must be good."

"Take Josh and Callum out and my lessons will be outstanding."

"That's for me to judge."

"I don't accept what you're saying."

"I'll be making another visit."

"What for?"

"I think it may be best to put you on informal support."

The "support" began at the start of the next term. Pam observed Sally eight times over six weeks and found half of the lessons unsatisfactory. She moved her onto formal support and did the same thing. Before the competency meeting, the union asked for a compromise agreement and for a mere £8,000 Sally was out of the door.

When she chatted to John about it as they prepared dinner he said:

"Single parent. Fuck. That was a bit tough."

"It's a tough world," she said.

"Sure is."

"People have to be competent in their jobs. Single parent or otherwise."

"They do."

"She wasn't cut out for teaching."

"Too many teachers aren't."

"I won't have anything but the best in my school. The children deserve it."

"'Course they fucking do," said John. "Is there another bottle of Sauvignon in the fridge?"

A NAZI HELMET

In the wooden garage were a gas mask and two helmets: one the standard issue Tommy's tin hat ; the other a black, close fitting, stylish Nazi model which covered your ears and protected the back of your neck. The swastika was undamaged. When little Paul Hawes played soldiers with his friends, he always wanted to wear the Nazi helmet; the British one reminded him of a plate; it sat on the top of your head like a recently-landed flying saucer; he thought it dim and plain. The Nazi one, on the other hand, spoke of intelligence and distinction. It was made not just to protect your head well, but to look good. Paul imagined that the men who wore the British hat must have been slow and helpless, like the boys in school who couldn't yet recite their tables, but the black helmet must have belonged to someone quick and independent who knew how to look after himself. Because he was a well-brought up boy whose mother insisted he observe Christian virtue, he never took the black helmet for himself but always offered his friends first choice; all the same, he would say:

"Which helmet do you want? This is the British one."

Usually that did the trick, but one or two boys would reach for the Nazi hat and Paul would feel humiliated: he thought he looked ugly and stupid in the green helmet. They played in the garden. There was a square of crazy paving in front of the oblong bay of the back room and a little rockery which dropped down to a five yard stretch of lawn, to the left of which ran the path of flagstones his dad had laid. To the right was a flower bed of mostly roses behind which was the thick privet separating the garden from the Haldane's. Then came the big square lawn where he played football and beyond that the lilacs and rhododendrons where he thought he'd seen a snake so his dad put on his boots and grabbed the hoe from the shed and came to sort it out; but it was merely a fallen black branch dotted with white fungus. All the same, Paul thought his dad a fearless hero. He'd been in Italy during the war and had told his son about getting up in the morning and lifting the snakes from his tent. What was a possible adder in the undergrowth to such a man?

The garage was to the left if you were facing the garden from the crazy paving and attached to it was a little sloping-roofed shed one of his dad's relatives had built. Paul loved both these constructions: the garage was a frame of thick beams to which tongue and groove had been nailed and the corrugated roof was held in place by strong timber triangles joined by heavy nuts and bolts. It fascinated the boy. Someone had sawn the timber, measured and joined and made this splendid thing stand. It seemed to him more marvellous as a construction than the house because its innards were visible. And the little shed too where the smell of the wood was still fresh and the joints fit together perfectly made him think it would be wonderful to grow up and be able to build such things. He had a little joiner's kit his uncle and auntie had bought him for Christmas and he sawed and hammered but nothing he made ever looked neat or held firmly. It was a mystery. One of those puzzles adults don't talk about, as if garages and sheds were the most natural things in the world.

On the crazy paving, Paul had built a den. He'd disobeyed his mother by moving some of the flagstones left over from the path, then in the garage he'd found a long piece of black hardboard which he used for the roof. He felt bad about not doing as he was told, but his mother said if he tried to move the stones they would fall on his toes and he'd have to go to hospital like David Bernal who fell out of a tree and broke his leg. It wasn't true. He'd moved them and his toes were fine. They weren't the full big stones. Just the bits his dad had broken off, so even he could move them though he was still only five and a half. He liked to sit in his den even when he was on his own. He had made it. It was his. Not even his big sister was allowed in it without his permission. It was much better, though, with a friend, even a friend he didn't like very much such as Nigel Heath. It was hard to find a friend you really liked. Most of Paul's friends were all right. The important thing was to have someone to play with. Paul knew he had to be kind, even to people he didn't like, because his mother told him that was a good thing to do and Jesus would love him for it. So he was kind to Nigel, most of the time. He let him wear the Nazi helmet if he wanted and he let him sit in the den, though Nigel said it wasn't much of a den because it only had three sides and no door or window. Paul wanted to punch him. He'd worked hard to move the stones and the thing about a den was you could hide there, even if it didn't have a door or a window. Nigel was always saying things weren't very good. He lived in a big house at the end of the avenue and they had a lounge where children weren't allowed to go. Nigel took him in there one day. It was just a big new-smelling room with a carpet, a sofa, two armchairs and a coffee table, but Nigel told him not to touch anything and to take his shoes off before he went in. Paul thought this very strange because children were allowed everywhere in his house. He could climb on the sofa with his shoes on and so long as they weren't muddy his mother wouldn't say anything. There was no room kept closed and giving off the odour of a furniture shop. Nigel said his mum and dad came and sat in the room on their own; his dad would drink whiskey but he wasn't allowed to smoke his pipe. The children had to stay in the long, narrow room at the side of the house. Paul liked that much more because the carpet and furniture were worn, there was a toy chest and you didn't feel as if you'd be sent to prison if you made a mess.

The day they went in the special room, Nigel showed him how to play a simple tune on the piano. It needed only one hand and three keys but Paul thought it remarkable. Why was there no piano in his house? He remembered his mum saying something about Uncle Harry having piano lessons because he was the oldest; she never got a chance. She said it in that funny tone of voice she used when she talked about things or people she didn't like or which got on her nerves. Was that why they didn't have a piano?

One day they were playing wars and Paul had the Nazi helmet. Nigel had no helmet at all because John Champland had taken the British one; instead he had Paul's dad's RAF cap. It opened out like an envelope and sat softly on your head. Paul said it had to be worn at an angle because that's how he'd seen it in a photo of his dad during the war. Every time Nigel ran to attack the McKernan's, the cap fell off. If he stopped to pick it up, he got pelted with clods.

"You wear this," he said to Paul.

Paul looked at the blue-grey object. It offered no protection. It wasn't the kind of thing to wear in battle. But it was his dad's. He'd worn it when he was fighting in Italy and Egypt, which were countries very far away where it was very hot. He took off the Nazi helmet, handed it to Nigel and pulled on the cap. He wondered if it made him look like his dad; but when he charged up the avenue towards the McKernan's it fell off and lay on its side in the road.

That night, after tea, he sneaked into his parents' bedroom and looked at the picture of his dad on the dressing-table. He was smiling in a special way; a big, beaming smile. It made Paul think of sunshine and happy days. His dad was young in the picture and very smart in his uniform. The cap perched on his head at a cocky angle. At the other side of the dressing-table was a picture of his mum and dad on their wedding day. His mum was very pretty and slim. Her dress had a long train and in her hands was a big bouquet. She was smiling too, the crooked little smile that everyone said he had and was just like hers. His dad wore a dark suit and very shiny shoes and his smile was as broad and sunny as in the air force picture. He heard the door open. His sister's head appeared.

"You'll get killed if they find you in here!"

By the time he was ten, Paul no longer played soldiers. The helmets were still in the garage somewhere, but he never thought of them when he parked his bike or turned it over to take off the wheels and clean it from one end to the other. His dad had taken him to a big warehouse to buy it. Whenever there was something to buy, his dad always knew someone. Paul got his football boots from Tommy Henderson who used to play in the first division and now had a little sports shop on Chapel St, on the way out of town. Henderson was a grumpy man and Paul hung back behind his dad.

"How are you, Tommy? Some boots for the lad. What have you got?"

The men shook hands but Paul noticed Henderson didn't look his dad in the eye. He disappeared into the back of the shop. Paul's dad looked down at him and winked. Henderson appeared with three boxes. From the first he took a pair of sleek, black and white boots in soft Italian leather with Di Stefano's florid signature in gold on the side. Paul tried them on.

"How do they feel?" said his dad.

"Fantastic."

"We'll have 'em, Tommy. Usual discount?"

Paul saw a shadow cross the shopkeeper's face.

"Not lost your cheek, Bernard."

"Get nowhere without it, Tommy."

Paul carried the boots to the car in the box. He couldn't wait to run out on the field in them, but at the same time there was a strange feeling hurting him. Later that day he heard his mum and dad arguing:

"Why can't you pay like everyone else?"

"What's wrong with it?"

"It's embarrassing, Bernard. You do it everywhere. When we went to the Vic and Station with Neville and Kath you had to go and find the chef and ask for ten per cent off."

"He's an old friend of mine. We were in Egypt together."

"And what did you get up to?"

"Don't start that."

"And Paul with you. Do you have to do such things in front of the child?"

"I got twenty per cent off those boots. Paul loves 'em."

"We aren't paupers. We can afford a pair of football boots for the lad. Have some pride. Pay the full price."

"What good's that?"

"What good is it? It means you can hold your head high."

"I can't?"

"It's demeaning."

"Why?"

"Because it's almost begging. And it's making use of people. Tommy Henderson is supposed to be a friend of yours."

"He is a friend. He got me free tickets to the cup final three years running."

"That's not what friends are for."

"I don't understand you, Jessie."

"I don't like it. It's not right. Just pay the asking price."

"What if people offer me discount?"

"That's different. If they offer you accept with grace. But to ask is ….."

"Is what?"

"It's not the way I do things."

"No, but it's the way I do. I've saved us a lot of money. When this house was rewired….."

"Yes, and you expected our Bill to do the joinery for nowt."

"He's your brother."

"That doesn't mean he should work for nothing. I wouldn't ask him. You shouldn't."

"I don't understand you. I don't understand your family."

"Don't understand just do as I ask."

Paul went to his room. He took the pristine boots from their box and ran his thumb over the leather. They were the most stylish boots he'd ever seen. None of his mates had any so neat. But what his mother had said troubled his heart. He hadn't liked what had happened in the shop. He would have been happier if his dad had just paid the money. It made him feel ashamed that Henderson had called his dad cheeky, his face had been stern and he'd kept his eyes lowered. He lay on his bed and thought of the day they went to the big warehouse. His dad walked in as if the place was his and bounded up the stairs. A man in a brown overall stopped them:

"Can I help you, sir?"

"Where's Stan Billington?"

"He's in his office, sir. Can I get you something?"

"I need to talk to Stan. Tell him Bernie's here."

"Bernie who, sir?"

"Just say Bernie's here. He'll know."

The man walked away across the cold wooden floor while Paul's dad started to lift and stack the bikes . He found what he wanted.

"This is the one, Paul. A belter! What d'you think?"

The frame was wrapped in brown paper so Paul couldn't tell the colour but it had drops and ten gears and was much smarter than the second-hand tracker he was riding round on. Billington appeared, a tall man with a bald head in a dark suit and shoes whose heels clacked rhythmically on the boards. He approached quickly and held out his hand to Paul's dad.

116

"Bernie, how are you? Haven't seen you for years."

"Fine, Stan. Bike for the lad. He likes this one. Can you do me twenty per cent?"

"Twenty per cent? That's our mark up."

"Aye. For an old friend, Stan. You want tyres you know where to come."

"Fifteen."

"Done."

The men shook hands and smiled. Paul's dad took out his wallet and counted the pound notes. He wheeled and carried the bike to the car and once home, Paul peeled off the brown paper to reveal the shiny blue frame of a BSA Golden Fifty. He rode it round the block. He went to the park to show it his mates. He cleaned it after every outing. But now he was confused: he loved his bike but the way his dad had behaved made him feel small. And what had he been getting up to in Egypt? Paul felt his mum was right, though he wasn't sure why. His dad was almost a stranger. It was funny how he was sometimes frightened when he was with him. He tried on his boots. They were belters all right, even if his dad had made Henderson sullen and grumpy.

One morning, Paul's dad wasn't in the house at breakfast time. His mum and his sister said nothing but he knew something was wrong. Then his dad didn't come home some nights and when he did he didn't stay very long or was gone in the morning. When he got up one day, still in his pyjamas, Paul sneaked into his parents' bedroom. The quilt and the covers were pushed back on both sides. He shoved his hands under and felt the warmth. Both his mum and dad had slept there. He was glad. There was something about a mum and dad sleeping in the same bed that was very good. He wasn't sure what it was but it made things feel better. Nigel's mum and dad had single beds and Paul thought that was strange. Nigel told him that sometimes his dad slept in the spare room and Paul puzzled over that. He pulled the door to quietly but when he got downstairs his dad wasn't there. He took a slice of toast from the plate in the middle of the table and sat down. His sister was reading a girls' magazine and his mother was fussing over breakfast.

"Get dressed, Paul. You'll be late."

She brought him a mug of tea, as he liked it, black and sweet.

"Did you see her?" she said to his sister.

She nodded.

"And what is she like? A tart no doubt."

The word he didn't understand stabbed at Paul's heart. The way his mother said it was so full of cold hatred he froze inside though he kept on chewing his toast. Who was she talking about? He knew it was something to do with his dad. He went off to school with his new boots in his duffle bag and during the day the thought of what had happened at breakfast time dwindled and he was happy with his friends busily getting on with his work. After school there was a match against Sacred Heart. There was always a special kind of rivalry when they played against Catholics. The Catholic boys called them proddy dogs, and sometimes, walking home on his own they would shout at him as they passed on their bikes:

"Hey, proddy dog!"

It was puzzling to him. He was friendly with Mark Clapham who went to Sacred Heart and with Joe Bylinksi who went to St Teresa's. It was queer to call people names because of the school they went to. All the same, he felt a little more nervous than usual about the match. It was six-a-side. Every year there was a tournament in the town and some schools struggled to get eleven players, so they made it six. Mr Keogh chose the best six players and they practised every Thursday night. Paul was ball monitor and took his responsibility of inflating the leather "casies" and keeping them dubbined very seriously. It was one of the nice things about Mr Keogh: he gave everyone something to look after so everyone had a little bit of importance and they all worked happily together and were an industrious and smiling class.

He laced his new boots tight, pulled up his blue and white socks, folded them over and adjusted the elastics his mother had made for him to hold them up. When he ran out onto the field, they felt so light and comfortable he seemed to move more swiftly and dribble more skilfully. He was on the right wing. Rob Kellman was on the left. Mr Keogh had taught them to get the ball to the wingers, take it wide and fast and cross it to Marty Nelson who was tall and strong and could jump for high ones. Paul loved those moments of zipping down the line, outrunning a defender and whacking the ball so it floated in front of goal. They were some of the most blissful seconds of his life. He didn't care about winning or losing, it was the sheer joy of having the ball at your feet, feeling the strength in your legs and getting things right; but he enjoyed the competition too. He liked to scrap for the ball, to fight off a shoulder charge, to leap over a sliding tackle.

The pitch was wet and muddy. The ball soon became heavy. He ran and ran and crossed and crossed till at last Marty leapt like a salmon and slapped the forehead covered by his blonde fringe against the sodden surface. The goalie threw himself towards the post but the ball sailed into the corner and Marty ran over to Paul, his face spattered with dots of rain-sodden earth. They scored six. Marty got four, Paul one and Rob one. They won six four. Paul's boots were wet and filthy. In the classroom where Mr Keogh had oranges for them, he took off his kit and pulled on his clothes. He walked home happy with his duffle bag over his shoulder.

His dad's car was outside.

He went through to the kitchen. His mother was doing the washing-up and crying. He stood and watched her a few seconds.

"We won six four," he said. "I scored one."

"Go and talk to your dad."

"Where is he?"

"In the front room."

Paul put down his duffle bag. He went reluctantly through the little dining room and into the front room. His dad was sitting on the sofa wearing his dark overcoat.

"How'd you go on?" he said.

"Won six four."

"D'you score?"

"One."

"New boots, eh?"

Paul sat next to him and looked at the coal fire his mother had set and which was flaring vigorously.

"Has your mum said anything?"

"No."

119

"Well, your mum and me aren't going to live together any more."

The boy sat quietly but didn't listen as his dad talked some more. At length, his dad got up and left the room. He heard his parents' voices and then the click of the front door latch and the sound of his dad's engine.

"Come and get your tea," said his mother.

In the days that followed a quiet gloom descended on the house. His mother went about her housework with a closed face and mouth and his sister washed her hair, put in rollers and sat at the table reading a girls' magazine as usual. He went out in the garden in his cleaned and dubbined boots to kick a ball around, or carefully rubbed between the spokes of his bike wheels with a cloth hooked over his index finger. One night, when he thought of riding to the park, he realised he needed new batteries and went to his mother.

"And where d'you think I'll get the money for those?" she snapped.

He went back to the garage and polished till his bike gleamed from crank to gear lever. In his bedroom he counted the notes and coins he kept in the top drawer of his tallboy; then he worked out how much he could save from his pocket money; but a terrible thought seized him: what if she didn't give him any? He wasn't old enough to get a paper round. Perhaps he should sell his tracker. It might bring a few shillings.

When he got up next morning and went down for breakfast, his sister was already in her grammar school uniform and his mum had a letter beside her on the table.

"Sit down and get some toast. Here," she said, taking half a crown from the pocket of her apron, "that's for some batteries."

"Thanks."

He put the coin in the breast pocket of his pyjamas.

"This letter is about school," his mother said, picking it up. "You'll be going to the secondary modern. You'll be all right there. Howard goes and he's doing fine."

Howard was his cousin, his mother's brother's eldest son, a talented artist who'd won a prize in the county competition. His sister chewed her toast and turned the page of her magazine.

"I'll make you a cup of tea," said his mother. "Then get dressed quickly it's nearly half past."

Paul went off to school with his boots and his ball in his duffle bag. He didn't know what to make of the news. There was something bad about it. His sister went to the grammar school and he knew it was supposed to be better. He knew that failing to get in was a bad thing but he was friendly with lads who were already at the Sec like Andy Black and Brian Gillespie who he played football with on the park and they were all right. In the playground, everyone was talking about the letters.

"Have you passed?" was asked a hundred times.

Nigel Heath came up to Paul and asked the question.

"No."

"You'll go to the thicko school. That's what my mum calls it."

Paul would have liked to punch Nigel's pink lips, but he turned away, took his ball from his bag and began kicking it against the school wall.

The following Saturday Paul was in the garage when the door opened and Nigel poked his head in.

"Are you playing?"

"Yeah."

"Have you still got those helmets. We could play war."

Paul went to the old cupboard with the rusty hinges, pulled open the doors and rummaged. He found the Tommy's hat first. Next to it was the RAF cap. The Nazi helmet had been shoved behind some half empty tins of paint. It must have been his dad.

"Here," he said, and he held the Nazi helmet out to Nigel. "You wear this."

Then he pulled the RAF cap down tight at the same angle as in the picture that used to sit on the dressing table and smiled as broadly as he could.

A FRIENDSHIP

The two boys were going from one lesson to the next. The smaller, who was slight and short for his age, tripped as someone clipped his ankles. He looked round to see a lad from the year above, much taller and broader and with an ugly sneer. He ignored him. Immediately, his friend stumbled, stopped and turned.

"Piss off," he said.

The smaller boy looked up at the two lads squaring.

"Or else what?" said the ankle clipper.

"I'll knock your spuggy out your mouth."

The tripper was taken aback for a second, stopped chewing his gum, pulled up his chest and started chewing again. The culture dictated that older lads picked on younger ones. A third year didn't stand up to a fourth year, especially a fourth year with friends. And Forton had friends: John Alston who'd pulled a knife on a lad at the youth club and was on probation; Alec Tasker who broke a first year's nose in the toilets. When you had friends like those, you did what you liked.

"Go on then," said Forton, sticking out his chin, and faster than he could have imagined Arkwright's big, tight fist smashed between his eyes. His head flew back and hit the lockers. He rocked forward. For a few seconds he looked as if he would fall. Life was sucked from his face like sparse rain hitting a parched desert. His eyes rolled upwards. Little Glasson looked on in amazement. Forton reached out to steady himself. Arkwright stood tall and strong and said nothing. The victim leaned against the lockers, ran his hand over his face. Blood had begun to drip from his nose. He raised his head and looked at his assailant but didn't dare speak. Arkwright turned and walked on and little Glasson hurried to walk beside him.

"Bastard," said Arkwright.

"Yeah," said Glasson.

"He tripped you first didn't he?"

"Yeah."

"Don't let the bastards bully you." Arkwright looked down at his little friend. "Nobody bullies my friends," and he put his strong hand on Glasson's skinny shoulder.

The event was a wonder to Glasson who had never hit anyone in his life. It wasn't just that he was small and skinny because he was quiet skilled and fast. He was the best tennis player in the school and a handy, neat footballer. Had he wanted to he could have swung a good punch and his speed would have kept him out of a lot of trouble, but he didn't like the idea of hurting people. Forton was a notorious bully and there were half a dozen like him in every year. Glasson knew you had to stay out of their way and if they provoked you it was best not to retaliate; but he couldn't help feeling excited about Tom's punch. He knew he was strong: he was left-handed but could arm wrestle anyone in the year with his right hand. He was very quick over four hundred yards. He built his strength by lifting the old square and oblong weights in his dad's garage. But Glasson had never thought he was a fighter, certainly not the kind of fighter to take on someone like Forton, and he was in awe of the power and swiftness of the punch which had left the bully reeling.

Arkwright liked Glasson because he was the only person he knew who didn't threaten him. Physical threat didn't worry Arkwright. He knew how strong and fast he was. There wasn't a boy in the school he feared. Not long before the incident with Forton, he'd been riding his bike home one evening when a gang of lads outside the chip-shop had shouted abuse. He turned back, got off his bike and confronted them. The quartet looked at one another. Who was this? Did he think he could take on four? One of them told him to fuck off and without a word Arkwright head butted him. Blood spurted from his nose. He crumpled. His chips were scattered on the floor. The other three stepped back. The chip-shop owner came running out.

"I'll get the police!" he called.

Arkwright calmly mounted his bike and rode off.

He mentioned the event to no-one but it bolstered his conviction he could take on anyone. It was important because people were menacing. They were full of nasty emotions: greed and envy and resentment. Arkwright had the feeling people were against him. His dad talked about it; the pakis arriving in droves and taking over the country, doing nothing all day and getting money for it. He found it worrying. Surely the adults were supposed to stop that sort of thing;

surely they were supposed to see that things were fair. Glasson was the only person who didn't make Arkwright uneasy. It was nothing to do with physical threat; after all, Glasson was five feet two weighed six stone and couldn't even do ten chin ups; Arkwright was five feet ten, eleven stone, without an ounce of fat and already stronger than his dad. No, it was that Glasson was genuinely a happy person. It puzzled Arkwright but he liked it. Little Glasson was always laughing. He seemed to laugh his way through life. When Arkwright was with him, he felt happy. He thought of Glasson as a good person and that was rare. People weren't good, they were out for themselves. They were out to get you. But Glasson wasn't like that. He liked people. He liked to ride his bike and kick a ball. He liked the girls. He liked music and he liked to have a laugh. Glasson was all right. There was no doubt about that. He was all right. Arkwright was glad to have him as a friend.

One Saturday morning they were in the woods behind the school. Glasson was running through the rhododendrons while Arkwright was hanging around with three other lads by the stile that led to the farmer's fields.

"Watch this," he said

He picked up a big, round stone that weighed nicely in his palm. When he glimpsed Glasson through the thick dark leaves he launched it with his all his strength and skill. He was aiming at the tall sycamore just in front of his friend. He wanted to give him a little fright and then they'd all have a good laugh. The rock flew fast and straight, hit the tree and ricocheted. Then they heard another strange noise and looked at one another. Arkwright went quickly through the bushes. Glasson was flat on his front in a little clearing of clayey earth, blood pouring from his head. What if he was dead? Arkwright was filled with fear. Had he killed his little friend? He stood still as the other lads joined him. Should he pick him up? He didn't dare touch him. Little Glasson. Poor little Glasson. Then all at once the body stirred. The boy got to his feet, stumbled a little, put his hand to his face and looking at the blood covering it, turned to Arkwright:

"Tom! My head! Carry me, Tom. Carry me home."

Arkwright shook his head in terror.

"Come on," he said.

He waited till Glasson was beside him and headed quickly out of the woods.

"Help me, Tom," said the little lad. "Carry me."

"Come on," said Arkwright. "I'll take you home."

Just as they emerged from the woods, where the few big houses stood at either side of the little, unmade road, a man was about to get in his car. Glasson ran towards him.

"Can you help me! Can you take me home!"

The man turned from putting his key in the lock, stared at the lad and said:

"My god!"

He got in and drove away. Glasson turned to Arkwright.

"Come on, Smiler," said the big lad. "I'll take you home."

They ran the length of the avenue of little semis, Arkwright terrified his friend wasn't going to make it. There was so much blood. It soaked into his windjammer. It ran down the arm the little chap held up to his wound. Arkwright looked at him as he ran. What would he do if he collapsed? Would he pick him up? He could easily do it, he was such a skinny thing. But supposing he died. Supposing he just fell and died, here on the ordinary pavement on an ordinary Saturday. Supposing he picked him up and carried him home dead. He had a horrible feeling that if Glasson fell he would leave him. He would leave him and run away and hope no-one would ever know he threw the stone. But the other lads would tell and what then? Would he go to prison? Was he a murderer? Was he going to be the murderer of his good little friend, good little Glasson who wouldn't harm a flea?

They passed a woman with a shopping basket over her arm. She took one look at the bleeding boy and turned away.

"Keep running," said Arkwright. "It's not far. We'll soon be there."

"Carry me, Tom," pleaded Glasson. "My legs are jelly."

"You can do it, Smiler. Keep running."

They crossed Crow Lane and came to Greenlands Drive where Glasson lived. It was fifty yards to his house. Surely he couldn't die before they got there. He was crying and staggering. Arkwright put his arm round him, tucked his hand under to support him.

"Nearly there. You can do it."

Then a horrible thought came to him: what if there was no-one in? What if his mum had gone out shopping and the house was locked? What would he do? Who would help him? Two adults had already turned away. What if Glasson died on his own doorstep. Why did he throw that stone? He hadn't meant to hurt his little friend. This was Glasson. He loved him. He was shocked to find himself thinking that he loved his little friend. It wasn't something he'd ever thought of. Lads were mates. That was that. But poor Glasson. Surely there'd be someone at home.

Glasson went up the drive. Arkwright stayed at the gate. The little lad pushed the front door. It opened. He went inside and Arkwright felt a great relief. But he couldn't go. Maybe there was no-one in and his mum had left the door on the latch for him. He couldn't go and leave Glasson to die alone in his own house. He waited an age before Mrs Glasson appeared. He thought she was going to tell him off. Maybe she'd call the police. She was a little woman, skinny like her son, but with a very pretty, serious face. She came to the gate and smiled.

"Thank you for bringing him home, Tom. You did the right thing, luv. You're a good lad."

Arkwright nodded.

"Thank you, Tom. He'll be all right. I've called for a taxi. I'll take him to the hospital. You go home, luv."

Arkwright nodded again, tried to smile and walked away.

It was a mile and a half home. The other lads had made off when they saw the bloodied Glasson holding his hand to his head. Arkwright went back through the woods, but he avoided the spot where he'd thrown the stone and the little bare patch where his mate lay as still as dead. He'd winged the stone to hit the tree. He couldn't have known it would rebound and hit Glasson. It was true he'd thrown it hard; and he was showing off. He could throw further and harder than any lad in the school. He entertained his mates by launching stones from one bank of the river to the other while most lads couldn't even get half way. Had he wanted to hit little Glasson? The idea made him panic. Why would he do that? He was his mate. He looked after him. But he couldn't kill off the notion that he'd legged the stone with a hidden intention to hit his friend. He'd thrown it in

126

his direction. He'd seen him leap through the rhododendron and he'd fired the little rock at once, right at the sycamore the boy was headed for. If he'd seen anyone else do that, he'd have thought they were trying to hit him, or at least, knew they might. The thought made his insides heavy. He thought he was going to cry. He hadn't cried since he was ten. One day he'd said to himself "I'm never going to cry again", and from that day he hadn't shed a tear. He'd thought about how it might feel if his mum died and imagined himself at the funeral, the only person who didn't need a handkerchief. All the same, he felt like crying. Would little Glasson be okay? Maybe he'd be permanently damaged? And everyone would know he threw the stone. The other lads had seen him and they knew he was showing off. If they told, everyone would think he aimed at Glasson. If it had been Forton or one of those bullies, he'd be proud to have split his head. To throw a rock that left Forton flat on his face in a pool of blood, that was an idea Arkwright liked. Forton deserved it. All those bullies deserved it. Lots of people deserved it. But Glasson. He didn't want to hurt Glasson in any way. He wanted to care for him. He wanted to protect him. It was odd. He didn't understand it. But he'd lobbed the stone. It was a good shot, no doubt about that; he knew as soon as it left his hand that he'd done it well. Was he trying to hit Glasson? No,no,no! He wanted to give him a shock. He wanted to see him coming out of the bushes with a look of surprise on his face saying:

"Fuck! That nearly hit me."

Then they'd all laugh and Glasson would come running up to Arkwright and try to hit him and Arkwright would push him away, like a father play fighting with his little boy. But if he'd wanted to nearly hit him maybe he wanted to really hit him. Maybe he'd gone too far because he was showing off. Suppose Glasson died. Suppose on the way to the hospital he just passed out and never came round and the other lads told everyone he'd thrown the stone and everyone would say he was a murderer. He wouldn't care if he murdered Forton or Alston or Tasker; he'd be proud. People could call him a murderer. Those bastards deserved to die. All the way home the picture of Glasson lying on the floor troubled him, the image of him with his hand to his head and the blood flowing like water from a tap, his worried voice saying: "Tom, carry me…. tortured his consciousness. He could have carried him. He should have. He should have picked him up and run home with him. He should have done that for his little friend.

He said nothing to his parents and all weekend he worried. What would happen at school on Monday? Glasson would be absent. People would be talking. They'd know. They'd be saying it was him. He did it deliberately and now Glasson was dead, or nearly dead or his brain didn't work properly anymore…

In the playground everyone had gathered round the little lad with the bandage on his head. It stuck up oddly from the site of the wound where they'd shaved his hair and ruined his quiff.

"What happened, Smiler?"

"I got hit by a stone, in the woods. Seven stitches."

"Who threw it?"

"Dunno."

Arkwright came up slowly with his loping stride, his demeanour of contained energy. He was very smart in his uniform. He liked uniforms and he liked to look neat. His black blazer hugged his broad shoulders and strong chest, his white shirt was ironed to perfection and the creases in his grey trousers sharp as the morning's frost; yet what you noticed first were his feet, not only because of the military shine of his shoes, but also because his feet were big yet not clumsy; they hit the ground with a surety and definiteness of presence which was at once impressive and threatening. He hung around on the edge of the crowd till little Glasson noticed him and smiled. When the bell went and the crowd dispersed the two of them walked to the boys' entrance together.

"Did the stitches hurt?"

"Yeah. Nurse was tasty though."

Arkwright laughed and put his great, strong hand, the hand that had thrown the stone on his friend's shoulder.

"Thanks," he said, as they were going through the double doors into the boys' corridor and past the toilets where the first thing that hit you was the smell of disinfectant mingled with the faint hint of urine, "for not telling anyone."

Glasson looked up with the charming smile Arkwright liked so much and which won him his nickname.

"Okay."

The little lad was pestered all day: "What happened, Smiler? Who did that to you? How many stitches? "Stone? Which bastard threw it?" But he didn't give away his secret. The lads who'd been in the woods heard him say he didn't know and decided to reveal nothing. Arkwright in his turn said nothing to them but it was a strange and marvellous thing that no-one would ever know he was the culprit. Why hadn't Glasson told anyone? He couldn't work it out: maybe because he suspected his injury wasn't entirely accidental and didn't want to get Arkwright in trouble; maybe because he knew, somehow, how bad Arkwright was feeling about things. In any case, it showed what a good person he was. There was no-one quite like him, Arkwright thought. Sometimes, he felt he could take on the world. He had that odd sense that everyone and everything was against him and he would gladly have punched everyone he met in the nose. But Glasson was the exception. He wasn't like the other lads. Even the things he was good at he just laughed about. Everyone went to him when maths homework was hard. He could solve equations as easily as eating ice-cream and when lads said: "How did you do that?" he just threw back his head and laughed, like he did when he got his report and was top of the class in nearly everything. It was queer. There were lads like Pete Norgate who was good at English and would stick his nose in the air and who had that funny little smirk when he got an essay back with an A or A+; but Glasson would have laughed if they'd given him the Nobel Prize. Arkwright felt a lot better. Glasson was his friend. He'd smashed his head with a stone but it had made no difference; the little lad was still the same; he still smiled, and he still always did the good thing. Arkwright was puzzled by that. How did Glasson know how to behave ? It would have been easy for him just to tell everyone what happened in the woods. He wouldn't have been blaming Arkwright. Most lads would just have told the tale. But there was some little difference in Glasson: he thought about other people and somehow he could read their minds. It was odd but it delighted Arkwright. If everyone was like Glasson, he wouldn't need to have his fists ready, he wouldn't have to practice his swing on the punchbag in the garage; he would have been able to relax and laugh his way through life like Glasson himself.

It was a few weeks after Glasson had the stitches out before his hair grew back and his quiff was in place. Arkwright was glad to see him looking like he should.

"Does it still hurt?"

"Itches," said Glasson "You can feel where the stitches were."

Arkwright ran his finger over the little arc of a bump under Glasson's hair. It was odd to think he would have this scar all his life because of the stone he'd thrown. Even when he was an old man, he would still be marked by their friendship.

"When you go bald everyone will see it," he said.

"I won't go bald. You will."

And they began their play-fighting routine, Glasson running full pelt and throwing himself at Arkwright who caught him and tossed him aside as if he were a pillow, the two of them laughing as if the world would never end.

Some months later, in the spring, Glasson cycled to Arkwright's house after tea. He was building a bike in the garage and Glasson went to watch and pick up tips. Arkwright's father worked in the aircraft factory, one of those men whose manual skill and mechanical intelligence allowed him to make or repair anything. From an early age he'd taught his son and Arkwright was quick and adept. He had the bike frame hanging from the trusses and was spraying it with a device his dad had rigged for him. It was plugged in the kitchen and the flex crept through the opening light and sneaked into the garage through the gap between the door and the frame. The nozzle delivered a fine mist and Glasson stood back and watched as the bare metal turned metallic blue. It was a wonder. When it was done, Arkwright showed him how to respoke a wheel. He had it fixed horizontally in a jig on the bench. He fed the spokes through the holes in the rim, attached them to the hub and secured them.

"You've got to tighten 'em one by one, you see."

He spun the wheel, stopped it, made an adjustment, spun it again.

"How can you tell if it's right?"

"Look," said Arkwright, "it's easy. Watch here."

Glasson watched but still wasn't sure how Arkwright knew just which spokes to tweak. When the wheel was spinning true, Arkwright went over to the punchbag and started whacking his fists into it.

"Have a go, Smiler."

Glasson's punches made hardly any impact and the two of them rocked with laughter at the difference between Arkwright's big, heavy fists and Glasson's thin, log-fingered hands. They decided to jump on their bikes and go to the woods. There was a fallen tree across the stream and they could balance from the roots to the branches. The clay banks were dry and there was a sweet odour in the air of the fructification of spring. They knew the seasons. The rank smell of decay in autumn. The metallic cut of winter air in your throat when you ran along the paths in January. They sat on the tree with the slow-flowing stream beneath them. They could see, through a break in the trees, the field where the cows were grazing and beyond it, the corner of the school building. Arkwright spotted someone.

"Hey, it's Norgate"

They stood up to get a better view. A lad was walking hand in hand with a girl, stepping high over the coarse grass and the bumpy surface.

"He's with Janice Nash."

"Yeah," said Glasson.

Arkwright had an instinctive dislike of Norgate. He was one of those lads who made him feel he just wanted to punch them in the face. He was captain of the football team and thought himself a great sportsman, but Arkwright knew he was stronger, faster and more skilled. He had little feel for team games and certainly didn't like pleasing P.E. teachers. He was the best runner in the year but was never picked for the cross-country team because Horseman didn't like him. He had his favourites. His flatterers. Arkwright felt it was stupid: he could have won every cross-country race for the school but because he didn't suck up to Horseman he was left out. Arkwright looked at Glasson who was watching the couple. There was a hint of seriousness in his face he'd never seen before. A grown-up look. He turned back to watch and saw the lad and lass kissing. Janice Nash was pretty enough. She was shapely and knew it and she could toss her blonde hair to break a young lad's heart. Arkwright knew Glasson liked her. He had a sudden surge of protective feeling towards him.

"Shall we give 'em a surprise?"

131

"No," said Glasson who sat on the trunk and turned his head away.

Arkwright looked over at the kissing couple again. He would have liked to go over and head-butt Norgate, to lay him flat in front of the girl. He didn't like her either. She'd flirted with him as she did with lots of the boys and he knew she'd batted her eyelids at Glasson to get him to do her homework. Poor little Glasson had taken it seriously but Arkwright knew a girl like that didn't like any boy as much as she liked herself. She and Norgate made a good pair. Arkwright had never thought much about Glasson's crush on Janice, but now it struck him she was a bitch. She played hockey for the county and her dad was friendly with Beech, the Headmaster; they were members of those funny organisations his dad was always ranting about: Masons or the Round Table or something like that. Arkwright didn't know anything about them but he knew the kind of people in them and he didn't like them; people who lived in big houses and went to church and looked down their noses at men in factories like his dad. Janice fancied herself. She was a snob. She knew she only had to stick out her chest and tilt her head like an inquisitive dove and any lad in the school would be following her around. Except him. Poor little Glasson thought she liked him because she nestled close to him in registration and got out her maths book. That was Glasson's trouble: he thought other people were as good as him. He thought she was honest. Arkwright knew a girl like that was as slippery as a pike. Some poor bastard would marry her. He'd never marry a girl like that. She'd give you the run around. He'd marry a girl who did what she was told.

"Let's go to the swing, Smiler."

Glasson got up and Arkwright saw real hurt in his face. That bitch. He'd like to sort her out. If she stuck her tits out at him again she'd be sorry; he'd shove his hand straight in her blouse. He'd show her not to mess with him. They followed the path to the big clearing where the light brown, dry bank cut away steeply on both sides. Arkwright had rigged a rope swing. He'd climbed the big oak to hook the rope around the branch. It hung three feet from the ground. Lads would take hold, run with it as fast as they could around the curvature of the sloping bank until the ground disappeared beneath their feet and they flew out over the stream, narrowly missed the willow as they swung back and arrived, slowing themselves with hurried little steps where they began.

"Get hold," said Arkwright.

Glasson took the thick rope in his slender hands. Arkwright pulled him back, edging up the slope with the weight of his friend on his right arm. When the rope had reached its limit, he launched it with all his might and Glasson, dangling from its end orbited, his legs almost horizontal, in a great whooshing arc till he came back to base and Arkwright grabbed him and stopped him abruptly. The two of them laughed madly. Glasson rubbed his palms on the thighs of his jeans.

"Get on again," said Arkwright, and he sent his little friend flying once more, watching him like a father watching his child rise and fall on a swing in the park, catching him in his strong, sure hands as his nimble feet struck dust from the dry clay. On they went till Glasson's arms could take no more. He lay flat on his back.

"Oh, my arms!" and Arkwright laughed to see how quickly he got tired. He was happy. It was easy to be happy with Glasson. It was odd: how could happiness depend on such a small, skinny, insubstantial thing? But it did. It was a miracle. He had no idea how it came about, but he was glad he'd met Glasson. He was the only friend he could trust absolutely. The only friend he knew would never let him down. Arkwright took the rope. He ran with a great, powerful, animal stride and launched himself and then still running when he hit the bank set off again and again and again round and round his strong arms holding him easily as Glasson watched and smiled and wished he were big and strong like his mate.

Just as they were about to go, Norgate and Janice Nash appeared from the bushes. He had that smirk on his face Arkwright wanted to wipe off and she looked coy and coquettish, pushing her hair behind her ears and stuffing her blouse into her skirt. Arkwright looked Norgate in the eyes and said:

"Been for a shag, then?"

Janice brought her hands up to her mouth and let out a little squeal. Norgate's face took on an expression that was half smile, half grimace.

"Like you," he said.

"Calling me a homo, Norgate?"

"What if I am?"

"Better send your girl-friend home before I break your teeth."

Janice looked suddenly serious and afraid. She tugged at Norgate's arm. Norgate turned to Glasson and said:

"She doesn't like you, you know. She thinks you're a shrimp."

"He's a better person than you, Norgate," said Arkwright.

Norgate laughed, that smirking, mean laugh Arkwright hated so much.

"She'd need a magnifying glass to find your dick."

Arkwright took a step towards Norgate. Janice pulled him away.

"Come on, Pete. Come on."

Norgate grinned, turned and the two of them disappeared into the bushes. Glasson was sitting down, his arms round his knees, looking at the ground. Arkwright almost went after Norgate. He would have liked to break his nose. But he didn't want to fight him with Janice there. It didn't seem right. Girls shouldn't be around fighting. It was for boys. But one day he'd get Norgate. On his own. He'd make him sorry. He looked at his friend. He felt pity for him that he was small and skinny and underdeveloped. It must be difficult when so many lads were big and muscular, almost men at fourteen. But Janice was an idiot. Who'd spend time with a bighead like Norgate when they could have fun with someone like Glasson? But in an instant he realised she wouldn't think like that: she wouldn't want to be seen with someone who looked still boyish and unready. She was playing at being a woman and wanted someone who was playing at being a man.

"Getting dark, Smiler. Got your lights?"

A few weeks later Glasson was at Arkwright's again in the evening. His dad had got him an old motorbike and was showing him how to strip it down and rebuild it. Arkwright had the engine laid out in bits on the bench. He explained to Glasson how it all fit together and what you had to do to keep an engine running well. Glasson picked up the clean, cold parts and examined them. He had little feel for mechanical things. He could do the maths to tell you how much energy the engine would use, but the physical matter of taking one to pieces and reassembling it seemed almost arcane. He wasn't too interested. What he liked was being around Arkwright. He liked the slow way he moved and the serious look on his face when he was paying careful attention. Arkwright was a good mate and Glasson was one of those people who learn quickly that all other advantages are worthless if you don't spend your time with people who make you feel good. The two lads, so different in such fundamental ways, were happy just to be in one another's company.

When it grew dusk and time for Glasson to go, Arkwright rode to the end of the avenue with him, to the little ginnel which led to the main road and there they said goodbye and Arkwright watched his skinny little friend stand up on the pedals to ride away done the narrow path. He went back to the garage to make sure everything was neatly put away, but he found himself wondering if Glasson would get home all right. Why shouldn't he? He'd done so dozens of times before. He couldn't understand why he was fretting, then he realized that while they'd been chatting at the end of the ginnel, he'd seen a lad pass by at the other end, a tallish, broad lad with his head tossed back cockily who'd looked their way as he took a drag on his cigarette. He was just the kind of lad to look for trouble. You could tell at once he was a bully. He fancied himself. You could see it in the way he stuck out his chest and the slightly sneering expression of his mouth. Arkwright jumped back on his bike, balanced along the little snicket and emerged onto the main road where he stopped. Thirty yards away Glasson was paused at the bus-stop, his legs astride his crossbar, talking to the smoker who stood too close to him. Arkwright knew what was going on. Glasson looked in his direction. Arkwright nodded and Glasson nodded in return. The big lad rode up to the pair. As he approached and the bully turned to see him, he stepped towards the kerb and craned as if to see if his bus was coming. Arkwright pulled on his brakes and stopped next to his friend. He was wearing a yellow woollen polo neck his mum had knitted for him. It was a little tight and showed the round profile of his biceps, the square strength of his shoulders and the athletic tapering of his torso.

"Trouble, Smiler?"

"Yeah."

"What d'he say to you?"

The stranger was moving from foot to foot. He kept his back to the pals and pretended to look for his bus.

"Asked me where I lived and what time I go to bed at night."

Arkwright got off his bike which Glasson held by the handlebars, he put his big, heavy hand on the intruder's shoulder.

"Want to pick a fight, lad," he said, "pick one with me."

The other lad didn't turn. He continued to crane and to smoke.

"Bully my little pal, I'll put that fag out up your nose."

Just at that moment the bus appeared. The stranger jangled change in his pocket. Arkwright removed his hand but stood beside him. The bus pulled in and he stepped on.

"Lucky for you it wasn't late," said Arkwright.

As the great, slow, red double-decker pulled away he turned to Glasson and smiled.

"Be okay now?"

"Yeah. Thanks, Tom. See ya tomorra."

Riding home, Arkwright wished he'd had the chance to punch the bully. He hated those people. Whatever he was, he wasn't a bully. He'd never pick on a little lad like Glasson. He'd never want to frighten or hurt someone smaller or weaker than himself. But a bully set his nerves alight and his fists itched. Glasson, on the other hand, was glad there hadn't been a fight; but he was chuffed Arkwright had come to his rescue. What would have happened? He knew those kind of bullies well enough. He might have hit him, or tried to pull him off his bike. It wouldn't have been too bad. He'd have got away; but he might have had a thick lip or a black eye. Arkwright had saved him and that gave him a good, warm feeling. Tom was a good friend. He'd put himself in the way of a fight to save him. Not that the other lad would have had a chance, but that wasn't the point.

Not long after this, the friends began to drift apart in that inadvertent way teenagers do. Arkwright spent more time with his engines and Glasson played more tennis; new friendships arose and though they had plenty of laughs together at school, they seldom saw one another at weekends or in the evening. They both left school at sixteen; Arkwright went to train as a ship's radio officer and Glasson took a job with a firm of accountants which he left out of boredom, got himself some A Levels and went to read maths at university. It was five years later, when Glasson was back at home for a while and got off the bus late one afternoon that he saw coming towards him a slow, broad, strong figure in a white naval officer's cap and blue gabardine. He recognised him at once and waited. Arkwright didn't hurry.

He held out his hand:

"All right, Andy?"

"Aye. Nice to see you, Tom. How's things?"

"Oh, not bad. Been to visit the folks. Don't see 'em often. Just got over a dose of the clap."

Glasson laughed.

"Not funny really," said Arkwright, "like pissing razor blades."

He went on to tell his adventures around the world, how he'd caught syphilis from a whore in Mauritius who'd no doubt been performing on stage with a donkey; the fight he'd had in a bar in Sydney when a sailor had told him to get out of his space at the bar, whipped out a knife and nicked his cheek before he got in the punch which broke his jaw and knocked him out; the scrap he'd had with a ship's engineer who'd told him he was going to kill him and how he'd punched him from one end of the ship to the other till he was so bad they had to get him to hospital. Glasson smiled and nodded. This was his friend. This was good Tom who had looked after him and probably still would. Glasson explained about his dull work in accountancy, his time at university thanks to Harold Wilson's programme of expansion and how he was now training to teach F.E. .

"Aye? You'll be good at that. Not wed?"

"No. What about you?"

"Aye. Baby due in January."

They chatted some more both wishing they could have longer time. There were the old days to bring back; so many little incidents. What a laugh they could have had.

"Better get on, anyway," said Arkwright. "Got to be on board by seven."

"Where you goin'?"

"South America. Pakis in the crew. I hate 'em. Throw the buggers overboard if I get the chance."

Glasson tried to smile. He didn't want to argue with his old friend. He owed him a lot even though he found his prejudices disgusting.

"Well, good luck to you, Tom. Take care of yourself."

"I always do."

"Hope to see you again."

"Aye," and Arkwright gave a little salute before setting off with his long, slow stride.

Glasson went down the lane of little semis and bungalows. It was safe and peaceful here. He was going to his parents' house where tea would be ready for him and he'd read Wells or Tawney or Lawrence and maybe go to the pub for the last hour; but he could hear the sound of the crashing ocean, feel the pitch of the ship in the unforgiving waves, see his friend with the earphones on his head, sending signals across the globe from his cramped cabin, smell the Tequila on the breath of a sultry, enticing, hip-waving girl in Lima, taste the blood that poured from the nose of some poor Asian sailor as the great, tight, hammer fist smashed into his nose, touch the soft pillow where Tom would lay his head in his narrow bunk dreaming of return to Lancashire to hold his new born baby in his powerful arms.

A LOVELY IDEA

Having no understanding of music, Laurie Wynter dreamed of being a pop star. What fascinated him was the hold pop stars had over their audiences. He was ten when The Beatles took off, and the sight of young girls in their thousands working themselves into hysteria in front of four young men of dubious talent sowed in his mind during the next few years the notion of easy success, adulation, and wealth.

"Why don't we start a band!" he said to his friends.

"What do you play?"

"Nothing. But I can learn!" and his characteristic, unconvincing smile stretched over his uneven teeth.

But music couldn't seize his attention and make him work. He tried piano but the task of scales and arpeggios bored him. He couldn't see any relation between these strings of notes and a tune.

"What's the point of playing scales?" he asked his music teacher.

"The point?" she said. "This is what music is made of. If you don't know this, you'll never be a musician."

He wondered if it would be easier to go straight to melodies on the guitar, but it was even worse. The contortions of his fingers to produce even a simple chord sequence made his hands ache. It wasn't worth the effort. The music wasn't worth the effort. He would've tolerated the discomfort for fame and money. Yet he just couldn't get near the music. He couldn't make it part of him. It was a strange, alien thing. He loved pop music. He thought Lulu a great singer. When *The Monkees* appeared he bought all their records. He was an ardent fan. But he wasn't competent enough in music to dare play rock n' roll in a pub.

It was a tremendous disappointment because he couldn't tolerate the idea of not being famous and rich. It seemed as obvious as night and day: the only thing worth doing in life was pursuing money and attention. He was bright. He was in one of the best private schools in the country. A place at Oxbridge was more or less guaranteed. When he was fifteen he read in *The Daily Telegraph* about lorry drivers going on strike for an increase to fifteen pounds a week. He thought strikes a disgrace but at the same time he wondered how people lived on fifteen pounds.

"Why do these lorry drivers earn only fifteen pounds a week?" he said to his father.

"That's how the market works," he replied spooning two more roast potatoes onto his Sunday dinner plate. "Labour is a commodity like any other. Its value is determined in the market like any other. Now, if you can predict how currencies are going to move, your market value will be very high. But any idiot can drive a lorry. That's why they earn so little. Because they're idiots."

The explanation appealed to him. It struck him they must be different: they couldn't be like his family. Something about them must make fifteen pounds a week appropriate. He knew his father who lectured in Economics earned seven thousand a year, but then he had income from books. His *Men and Markets* had sold tens of thousands in paperback. He was also invited to lecture abroad and made a lot in fees and expenses. He'd laughed at the dinner table about making £500 for an hour's talk in Paris. It was strange. Why was the world divided between people like them and lorry drivers, coal miners, factory workers, shop girls, milkmen, postmen, joiners, all kinds of people who earned next to nothing? It could only be that it had to be. It was the way things were and it couldn't be that the way they were was a mistake. Such an idea would have shaken his faith in life too radically. For a moment the horrible possibility had emerged that those lorry drivers were hard done by. Their lives must be restricted. They must struggle. But this was an idea which couldn't be permitted to mature. Having pictured their misery utterly clearly, he had to deny it. His diligently formulated defence was that God intended the world to be this way. The rich deserved to be rich just as his father deserved to be well-off. And those with little had their rightful place. It was a scheme of things which couldn't be altered. Of course, people had the right to better themselves. It was a phrase his father used often. That was fair. Everyone had the right to better themselves but some didn't make it. Fate decreed they must be at the bottom. Then that life must be right for them. They couldn't be allowed to starve of course. There was a Christian duty to keep people from absolute poverty. But it was clear to him things were as they were for a purpose. A force greater than himself had chosen him to be among the best. Who was he to deny it? It would have been perverse. It would have been to fly in the face of the facts.

140

These ideas made him comfortable and confident. He would do well. He'd make money. He'd fulfil the destiny decided for him by God. But what troubled him was fame. He had a sense he was destined to be famous. If he joined the Civil Service of the Foreign Office, if he went into business or the law he could make big money. He had to make big money. Imagine being like one of those lorry drivers or even a teacher or a lecturer. Oh, you could get by. But the humiliation of seeing others with millions. The shame of living in a world where fabulous wealth was possible and to have nothing more than a decent semi in the suburbs, a car, a caravan, holidays in Cornwall. It was too distressing to think of. It was wrong! It was unjust! People like him were meant to be very wealthy. It was the working out of what was written in his nature.

"What do you think you'll do in life?" he asked one of his classmates.

"Foreign office."

"Why?"

"My father has contacts. I'm a linguist. If I'm lucky I'll get an Embassy. Paris would be nice. Keep your nose clean and it's a cushy life."

"Yes," said Laurie, "but don't you have a desire to be known?"

"By whom? The plebs? Who cares about them?"

For a while, he thought of becoming an actor. He enthusiastically pushed himself forward for roles in school plays. He was The First Knight in *Murder In The Cathedral*, Bagot in *Richard II* and finally, in the upper sixth, *Tesman* in Hedda Gabler. But acting made no more sense to him than music. Acting out , he understood intuitively. Enacting little mental fantasies and then behaving according to them. He did that all the time. Wasn't that how life worked? Didn't everybody do it? Acting though, this business of getting into character and having to take that seriously. It was a lot of hard work for little reward. Nor did he understand what a character like Tesman was all about. It seemed hopelessly silly, and on stage professional actors were seen by a few hundred people each performance. Six times a week for a run of two months. You might be seen by no more than thirty thousand people. What good was that? He thought of football crowds, pop concerts, the Nuremburg rallies. Those were audiences worth having. Hollywood actors could attract such adulation. He read in a Sunday supplement about the young Marlon Brando being handed keys to hotel rooms by women he didn't know. The idea of that power fascinated him. He wondered if he could attain the same kind of effect: if he became a sort of celebrity within his circle, would the girls all want to go to bed with him? It was an intoxicating idea, but it wasn't intimacy which appealed to him but power. It was the fact that women who had never met Brando were willing to have sex with him just because he was famous. It was strange. People were prepared to hand themselves over to those who had achieved fame or notoriety as if by so doing they gained a little of the fame themselves. Fame was even more attractive than money. Of course, he read in the Sunday papers too about rich men who had strings of women. But didn't fame and money go hand in hand? He tried to think of someone famous who didn't have money. He'd been told Mozart died a pauper and he knew artists and writers could be ignored and left in poverty. But that was different. Most people took no notice of them anyway. Who but a few precious intellectuals or pious social climbers listened to Mozart or read James Joyce? No, in the culture that mattered, popular culture, the famous were all rich.

By the time he got to Oxford, he'd put stage acting behind him. Music and theatre had let him down. What else was there? He worked away at his degree, had one girlfriend after another, found the whole business a bit disappointing, and began to think he would have to resign himself to being rich. Yet every time he watched the television he was hurt by the thought of his potential obscurity. He could go through life, make a fortune, live well, have houses in several capitals, drive a Rolls, fly around the world, but what did it all mean if his name wasn't known? What were the lives of obscure people worth? They lived, they died, they were buried. They mixed with the earth. It was as if they had never been. A few relatives retained their memory, but what good was that? Did he know anything worth knowing about his great-great-grandfather? The aristocrats treasured their lineage. But the common people? They were forgotten, dismissed, their memory wiped out. He didn't think of himself as one of the common people, but he wasn't aristocratic. He wished he was. How easy it would be if you were born into royalty, even into a minor branch. Money would be yours, contacts. You were important by birth. The fact was, most people weren't important. Their lives were worthless. In truth, only those who had a place in history were worth anything.

In his final year he was delighted when he met Caroline Winstanley, daughter of a Duke. He visited the seat in Berkshire. At once he felt lifted out of ordinariness. He soon discovered the family had contacts in every important arena of life. Caroline's brother-in-law ran a television company. Her uncle was in finance. There was no door the family couldn't open. She was the girl for him.

Her uncle found him a job in merchant banking.

"What exactly is merchant banking?" he asked naively.

"Banking for the rich," replied her uncle pouring another glass of *Veuve Cliquot*. "Banking is a bit of misnomer but it sounds respectable. People think of suburban managers of impeccable probity. What we do is get round the law to make the rich richer."

The idea appealed to him. He was as complaisant as possible and this flexibility, his absolute lack of principle which made adjustment to every circumstance easy, served him well. The complexity of some of the finance was a little troublesome, but he discovered no-one cared too much about grasp of detail: commitment to the cause was what mattered. His work was all about gambling on the economy. Would this flourish, would that fail? There were wonderful little tricks by which great fortunes could be made. What pleased him most was how it was all a mystery to the general public. They might fool themselves about democracy, they might believe their votes made a difference, but they were dupes: the people who ran these elevated, obscure financial institutions had much more power than mere MPs. They could make or break entire nations. In fact, they could bring the whole world economy crashing around the ears of the benighted masses. And why shouldn't they? There was a powerful attraction in the idea of ruin. To lay waste the planet rather than give up having things your own way! Wasn't that a marvellous notion! The power was vertiginous. By the time of his sumptuous wedding to Caroline he was earning £100,000. She was working for her brother's company. They bought a huge town house in South Kensington. There was no doubt about the millions to come. Sometimes he wondered if he might even be a billionaire. Yet the nagging sense of obscurity dragged him down. He read about criminals who served their sentence and wrote their memoirs. They were celebrities. Didn't people love and admire the Krays? It really didn't matter how fame was attained. Once you had it, its effect was magical.

He was tormenting himself over ways to attain fame when the news came that his father had suffered a stroke. The doctors saved his life but he was paralysed down his left-hand side. Curiously, he denied the deficiency. The specialist explained that the damage to the right-side of his brain had diminished his sense of reality. Laurie was amazed. There were so many things he barely understood. He paid for the best care but the initial intervention had been by a public hospital. Without the ambulance, the doctor, the nurses, his father would have died. The fact of having him moved to a private facility as soon as it was safe couldn't obliterate the fact. It troubled him enormously. It made him feel he had some intrinsic connection to those foolish millions who relied on public services. If only his father had taken out insurance and been taken straight to a private bed.

"He was lucky to be brought here," the doctor said to him.

"Why's that?"

"We're the best in the country. It's our speciality. No-one else in the region can do what we can do for stroke victims. If he hadn't come here the outcome might have been very different."

"Unless he'd gone private," said Laurie.

The grey-haired doctor raised his brows and gently shook his head.

"No. There's no private facility he could have got to in time which can do what we can" he said with a quiet smile.

Laurie was appalled. Was that true? It shook his faith very badly. It seemed terribly wrong that public money should buy better care than private millions. It was an insult. Then it struck him that it was just what was wrong with the country! People could work hard to make fortunes yet any low-level nobody, any unemployed bricklayer or unambitious school cleaner who fell ill might get better care from the State! It made a mockery of everything he believed. What was the point of driving for money and fame if they didn't bring great advantage? He realized in a flash of insight that the whole idea of a free, universal public sector was a mistake. Services should be businesses! If people can make money from them, then they will work as they should. Most importantly, people shouldn't take them for granted. They must accept business as the model of provision or renounce provision altogether. The ideal would be to close down the public sector and make people pay. No-one expected to have their shoes provided by the State, why then education or health care? And wasn't it obvious people were willing to spend their money on cars or holidays or booze while expecting other people's taxes to provide services? But once his ideas had run to this extreme he began to temper them with objections. Children had to be educated. It couldn't be left to the market. Nor would it do to let people die of appendicitis. So a half-way house was necessary. The public sector needed to lose its dull character. It was a heavy, oppressive beast which squatted in the middle of the economy like a hippo in a mud pool. It needed to sharpen up, put on a smart suit, take on some of the grinning chutzpah of popular culture; it needed to be run by people with business brains and above all the people who used it needed to be customers. A customer, after all, was empowered. When he went to buy a new car, he could make demands because he was handing over £15,000. A customer has the right to be uppity, bolshie. Yes, that was where it was right to be up in arms, to be importunate and demanding. The foolishness of trade unionists was their dispiriting collectivism, their ponderous insistence on rights in the workplace, their perpetual criticism of successful people who had made fortunes. People as individual customers, that was the point. Once they were consumers of education or healthcare, well, the schools and hospitals would have to operate like businesses. Let money follow the customer. The bad schools would close, the poor hospitals decline, people would have real choice.

During his father's long, slow recovery, he began to pay more attention to political speeches. He thought Mrs Thatcher marvellous, especially the feeling of the sermon in what she said. In her tone of voice he could hear a disdain for debate. Her intonation contained no acceptance of dissent. He liked this sense of a message, a revealed truth which must be directly communicated. Then one evening, at the height of the bitter struggle within the Labour Party in the early eighties, he went with some friends to hear Tony Benn, just for the sake of it. Though he disagreed with almost every word and was mystified by the idea of a struggle between left and right he was mesmerised by the delivery. To be able to speak like that! To move audiences, and through electronic media to be able to influence millions at a time; there was power!

"What's all the stuff about left and right?" he said to one of his banker friends over a drink afterwards.

"Jealousy," the young man replied. "That's what they mean by the left. They're envious of our success and want to take our money from us. It's nothing less than theft."

"I just don't get it," said Laurie, " the idea of some showdown between irreconcilable interests. Why don't they just get on with things? Make it work."

"They don't want it to work. They want to ruin the economy just because they're losers. That's why we need strong laws to keep them in their place."

"Funny though. A man like Benn. Tremendous talent. Why does he talk all that rubbish?"

"Oh, he thinks he's some kind of messiah, I suppose, come to save the poor from the dreadful rich. Where would the oiks be without the likes of us, eh Laurie? Swinging through the trees and living in caves. No gratitude. That's the problem with the masses."

Laurie thought hard about these questions. He began to read around politics. Whenever he came across terms like alienation, exploitation, class struggle or even capitalism, he wanted to laugh out loud. What was it supposed to mean, alienation? He had no idea. Even capitalism. Why did left-wing intellectuals use it as a term of criticism? What was to criticize? It was the most natural thing in the world. Getting on. Doing the best for yourself. Making your way. Doing better than your neighbour. That was just human nature, why call it capitalism and try to analyse it? Intellectuals made him impatient. Once, he'd tried to read Einstein's Relativity, out of a belief that as a well-educated young man he should know what it was all about, but it was so searingly objective, so bereft of anything personal, he couldn't find a way to accommodate it. He put the book aside with the sense that physics was for a handful of weirdos. He began to develop the same feeling about politics. Normal people had no interest in it. Really, there was no need for it. Why didn't we all just get on and do what needed to be done? Whenever he heard someone like Benn or Foot he was deeply uncomfortable. The suggestion that something was rotten in the state of the nation; it made him wince and his mouth curled into a little snarl of distaste. The essential was to be always positive and how could you be positive if you thought the system, or whatever it was termed, was flawed? No, he couldn't stand it. It sickened him. What he loved was the endless glee of popular culture. Pop music in particular. And didn't people like it? Weren't people more interested in Donny Osmond than Neil Kinnock or Brenda Dean or any of the rest of the dull tribe of naysayers, do-gooders, reformers or would-be revolutionaries? That's how politics should work! Give the people what they liked! Give them what they wanted? Who wants the pain and trouble of thinking about how bad things are and having to struggle to find answers? In any case, things weren't bad. Things were just great! And then the idea came to him: politics was the way to fame!

When he told Caroline he was going to join the Labour Party, she was taken aback.

"To change it," he said. "You see, what's the point of joining the Tories. I mean, I'd be just another Tory. I think like a Tory. The thing is, the Labour Party needs to be changed. We need to get rid of all this stuff about socialism and turn it into a party which gets on with things."

"But they'll never accept that," she said. "They're always banging on about the poor and closing the gap and that kind of thing. They'll never listen to you."

"Well, I'm not going to tell them! That would be guileless. I'm not going to say I want to eliminate all trace of socialism and all talk of equality from the Labour Party and make it a party the rich are happy with. You have to say what your audience wants to hear. Then once you've got a bit of power, you do the opposite. But no-one remembers what you said anyway!"

"I don't see why you can't join the Tories if you want to attack Labour."

"You know," he said blenching as if from a blow, "I wouldn't have as good a chance of getting on in the Tory party. I can be the new man in Labour. I can be the man who stands for change. They'll lose the next election badly. Foot is hopeless. That'll be my opportunity. They'll all be down in the mouth and looking for a way to win elections again. I can do that. You see, the way to win elections is to stop talking about politics. No-one likes it. No-one wants to hear it. Like that speech by Jimmy Carter. That was terrible. No-one wants to

147

know the country's suffering from a moral malaise or a crisis of confidence. People want cheering up."

"He was talking about the energy crisis wasn't he? That's a real problem."

"Not if we assert ourselves! Look, we are the democracies. We have the moral right to lead the world. If other countries try to get in our way, we just have to tell them no. It's a simple as that. The important thing is to stop all this talk of left and right, rich and poor, private and public. It's all one. It's all about aspiration. That's the key. People getting on. If you make them feel they can do that the problems will evaporate."

He sent off his application and the secretary of his local branch came to see him. He had to go to the meetings. He had to show willing. It depressed him terribly. The people were wretched. He talked to a nurse who devoted hours of her time to the party. He could hardly keep from sneering at her. How did people live these reduced lives? Was that the limit of her ambition? To work as a nurse and push leaflets through letterboxes at election time? Why didn't she start a business? Why didn't she have some push! But he had to smile and pretend he was comfortable. He heard arguments which made him want to thump the table or walk out. People kept talking about unemployment and poverty, this protest and that demonstration and how Thatcher was destroying manufacturing. It all seemed so silly. What was Thatcher doing but modernising! These people talked as if we were still in the nineteenth century. Thatcher was right: strikes and unions and restrictive practices were ruining the country. Who needs manufacturing? There was a bright new dawn ahead in financial services. If only people would back Thatcher instead of sniping at her, then unemployment would fall. People could get jobs in banks or insurance companies. These people were starry-eyed about coal miners or ship-builders. And they despised the rich. Whenever he heard one of them talk about closing the gap between rich and poor it set his teeth on edge. Why should the gap be closed? The rich deserved their money and they were something for the poor to aspire to. The poor, after all, were just a set of miserable losers. What hope was there for a political party which focused on them?

All this low level, disheartening stuff had to be escaped as soon as possible. He was searching for a safe seat. It meant being friendly to trade unionists he despised. One of them, Ken Topping, a life-long

TGWU man, took a shine to Laurie and offered to help him. The MP in his constituency was stepping down. He'd put the word out.

"Why do you think he likes you?" said Caroline.

"Oh, because I'm young and bright and he sees that I might do well in parliament. You see, that's human nature. He'd like me as his MP so he can feel close to power. He's more interested in that than justice or equality."

To try to work out how to hone his speeches he went to hear other MPs and candidates. John Prescott, in jeans and an open necked-shirt, called for the nationalisation of the commanding heights of the economy. Laurie was appalled. Surely Mrs Thatcher was right about that. The days of nationalised industries were over. Privatising was the way to forge ahead. He thought Prescott ridiculous, but what he liked were the jeans and open collar. That was the way to relate to the people! That's what the country needed: a Prime Minister who wore jeans in Downing St. He went to listen to Dennis Skinner and though he found him amusing was shocked. What bitter antagonism to the rich! What irrational prejudice! Why did people elect such a man? It was from people like Skinner the Labour Party must be saved. What was he but an ignorant, old-fashioned, cloth-cap demagogue? And he criticised America! The richest country on earth. What kind of fool criticised that sort of success! It was beyond belief. But it was listening to Neil Kinnock which really made his heart shrink. He was smart enough to do very well, yet he retained his boy-from-the-valleys demeanour. He spoke for the poor minority. Didn't he get it? The poor were no more than twenty per cent! How could you win elections appealing to them? In any case, who else could they vote for? The clever thing was to take the votes of the poor for granted and skew your politics to the middle-classes. And Kinnock invoked the memory of Nye Bevan who stood for everything Laurie hated. It was a great pity he hadn't been expelled from the party. He was a disgrace. Calling the Tories vermin! Establishing a health service which had become a bureaucratic monster. That was socialism. From the first, Laurie believed, health care should have been privately delivered. And the better off should have been able to buy better treatment. He thought the NHS as conceived by Bevan a disaster. But Kinnock loved this stuff. Laurie thought him laughable.

"You know," he said to Caroline, "I really have a sense of destiny about this."

149

"Destiny?"

"Yes, as if God wants it to be."

"If he does, he'll find some way to reveal it to you."

"I know," he replied excitedly, "I think he already has."

"How?"

"Well, you know, just the sense of rightness. I've prayed for guidance and I've never had a moment's doubt. Now if God didn't want me to do it, he'd find ways to make me doubt wouldn't he?"

"We shouldn't presume to know the ways of God, Laurie."

"Of course not! But we expect guidance don't we? We expect a spiritual crisis over a choice which entails moral peril. But I feel nothing but assurance."

"Perhaps you should talk it over with Father Noblett."

"Yes. I will."

Caroline's father had married a Catholic and converted. Mother and daughter shared a devout, nervous faith. Laurie had renounced his Anglicanism after his wife convinced him that to presume direct contact with God was blasphemy. The Protestant notion of everyone making their own pact with God effectively made a church and priests redundant, and why would Christ have founded a church if he'd wanted that? Laurie discovered he agreed. The idea of a Pope who had special access to God appealed to him. Protestantism was a kind of anarchy and it embraced the plain, non-conformist denominations he'd always disdained. They were the religious equivalent of socialists. The authority of the Catholic church reassured him. He saw the connection between Church and political party: a strong, central authority was vital.

"I have a sense of being chosen, Father!" he said with his fixed smile in place.

The elderly priest looked at him over his glasses. Huge, ungainly, the athleticism of his youth had long left him. After God, food was the great love of his life. His enormous belly made him move slowly and puff and wheeze. He sat down. On the little round table in front of him was a plate of sliced fruit cake, chocolate cake, scones filled with luxurious jam and cream, chocolate biscuits and two vanilla slices oozing yellow custard.

"Would you like a vanilla?"

"No thanks, Father. I try to stay trim."

"Every credit. A young man should. You don't mind if I...."

"Not at all, Father."

The older man bit into the confectionery making the custard over-hang and plop onto his black cassock. He scooped up the blob with his fat index finger which he sucked with relish.

"Chosen?" he said once his mouth was half empty. "What makes you think so?"

"Well, you know. I have no doubt. That's what impresses me, Father. No doubt at all. I'm absolutely convinced it's the right path for me."

"Sometimes our minds play tricks on us."

The remaining half of the cake was shoved into his gaping mouth and slowly chewed. Little bits of pastry and icing clung to the corners of his lips.

"Yes, but I suppose it's like you. You must have known you were intended for the priesthood."

Father Noblett nodded as he drew the back of his hand over his mouth. He reached for a slice of chocolate cake.

"Help yourself."

Laurie shook his head.

"Intended for the priesthood? I wish, like you, I'd been without doubt." He laughed. "My life has been continual doubt. A torment."

He licked his fingers, bent forward to study the plate and picked up a scone.

"Don't assume," he said before the first bite, "you can know what God intends. If you feel called to politics then to act on that is sensible. But the Devil's temptations can leave us just as convinced as God's guidance."

"Of course, Father. But I'm a convinced Christian. I can't imagine God would leave my prayers unanswered."

The priest lowered his head to peer at the young man.

"Sure you wouldn't like a scone? My housekeeper makes them. A most obliging lady."

He ate a second scone without speaking, picked up the big, china teapot and poured two cups.

"So what's your ambition?"

"Well, you know, to get as far as I can and make a difference."

"Prime Minister?"

"Who can say!" and the great billboard of a smile was on his face.

"For a Catholic, the church must come first. You will have to make your politics fit your faith. Consider abortion, for example."

"Yes, I'm opposed to it," said Laurie. "Of course, I wouldn't be able to abolish it. We have to be realistic. But I'd campaign for a lowering of the legal limit. We must make it difficult for women."

"Good."

The priest having drunk half his tea, reached for a chocolate biscuit which he slipped whole into his mouth as if a holy wafer.

"It's true," he said as he chomped, "in certain places the working-class have always seen the Catholic church as a friend. It's a great help to us."

"Of course."

"So long as we don't dally with Godless socialism or that Liberation Theology rubbish. The point is to sympathise with the lot of the poor the more completely to have them in our power."

He lifted a second biscuit, bit it in half and laughed.

The business of finding a winnable seat meant he had to address little branch meetings and sound like a socialist. He even used the word and though at first he felt acutely uncomfortable, little by little he was able to produce it as if he meant it. Part of him concluded people were infinitely gullible, but another that he was extraordinarily con-vincing. It was really just a matter of selling yourself. It simply was salesmanship!

"You know," he said to Caroline, "most people have no interest in politics."

"I suppose they find it boring," she said.

"No, it's not that. They're just focussed on other things: their gas bill, promotion, getting their kids into school, sex, friends. Politics isn't on their radar."

"They leave it to the professionals."

"That's right. But, you see, why should we be interested in politics if the people aren't?"

"If you're going to be a politician, Laurie, you've got to be interested in politics!"

"Why? Look, if we take the politics out of politics, what are we left with? Management. That's what we should do: manage the country. That's the way to put an end to all this left right nonsense."

"I wouldn't say that in your selection meetings."

He laughed.

"I've discovered I've got a real talent for convincing people. I think I could convince them I can walk on water. The thing is, we've got to get the people who think politically out of the leadership of the Labour party."

"That's not going to be easy," she said brushing burgundy varnish onto the nail of her big toe. "It's a political party, it attracts people who think politically."

"We'll change the culture. What we want is people who are looking to get on. Politics is a career like banking or the law. It's a job. We need people who think of it that way. All this hysterical stuff about changing the world has to be cast aside. What matters is being modern. Keeping up with the trends."

"But they'll find you out. You won't be able to pretend to be apolitical for very long. You'll have to vote in parliament and they'll watch you."

"Oh, I can vote for this and that to keep them off my back. The important thing is to get power. It's like the church. A few people at the top make the decisions. You just have to be one of those few people and you can change things."

"You make it sound easy, but I don't think the Labour party is going to give up on socialism overnight."

"They will if socialism loses elections! That's the trick. Win elections. That's the thing a party has to do and if we can do that we'll be untouchable."

"Do you really believe winning elections is easy? If there were some formula, someone would have found it by now. People don't vote rationally, Laurie. If they did, elections wouldn't be necessary."

"No, there isn't a formula but look, Labour appeals to the twenty per cent at the bottom. Very clever. You have to win the middle-ground. Give the middle-classes what they want."

"You aren't even an MP yet. There'll be a hell of a fight for the leadership if they lose the next election."

"There's no if, Caroline. They'll get slaughtered. That's what gives people like me the chance. Of course, they'll probably do something mad like electing Kinnock leader. So we'll have to wait for him to lose, but in the long run we've got a real chance."

"I don't see it. They'll always be socialists."

"On the other hand, they've never been socialists! When they get power they have to make things work. Denis Healey isn't a socialist, he's a reformed communist and they're the most reactionary of all. You see, the system just makes it impossible for them to do anything really radical. On the one hand, there's too much careerism and self-seeking in the party, on the other, they've got to get on and manage the economy. The really radical thing is trade unionism in the workplace, but Thatcher is dealing with that. By the time we get our hands on power the unions will be decimated."

"Isn't is all Buggins' turn? You'll have to wait and you might be too far back in the line to get any real power."

"Well, you have to subvert all that stuff. It just takes a few people willing to conspire in the right way. You see, when you have a Buggins culture no-one expects you to defy it. That's what Thatcher's done. She's ridden roughshod over the polite deferences of the Tory party. I'll do the same. I'll ambush them. That's what life's about after all, taking your opportunities. To do that you have to take people by surprise."

"But if they see you coming, Laurie, do you really want to spend your life as a backbencher or a junior minister?"

"Oh, I'll get promoted to the Shadow Cabinet. I've got the skill, you see. I can talk. I can convince people. And you know what the secret is? A little judicious slyness. Never quite say what you mean and you can convince people you stand for anything. You see, they project their hopes and ideas onto leaders, then they really believe the leaders are saying what they think. It's the way celebrity works. Everyone pours into the celebrity their own potencies, dreams, aspirations, and all the negative stuff too. I suppose it's a kind of social madness or mass hysteria as they used to call it, but who cares if it works?"

"Well, I'm still going to vote Tory."

He laughed again.

"If I succeed, there won't be any need to vote Tory. I'll offer everything the Tories stand for. It'll be the abolition of politics. The murder of everything left of centre. Isn't that a lovely idea?"

"Yes it is. It is."

And she added the final stroke of varnish to her little toe.

A DISTANT COUNTRY

The Soviets had just invaded Czechoslovakia. Katie was on her way to work on the number 8 bus which went north out of the town past the two big council estates her mother talked of as trouble, onto the road to Longridge and the hills beyond. The little industrial estate where she worked, just after the crematorium, was a mile from the village of Grimsargh where they sometimes went at lunch for a snack and a drink in The Plough. The landlord, Harry Barker, was a Tory councillor; a pot-bellied, short-sighted, spluttering, man who treated his customers as an inconvenience, a perilous river to be traversed between him and their money. Katie was thinking about him as she read *Loving*, because he'd stared at her crutch yesterday while she sat on a stool opposite the bar eating her prawn sandwich. It was disgusting to be ogled by a fat, ugly old man. She didn't wear miniskirts to attract him. Being ogled by Billy Capstick was another matter. He was sitting next to her reading *The Daily Telegraph* which he bought for the crossword.

"Bastards," he said.

"Who?"

"Soviet Union."

"Why?"

"They've just invaded Czechoslovakia."

"Where's that?"

He folded the paper and turned to her.

"A distant country of which we know little."

"What?"

"Our stop."

He followed her down the stairs. She was aware of him looking at her hair which she'd brushed for twenty minutes before leaving home. It went right down to below her waist but she tucked it inside her leather coat to keep it neat. She knew he liked her hair because he'd said to her:

"A wig-maker would pay a fortune for that."

She'd hit him, as she often did when she thought he wasn't serious

156

enough. On the other hand, his seriousness frightened her. She'd been reading an article about sexual positions in her magazine. A girl said she liked it from behind: she put her face in the pillow and her backside in the air and her boyfriend slid it in and, apparently, it was wonderful. She'd never done it that way but was thinking she should. If other people did it, if it was the thing to do, she didn't want to miss out. The problem was, she'd finished with Barry and wasn't having sex in any position just now. Sex with Barry was okay. She had orgasms often enough. But he didn't turn her on. She felt being turned on was essential. She wasn't sure what it meant but it had to be something more than the mere physical fulfilment of sex with Terry. She felt awkward afterwards. She liked to get away from him. Something wasn't right about that. But she wanted very badly to be turned on. It was the kind of thing her mother would disapprove of. The kind of thing her mother approved of was being the first in the avenue to have colour television, never having been without a fridge, having a holiday every year and a car not more than three years old. Katie was bored to the point of insanity by carpets and three piece suites and wallpaper and double-glazing. She was itching and she needed to scratch; but just what she was itching for she didn't know. She was eighteen and had decades ahead of her to find out. For the time being. she had to work. Billy was walking beside her tapping his thigh with his rolled paper and whistling in his irritating way.

"Stop it," she said.

"Don't you like Mozart?"

"No."

"Shall I whistle Beethoven?"

"No."

"Verdi?"

"Don't whistle at all."

"I can't go into work quiet. Brydon might think I like being here."

"Don't you?"

"Do you?"

"I don't mind."

"Not minding is typical northern resignation. You put up with it, but do you like it?"

"You're getting on my nerves."

He held the door for her.

"The canapés and champagne are to your left, madam."

She ignored him and went into reception where Bernadette was already at her typewriter. She trilled a cheerful good morning, as she always did and Katie did her best to sound happy. She took off her coat, hung it on the back of the door and sat down. A terrible sense of closure descended on her. What was she doing here? The typing had nothing to do with her. There was a little pile of the yellow Vehicle Hire Forms by her machine together with hand written details. It would take her the first hour to get them done. But what connection did she have to them? It would've been all the same if she'd been typing death warrants. There was no link between her activity and the purpose it served. She was sure the forms must be necessary. Once they'd been signed by Mr Brydon they went up to Billy and Leo. What did they do with them? They must keep one copy and send the other two out. What did it matter? Her business was to type them, what happened after that didn't need to bother her. She tried hard to forget her disturbing thoughts, what her mother called those funny feelings we must ignore. If she could just get through to the arrival of the tea trolley, a Kit-Kat, a sweet tea and a chat to Bernie might do the trick. But things were different for Bernie because she was having an affair with Mr Brydon. She could get whatever she wanted. Katie knew her colleague was being paid more than the deputy depot manager while she was getting only £600 a year. Of course, money wasn't everything: she was living with her parents and they asked for only £3 a week; all the same, Bernie was on £1,400 and that was a big difference. Vaguely, Katie felt if she had more money everything would be easier. She didn't think through how, but she felt it might even help her get the right boyfriend and feel really turned on. By the time Mrs Rutherford arrived with the tea and biscuits she was ready to pull on her coat, walk out and never come back. One of those women who had left school without any education to speak of, Mrs Rutherford had made her way as best she could. She ran the canteen though her cookery skills were negligible. Katie had asked her many times for weaker tea, but the brew still made her shudder and left a bitter film in her mouth. Even the Kit-Kat snapped with a soggy sound. The sight of the big woman in her white coat, her thick hands gripping the cups and the money, her huge backside waddling as she pushed the trolley to the lift, depressed her. It was a horrible lonely feeling. Mrs Rutherford was a widow bringing up two teenagers. How did she scrape by? Might that happen to her? Might she marry some good-looking boy like Billy, someone full of life and fun only to be left on her own with no money and children to look after? It made her feel it was hardly worth setting out on life's adventure. She'd left school at sixteen hoping work would be exciting and she'd meet all kinds of interesting people, but it was worse than being in the classroom. She was eighteen. How long was she going to spend her days like this? What was the way out?

"And I said to him, I'm not going there. You can take me somewhere better than that. Have you seen it? Coons go there."

Bernie was talking about her boyfriend Ian who ran a car business and drove an Alfa Romeo. He was always asking her to marry him but she rebuffed him, made him buy her ever more expensive presents, take her on flashy holidays and to posh restaurants, while two or three times a week she took her knickers off in the back of Mr Brydon's car.

"Oh."

"I said to him, I said, I like a nice place. High class. I like to be seen among the best people. You can't take me to a place full of niggers."

"Is it full of niggers?" said Katie.

"Well, my friend Wendy, you know Wendy the one with the big breasts and the funny teeth? She went there and she said there were four coons at the next table. Ruined her night. Well, it would wouldn't it? You don't pay good money to eat with savages do you?"

"No."

Katie didn't like coons either. Her mother was very proud of living in an area without blackies. Sometimes Katie wondered if niggers were as bad as her mother said and Terry had a West Indian friend who was nice and bought her drinks and was always laughing and smiling. But she thought that must be an exception. When she saw coons and pakis on the street she felt it wasn't right. They should be in their own country. What were they doing here? When she was a girl there were no pakis in the town, then suddenly she would see these women in their bright dresses walking down Market St or across St John's Sq. How did they get here? It was all a mystery to her, but it seemed wrong. This was her town. There were no black people where she grew up. Her parents bought one of those little three-bedroom semis built between the wars; in truth no bigger than some of the terraces in the town, but with a garden back and front, a garage and privet hedges, they granted status and allowed their occupants to identify with the rich who owned the six bedroomed places with an acre of lawn and a garage big enough for two Jags. Mr and Mrs Heywood inherited £600 when her father was killed at work by a falling steel beam. They used it as a deposit on 17 West End Way, took out a mortgage for the remaining £700 and felt they were safe. Brian Heywood was a traveller for a fabrics firm. Duteous, obedient and with a faith in business as unflinching as a medieval peasant's belief in god, he worked his way up to Regional Manager which meant when Katie was thirteen they were able to build an extension.

"Four bedrooms," said Mrs Heywood as they ate braised steak and chips one Friday tea-time, "not many people have four. And a garden back and front. Think yourselves lucky."

But Katie didn't feel lucky. Even at thirteen she felt oppressed by her mother's snobbery and ambition for her and her brother. Neither of them was clever. They progressed from St Theresa's Primary to Blessed Edmund Campion, worked hard and left with a couple of O Levels each.

"You don't need qualifications to make money," said her mother. "Look at your father. He left school at fifteen and we've never been without a fridge since the war."

Her brother trained as an electrician, set up on his own and was soon earning £100 a week. Katie wanted money too, but not the boredom of work to earn it. There was another world. The first record she bought was *Livin' Doll* by Cliff Richard. She played it over and over on the radiogram. Then she bought Helen Shapiro's *Walking Back To Happiness*. Perhaps she could be a singer. Then she would receive the attention she felt she'd always lacked. People would love her. Her picture would be in *Loving, Living* and *Woman's Own*. She'd earn millions and be able to live exactly as she liked. She practised singing and making the right movements in front of the mirror. She felt she'd perfected an agonised facial expression which fitted perfectly with the strained emotions of the hits she sang. But how to move from bedroom performances to the real thing? She had no idea. She supposed she might need a manager. How to find one? Then there was the question of her singing: was it any good? She knew nothing about music so was nervous about approaching musicians. What did it mean to sing in this or that key? When she was sixteen she met Roy Askew who played folk guitar and wrote his own songs. She was taken aback by his playing. He invited her to his house and in the front room he finger-picked and played nifty chord sequences which took her breath away. She confessed her desire to sing but when she tried one of his songs, she ran out of high notes and collapsed into coughing. He explained she needed to start lower. She couldn't get enough volume. He told her she needed lessons to build the dynamics of her voice and he offered to teach her music. He gave her a set of songs to practise but she found they undermined her confidence. The thought of standing in front of people and finding her voice diminishing to a squeak or being unable to sing loud enough for people to hear brought the carefully assembled dream of adulation and wealth crashing into a nightmare of humiliation and rejection.

She renounced her ambition to sing and replaced it with the idea of becoming a groupie. There was a rock group in the town which had recently made a record: *Soft Orange* consisted of four men in their early twenties, the customary assemblage of rhythm guitar, lead guitar (and vocals), bass and drums. The drummer, who was small, muscular and energetic, modelled himself on Keith Moon: if he wasn't drunk he was stoned, at the end of each performance he threw his kit across the stage, and he seduced any willing girl or woman. Katie and her friend Alison started to follow them. They hung around. They smiled. They made it clear they were available. But they weren't. The first time they were invited backstage, Colin Wignall, the stocky, wild little drummer, grabbed Alison and shoved his hands up her jumper. She hit him with her ineffectual fists and backed into the corner as Terry Millom, the tall, slow, bearded singer whose hair came halfway down his back, pulled him away and shook his head wisely. Pale and shaking on the bus home Alison said:

"That's the last time I see them."

"I know," said Katie, but she couldn't give up on the possibility of attracting Terry, who seemed to her the embodiment of rock stardom. If their record was a hit, they might become millionaires. He would buy a stately home or a chateau in France. They would drive everywhere in his white Rolls. They would fly in his private jet to Sydney or California. She would never need to work again. Her photograph would be in *Loving*; arm in arm with the tall, inscrutable guitarist, she would look out defiantly at the world which would envy her. She would be the centre of interest. Everyone would treat her with deference. She understood Alison was upset: Wignall was a madman and it wasn't nice to have a rampant lunatic grab your breasts in front five other people, especially when he didn't even know your name; but she felt she was exaggerating. This was the nearest Katie had ever been to fame and wealth and she wasn't going to let it slip because Wignall was a sexual molester. To give up on this was to contemplate years of dull office work and, if she was lucky, marriage to some halfway decent joiner or postman and the comfort of small snobberies which were all that kept her mother from despair.

"I should report him to the police," said Alison.

"Yes," said Katie.

"Little pervert."

"I know."

Katie tried to interest other friends in following the band, but they quickly became disillusioned and fell away. There were long hours of hanging around before being invited backstage or into a van for a spliff, a snog and a grope. Katie wasn't sure she liked sitting on Terry's knee while he ran his hand up her skirt in front of the other band members and their girls, but she reasoned it was one of those things you had to put up with in order to arrive at something better, like boring lessons, incomprehensible Latin masses and hours of stupid work. She felt if she persevered, she would become his girlfriend, rather than just the girl he favoured for an after-gig bit of heavy petting. It was difficult though to balance the degree of her willingness with the extent of his commitment; he was as uncommunicative as a wall. His conversation was carried out in a few grunts and the odd word, winks, a toss of the head, a shrug of the shoulders. She went along with it, curtailed her chatter, tried to make herself as intriguingly laconic as him. When she finally gave in to him and he seduced her in the back of the van, between two towering speakers, her head jammed against a guitar case, he slipped inside her without a condom and she spent a worried two weeks.

"What if I'm pregnant?" she said.

He shrugged and lit a spliff.

Henceforth, she insisted on protection and though the sex was frequent, she felt he was becoming less intense. Perhaps she should let herself get pregnant, then he'd have to marry her and if the group became rich and famous she'd be able to hire a nanny and not need to attend to the baby. She was thinking she might do this when one night, after a gig in Barnoldswick, he ignored her and went off with a black girl in a skirt so short she couldn't sit down without showing her crotch. Katie went backstage.

"Where's Terry?"

"Shaggin' in the van," said Wignall.

She went out to the battered, white Bedford. The doors were locked. She hammered on the side, lit a cigarette and waited. When Terry came out of the back doors with a spliff in his fingers, he nodded at her and walked on. The black girl trotted behind him on her stilettos. She thought she would go backstage and give him a tongue-lashing, but she knew he'd sit and smoke, nod and wink and her words and the anger and humiliation behind them would run off him like rain off new slates.

"Coon," said Katie to Bernadette as she bit into her Mars.

"No!"

"Yeah. In the back of the van."

"Fancy doing it with a coon. He'll be sorry if he catches something."

Katie was almost tempted to say, so will you, but she held back. To her knowledge, Bernadette had had sex with Brydon, her boyfriend, Stan Glynn the office manager, Tom Sutcliffe the cold-store supervisor, Jack Minshall one of the lorry drivers and Dick Wheeler the soap powder sales rep. That was in the past eighteen months and they were the ones she knew about. She wondered if they always wore condoms because she knew Bernie was on the pill. Still, she wasn't likely to catch anything from Brydon who probably wasn't even having sex with his wife anymore, but Stan Glynn was known to be putting it about.

"I hope he does," she said.

"He deserves to. Some people have no morals."

Katie had to give up following *Soft Orange* which brought her anguish when they had a record in the top hundred and a double-page picture in *Loving*. She read they'd met the *Beatles* and the horrible sense of missing out ran through her veins. Was that randy little coon meeting John Lennon just because she was willing to open her legs in the back of a van? But then she'd done just that and got nowhere. Did coons have something white women didn't? It was all too horrible to think about. She wondered if she should start going to their gigs again. Maybe Terry was missing her? But the need to save face was more powerful than her distress and she renounced her life as a groupie once and for all.

It was at this time she started going more regularly to the youth club. It was housed in a little building on the corner of Church Lane and the main road so the youngsters hung around watching the traffic, leaning on the safety barrier, smoking and looking cocky. There was a small room downstairs with a tall bar which served coca-cola in plastic cups. The DJ had his turntable behind it. The amplified music made conversation impossible. The room was dark except for flashing purple lights which sent intermittent beams criss-crossing so that faces were suddenly lit up ghoulishly. The girls wore mini-skirts. The boys, tight jeans and leather jackets. Upstairs was table-tennis in a bare space lit by a single neon tube. But for the young people of the suburb, this was the place to be. The other youth clubs were tame by comparison. Only St Jude's had a darkened room and thumping music. At the Congregational club they had a Dansette and a snooker table in a dusty scout hut. But Jude's had the feel of an ante-room to a night club. They could begin to feel grown up. They were on the cusp, though of what they weren't sure but it felt exciting and a bit dangerous. Everyone knew that after Jude's the next step was the town pubs, *The Fish* and *The Joiner's Arms* where the *jeunesse doré*, or at least silver-plated, gathered at the weekend and where the souped-up minis and the MG Midgets roared away in a little cloud of fumes and a screech of rubber while the carless stood by smiling enviously.

Billy Capstick was a regular. She quickly realised he was sought-after. He was good-looking enough but he had an easy, friendly way which charmed the younger girls. As soon as she knew most of them wanted to go out with him, Katie decided she would target him. One

Wednesday she was sitting with Alison, a cup of coke in her hand, the music shaking the walls, when he walked in. She caught his eye and smiled thinking he would understand. He smiled, nodded and walked straight past her to go and talk to Janice Bush. Katie was offended because she thought she looked particularly attractive that night. She'd washed and brushed her long blonde hair, taken a bit of time over delicate make-up, chosen her clothes to match perfectly and was in that mood where she believed no boy could look at her and not be moved. It wasn't her way to smile first. She cultivated an aloof demeanour. She expected to be paid attention and if a boy exuded the right degree of willingness to please, she might give him a nice smile, eventually. To come right out with it and smile at Billy was such an unusual act, so much of her self was given away by it, she couldn't believe he would walk by. And Janice Bush? What was special about her? Katie had always thought she was vulgar. She might be quite pretty but she wore that garish red lipstick and her thighs were too fat. It was hard to accept Billy could prefer her.

She was so mad she convinced herself she wanted nothing to do with him; but then he started to pay her a bit of attention at work. At the Christmas party he held a sprig of mistletoe over her head and kissed her on the lips. Sex was taking place in darkened corners all over the depot but Katie had had enough of that kind of thing in the back of Terry's van. If things were going to kick off with Billy, she wanted them to have a chance of lasting but she wasn't at all sure she did want them to kick off. He was a strange boy. She was never sure of what he meant and he talked about things she didn't understand. Then one evening when she was working late catching up with typing, an evening when Bernadette was entertaining Mr Brydon, Billy appeared from upstairs already buttoned in his navy-blue overcoat, a scarf wrapped roughly round his throat and leather gloves on his hands.

"Overtime?" he said.

She refused to look at him, sat primly on her stool and typed as if she believed in it.

"Obviously."

"You'll be having tax problems."

"Like you."

"Like Bernadette."

165

She refused the dangled, tasty fly.

"You must be the fastest typist in Europe."

"I am."

"You should ask for a bonus."

"You don't get one for fast typing."

"What do you get one for?"

She refused again. He turned his back on her and looked out of the tall, wide window at the dark industrial estate. She raised her eyes to look at him and it struck her how handsome he was from behind, how his thick, brown hair shone and nestled gently on his collar. He was tall and nicely slim but his shoulders had a look of strength and vigour which pleased her. Then she noticed he'd spotted her reflection. Damn! She pretended to focus ever more intently on her work. He turned and looked at the clock.

"Next bus is twenty-five minutes," he said.

"Better get walking."

"Could do with some company."

Her heart gave a little kick.

"Frightened of the dark?"

"Need someone to hold my hand."

"Cissy."

"I might get attacked out there. Things you read in the papers."

"Should be able to take care of yourself."

"I can run fast but I don't fight. I'm a pacifist."

"What's one of them?"

"Someone who doesn't believe in war."

"How can you not believe in it?"

"Cissies like me think there are alternatives."

"You're crazy."

"You're the second person who's said that to me this week."

"Who was the first?"

"My psychiatrist."

"You pay someone to tell you you're mad?"

"No, I pay him to make me sane."

"He's a failure."

"You should have seen me before he started."

"I did."

"Then you'll have noticed the difference."

"You get madder by the day."

"There are no degrees of insanity. It's like virginity. You are or you aren't."

"And you are."

"How did you know I'm a virgin."

"You're not a virgin, you're mad."

"Do you mean if I was a virgin I'd be sane?"

"You'd be mad to be a virgin."

"But I am a virgin."

"You must think I'm mad to believe that."

"I think you're perfectly sane, but I'm mad."

"You're driving me mad."

"It's a quality of madness, it's contagious."

"If it was contagious everyone would be mad."

"Chickenpox is contagious but I haven't got it."

"Did you have it when you were little?"

"What, madness?"

"No chickenpox."

"I've no idea. I'm too mad to remember."

"I think you should go home."

"You'd send a madman out in the dark on his own?"

"Why not?"

"Who knows what I might get up to."

"Behave yourself or you'll end up arrested."

"I am arrested. At least my development is. According to Dr Freud."

"Who's he?"

"A psychiatrist. He had to flee the Nazis."

"Why?"

"Because he was Jewish."

"I don't like Yids."

"How many do you know?"

"None."

"How do you know you don't like 'em, then?"

"I don't need to put my hand in the fire to know I don't like being burned."

"You're a catholic ."

"I am."

"Jesus was a Jew."

"Was he?"

"You should know, he wants you for a sunbeam not me."

"Don't you go to church?"

"They kicked me out."

"Why?"

"For being a communist."

"Are you?"

"Only during the week. I'm a liberal at weekends."

"Are you a member?"

"I used to be a member of ABC minors but I tore up my card."

"Why?"

"I couldn't stand the bad behaviour."

"You're mad."

"This conversation is going in circles. Harold Pinter couldn't put up with it."

"Who's he?"

"A writer sympathetic to communists."

"He should live in Russia."

"They wouldn't have him."

"Why not?"

"He's a communist."

"The Russians are communists."

"So are the Czechs."

"Who?"

"The people the Russians have just invaded."

"If they're communists why have they invaded?"

"The Russians don't like communists."

"They are communists."

"Only at weekends. During the week they're straightforward ty-rants."

"It's too complicated."

"It's very simple. The world is mad but only the mad can see it."

"You're interrupting my work."

"Work is a waste of your youth and beauty."

Her pulse accelerated again.

"I want to go home."

"Let me escort you."

"I'm going to miss the bus if you keep talking to me."

"Will it arrive later if I'm quiet?"

"It's time to go, Billy."

"I'll wait for you in perfect silence if you let me buy you a drink on the way home."

Her fingers flicked out more quickly from the home keys and her eyes focused more resolutely on the words being imprinted on the yellow form:

For the provision of one ten-ton, uncovered trailer and driver for 8 hours on 2nd October 1968......

In less than a second the thought of sitting in a nice pub, nestling next to Billy drinking a lager and lime made her breath quicken but at once the idea of being grubby from work and still in the clothes she'd worn all day, her hair unwashed since the morning filled her with dread.

"I'm in a hurry. I'm washing my hair tonight."

"So am I."

She didn't look at him. He stood by the window for a few more seconds.

"See you tomorrow," and he was gone.

She banged furiously at the typewriter. Each little form seemed to take an hour. She yanked the completed one from the roller, turned the serrated black knobs to insert another. How she hated those forms! She was alone in the depot now apart from Willie Crawford the warehouse supervisor who appeared in his white coat, rattling his keys.

"I'm nearly done."

Three minutes before the bus was due, she pulled on her coat, switched off the light, skipped down the steps and ran to the stop, expecting to see Billy. He must have set off walking. She peered down the darkened road. It was getting chilly. She lit a cigarette and waited till the tall, illuminated, slow number eight appeared round the bend. She put out her hand. She was the only passenger upstairs all the way to town.

It was a month later her mother bought her a car. She didn't like her travelling on the bus and a car was sign she was getting on in the world, a little. An insurance policy matured, there was a bit of spare money. They bought her a mini, taxed and insured. She had to pay the running costs. Every morning she passed the stop where Billy waited with his rolled newspaper in his hand. The first few times, she pretended not to see him. Then one day, when the queue was small and he was leaning against the shelter in that careless way she liked so much, she pulled into the lay-by and he climbed in.

"Won the pools?"

"Robbed a bank."

"You should've robbed a bigger one, there's hardly room for my legs."

"Don't complain or you can walk."

" I'm not complaining." He paused. "How comfortable is the back seat?"

"Billy!" she reprimanded.

She arranged to pick him up each morning and things went well for three weeks, till she had to give her mother a lift into town because her dad was ill.

"Do you give Billy Capstick a lift every day?" said her mother over beefburger and chips at tea-time.

"Yes."

"How much does he pay you?"

"I don't charge him."

"You should. What's the bus fare? Ninepence into town and a shilling out to the depot. One and nine a day. That's eight and ninepence a week. Nearly two pounds a month. That's twenty-four pounds a year. The cheeky monkey. He could have offered something for petrol."

"He did."

"Well, why didn't you take it?"

"I'm going there anyway. What difference does it make?"

"What difference? Twenty-four pounds a year that's what difference. He can pay up or you don't take him anymore."

"I can't ask him now."

"Why not?"

"Because he's a friend."

"He's a free-loader. Either he pays or you don't take him. Just remember who bought that car."

Katie picked him up a few more times, but she knew her mother would find out and she wouldn't put it past her to take the car off her.

"I can't give you a lift tomorrow," she said as they got out at the depot.

"Okay. Why's that?"

"I'm not coming by car anymore."

She knew it was a stupid thing to say but she couldn't think of better.

All day she tried to work out a route which would keep her from passing his bus stop. Or she could set off earlier. But then he'd see her mini in the car park anyway. Why didn't she just ask him for the money? She didn't understand why but she didn't want him handing notes and coins to her every Friday. She didn't want to feel like a taxi driver. She'd rather not take him than take money. The next day she pretended not to see him as she sped by the stop where he was leaning nonchalantly as usual. Contact between them at work dwindled. Months went by, she still had no boyfriend though she'd tried half a dozen, and Billy no longer joked with her.

"Can you work late tonight, Katie?" Bernie said to her one lunchtime as they were eating their sandwiches in the sunny reception.

"I'm going out."

"Where to?"

"Pictures."

"Who with?"

"A boy."

"Is he nice?"

"He's all right."

"What time's it start?"

"Don't know. About half seven."

"Oh, you could stay till six."

"What about you?"

"I've got to go to a meeting with the boss."

Meeting! Katie bit into her prawn sandwich imagining the pot-bellied manager, his y-fronts round his ankles, his trousers round his knees, his jacket on the front seat, his tie on the floor, his shirt unbuttoned and his string vest on show, grunting as he pushed in and out of the squealing Bernie whose buttercup yellow mini skirt was up round her waist. And for that, she had to work late. How could she do it? How could she let a leering old man like Brydon do it to her? She wondered what they got up to? Did she suck him off? It was disgusting. She put her sandwich back on the plate.

"Where's that?"

"Oh, Manchester or somewhere."

172

Manchester! Parked up by the canal or behind the depot. She felt impossibly lonely. Why was it Bernie was shagging with Mr Brydon and she, who really wanted a boy she could love, was all alone? Was this how the world worked? Should she be getting her knickers off for Brydon too? Should she be increasing her salary by stroking his balls? It was too atrocious. She felt as if the world were spinning away from her. Were all her feelings wrong? Was it better to be like Bernie?

"So you can stay till six then?"

"Yes."

"Good. Make sure all those VHRs are done."

She would have liked to have said, Make sure you give him a good time, but she picked up her mug of coffee and turned the pages of *Loving*.

When she left the depot at five past six she could have cried with weariness, boredom and isolation. She revved the engine of her little car and zoomed off down the quiet road. She wanted to drive impossibly fast, to screech round the bends and bang through the gears at roundabouts; but as she was nearing the motorway bridge she caught a figure in her headlights, walking briskly, swinging his newspaper. She smiled and her heart began to thump with excitement. She passed him. There was a lay-by. She pulled in. In her mirror she could see him walking. Then he began to trot. She smoothed her hair. Was her mascara smudged?

"Thanks," he said, out of breath. "Very kind of you."

"S'all right."

"Drop me at Midgery Lane if you like. Plenty of buses from there."

"I'll take you home."

"Get some petrol on the way. I'll pay."

"Don't need any."

They were heading for town. She wanted the journey to last but the road seemed to be gobbled up, even at thirty. Once they hit the centre there'd be nowhere to stop. She wanted to stop. She wanted to be parked up somewhere quiet with Billy. Right now Bernie was doing it with Brydon. She was letting him stick his dick in her so she could get more money and do what she liked at work. But Katie wanted to be with Billy because she liked him. She did like him. He was handsome, funny and kind. Even if he did have strange ideas. He was the sort of boy her mother disliked. So much the better. She wanted him to kiss her. She wanted to climb in the back seat and let him take her knickers off. As she approached a roundabout an idea seized her.

"I've forgotten something."

She did 360 degrees.

"Must be important."

"It is."

" Your make-up."

"No."

"Fags."

"Got 'em."

"Must be your purse."

"Nope."

"I give up."

"I've forgotten to leave a note for Bernie," she blurted without thinking.

"Will she miss you that badly?"

She slapped his leg.

"Something she has to do. She'll be in before me in the morning."

"Wasn't she working overtime?"

"Gone to a meeting with the boss."

"Ah, if that's a meeting, I know it well."

"What?"

"Are you familiar with The Ecstasy of St Teresa?"

"No."

"It's worth getting to know."

The depot was in darkness. A dismal, two-storey, squat building made up of offices at the front and a warehouse behind, it looked more depressing in the dark. At least during the day there might be a little sunlight hitting the windows or with the lights on at dusk you could project a degree of warmth onto its brutalist structure. The big, grey metal gates were padlocked. She pulled up outside, turned off the engine and the headlights. All the other buildings on the estate were closed for the night. The place was black and deserted. It had served its daytime business function. The workers had gone home. With that violent division between working life and the rest, the estate became a lonely, empty, threatening locale, a no-place between the town and the villages people who could afford it lived in to fool themselves into the myth of perpetuating rural life. The street light outside the depot was out. A single, sad orange bulb glowed forty yards in the distance. A few cars sped by on the main road: workers from the town heading home. Katie stared ahead. This was a horrible place. The horrible place she came to every day. Why did they build these things outside the town? It would be much better if she worked in the centre. What was she doing in this place? Billy was beside her. He was looking up at the darkened windows.

"Who was in when you left?"

"Willie Crawford."

"Not there now."

"No," she said, "but we are."

She didn't move. She imagined her meaning was clear. It was an invitation. How could he resist? She thought he would lean across and kiss her or touch her thigh. She would let him do what he liked. She wanted to be naked with him, even here in the sordid circumstance of her car parked outside the depot. She thought he couldn't fail to understand. To turn to him, to look him in the eyes and smile would be going too far. She'd said what she'd said. That was enough. She waited. Hours went by. He didn't touch her. He didn't lean over and kiss her.

"Want me to break in?"

It was all she could to hold back her tears. She didn't know if he'd failed to grasp or wasn't interested. Could it be the latter? She'd never let the idea pass through her head. Ever since she'd smiled at him at the youth club and he'd started to be friendlier to her at work, she'd assumed he would climb barbed wired walls to get at her. It was a terrible shock to think he'd changed his mind. She couldn't believe it. But why was he so stupid? She was there, she was sitting waiting. What did he think she was sitting there staring out of the windscreen for?

"No."

"Guess Bernie'll have to go without her note."

"You think so?"

"Unless you stick it to the front gate, but then anyone could read it. Some bloke walking his terrier at midnight would stop, pull off the sellotape, get his torch out of his pocket and read, Bernie, don't forget to water the aspidistra. He'd think it was code and the Soviets were about to invade, charging up the M6 in their T54s Next thing you know, the depot'd be surrounded by marines. We'd arrive in the morning and they'd arrest us as spies."

"You're mad," she started the engine and switched on the lights.

"You'd be okay because they'd look in your bag and find a copy of *Loving*. But when they pulled Theses on Feuerbach from my pocket, I'd be done for."

She didn't reply. What was he talking about? She'd just offered him her body. She just offered him love, albeit on the back seat of a mini, and he was too stupid to understand. What did he expect? Did she have to take her clothes off in the front seat? She hit the roundabout a forty, touched the brake and the car screeched and rocked.

"Who's after us?" he said.

She didn't speak. The journey lasted years. They climbed the hill to the suburb where they both lived. She pulled in outside the chip shop; kids were hanging around on their bikes.

"Steak pudding, chips and peas?" he said.

She turned to him. For the first time since he'd got in the car, she met his eyes. He really was very handsome, and nice. She smiled. For a second she hoped he wouldn't get out.

"Okay. Thanks for the lift. See you in the mornin'"

She wanted to say: No, don't get out. Let's go for a drink. Or park up somewhere. I could go home and get changed. We could meet in *The Plough*. Or I could pick you up. But he was gone.

Her mother had made fish for tea.

"That's fresh salmon. Do you know how much that cost?"

"I don't bloody care."

"Katie Dyet, don't you swear at me! Your own mother."

176

When she'd eaten Katie had a shower then sat on the sofa with a mug of tea. Her father was watching the news. There was something about the Soviet invasion of Czechoslovakia. She went up to her room and read an article about how to turn men on in *Loving*. When she switched out the light and pulled the duvet round her shoulders an inexplicable tear trickled down her cheek.

Next morning she pretended not to see Billy at the bus-stop. He never travelled in her car again.

LET'S KILL THE TEACHER

We were sitting in the staff-room towards the end of break when Dransfield sighed heavily, closed the *Times* whose international pages he'd been scanning, got up with his usual refusal-to-be-hurried slowness, took his mug into the kitchen and slouched off to his class. We knew things were tough for him, being of the *old school*, nearing retirement, one of those teachers who grew up in the fifties, took learning seriously, knew his subject inside out, had read a thousand books to get his degree, and was dismayed that pupils in his classes replied "Whatever!" when he told them they'd missed off an accent or got a tense wrong. His mind and those of the young he tried to teach had been formed in contrary circumstances and the almost physical distaste he experienced at mental slovenliness was unknown to them. Every lesson drove him a little nearer despair. He'd become convinced our culture was declining so quickly, heading so gleefully towards suicide, the future would be dominated by minds capable of no more than three-minute concentration, bereft of a sense of posterity, locked into instant gratification. For those of us who were young, these seemed the musings of a sad old man who'd chosen a career well below his capacities.

The first two lessons had gone badly. At nine, the year eights came into his room with their usual raucousness, showing-off and lax indifference to his presence. The previous evening, while his wife slouched in front of some mindlessly glamorous American movie on Film 4, he'd produced six separate tasks which were now laid out on the six tables in piles of thirty. He'd been pleased with his work and had gone to bed hoping, like some naïve rookie, this time they would rise, appreciate his effort and respond to it with their own.

"Is it a test?" called Ashley Brimley.

"Test!" shouted Sam Hothersall. "I'm not doin' a test!"

"Why are we doin' a test?" screeched Jake Sturrock in a voice not yet broken.

"It isn't a test," said Dransfield, but no-one seemed to hear him.

As usual, he stood behind his desk waiting vainly for a reduction in noise that wasn't going to happen, and when, all the boys finally in the room, at last seated but no more attentive to him than a monarch to his flunkeys, he raised his voice and called for quiet with one of his customary polite formulations:

"Can we settle down now, please?" or "Shall we make a start, gentlemen?"

There was a momentary dip in the racket, one or two pairs of eyes shot a glance at him as though he might be more than someone who had wandered in off the street and who was worthy of neither respect nor silence, but quickly the collective need to be lost in chaos, to be able to justify ignorance by claiming it as the class's norm, reasserted itself and only by shouting like a drunken football fan after a bad defeat could he bring some calm.

"Right, that's enough! I've been polite, now comes the nasty stuff. Either you shut up, this instant, or you're in detention."

"Is it official, sir?

"No, departmental."

"When is it, sir?"

"Wednesday."

"I can't do Wednesday I've got a football match."

"If I put you in detention, you're doing detention."

"I can't do Wednesday either, sir. I've got to go the Mosque."

"You'll have to bring a note."

"Can I bring a note, sir?"

"Can I?"

"Can we all bring a note, sir!"

"I've got to go to the Mosque, sir."

"You're not a Muslim, Hooper."

"I've had a conversion, sir."

The noise, which had diminished for thirty seconds to a level which would have allowed him to deliver his lesson in a normal voice, had risen again to a birthday party hubbub. Ashley Griffin, a big, blond lad convinced he was going to be elevated into the stratosphere of super-rich celebrity if only he behaved in every context with the self-conscious, before-the-camera, false exaggerations of *Big Brother* , was on his feet in the middle of the room, and Gavin Barton, a wick, skinny little boy with a mop of curly hair which he shook compulsively as he practised the drumming which he was sure was going to turn him into a super-star, teenage rock sensation, was on all fours under the desk.

"Sit down, Ashley!"

"But he's got me pencil-case!"

"Sit down even though he's got your pencil-case."

"Where's me pencil-case?"

"I haven't got it!" said Gavin emerging from under the table.

"Sit in your chair, Gavin," said Dransfield.

"I was just getting' me pen lid."

"Sit in your chair."

"Where's me pencil-case!" called Gavin as he scanned his place.

"Well you took mine!" called Ashley.

"Sit down, both of you'!"

"But I don't know where my pencil-case is!" called Ashley with the pathetic intonation of crisis.

"What do you want me to do," retorted Dransfield, "call the FBI?"

The class, which apparently hadn't been listening, erupted in an orgy of jeering as they always did if a teacher dared make a joke or employ a witticism which raised him or her above their level. There was nothing Dransfield could do but wait for the bedlam to subside and in those few seconds it came to him how sunk they were in this culture which would admit nothing better than itself, a distortion of the ideal of democracy and even of equality, it was a vicious dismissal of all values which existed beyond their narrow horizon, a reduction to immersion in the moment, rejection of transcendence, a mental return to the cradle where nothing could exceed their immediate needs; yet it wasn't their needs these boys were attending to, on the contrary, they ignored them with all the studied cynicism of their wilful refusal to pay heed to him; it was their desires that overwhelmed them, desires engendered by a slick commercialism for which there was no distinction to be made between a child and an adult - they were both consumers, and in fact, the child was a superior consumer because of its inability to see long-term advantage - and without

180

such a distinction why should they acknowledge him, believe he might have something to offer, recognize his experience, respect his learning? These boys' heroes were tv stars, young, rich, loud-mouthed, overnight sensations, or multi-millionaire footballers flaunting their lavish lifestyles, or even criminals, if criminality had made them rich and notorious. Everything Dransfield represented they despised: the slow accumulation of skill and knowledge, the struggle to master content, the high value attributed to objectivity, steady, honest work for modest reward, a hierarchy of values and priorities, the recognition that our desires can trick us into folly, an unassuming demeanour, a high-minded striving against vulgarity; they were willing to get on with something, but only on their own terms and they feared whatever surpassed them, like savages whose animistic understanding makes them respond violently to whatever is different and therefore incomprehensible. They behaved as they had to, for their context controlled them; they'd been sold i-pods and mobiles and PSPs and the virtual world these represented was more real to them than the flesh-and-blood world which was lurid and slow and demanded attention; they were middle-class boys whose homes made the school, even in its newest extensions, look shabby and cheap; their parents had lived the whole of their teenage and adult lives under the illusion that *there is no such thing as society* and had worshipped at the altar of property as a proof of worth so their children, required to prove themselves at every moment of their lives, lacked any secure sense of esteem and acted out like perform-ing seals or trained dolphins; the political culture which had once provided a rough-and ready guide to the choices available in modern life was now so confused, most of them wouldn't have known whether conservatives stood for reforming capitalism out of exist-ence or socialists for the supremacy of the Stock Exchange; some of them came from homes where there were more televisions than books and hardly any of them ever visited a library; many of them had never played a street game and certainly never invented their own rules or composed their own rhymes; all of them had televisions in their rooms and watched late night pornimagery of some kind; few improvised their own games of cricket or football on the local park because their parents worried about the danger, taking them instead to organised practises where they were driven to *perform* by ambitious, sideline would-be managers and coaches; they bought chocolate bars, sweets and crisps on the way to school and ate them

181

before the first lesson; they thought the MacDonald's big, red M the symbol of freedom; from the American series they watched they derived the idea that there is one mode of behaviour, one tone, one demeanour which is suitable for every place and time, for that is the expression of *you* and any deliberate, conscious restraint would be a denial of your very existence; they believed they had a right to whatever they desired to do or have and anything which curtailed that right, even for an instant, was unjust.

"Sit down, Ashley."

"But where's me pencil-case?"

"I'm going to count to five and if you aren't in your seat I'm taking you to Mr Doyle."

The boy sank reluctantly into his chair, resting his head on his folded arms.

"Sit up properly."

"Where's me pencil-case!" he exclaimed, raising his head, as affronted as John McEnroe on a bad day.

"Gavin! Gavin! You sit down too."

"Sir."

Apparently compliant, the boy moved to his seat but just before sitting grabbed a pencil-case from the desk and hurled it across the room at which its owner, Jordan Batty jumped up:

"You bastard!"

"Watch your tongue, Jordan!"

But the boy was away after his belongings, the noise was becoming painful, Gavin grabbed another pencil-case, Ashley got briskly to his feet again and Dransfield, knowing there was nothing else for it, bellowed:

"Si'down at once! Count of five if you're on your feet you get an official!"

The spectacle of a man as old as some of their grandfathers having to bawl like a commodity trader in the midst of market meltdown made them smirk and quieten and watch him. He was their prey and they had him in their talons because, although they obeyed, they'd won by making him look ridiculous as they did to all teachers, if not by forcing them into this kind of howling, then by making them teach against their noise and unwillingness, forcing them to strain to entertain them, refusing to allow them their simple status as adult professionals which should have been enough to command their cooperation.

"Your behaviour is disgraceful…" Dransfield heard himself begin, launching into one of those petty homilies, full of anguished disbelief and stressing their inability to behave socially, to adapt to the context, to uphold their responsibility to take education seriously; and though this chastened them enough to permit him to explain what they had to do, within two minutes of them starting the work the noise was filling the space as inexorably as the waters of a burst river fill the cellars of the bankside houses. He went from table to table, urging each quartet to make progress.

"Come on, you've six minutes only to get this done then you move to the next table."

The noise was awful but he decided to do no more than urge them to quiet as they were at least launched on some work and as he went around the room, verbally prodding them as a farmer prods cattle, he reflected that what he'd said wasn't true: they *were* behaving socially, they were simply adhering to a set of social rules which contradicted absolutely the ones he was trying to teach by; on the one hand, the system worked by coercion: they were required to be educated and that meant, for almost all parents, school, so the inordinate power of the State compelled them to be here and to follow the National Curriculum, to stick to the school's timetable, to wear a uniform, to do homework, to run the cross-country; on the other hand, the air was thick with the boomerang rhetoric of choice, diversity and personalisation, the glib falsehoods of politicians cynically making use of the system to keep themselves in power. Yet the falsehoods became policy and the ambitious had to follow it just as the parents, naively, imagined that there was no dislocation between the highflown words of a Minister desperate for advantage and the daily reality of classrooms where teachers battled for enough order to get something done or gave up on education and sank to the level of entertainers, putting pupils in front of computer screens where they could play games with a little added, putatively educational content, showing them endless videos, or turning every aspect of learning into a game that flattered their childishness and never brought them up short against the hard demands of disinterested mental effort.

The chatter got badly in the way of their attention, but all the same, most of them were getting along with the work because he'd reduced it to the candy-floss simplicity the system demanded and as he went round seeing them selecting items of vocabulary and slotting them into passages of nursery-rhyme redundancy or asking one another the way to the railway station or the town hall in phrase-book French, he felt for the ten thousandth time that dreadful collapsing sense of playing his small part in the demolition of intelligence.

"Sir, what's the French for street?"

"Well, it's there, look."

"Where?"

"Look," and he pointed to the helpful list of vocabulary at the side of the worksheet.

"Oh, yeah."

There came the usual noise of a kerfuffle behind him and turning he found Jack Cronshaw sprawled across the desk, the worksheets on the floor like discarded bus tickets. A great jeer arose from the class and Cronshaw, relishing his fifteen seconds of limelight, kicked his legs and flailed his arms like a non-swimmer in a wild sea.

"Get back in your seat, Jack!"

The three boys at the table were giggling like giddy four-year-olds high on E numbers.

"He's swimming the channel!"

And Cronshaw agitated his limbs more ferociously, rocking the table and raising another loud jeer.

"Jack, get back in your seat!"

But the boy was enjoying himself, the class had broken down, no work was being done, what they were there for was forgotten, they'd tilted the little vessel of education in which they were used to being pandered to till it had capsized and were now frolicking in the waves, excited as six-year-olds on an August holiday; why should they pay any attention to Dransfield, what did he represent? He belonged to a past they were ignorant of and disdained because everything in the past denied the bright future that was theirs.

184

"Jack! I'm going to count to ten then I'm going to take you off the desk. You're risking injury behaving this way in the classroom."

At this provocation the boy behaved as if a sudden surge of electricity had passed through his body, the two desks, pushed together to make one, came apart, books, pens and pencil-cases cascaded to the floor and at the end of his very short tether, Dransfield grabbed the boy by the collar and yanked him to his feet.

"You hit me!" Cronshaw exclaimed.

"No I didn't."

"I've got witnesses. That's assault."

"I wish you luck in your career as a barrister... Now sit down."

"I'll get my dad."

Around the room were cries of "Sue him, Jack!", "Get him sacked!", but Dransfield remained as calm as a man contemplating the roses in his garden.

"Good. I'll be glad to talk to him. Now sit down."

He pushed the tables together, picked up the belongings and went once more around the room.

"That's six minutes. Change tables, Clockwise round the room, please."

They stood up and grabbed their bags.

"Listen, there's no need to take your bags. Leave them where they are. You'll come back to where you started from. Leave your bags."

"I'm not leavin' mine, someone'll nick me stuff."

And that collective opinion meant thirty boys hoisted their bulging rucksacks onto their shoulders, began shoving and jostling like bumper cars on a bank holiday, moved in various directions, pushed the desks and chairs aside and, enjoying the low-key melee, refused to listen when Dransfield called:

"No, no! Clockwise. Go clockwise to the next desk. Come on! This is simple. Just go clockwise."

They relished their sullen defiance like a tired two-year-old in the supermarket, milled and shoved in their bovine progress to their next task and when, finally, they were all seated again, Dransfield found they'd deliberately muddled the worksheets.

185

"Who's done this?" he said holding up a sheaf, and though he was on the verge of letting fly, he restrained himself, forced his voice away from stridency and his demeanour from tension. "Pathetic. It really is pathetic."

Patiently, he went round the room resorting the papers till each table had its correct pile.

"Okay. Six minutes from now."

"Sir, he's got me ruler!" Ashley was on his feet.

"Sit down."

"But he's got me ruler!"

"Fine, but sit down."

He went to the table knowing that he'd ask Gavin to give back the ruler and he'd say he didn't have it.

"Give him his ruler, Gavin."

"What?" said the boy, spreading his arms, his fingers splayed, his mouth gaping like the Mersey Tunnel.

"Just give him the ruler, enough's enough."

"I haven't got it!"

"Either give him the ruler or you'll have to leave the room."

"But I haven't got it! Look! Can you see any ruler?"

Ashley lurched across the desk and grabbed Gavin's pen which he sent skidding across the floor.

"See that! Get it!" and Gavin was on his feet.

"Sit down, Gavin!"

Ashley jumped up and grabbed Gavin round the neck, the two of them toppling like an over-stacked pile of books, at which another great jeer soared at the boys wrestling on the floor.

"Get up the pair of you!"

As calmly as if he were lifting a baby from its cot, Dransfield separated the fighters who were now red-faced, over-excited, dishevelled and delighted at being the stars of the moment.

"You aren't being filmed," said Dransfield, "this isn't *Big Brother*. Now sit down and calm down."

"But where's me ruler!" cried Ashley his arms spread like Christ on the cross.

Dransfield put his face close to Ashley's and spoke very low:

"At the end of the lesson we'll conduct a search and investigation and if your ruler doesn't turn up, I'll call for International Rescue immediately. Okay."

In response to the teacher's proximity to their classmate, hoping he might have been pushed far enough to make a mistake which could allow them to disperse through the school exaggerating grossly the story of Dransfield attacking a pupil, and listening intently, for the first time in the year, in case he might say something they could report to their parents, thrilling at the possibility of getting a teacher in serious trouble and possibly sacked, they had become utterly quiet and as attentive as infants in front of their first Punch and Judy. Dransfield stood back smiling and surveyed them.

"That's very good. Now get on with the work."

At once the racket exploded, they turned to one another and began chatting about their inconsequential obsessions paying flitting attention to the work and Dransfield, walking amongst them, wishing he could simply go out of the door and never return was struck by how precisely he could locate the time at which the behaviour of the pupils turned and from being mischievous but essentially biddable, they became malicious, conscious of their power, keen to assert their rights, and ready, at the slightest opportunity, to make accusations. The ancient recognition that children, being immature, can't share adult rights nor assume adult responsibilities had been discarded and now the absolute equality of the generations was asserted as a law. As his mind had done thousands of times, it quickly ran through the demented logic that had made this happen: visceral and irrational hatred of the public sector, fear of educated masses, a wayward belief that individual freedom isn't socially guaranteed, a terror of organised labour, a compulsive need to control and manage every detail, the need to open up new markets by turning children into vigorous consumers, the emergence of a political elite detached from the population and determined to manipulate its way to power and stay there, the superstitious conviction that any putative knowledge or skill can be reduced to the numbers by which it's measured, and hovering above it all the preening egotism of the very rich who

187

wanted the world made safe for themselves, whatever the cost in accumulating despair and misery. He recalled the precision of the change: September 1992, the introduction of OFSTED, a message to pupils and parents that it was open season on incompetent, feckless, left-wing, lazy, teachers.

"Six minutes! Move to the next task. Clockwise and don't take your bags."

But it was hopeless, the more they ignored and defied him, the more they loved themselves, like a child who discovers for the first time that its parents can be controverted without the sky falling in. His well-planned lesson descended into the chaos of paddling-pool time on the lawn in summer as these heedless, self-centred boys chatted, messed and frittered the hour away. He wrote some perfunctory homework on the board, told them to take their completed sheets with them and dismissed them on the bell. When they'd left, the room was littered like a nursery after paper pattern making and as he hurried to clear up, bending and reaching for the discarded work, some of it bearing crude emblems of male genitalia, his next class began to arrive. They slobbed in and threw down their bags. Dion Clovelly spread his arms and buzzed around the room:

" What are we doing today, sir!" he called

Miles Blashaw stood pouring coca-cola down his throat from a two-litre bottle like a kid taking a break from a playground football game.

"Put the bottle away, Miles."

"But I'm thirsty!"

"So am I but you don't see me getting a bottle of brown ale out of the cupboard, do you?"

"Have you got brown ale in there?" shouted Clovelly, spitfiring between the desks.

"Put the bottle away."

"I'm thirsty," said the boy, "it's my human right to drink."

"Not here and now it isn't."

"If he dies of thirst you've had it," called Thomas Gold.

"If he dies of thirst they'll bury him in a coca-cola bottle shaped coffin."

"Did you hear that?" called Ryan Stanford. "He said he wants you to die of thirst!"

"Sue him, Miles!" called Gold.

Dransfield stood behind his desk and surveyed the noisy, disunified group, each boy in his own little bubble confirming that there is no such thing as society, and though he knew they weren't to blame, were merely the unwitting victims of a debased culture, he despised them because finally they did have a choice, young as they were; they needed to choose against their culture. Raised in a time which proposed that the individual is made against society they exhibited a hypomanic sense of self-esteem, thrusting themselves into every situation as though they could define themselves from within. The irony was that this radical individuality was socially imposed and the originality they attached to their behaviour was in fact the most reduced conformism. Unable to address them as a class because of their noise, he went from table to table:

"Do you have your exercise book? Can you get it out, please? The date and title are on the board."

It was as effective as herding lemmings from the cliff face. Reluctant, slow, uncooperative, loud, fiercely determined to do as little as possible and to sabotage the lesson, they refused to work as a group, wouldn't raise any pace, relished Dransfield's discomfiture. They were doing, he knew, the work of the politicians, the leader writers, the bureaucrats, the target-setters, the self-appointed experts, the glib commentators, systematically destroying intellectualism, debasing the value of learning, asserting the rights of reduced consumerism; they were customers and they couldn't be wrong. He battled through the lesson. Clovelly threw a text-book through the open window.

"Come with me, please Dion."

"Where'm I goin'?"

"I'll have to put you in another room."

"Which room?"

"Just come with me and I'll show you."

"Do I need to bring my stuff?"

"Yes, please."

Agonisingly slowly, the boy gathered his things, calling comments to his mates all the while as Dransfield stood by the door. Once his bag was packed, he deliberately picked it up awkwardly so its contents spilled on the floor. Another great jeer filled the room. Dransfield waited, his heart beginning to pound with anger and humiliation. Daily he was put through this and though he knew his sensibility was partly to blame (intellectual, liberal, thoughtful, questioning, these boys hooked on celebrity and electronic gizmos found him impossible to fathom) he despised the system that left him facing such classes and which told him their behaviour was the result of his uninteresting teaching. One of those liberals who had come into teaching out of idealism, convinced that voluntary compliance could replace coercion, he had witnessed the invasion of supermarket ideology, the arrival of the idiocy that outcome is all and process meaningless, the virus of blame according to which a Secretary of State bears no responsibility for failure and can even declare publicly that she wouldn't touch some schools with a bargepole, the wretched notion that there is one kind of effective lesson only and if it doesn't begin with a *starter* and end with a *plenary*, it's a failure, the mind-destroying concept that boys do well at Eton and badly in Brixton because in so-called *failing* schools the teachers are no good, and above all the time-serving cynicism of self-exculpating politicians for whom the education system was nothing but a means to garner votes, to hang on to power for a little longer, to line their pockets, to win a place in the history books at any price, and of course, who did the bidding of the rich who saw the school system as an expensive white elephant and wanted it reduced to a training scheme to turn out obedient and mindless employees.

Two lessons done and Dransfield was already weary, frustrated, at the end of his tether. At half past three a group of us were in the staff-room chatting and laughing before going to the pub. We were young. We'd grown up with the cynicism Dransfield hadn't adjusted to, viewed idealism as a folly and didn't care too much about the future, except our own. We saw him come in with his briefcase, sit down and scan the paper as he ate a sandwich left over from his lunch. He cut a lonely figure and in a way we felt sorry for him, but at the same time we knew he belonged to the past: things had changed and he hadn't, he was out of step with his culture and secretly we despised him for his high-mindedness, his belief in principle. We'd been trained to use our elbows, to look to the main chance. There might be such a thing as society, but we knew it was a jungle and we relished its cut-throatism. What did we have to do to get on, to have the big house, the fast car, the good-looking spouse? Just tell us and we'll do it. But Dransfield wouldn't. He insisted on values and principles and that was his downfall. He sat for a few minutes, dropped his crust in the bin, stood up and pulled on his coat and with his briefcase seeming to weigh inordinately went out to his car without speaking to anybody. We were glad to see him go. His presence disturbed us. He was out of place. We were the new world. Like the kids, we were consumers, we asserted ourselves, we wanted our place and Dransfield's resistance to the present bewildered us.

Soon after that he took the reduced pension, made a down-beat speech when his cheque was presented and disappeared. No-one has heard of him since.

MALCOLM LOWRY AND THE BEAUTIFUL BOY

It was one of those crisp autumn days when the cloudless sky and the still air bring memories of summer but the chill made him wrap his brown scarf round his neck, pull up his suede collar and the anticipation of wind and rain brought him a quick shudder; the campus was swarming with warmly-clad students and as Frank Womack emerged from the little newsagent in the corner of the square, he was overwhelmed once more by the sense of possibility they presented. He tucked his TLS under his arm and following a huddle of chatting, light-hearted undergrads, tried to appear mature and professional, to assume a preoccupied air as if thinking of James Joyce's prose style or the architecture of *The Fairie Queen*. On his short journey to his room, he noticed three or four particularly attractive young men. Being small, he'd always been impressed by height. They almost frightened him, but it was a delicious sort of nervousness. What he noticed about the boys was the thick, shining health of their long hair, or the boyish freshness of their complexions, or the quick strength of their stride; and there were so many of them, so many young men, each with something beautiful or at least attractive about him; his mind dissolved at the thought of this cornucopia. In his room, he quickly prepared himself for his seminar. This would be his first encounter with the group of freshers who had been lectured on and were supposed to have read *Under The Volcano*. Most wouldn't have got to grips with it; he could lord it. He would, as usual, quote from his own study of Lowry. The experience would be a mixture of frustration at the poor quality of undergraduates and delight in his own use of language and ability to appear a towering intellectual before these sons and daughters of largely provincial, predominantly middle-class, intellectually limited parents. He would lounge in his armchair in the corner (it was important his skill seemed effortless); he would be polite and solicitous; he would talk slowly and adopt a far-away look at his moments of supreme inspiration. He placed a copy of the novel on the desk beside his chair. There came a timid knock at the door.

Meeting a new group of students was always exciting, unnerving, slightly tedious and ultimately disappointing; he always hoped the group would include a mind to match his own, a boy or girl with a passion for literature who had read more than the set texts and could speak well; or a beautiful boy, a slender, untried youth he could impress and corrupt. But year in year out the undergraduates were neither brilliant nor beautiful; they were ambitious, relatively diligent, plain, ugly, taciturn, willing to please, on occasion stunningly poorly read and for the most part highly forgettable. This group came in rather sheepishly and stopped talking before crossing the threshold, laden with ring-binders and unthumbed copies of the novel.

"Do come in, do come in!" he called. "Make yourselves at home. Shall I close this window, there may be too much of a draught? What do you think?"

He directed his question at the plump girl in the green coat whose brown hair fell in unwashed strands along her cheeks and touched her narrow shoulders as she was about to take the seat with its back to the window. She turned her head, looked at him with flushed cheeks and smiled.

"I'll close it then, shall I? Come in everyone. Is there room? I think so. We'll just about fit in won't we?"

He popped his head into the corridor and looked both ways before closing the door with that fatal little click which meant the next hour might be one of atrocious boredom and frustration. The students were entirely silent. Most had kept their coats on.

"Do take off your coats if you feel like it. It's warm enough in here, don't you think? I've closed the window, we don't want anyone catching the flu do we?"

One girl slipped off her brown, waisted jacket and hung it on the back of her chair; a boy unzipped his anorak. Womack sat down, crossed his legs, rubbed his palms together in his characteristic way and began:

"Well, we should get to know one another a little shouldn't we?"

He looked round at the thirteen students and his heart almost stopped. Twelve were the normal run, but in the corner, his chair pushed back a little from the circle, the books stacked high on the shelves behind him threatening to totter if he nudged, was the beautiful boy he'd dreamed of.

"Oh, do be careful there!" he called leaning forward, " those books above your head may topple if you push your chair against the bookshelves."

The boy looked at him with big, round blue eyes which captured the light from the window opposite, and gave a tiny smile of recognition.

"Perhaps you should pull your chair forward just an inch. I would hate you to be clobbered by the Nonesuch Donne in your first seminar!"

He'd hoped there might be some recognition of what he thought of as wit, but the students remained silent. The boy edged his chair forward a little.

"As you know, I'm Dr Womack and I'll be your tutor for the year. After each lecture you'll have a seminar with me in which we'll try to discuss what you've read in some detail but I'm quite happy to spend more time on the authors which interest you most. Today, of course, we're going to begin with *Under The Volcano*. Now, have you all managed to read it?"

The novel was included at his insistence. Some of his colleagues had protested:

"It's a hard text, Frank. As the first novel they encounter. We should ease them in gently."

But he stood his ground. Lowry was the subject of his PhD, of his only book, of a little snowstorm of papers and the fact it was hard reassured him. The students needed plenty of exposition; Lowry was new to almost all of them. Lawrence, Joyce, Conrad, Murdoch, Lessing, Golding, they might have encountered at A Level, but this took them into new territory: a great but not popular novelist and a minority taste because he was difficult. Womack liked to bring attention to minority tastes, it was almost a compulsion.

"We'll get to know one another as we go, shall we? So who would like to begin? Tell us what you make of this book. Anything at all, anything that struck you when reading it? Mmm."

And he brought his hands together as if in prayer, his thumbs tucked under his chin. He knew there was going to be one of those long, awful pauses after which he'd have to wade in and explain what his writer was about. He thought for a second he might fire a set of questions around the room: when is the novel set? how long a period does it cover? who are the major characters? what would you say are the major events of the book? But he dreaded the lowered eyes, the embarrassed fiddling with papers, the flushed cheeks, the silence.

"Lowry," he said, lowering his hands, "there he is," and he pointed to the famous print of the author looking rather Hemingwayish, reclining in his shorts, his glasses in his hand, a book resting on his thighs, half literary intellectual, half Hollywood pin-up, "was, of course, like Geoffrey Firmin, a troubled man. An alcoholic. In Firmin's drinking we have a metaphor for a sense of malaise creeping through British society. Firmin is an ex-Consul, a minor diplomat, a representative of his country, but a man broken by drink. A man who knows at every minute of the day exactly where every drop of alcohol in his house is hidden. Obsessive. An addict. He can't help himself. His cravings destroy him yet he can do nothing about them. Mmmm? Aren't we all a little bit like this?"

There was the expected silence and no-one met his eyes. He paused a few seconds, entwined his fingers and was about to go on when the beautiful boy spoke. He had an obvious northern accent but Womack couldn't place it and he spoke slowly and without apparent effort.

"Maybe a bit, but Firmin isn't typical. He's too extreme a case for us to feel much sympathy with him."

"Oh, but we do feel sympathy," said Womack, "it's an inordinately touching portrait of a man pursued by his demons. You see, in taking the extreme case and you're right, you're quite right...I'm sorry, what's your name?"

"Joe Bryning."

"Yes, Joe, sorry. Yes. In taking the extreme case, Lowry illuminates the ordinary. Pathology is the royal road to understanding health. And Firmin is a man who seeks out hell. Remember. He says that. He says he loves hell. Now, that's the mystery. How can we love hell? How can we shun what brings us happiness and run headlong to our misery and destruction?"

"He couldn't be an alcoholic if there was no alcohol," said the beautiful boy.

"Sorry?"

"It's cultural. He needs an alcoholic culture to destroy himself. If he lived in a country without alcohol, he couldn't do it, or he'd have to find another way."

The other students were looking at Joe. One or two of them made notes.

"That's true, Joe. That's a very good point."

There was a catch in Womack's voice which suggested the opposite.

"But it's a sociological point. Not that I'm putting that down. Only, this is a book which deals with the tortures of the human soul. Geoffrey Firmin is one of God's creatures. The essence of the novel supersedes sociology and takes us to that territory where we live very much alone. It's the spiritual torment that involves us. You see, Firmin is a kind of Christ figure, wouldn't you agree? Only his cross is booze."

He lifted his praying hands to his pursed lips and looking at Bryning, nodded slowly.

"Perhaps he just needs a good psychiatrist," said Bryning.

"Don't you think his problem is a little beyond psychiatry?"

"Well, he's a portrait of Lowry, more or less. He was an alcoholic. We can probably find the cause of his problem in his upbringing or his culture. Or maybe he was just predisposed to addiction."

"Predisposed?"

"Perhaps some people are, like some are more likely to have heart attacks or hay fever."

Womack threw back his head and laughed loudly, a cracking almost unhinged laughter that made the students sit straight in their chairs and widen their eyes.

"Yes, that's good, Joe. But you know, a great spiritual crisis is a little more overwhelming than hay fever. Predisposed to drink or otherwise we are dealing with a man tormented to the point of despair by his demons and we are forced to see this as a struggle between good and evil. Firmin is, after all, an essentially good man, but a man with a fatal weakness."

Bryning raised his eyebrows and tilted his head in grudging agreement. Womack looked him in the eye. Their exchange required it. He felt no embarrassment, even though he held the look too long and the beautiful boy looked down at his red ring-binder. He really was extraordinarily beautiful, unearthly: his long blonde hair and clear blue eyes, his slender frame and artistic hands seemed sent to torment him. Before the seminar was over, he was in love with him, and when he said to his wife at the table that evening:

196

"There's a very bright young boy in my new first year group. I can't remember anyone making such an impression on me for years."

He wasn't thinking about his peculiar comments on Lowry, but how it might be, at last, to get into bed with such a creature. Had he known that at that very moment the beautiful boy was in his room with a stunningly pretty girl who, like Womack, wasn't able to hold back; had he known she was unbuttoning the white top which clung to her narrow waist, was revealing herself and surrendering because he was the most attractive boy in the year and in that curious quirk of the mind which makes people choose partners of comparable attractiveness, she felt impelled to possess him; had he known the beautiful boy was without defence against her and was falling headlong, he would have got up from the table without touching his meal, would have left the house, would have flown into one of those inaccessible moods which set him at odds with his wife for days. As it was, he was running through little scenarios of seduction which softened his mood and made him complaisant as a well-fed dog.

He met the group once a week. He was careful to dress attractively. They moved on from Lowry to Yeats, Conrad and then Gerard Manley Hopkins. Though Womack hadn't published on him, he liked to linger over his work. The students said they'd like to study Beckett, Joe Orton and Brian Patten. Womack hated Beckett who lent himself easily to atheistic interpretation, had a horror of Orton for his remark "I think Christianity is a mistake" judging him a superficial farceur, and considered Patten's work unable to sustain serious interpretation. He spent one seminar on *Waiting For Godot*, which he dismissed as the literary equivalent of executive toys; one on Patten who he claimed couldn't hold his own with the great poets any more than pop music could compare to Bach, and ignored Orton altogether.

He devoted five seminars to Hopkins.

"Praise him," he said. "Praise him. It's direct, isn't it? But its directness is prepared by the preceding lines. It is the only possible conclusion. And therein lies the genius of the poem."

No-one said anything and feeling himself on the cusp of one of those few minutes of dazzling brilliance which left him light and at ease for days, he was about to continue when the beautiful boy said:

"I don't think it's the only conclusion."

"Don't you?"

197

"Well, if you see all the things he mentions as products of evolution, they're even more amazing."

Womack threw his head back and laughed once more.

"Yes, of course. But Darwin merely uncovers a mechanism. He can't tell us what's behind the mechanism.

"Perhaps there isn't anything."

"But that just leaves us with an absence, doesn't it? And Darwin has explained nothing. No, we have to see that what Hopkins is pointing to is the mystery of beauty. Why do some things strike us as irresistibly beautiful? Why are we unable to restrain from crying out at the sight of a truly exquisite wonder of nature? We are taken out of ourselves, our hearts are ripped from our breasts, we are no longer in control....."

"But all that could be explained by evolution."

"How?"

Womack's abrupt question and his staring into Bryning's eyes discomfited the student and he struggled to find a response.

"No," the academic resumed, "we have to put evolution in its place. It fails to explain our spiritual responses. That's what Hopkins is getting at: our spiritual response to beauty."

"Maybe it's just a trick of the brain."

Womack was taken aback. The reduction of the most refined human responses to a debased materialism struck him as profoundly cynical. And that such vile thinking should come from his beautiful boy!

"Praise him, praise him," he said to recover his sang-froid, "that's the way to keep cynicism at bay."

Bryning looked him straight in the eye, but said nothing.

That week, Womack set their first essay: Attempt a definition of the short story. He knew its abstraction would trouble them, that most would struggle and the marks would be low, but he liked that. Some of his colleagues set straightforward tasks: From the stories you have read, explain what you consider to be the major preoccupations of Conrad. How successful is he in realizing these artistically? Then they would mark them generously and the most diligent would achieve 75% or better; but Womack liked to make the students aware of his intellectual superiority and the process of dealing with an aggrieved undergraduate desperate to know why their work was worth no more than 37% and worried they were going to fail the year, always gratified him. They pleaded, he shrugged. They objected, he smiled wanly. They cited their hours of effort, he pointed out university wasn't meant to be easy. It was true, his students usually had the worst results in the year, but most scraped a 2:2: in his view, all they were worth. Occasionally, a very good student would get a 2:1, but he drew the line at a First. Having achieved that himself, he considered it reserved for a very small elite, and in his twenty-three years teaching had never encountered a boy or girl up to his own standard.

When the work arrived, he was delighted to find a number of abstract responses. He was able to make dismissive, derisive remarks: You should have referred to the work of a number of writers! This isn't literary criticism, it's cod philosophy! Even those who'd taken some stories by Chekhov, Katherine Mansfield or Henry James and examined them in detail were given short shrift: This is all well and good at A Level, but I know the stories! What about answering the question! An essay which left specific work aside to try to pin down the abstract essence of a short story, failed as inevitably as one which stuck to the particular but made no attempt to pull together an overarching definition. He left Bryning's essay till last. It began:

To attempt an abstract definition of the short story would invite failure. All we have are the stories written so far. By examining some of the best in detail we may be able to tease out some general characteristics, but to go further would be to risk a foolish prescriptiveness. What will the short stories of the future be like? We have no idea....

He went on to analyse *Odour of Chrysanthemums*, *The Secret Sharer, The Lady With The Little Dog*, and *No Pain Whatsoever*. Womack hadn't read the Richard Yates and was about to underline in red and scrawl Who wrote this? when he paused. He wondered if his assumption that it must be some second-rate piece by an unworthy populist might be mistaken. Who was Richard Yates? Before he could mark, he had to find out and the trip to the library, looking up the references and finally sitting in his armchair after dinner with a glass of red reading the story itself left him badly annoyed. When he went back to the essay, he was infuriated by its diligent explication of technique and little sentences like, *Perhaps we could say that Lawrence's maxim of adorning a tale and pointing to a moral is a defining feature of the short story*, made him want to cry aloud. He put a double red line under this particular example. Pure Lawrentian bunkum! What moral is pointed to in *The Secret Sharer*? Once again, he hesitated a moment. Perhaps there was a moral in Conrad's piece, but he'd run out of patience, and fifteen pages of sedulous first-year tutor-pleasing left him in that sullen frame of mind in which he felt he was wasting his life on trivialities.

"These students drive me mad!" he said to his wife. "I should be writing books for a living, not wearing out my eyes reading this drivel."

The following morning he put his highest mark on Bryning's essay as he ate his toast: 41% You evade the question and stick to safe specifics. There is no definition of a short story here! To his surprise, the beautiful boy didn't come to see him. Three or four of the group arrived. One girl who received 31% was in tears. She'd got an A at A Level? How could she be doing so badly? He explained she'd probably come out with a pass degree, which was better than nothing. But why didn't Bryning turn up? He'd been sure he would. How could he be satisfied with 41% for all that effort?

"Everyone happy with their essays?" he chirped in the following week's seminar.

Bryning didn't meet his eyes.

Womack fretted for a few weeks over the boy's lack of response, but having turned to drama and studied *The Wild Duck* and *Hedda Gabler* , the students were ready for their second essay. He typed the title and pinned it to the notice-board:

Greek tragedy is the tragedy of necessity, Christian tragedy is the tragedy of possibility. Discuss.

What would the beautiful boy make of it? It'd become clear he was an atheist. Disappointed, Womack nevertheless still found himself imagining an affair. Did Bryning suspect? Was that why he hadn't come to see him? He'd made his interest clear enough, he supposed, but surely hadn't given himself away entirely. He dreamed of Bryning handing him a thick manuscript, written in a tiny, neat hand. It took him days to read and revealed a huge knowledge of western drama. When the boy came to his room, he attacked him with it, beating him around the head till he fell to the ground. Instantly, he was naked. Womack woke with the image of the beautiful, long, pale body in his head; the buttocks were small, tight and round and the

200

prostrate boy's face was buried in the carpet.

When the essays came in, he marked Womack's first. It began with Aeschylus and followed with long paragraphs on the major Greek dramatists; the influence of the Greeks on Seneca led to a discussion of what Shakespeare had taken from the Latin writers; a survey of dramatists from the Miracle Plays to Arthur Miller came next and in conclusion he argued that determinism was at work in western plays: in the Greeks it was more obvious because of their mythology, but wasn't the death of Willy Loman just as inevitable as Oedipus's murder of his father? Womack gave it 30% and scrawled across it in his most hurried, academic hand: Not enough stress on the Christian element.

Bryning came to see him.

"Come in, come in, Joe. Do sit down. Turned much colder hasn't it? Is it warm enough for you? I've a little heater I can plug in."

The boy settled himself and unbuttoned his coat.

"So, Joe. What was it you wanted to see me about?"

"I wanted to ask," he said, "why I got 30% for this essay."

"Didn't I put a comment on it?"

"Yes."

"What did I say?"

Bryning read the comment.

"Ah, yes," said the little academic, bringing his praying hands up to his lips. "The title does make that clear doesn't it? I was looking for a discussion of Christian drama."

"What falls within that definition?"

"Well, all western drama since the birth of Christianity."

"But some of that was written by avowed atheists."

"Oh, but that makes no difference. The form of drama Brecht is working with, for example, is part of the Christian tradition. His atheism is super-added. The essence is that Christianity brought to drama the sense of free will, of Christian conscience and that shaped the form. That's what I was asking you to get at."

"Yes, but Shakespeare isn't a Christian writer…"

201

"My goodness!" exclaimed Womack. "He's altogether a Christian. His work is replete with Christian references."

"I know what you mean, but in what way does King Lear express a Christian view of things? It's about power and how it drives people mad."

"Of course it is, Joe, but within a Christian frame of reference. It's men who make the decisions. The gods are no longer in control. Free will rules the world because that is the gift of the Christian god."

"I see what you mean, but it stretches the definition of Christian drama a bit thin…"

"No, no, not at all Joe. You're quite wrong. That's why I used that form of words in the question. You see, you're only just starting out. You've got a lot of reading to do. You don't yet understand just how overwhelming the Christian contribution to our culture has been. But I think you've got potential. You're a bright young man, Joe. In fact, if you like we could meet and I could help you with your essay writing. You could come to my house for example, one evening. A more relaxed setting than a seminar. What do you think? Mmm?"

He leaned forward, his elbows on his thin thighs and peered into the boy's exquisite face. It was extraordinary just how the simple symmetry of that little bit of flesh and bone could strip him of all will to resist. It was as if Bryning had been made for him. How could he believe otherwise when the mere sight of him sent his desire to such a pitch, nothing else mattered? Yes, even now, staring into his eyes, having just invited him to his home, he knew he would be in trouble if the boy reported him. It was a proposition and he could lose his job; but what was his job, his wife, his publications, his reputation, what was any of it compared to possession of such beauty? To run his hands over that slim body, to kiss those gorgeous lips, above all to be on top of him, pressing down on him.

Bryning sat quite still and composed staring back at him.

Womack's sense of command suddenly left him. He collapsed inwardly like an animal shot through the brain. He'd seen in Bryning's eyes a confidence and refusal which stunned him. This was nothing but a boy! An eighteen year-old fresh from some dull sixth-form and here he was, in a position of superiority! A dreadful panic seized the academic's mind. He stood up, began to busy himself with papers on his desk, then slotted some books into his shelves.

"So I think that's all, is it?" he said, his back to the student.

"I'd like this essay remarked by another member of staff."

Womack turned and confronted Bryning, his face taut with indignation.

"Are you putting my professional competence in question?"

"No," said the young man calmly, "but I think your own convictions prevent you seeing the value of my work."

"The value of your work! Young man, let me tell you. Your work has no value. Objectively, no value at all. You're a first-year undergraduate who'll be lucky to come out with a 2:2. That's how much value your work has. When you're set an essay, your business is to answer the question. All my colleagues will support me. Your essay simply fails to address the issue of the difference between the determinism of Greek tragedy and the possibility of Christian tragedy. I've offered to help you. Here, this morning, I've offered to give up my time and energy to improve your essay writing. That's because I'm behaving professionally, because I recognise you've some potential. But potential comes to nothing without hard work and the right guidance. At the moment, your work is no better or worse than the general run of undergraduate essays."

"All the same," said Bryning, "I'd like a second opinion."

"Then get one! By all means. Go! Go and get your second opinion."

The door clicked. Left alone, Womack went on tidying compulsively but what the papers were he didn't know. His mind was in the grip of the fear that Bryning was knocking on the Head of Department's door. Asking for a re-mark would get him nowhere: Walter Byron was as dismissive of student complaints as himself. But if he mentioned the invitation! It was innocent. He was trying to help the boy. He's misinterpreted it. He's too immature to comprehend. You know what undergraduates are like, their heads are full of sex. I'm a married man. My wife would be at home. We'd give the boy a meal. I was trying to help him along because I can see he could make something of himself. As a matter of fact, I mentioned it to Sue. I told her I had an exceptional boy in my group. Now, would I say that if I had designs on him? Absurd!

He went to Byron's room. No answer and it was locked. Heading for the Senior Common Room he crossed Frances Povey carrying a little burden of files.

"Morning Fran! Hard at it?"

He was impressed by his everyday cheerfulness but his heart beat fast and heavy.

The Common Room was a low-ceilinged, depressing oblong with round, squat coffee tables dispersed to look casual and impossibly uncomfortable orange chairs with wooden arms. As usual, Colin Kirkham, taking a break from work on the fourth volume of his history of the Russian Communist party was smoking his pipe in the corner next to Ernie Staples, the Cambridge-educated Marxist whose recent book, Marxist Poetics, was selling thousands. Womack hated the pair more than he hated the place. He looked round as he approached the counter and spotted Walter Byron peering through his glasses at the arms-length TLS.

"Hello, Walt."

"Morning, Frank."

He sat down with his coffee and sighed like a man whose genius could save the world if only the world would listen.

"Essays! It wouldn't bother me if I never marked another."

"Did you know Somerset Maugham was a faggot?"

"Yes."

"I didn't. Seems he had a taste for little boys. Should cut their bollocks off. What did you say about essays?"

"You might have a student coming to see you."

"I'll keep my door locked."

"He thinks I undervalue what he calls "his work"."

"What did you give him?"

"Thirty per cent."

"Must've been bad."

Byron turned to look Womack in the eyes and the younger man could see the scepticism in his glance.

"Oh, you know me Walt, I like to chivvy them along. I don't give marks for nothing and he hadn't answered the question. I offered him extra tuition. The boy is bright, but he needs forming."

Byron shifted in his seat. His heavy bulk twisted towards Womack as he leant over the arm of his chair. Womack noticed the thick, black hairs which sprouted from his ear. He found Byron's physicality obscene. He was sixty-two, bulky and slow, stank of stale tobacco and poked his finger in his ear, wriggling it vigorously in complete disregard of others.

"This extra tuition. Knock it on the head. Seeing students outside the allocated hours is risky. Remember what happened to Stan Heron?"

"Oh, I'm not up to anything like that! In any case, I never invite girls."

He met Byron's eyes, in anticipation of confirmation, but there was an incipient sneer on the old buffer's lips and his dull eyes under their drooping lids refused to be convinced. He felt small and accused.

"What's the little bugger's name?"

"Joe Bryning."

"If he comes to see me, I'll send him away with a flea in his ear. Have I time for a drink?"

Reassured, Womack got on with what he had to do but at moments the melting thought of Bryning taking a complaint to the Dean turned his intestines to slush. In seminars, the boy never spoke, but sat self-possessed and incredibly handsome, as if to taunt him. He thought of firing questions at him, of trying to make a fool of him, but resisted. |He hoped one day he might bump into him, in the library or the bookshop and start an inconsequential conversation which might lead to inviting him for a drink, or, even better, the knock would come and the beautiful boy, a timid supplicant would enter and say:

"About the private lessons."

When his third essay arrived (he allowed them to devise their own title and Bryning came up with: Saint Joe: innocence in the plays of Joe Orton) he read it with disdain. The thesis was inane: Orton's theme is abused innocence and he leads us a merry dance through corruption and manipulation the better to reveal what it means to be pure of heart! Under normal circumstances, he'd have awarded 25%, but he forced himself to give 44.

Then he waited.

Bryning made no complaint nor did he contribute any more to semi-nars. One day, Womack was heading to his car parked on one of the outer bays when he came across him hand in hand with his girl. He stared at her thick auburn hair, her green eyes, the lovely white teeth of her big smile, her sweet little pointed chin. Looking into Bryn-ing's face, he knew he must be giving himself away badly. He couldn't speak or acknowledge the boy. He slammed into his car and drove too fast down the quiet lanes home.

"If students devoted as much time to reading as they do to sex I might have some essays worth marking," he snapped after his meal.

His wife took away the dishes.

It was the custom in the department for exams to be marked blind. Tutors took home bundles of essays by students they'd never taught. Bryning's end of year exam was marked by Fran Povey. The scripts went straight to Walter Byron.

"Looks like we've got a genius on our hands," he said to Womack as he joined him in the Common Room.

"Really?"

"Your young Bryning, Fran Povey gave him over eighty per cent for each of his three essays."

Womack swayed a little in his chair.

"That's absurd. He must've cheated."

"How?" said Byron abruptly, fixing him with his ugly, bulging eyes.

"I don't know. Who knows what students get up to these days. They're high on pot and LSD half the time and the other half they're occupying the administration building."

"I've read the essays," said Byron without flinching, "the boy's bloody good."

"Well, I'm glad to hear it," said Womack picking up his coffee, "if he's got his head down and done some reading at last, so much the better. Good for him. Yes. Good for him."

MANAGEMENT

Jill Texas loved America and Meryl Sprick loathed Jill Texas. Texas loved the place because it was big, because it was rich, because it was powerful. She was born into the Liverpudlian working-class. Her parents were socialists. But the lure of American glamour was irresistible. She went there as often as she could, taking her family each summer to Florida or Dallas, three weeks at a time. Once she went to New York. It was a great city but she preferred Florida. There was something suspect about New York. Some of the people weren't typical Americans. They had the accents but their attitudes were cosmopolitan. Sprick scoffed. Texas delighted in Texas. She changed her name from Higton. Her motto was a slogan she'd learned in Dallas: There's no such thing as a free lunch.

"There is no such thing as a free lunch," she said to Sprick after telling her she wasn't giving her a discretionary pay rise.

Shortly after, she took a sixth-form assembly. The theme was: There is no such thing as a free lunch. She felt very pleased to be able to influence the students with her homespun, American wisdom.

"Before long, you will go out into the world. It's a big world out there. There are opportunities. You will have to make your choices. What are you going to do? You might do this thing, you might do that thing. You might think it's all coming on a plate. But it isn't coming on a plate. And do you know why? Because there's no such thing as a free lunch. If you want that thing or the other thing, whatever thing you want, you'll have to work for it. That's why you should be working hard now. Every summer I take my family to America. It's a great country. But you know what? Even in America….."

The bell rang and Texas was still talking. The students began to fidget. The staff shuffled. Sprick twisted the papers in her hands. This was her assembly. She was Head of sixth-form. But Texas had usurped her without asking. She had merely announced:

"I'll take the assembly on Thursday."

Sprick believed in hierarchy as much as the next woman. There was nothing unconventional about her view of the world. She had faith in the necessity of authority. She'd worked at Highfield for thirty-five years. All her adult effort had gone into this one job. When she arrived, it was a Grammar so she felt comfortable, having been at a minor public school. The mistresses went around in gowns; the prefects punished younger girls; there was a matron; the sports fixtures were against private schools; lesbianism was rife; everyone kept quiet about the games mistress.

But there had been the sixties.

Sprick had started at Bristol in 1964. They stayed up till three in the morning listening to Bob Dylan, drinking plonk, talking about socialism. Harold Wilson was going to change the world. He was elected by working class votes in remote places called Rotherham, Middlesbrough and Tredegar. To Sprick these were just names and what the working-class might be like she had no idea. But it was impossible not to rally to the idea of the working-class, the ideal of socialism, the atmosphere of change. Her parents were Conservative Anglicans. To vote Labour was an act of rebellious independence. And Dylan sang rebel songs like Guthrie, *The Beatles* came from the industrial north. She became a Liverpool supporter though she knew nothing about football and had never been near the city.

"The point is, man, we've had a fucking revolution in this country! A bloodless revolution, but the working class have got schools and hospitals and pensions by organising and using their votes. The rich can't fucking stop it! It's a democratic revolution and only the antediluvians are against it."

Sprick listened to the mouthing politicos and felt she was part of something noble and irresistible. Her parents and the sadists who ran her school were the antediluvians. She nailed her colours to the mast of the bright future of democratic socialism.

But then came the eighties.

She was in her mid-thirties, a mother of two young children; socialism was disappearing like the rain forests; the Tories were selling off the people's assets. She bought shares in everything. She gave her copies of E.P.Thompson and R.H.Tawney to the Oxfam shop. When the miners struck, she joined in the general excoriation of Arthur Scargill.

"Tunnel vision type!" she said.

She resigned from the union to help her promotion prospects. She began to talk about the immutability of human nature. When the fleet returned from the Falklands, the waving flags and the bare-breasted girls brought a tear to her eye. She believed competition would make the railways more efficient.

Now Osama Bin Laden was sending planes to crash into tall buildings and Texas was Headteacher, because they could find no-one better, because someone had to be. She'd been appointed after the second round of interviews. The county adviser didn't rate her. The governors weren't sure. She made a nervous start. Highfield wasn't what she was used to. She'd always worked in comps and made her way through obedience. Anxious that the staff were stick-in-the-mud she threw her weight around. She'd read in an American book of management techniques that playing one person off against another is a good way to maintain control.

"When Joan Cairns retires I'll be able to do things differently in maths," she told a young mathematician.

She approached a teacher in the corridor and asked if she was considering early retirement. She never missed an opportunity to criticise one member of staff to another. She promoted hockey which she thought more democratic than lacrosse. She feared the authorities would be on her back for being laggardly; the place had to change and she had been appointed to change it.

Sprick knew the school couldn't stand still, but its recent past was her life.

"Parents like tradition," she said to Texas.

"Tradition is an excuse for laziness."

Sprick spread the word among the staff: Texas thinks you're lazy. What she'd said to one member of staff was repeated to another. The negative feeling towards her began to grow. People felt she wasn't on their side, they were undermined. They watched askance as she strode through the staff-room, her head cocked back, her fixed smile showing her large teeth. They detected criticism in her tone of voice. They believed every new policy was a plot against them.

Texas needed to win them round. For a long time most of the staff had wanted the one-hour-fifteen minute, decades-old lunch-break shortened. It remained because the P.E. staff had lacrosse turnouts. Lacrosse was sacrosanct. The school had produced a long line of county players and even a couple of internationals, but the eternal pause left most pupils idle and finding mischief. In the afternoon, they were over-excited, tired, unwilling. No-one wanted to offend the sports staff, but everyone wanted a shorter break. Texas thought the existing arrangement un-American. What would they do in Dallas? Why, they'd do what was modern! Traditional values in a modern setting! And wasn't lunch for wimps? Wasn't this the change to win the staff to her side?

Indifferent, Sprick went with the sportswomen for the sake of taking on Texas.

"But the survey shows clearly most staff want a change."

"So?"

"So they're unhappy with the existing arrangement."

"Tough."

"I think that's unhelpful."

Sprick snorted and shrugged her shoulders.

"I've drawn up three possibilities. We'll get the staff to vote and then I'll confirm the choice with the governors and the county. We should be able to shift next September."

"Lacrosse is very important here. Lots of parents send their girls because they'll play for the school. And sixth form numbers depend on them. Undermining lacrosse undermines the school."

"I'm not undermining anybody, it's what the staff want."

"It's weak leadership to give in to the staff."

Texas blenched. She stared at Sprick who sat stiffly staring back at her blankly.

"I'm behaving democratically. If I impose my will on the staff they'll be up in arms."

"You can't be a Headteacher and a democrat."

Texas looked at her opponent. She would do anything to controvert. And she was spreading disaffection amongst the staff.

"I'm the Head. I've been appointed to change the culture in this school...."

"What's wrong with the culture?"

"It's out of date. It needs modernising."

"Lacrosse isn't out of date."

"That's ridiculous! I'm not opposed to lacrosse."

"But you're making things impossible for the sports staff."

"They can practice after school."

"Not in winter."

"The needs of lacrosse can't dominate the school!"

"Why not?"

"Because that's what's wrong with this place. It thinks it's a little Roedean and it isn't. It serves everyone. It has to become inclusive."

"Spare me the buzzwords."

Texas put the alternatives before the staff who voted heavily for the shortest option. She ignored Sprick, had the plan passed by the governors, ratified by the County and implemented on 1st September.

What the majority of staff had long argued for, they had won. Texas had given it them. Yet their suspicion of her grew.

"Waste of space!" they could be heard to say.

Sprick was delighted. She and Texas stopped talking to one another. Sprick had sensed from the first Texas's lack of confidence. Her public school mentality clicked in. People who lacked confidence, shy people, quiet people, people who didn't use their elbows and knees, who didn't push to the front of the queue and promote their inflated view of their importance and competence were natural victims. She'd witnessed some nasty bullying as a pupil. There was a girl in her year who feared water. The P.E. mistress forced her into the pool. She kicked and spluttered and panicked. She couldn't even swim a width with a float held before her. The bullies waited till the P.E. mistress left the side and dragged the victim to the deep end, shoved her head under till the bubbles rose.

"Get that girl out of the water!"

But secretly the mistress sided with the bullies. She hated a weakling. She loathed a girl who couldn't swim or run. The school turned a blind eye to most bullying. It was looked on as character-building. Only the worst examples, when a girl lost an eye by being locked in a laundry basket while sticks were poked through its sides or another had hair spray forced up her nose, resulted in firm action. But the matter was always hushed up. Above all, the reputation of the school must not suffer.

Sprick didn't want to take part in bullying but nor did she want to be bullied. She was a big lass, athletic and able to take care of herself. But the bullies were sly. They never left themselves vulnerable. They operated in groups. If they chose you as a victim, your time was very hard. So Sprick joined in the mockery of the weaklings, the outsiders. They were fair game. And the bullies left her alone, apart from the odd nasty incident when some ugly-minded prefect would whip away the glasses without which she was helpless.

"Can you see me, Sprick! Come and get your specs. I'm over here."

But when she moved, she was tripped and, flat on her face, was laughed at. She learned to stand still, back into a corner and wait. She was poor sport. They never made her cry. They grew bored.

Now, thirty-five years after leaving school, the smell of a weakling stirred the old responses.

Sprick had believed she would be a Headteacher but once she'd started to climb at Highfield, she didn't want to leave. It was a prestigious place with a large sixth-form, a middle-class catchment, an impressive tradition. If things fell right, the headship might come to her. So she pushed, played the game and waited. On the first occasion she was too young and on the second too old. She'd risen to Head of Sixth-Form and Deputy Head. She would have to be content.

But Texas provided an opportunity.

If she were to fail, if she were to leave, if she were to be forced out, there might be a chance, even if only temporarily. And if that temporary elevation fell within her final three years, it could make a significant difference to her pension. Might there not be a chance of a long-term promotion? She'd done it before. She had never had to make an application, fill in a form, go through an interview, and she'd slid up the greasy pole all the same. To end her career as Head, to see her salary go up by ten grand , to have a much bigger pension: it was attractive and satisfying. But she couldn't do it alone. She and

Texas at loggerheads wasn't enough. The staff had to turn against her enemy. She had to be isolated. She had to feel the negativity of her colleagues, day in day out. Sprick knew that a little poison can spread swiftly. She was subtle, almost understated. But she talked frankly to her confidantes on the staff, those she had taken under her wing, the future of the school.

Sprick noticed Texas spent more and more time in her office. She knew the major concern of the staff was discipline. Pupils were defying teachers at every turn. Some classes were unteachable. The school would get to the point of permanent exclusion; the parents hired a barrister; there was a technicality. The daily humiliation of being treated as skivvies by cocky teenagers drove some staff into depression, others ran for early retirement, some gave up the ghost and the pupils ran riot in their rooms. Sprick encouraged her colleagues to put pressure on Texas. She dug in her heels: poor discipline was a result of poor teaching. It was the government's line; it was an American idea; she liked it. But being blamed for the epidemic of regression and boorishness among young people made the staff resentful. Why doesn't she do something? She's the Head! She should set the tone. Finally, Texas gave in. She would speak to the whole school in assembly.

She stood on the stage, Sprick seated to her left.

" I have to speak to you this morning about something my staff have asked me to speak to you about. It's not a thing I like to have talk about but I have to talk about it. Some of you and I know it is only some of you aren't doing what you're here for. I'm not happy. My staff aren't happy. If you think it's funny to talk all the way through a lesson. If you give cheek to your teachers. If you never do your homework. What do I say to you? I say maybe you shouldn't be here. Why should you be here? Some of you think the rules aren't for you. Well, the rules are for everyone and the rules will apply to everyone. I've seen things around the school, it may be the graffiti thing, it may be the litter thing, it may just be walking around with your blouse hanging out, but I've seen things I don't like. I don't like them. I want them to change. They will have to change. We've had new toilets. I go to those new toilets and what do I find? Someone's turned on all the taps and left them running. Is that funny? Is that the way to treat what's provided for your benefit? It won't do. And you know what my motto is? It's something I learned in America........"

Sprick's mouth curled into a smug, sardonic little smile. To stand in front of the girls, of the entire school and by implication suggest they were all letting her down, was the very worst thing she could do. By goading her into it, Sprick had hastened her downfall. In truth, Sprick had no complaint about the girls' behaviour. The truly disruptive and disaffected were no more than a passing irritant. In the solvent of middle-class conformity their recalcitrance quickly dissolved. She'd talked up the seriousness, claimed teachers were swimming against an impossible current, predicted a parental revolt. Texas had gone for it like a salmon for a fly. Now she was going to be caught as she leapt and clubbed to death.

Most of the staff were pleased, but many pupils, as Sprick predicted, turned sour. They weren't to blame. They felt they were being told off for nothing. The ill-feeling spread and within days someone spray painted on a wall : TEXAS MUST GO. Sprick was thrilled.

The pupils' behaviour didn't change. Texas stayed behind her office door as much as possible. At a morning briefing, someone asked her to explain a decision.

"This isn't the forum," she said.

The teacher protested, Texas lost her temper, closed the meeting and ordered the staff to their classrooms. The following day she was absent. Sprick started to feel sure the Headship would fall into her lap. She walked past Texas in the corridor and ignored her. She kept feeding stories of incompetence and stupidity. Whenever Texas appeared before the staff, the atmosphere was sinister. It was that vicious and cruel mood that seizes groups when they're sure they are right and have an enemy in their sights; the mentality of the pack baring its teeth; the howling of the crowd that drowns the modest voice of reason. People whose true judgement of Texas was essentially neutral found themselves drawn into the vortex and condemned her out loud. Cowards who would never have stood up to a strong Head they knew was wrong, began to throw their weight around.

After the Christmas holiday, Texas announced she was leaving. Sprick knew they would never appoint in time for the next term. She was home and dry. She began to feel justified. Shouldn't she have been appointed to a Headship long ago? But when she took over, she found herself fearing the staff. Supposing they turned on her? Supposing they saw her as weak? Supposing they put two and two to-gether? Those loyal to her who knew they would be rewarded put the word out: she was working hard, she had the best interests of the school at heart, everyone should back her. The mood swung behind her, though in truth, little changed, but she surfed the wave of popu-larity and buffed-up respect. One day she brought sheaves of docu-ments and armfuls of files into a staff meeting and dumped them un-ceremoniously on the table to show how overwhelmed she was.

She managed a paltry term as Acting Head. The following Septem-ber a new, young woman took over. Sprick made herself like her. Undermining one Head was enough for anyone, and in any case, there were no stakes to play for. The new woman did much the same as Texas, but she was subtle, discreet, diplomatic. Put in the picture by the school adviser, she kept carefully on the right side of Sprick. She was on the verge of retiring. No need to face her down.

"You know," one member of staff remarked to another, "one of the things everyone hated Texas for was not allowing school trips. But have you noticed, this new woman is closing down even more."

"Yeah, do they ever change?."

It was suggested Sprick might intercede on their behalf. Two older colleagues who thought themselves close to her were delegated.

"People feel closing down on the trips is narrowing what the school offers."

Sprick nodded.

"Some of these are long-established. A lot of hard work has gone into them."

"I know," she said.

She held out her palms and raised her shoulders. Her mouth turned down in sympathetic regret.

"It's the new ideology," she said. "Children should be in the class-room."

When the supplicants left, Sprick went to speak to the Head.

"I'd better warn you, people are getting hot under the collar about trips. I've told them where you stand, of course."

"Thanks for that, Meryl."

As Sprick's career neared its last few weeks, she began to put in review her years of making her way, playing one rival off against another. She was proud of her strategy. To think of herself as Machiavellian gave her a sense of esteem. She'd made it to Headteacher, however briefly, and the boost to her pension would be a constant reminder. Nearly forty years. It concertinaed in her mind. She could run through the major events in seconds. She'd made a memorable contribution. Yet in spite of herself, in defiance of her efforts to convince herself it had been a bagatelle, she couldn't help returning to the thought that her ousting of Texas was her greatest achievement.

BIRTWISTLE & BEETHOVEN JUST WON'T DO

Sycamore Primary served the poorest estate in town, and the town itself was poor. Once there'd been industry: after the war, trucks were made in a large, low factory of yellowish brick on whose roof sat proudly a shiny, finished red lorry, symbol of free enterprise, craftsmanship and progress; a metal tubing factory was established in a former warehouse with impenetrable windows and pipes rising high above the slate roof from which smoke and steam drifted skyward day and night. These two big works gave employment to thousands of men, trained dozens of apprentices each year and kept the local economy buoyant. Throughout the sixties the little place flourished, in a small way. It was provincial and unimaginative, but people found work, some choice housing was built in the leafier parts, its heart beat steadily and no-one had reason to think this might not go on forever, or at least long enough. Even then, of course, there was poverty and a big gap between the thriving and the make-do-and-menders. But socialism was in the air, the future would see the rich get poorer and the poor get richer, and the liberalism of the time meant the children from the council estate went happily to their school each morning, where their teachers did their best, there was a passing scent of joy in the air, a bit of grass to run around on and the big question of how to prevent the poor being failed was dealt with where it should be: by those who claimed to have the answers and asked for votes to prove it. But the oil price shocks of the early seventies applied the brake and little by little, things went into reverse. Mrs Thatcher's dislike of industrial workers and fawning complaisance towards financiers, ensured the closure of the factories. Shops were boarded up. Drug pushers hung round the bus station. At length two big, downmarket supermarkets opened. The qualified middle-classes found work in the nearby cities, but those at the bottom sank into the sludge. Sycamore Estate was a place people lived only if they couldn't move elsewhere. When the OFSTED inspectors arrived they found serious educational weaknesses. The Head put pressure on the staff and they pulled it round. But a collapsing gable-end can only be propped for so long. Eventually, the place was put in Special Measures and the witch hunt began.

Jeanie Isaacs, one of those women from the working-class who made the best of the educational opportunities that were part of the post-

217

war consensus, and wanting to get on a little, as society urged, had nevertheless felt a keen desire to put something back in recompense for all she felt she'd received, and had chosen teaching because it provided simultaneously a decent income, a sense of purpose and of staying in tune with the undogmatic, democratic socialism of her parents. She'd been Head for eleven years, had done everything she could think of, was respected by her staff in spite of her abrupt manners, popular with the parents because of her firm hand on the tiller, but knew they were coming for her.

"Maybe I should just throw in the towel," she said to her husband. "No, remember Clive Jenkins's old mantra: never resign, always make them sack you, it's more lucrative."

"This isn't the seventies, Jim."

She was old style. She didn't like numbers in boxes, she liked children. The slick inspectors, trained to find evidence like sniffer dogs to hunt out cannabis, turned up a miserable catalogue of failures. They even told her her desk was untidy.

"I couldn't believe it. He stood in front of me in my own office and said "Such disorder is indicative". I was speechless."

"Bloody fascist," said Jim.

"How can I stop them?"

"Build an underground resistance."

There was no doubt, according to the new strictures, the need for every human relation to be reduced to a number, for every advance in a child's perilous and difficult progress to mastery to become a statistic, for teachers to cease to be imaginative purveyors of their enthusiasms and to be transformed into operatives mechanistically applying what was decided facelessly elsewhere, she was a failure. Judged by a different set of criteria, she might have been deemed brilliant in spite of her third-rate mind, her lack of reading and her tendency to believe the mere fact of being schooled could correct every perversity, dissolve every evil inclination and create in society at large the atmosphere of a Methodist Sunday picnic. But the barbarians had come through the school gates. They wore power suits and spoke a curious language composed of a series of assertions expressed in an impenetrable jargon, which admitted no dialogue. The chief of the invading tribe was Scott Tyebard whose oddly set expression which modulated hardly at all when he spoke, as if one mood were enough for a human mind and all the music of his heart were played on a single string, was enhanced by his prominent, heavy glasses with thick, gold-plated arms which lodged behind the ears his short cropped hair made sit out from his bullet head. He had a chunky, rugby player's build and wore his collars and suits tight so he looked as if an atomic explosion were about to take place in his thorax. At once he reminded Jeanie of those thick-necked, swollen-chested terriers on short, thick leads held by skinny young boys and girls who struggled to restrain the vicious energy of their pet: animals with a hunting instinct and a fierce protectiveness of their narrow territory, ill-suited to human communities, creatures of muscle and tooth whose brains have not been civilised by long contact with people, whose instinct to fight and kill has never been layered over with more emollient intentions.

His intervention team, descending on the school like hyenas on a wounded gazelle, lost no time in tearing out its heart, devouring its liver, strewing its guts in the playground and dumping the blame on Jeanie like Saudi Arabian fanatics dumping stone on an adulterous woman. She refused to resign. They sent her to see the Senior Human Resources Officer at County Hall. The building was square and squat in spite of its six storeys. Built by the thrifty yet ostentatious, hard-working Victorians, a monument to their civic pride, the staircases were wide marble, the banisters polished oak, the corridors as expansive as football pitches, the Committee Rooms panelled and carved like the sitting-rooms of country estates; but Ms Bewley's office was modern. It was tucked away up three flights of skinny, vinyl-tiled stairs and accessed through a redundant little staff kitchen. The table was veneered and had metal legs. The chairs were plastic. The ceiling had been lowered to save on heating. The walls were bare. Ms Bewley herself was a smart, efficient young woman who wore her officiousness like a veteran wears his medals. Jeanie who was fifty-five and had three children older than her, sat opposite with a sense that she was about to be put in her place by an infant. She stiffened. She'd spent thirty-three years in control.

"Given the position of the school…" the young woman said, looking down at her notes.

"I'm sorry?"

Ms Bewley looked up, her dark eyes blank.

"Given that the school's in Special Measures, your position becomes untenable."

"The school is in Special Measures because it serves the poorest children in the catchment."

"I'm afraid I can't enter into that kind of discussion…"

"Enter into it? You began it. You're telling me I have to lose my job because the school's in Special Measures. That's just another way of saying I'm to blame. If you're saying that, you should be able to support it."

"I'm afraid that's not part of my job."

"No. Your job is to tell me to resign or I'll be sacked."

"I wouldn't put it as brutally as that, Mrs Isaacs."

"How would you put it?"

"Given the circumstances of the school the authority judges that in the interests of efficiency…"

"Just as I said."

The young woman stuck to her brief, as she'd been trained, and as she believed was her right and duty. She'd taken an M.A. in personnel management and had never found any reason to question what she'd been taught. On the contrary, dutiful adherence to the letter of instruction had brought her quickly to her elevated position, her competitive salary, her one-bedroomed flat in the city centre overlooking a once attractive little square, her two-seater BMW and three foreign holidays a year. She was a great believer in the power of education to create opportunity and advance talent. In her eyes, Mrs Isaacs was a dodo. The struggle for existence, being inherently progressive, must have its victims. Had a dinosaur sat on the other side of the table, she couldn't have been more convinced she was looking at a doomed species. Had she possessed the means to intuit the anguish in the older woman's mind, she would have been astonished. It seemed to her as natural as the rotation of the planets that young people like herself should rise and the old, and she saw Mrs Isaacs as distinctly old, with their outdated ways, their reliance on their judgement, their belief that motivation matters as much or even more than outcomes, must be swept aside. Of course, she didn't want them thrown in dustbins and dumped in the nearest landfill, but that they should retreat from the public scene, tend their gardens, look after their grandchildren, play dominos, do a little voluntary work, take advantage of their bus passes, bake, fettle, undertake some light reading, join a yoga class, research their family history, get to know the tow paths of the local canals, organise charity coffee mornings and be as unobtrusive as possible seemed obvious.

Jeanie left the interview impotently seething

"I have to resign," she said to Jim over coffee in Starbucks.

"Why?"

"Otherwise they sack me. If I resign, I go without working my notice and I get three months pay tax free."

"Buggers!"

"I wish I could afford to make them sack me and take them to tribunal."

"We're not on our uppers."

"We're not millionaires either."

"Principles are always costly."

"I never thought I'd end my career like this."

"I believe those were Mussolini's last words."

"Stop being facetious, this is serious."

"Yes, Jeanie, it's so serious we've got to learn to laugh at it. Sooner or later the tide will turn and these miserable time-servers will be consigned to oblivion. But for the time being, we've got to get by and the best attitude is to take the piss."

There was a tearful little ceremony in the school hall where the children applauded loudly and cheered heartily, in their benign innocence believing they were sending away the grandmotherly Headteacher to a pleasant land of desired and blissful ease. Jeanie was gracious and beaming but once at home she collapsed into weeping and couldn't stop thinking that her school, her children, her life's meaning had been cruelly taken away.

In her place they appointed Ms Milner, a no-nonsense Welsh woman who had always managed to conceal her mediocre intelligence through extreme effort and obedience, powered by chronic fear of failure and punishment. She understood her brief. All her life she'd been a conduit so she slipped easily into the role of carrying out the bidding of her masters. Cascading from the Department For Children Schools and Families, affectionately known as Carpets and Soft Furnishings, descending as irresistibly as a boulder down a mountain came the conventional wisdom, which like all such stupidity was as empty as it is rigid, that schools never fail because their intake is impossible; because the odds are just too great; because the children come from homes without rich conversation where they hear a reduced vocabulary and numeracy goes no further than the lottery numbers; where they are read to not nearly enough and from which they venture out into the wider, enlightening world of society and culture hardly at all; where the expectations are low , the intelligence defeated; where there are more televisions than books. No, if schools don't rise to the required level, if the statistics don't please the bureaucrats for whom a child is a set of results, the only explanation, the sole possible cause, is that the teachers aren't up to scratch.

From her first day in the place, Ms Milner was looking for victims, because without them, how could she convince her superiors she was doing her job?

Only child of a pair of teachers who had supervised her homework with the discipline of diligent Chapel-goers, she had never ventured an inch from the path laid out for her and thought her success proof of the rightness of her judgement; but like all such people, whose sense of self rests entirely on the admonition of authority, she was haunted by the fear of falling. The problem of walking a tightrope put in place by others is that although it spans a trickling stream only two feet below, the anxiety attendant on refusing to walk it makes it appear to stretch over a bottomless abyss of shame, misery and perdition. Kirsty Milner's mind was constantly offended by what she saw as shortcomings in others. And just as our brains are apt to deceive us into conflating beauty and virtue, in people's physical defects we often believe we have spotted a fundamental flaw in character.

It was Mary Birtwistle's misfortune to be excessively thin.

As soon as Milner saw her, she thought of anorexia. In fact, Mary ate hearty. She was a happy if somewhat heedless little woman who indulged a taste for crisps, dark chocolate, especially filled with nuts, Dandelion and Burdock and red wine and who, to the despair of her slimming friends and relations, never gained an ounce.

"It's because she's never still," said her boyfriend. "She's wick. Even in bed she fidgets like a kid with chickenpox."

"You exaggerate, Tom," she admonished, pushing another fist of crisps into her mouth.

But it was true. She was one of those people forever on the go. She seemed to meld with her activity and her leisure might amount to ten minutes in front of the television, or quarter of an hour with a contentless magazine, before she'd jump up and tidy the entire house, or hoover every corner, or climb a step-ladder to clean the windows, or take the hoe to the weedless flower beds or tackle an Annapurna of marking or spend hours on elaborate preparation. Not that she was always as effective as busy. It was the sheer joy of being immersed in something which propelled her and if the windows were a little smeared, her books not perfectly marked when she'd finished, she merely laughed and shrugged. She'd enjoyed herself and prevented time weighing heavy.

She'd always wanted to be a teacher because she loved being with children and there was no idle time. She'd worked away blithely at Three Moons for seven years without ever having a complaint made against her, taken a small responsibility and moved through the ludicrous Threshold, never had any reason to seriously doubt herself and in spite of everything, the sometimes difficult parents, the children who found learning alien, the mad prescriptions from on high, the inadequacy of resources, she loved her job. Sometimes she found herself temporarily confused by what she had to teach. Maths and science strained her mind and there were moments when she would have to stop, pick up a pen and paper and laboriously work out what was half of three eights. What came easily into her head was that it must be one and a half eighths, but then she had to take a number, sixteen for example, divide by eight and multiply by three. So if three eighths of sixteen was six, one and a half eighths must be three and then it struck her that half of three eighths must be three sixteenths. She was always undermined by having to do this and wondered why she couldn't simply remember. At times she would sit with her cup of tea in the little upstairs staff-room that looked out over the playing fields and her confidence would seem to fly from her like the birds heading for the woods. But she always perked up and dismissed her self-doubt. Some of her colleagues couldn't spell Mississippi or Mediterranean without a dictionary. She just had a little quirk with figures. What mattered was her enthusiasm, her commitment, her love of the job and the children.

Milner was under pressure from the start. The Authority wanted action and that meant nailing the weak teachers, an essentially savage process much like a pride of lions' instinct for the weak or spavined in a herd of wildebeest. As Milner had to find weak teachers there had to be some. Had all the teachers been excellent the least excellent would have been brought down. Mary's skin and bone build setting in train Milner's negative responses, her absence of punctiliousness and preference for enthusiasm over detail, her lack of affinity for pernickety record keeping and hair-splitting form-filling made her a natural victim as surely as a hobbled new-born on an African savannah. So, in accordance with the improvement plan drawn up by the governing body, a document of such minute, redundant detail and mindlessly restrictive intrusiveness it contained wisdom such as: *raise the standard of teaching and learning by raising expectations of what children can achieve* as if somehow or somewhere teachers had ever believed it possible to raise standards by lowering expectations of what children can achieve; or such innovatory and soaringly insightful targets as: *all classroom staff know the progress that children are making and intervene as necessary*, a prescription for teachers as enabling as to say to bricklayers, all bricklayers, know what a brick is and can lay them in straight lines; or exotic enlightenment such as: *pupils are informed of their progress after assessments have been completed*, just to put a stop to that age-old practice among educators of telling pupils their progress before it's been assessed; in short, a document as empty and worthless as a statutory manual for cyclists dictating that: cyclists shall put one foot on each pedal; they shall make the wheels turn by exerting pressure on the pedals: they shall steer the bicycle by use of the handlebars; they shall slow or stop the bicycle by applying the brakes; they shall change into an appropriate gear for climbing hills; they shall cycle on the left.

Milner began to stalk her prey.

If a woman has decided her marriage is at an end, if in her deepest, hidden self, that realm where thinking takes place in images whose primitive power overawes all language and logic, she knows she no longer wants to stay with her husband, nothing he can do will bring her round. He might be the most devoted and irreproachable spouse

224

in history but she will see him negatively. The very way he laces his shoes will drive her mad. Nothing the Jews could have done would have changed Hitler's mind. Once an irrational prejudice is unleashed, trying to resist it with reason is as futile as trying to stop the earth turning. So it was in schools. For decades the idea had been abroad that the profession was riddled with incompetence. One Secretary of State after another, puzzled, bemused and defeated by the stubborn failure to succeed of hundreds of schools and tens of thousands of pupils, looked for an exculpating explanation, for none of them was willing to admit they were in charge of a system whose workings were as mysterious to them as sexual attraction, nor to confess it was overburdened with expectations and the problems of deprivation and its attendant evils couldn't be resolved by learning to order a cup of coffee in French or to find the area of a sphere. The malicious genius of ambition and careerism which drove mediocrities into politics, gave rise to the easy notion that the teachers were hopeless, feckless, left-wing, lazy, chaotic, feather-bedded, unambitious, trendy; in short were failing the children and must be stopped. The evil genie released, it wasn't long before figures were plucked from the air: was it fifteen thousand teachers who should be sacked or seventeen thousand? Did it really matter? Finally, weren't they all guilty, even if some were less guilty than others? The apotheosis of this Salem mentality arrived, as was to be expected, in a demented and laughable distortion of language according to which satisfactory is not good enough. The original sin of a teacher was to be a teacher and that the regime celebrated the good or outstanding few only condemned more definitively the satisfactory, and therefore unsatisfactory, majority.

Milner had absorbed the precepts of this twisted and destructive culture as though her life depended on them. Mary Birtwistle had undoubtedly been a satisfactory teacher for years, and that was proof beyond question of her incompetence. All that remained was to gather the evidence. Before her first observation, Milner went through the children's folders at the end of the day once the other staff had left. As she leafed through the pages of appropriate work, all duly marked according to the school's declared policy, she experienced a little tension of disappointment and irritation. She might find one or two incorrect answers given ticks, but that wasn't enough. Then, like a stranger lost in an unfamiliar city who unexpectedly emerges from an unrecognised side street onto the square where her hotel lies, she found an unmarked piece of writing. Hurriedly she went through file after file and to her delight the same piece was without red pen in all of them. It was merely one piece of work, but it was the sin of omission that pointed to damnation. When, a few days later she observed Mary's lesson, one no worse than many she had taught herself when her work was in the classroom, a lesson neither perfectly planned nor executed, but one which kept the fifteen children working and intent for the greater part of the time and left them, if not with a precise understanding of the nature of the way physical forces work on an object, a precision, of course, lacking most of the time in ninety percent of humanity's minds, at least the beginning of an understanding to be subsequently revived, deepened and extended, she picked up the minor mismatch between the plan and the delivery, inevitably thought the pace too slow, pace being as much an obsession of inspectors as masturbation or contraception of the Pope, made a note of a modicum of untidiness on the teacher's desk and went away with her clipboard as satisfied as a licentious husband after a visit to a whore.

The following day she called Mary into her office and handed her the report of her observation.

"So, what do you think of that?"

"Well, not too bad."

"Do you accept my criticisms?"

"In a way. You might be right that I didn't deliver the lesson exactly as planned, but that often happens."

"But that's not okay, is it?"

Mary suffered that little nervous shock we all experience when we discover, like a child lifting a rock in expectation of some hidden delight only to find a crawling mass of beetles, leatherbacks, centipedes, ants and the wriggling bodies of swollen worms, our positive, generous mood isn't reciprocated by our interlocutor, friend, colleague, lover or spouse. That sudden expulsion from what was thought to be a territory of friendliness into a barrenness of loneliness and alienation can be set off by the smallest harshness, the most apparently trivial brittle hauteur. She looked into Milner's eyes in a reaction more automatic than conscious, hoping, as everyone does in such moments, to find some small glimmer of tenderness or understanding that might provide an exit from isolation, but the other woman had raised her chin and slightly narrowed her eyes in a judgemental demeanour. Mary looked down at the report pretending to read, too flustered to focus.

"I don't say the lesson was perfect."

"No-one expects lessons to be perfect but we do expect them to meet the minimum standards."

This suggestion that, after seven years of happy, untroubled service what she had been doing day after day, lesson after son wasn't even minimally adequate couldn't have undermined Mary more than if the floor had opened up beneath her chair. At once she saw what was ahead of her. There came in to her mind the heart-rending image of her leaving the school having been sacked and at the same time she felt all the means she might have had to defend herself collapse like an insolvent bank. She knew there was nothing more to say and in Milner's look detected that essential cruelty of the time-server who, finally, will comply with any stupidity, recycle any lie, be minutely conscientious in unfairness before they will put their own advancement at risk. In the simplicity of this relation, that Milner would do nothing to jeopardise her own position and everything to defend it, Mary saw the inexorable working out of her   demise.

"What I've decided to do, Mary, is put you on informal support. There'll be a meeting with someone from HR and you are entitled to have a friend or union representative with you."

"What exactly is informal support?"

"It's a programme of monitoring and help to try to eliminate the weaknesses from your teaching."

The benign definition did nothing to allay Mary's sense of unfairness; on the contrary, the apparently bland formulation only reinforced her appreciation of the nastiness behind it, just as the neat brevity and uncluttered clarity of the final solution could only bring dread into a sensitive mind. She left Milner's office a changed woman and in some quiet corner of her mind whose workings she never put into words, knew the life she had been living was over, just as a bereaved relative knows that though grieving will alleviate the anguish, life is forever, irrevocably changed. All day she went about her tasks in a way that wouldn't have alerted a casual observer to the transformation within; she sat in the little staff-room at lunchtime eating her sandwiches and chatting about nothing in the way that had once brought her such pleasure but which now seemed empty and false because as she talked she could eliminate neither the consciousness of the insult she'd suffered nor the expectation that an inexorable process set in train by people in power, backed by law and undertaken to justify the rackety ideas of politicians, would, like a Stalinist show-trial or some Kafkaesque fantasy, prove her unworthiness and leave her bereft.

"She's putting me on informal support," she said to Tom.

"What does that mean?"

She heard the quake in his voice which meant he feared what was to come, didn't know what to do about it and wondered whether it was, in some arcane way he knew nothing about, justified.

"It means I get observed every week, my planning is checked, my marking is checked, the MIT team come and see me and if everything isn't perfect I'm going to be working in Tesco."

"They can't sack you, surely!"

"They can do it in no time. It's a rapid process, Tom. There's no gentleness about these things any more, no recognition of past service. If they need victims to make it look as though they're doing something, they find 'em."

"Have you contacted the union?"

"I've left a message."

"Well, they'll know how to deal with it."

"We're up against a juggernaut."

"But they can't sack you if you do everything they ask."

"I'm already working till eleven every night. You see how impossible it is. It's a good trick isn't it, burden people till they can't cope then come after them for not coping."

"I thought the union had a policy on workload."

"Oh yeah, don't do bulk photocopying or collect money. That's going to help me when they come looking for every speck of dust in my classroom."

The union's District Secretary arranged to meet, so late one afternoon they got together in Starbucks, two women who might have met for an anodyne chat after shopping, sitting at a table in the corner by the window, trying to keep their voices down. June Egger was in her late fifties, a former P.E. teacher who now filled her timetable with R.E. and humanities and had taken over the union role because no-one else wanted it, even though it gave a full day a week away from teaching, and though she did her best in this as in everything else, hers was a finger-in-the-dyke role, first aid for the bullied, the worn-out, the weary, the earmarked, and once matters became really serious she passed them up to the Regional Officer who understood the recondite provisions of compromise agreements and severance deals. She listened sympathetically, read through the paperwork and said she would do all she could to help, but Mary was left with the sense of a woman almost at the end of her career, well-meaningly fulfilling a union role but without any real bite or potency. Two weeks later they met with Milner and the Senior HR Officer to be presented with a detailed programme laid out A4 and landscape with the pages divided into five columns headed: Problem area, Current performance, Expectations, How to achieve, How/who monitors. The first column contained formulations like*: Numeracy unit plans lack personalisation* and in response the second column had: *Personalisation of planning meets the needs of the class*. It was one of those bureaucratic documents, devoid of simple, direct expressions and swollen with pomposity as if a parent were to say to a teenager: Your bedroom shows little evidence of preoccupation with personal hygiene. Mary was hoping June would know how to pull it apart but she simply sat and listened, nodded and afterwards stressed to her how important it was now to meet all the expectations before the next review.

The more Mary read the plan, the more her head swam. It was an are-you-still-beating-your wife document, her guilt and inadequacy seeped from it like the stench from a bin of rotting food.

"It reminds me of the days I used to knock around the pubs and clubs as a teenager," said Tom, " and some kid would come over and say: 'Are you lookin' at my girlfriend?' And you'd say: 'No." And he'd say: 'Why not?"

"That's exactly how I feel, except in your case you could always have asked the kid outside."

"Oh yeah, but he had his mates waitin'. Thirty of 'em with knuckle dusters and studded belts. When people are lookin' for trouble, they're lookin' for trouble, and these buggers are lookin' for trouble."

"I don't think I can go through with it," said Mary.

"You have to. Think on your feet. Use your wits. Be cleverer than they are. They're only a bunch of arse-licking bureaucrats after all."

"But like your bully, they twist your arm up your back and push you into a corner. Whatever you do won't be good enough."

"There must be a way round it."

"They've got their mates with 'em, Tom. Knuckle dusters, studded belts. The politicians behind this are the ones who brought barbarism to Iraq. What do they care about a few teachers put through the mill?"

"There'll be no teachers left if they don't back off."

"Maybe that's their plan. Staff the schools with teaching assistants and save a fortune."

Tom sat back in his armchair with the air of a man thinking about something for the first time, like a child told gravity is a phenomenon of universal attraction which conforms to a very strict law of distance, and whose simple view of things falling to the ground just because the earth attracts them is dispelled forever and replaced by something much more abstract, difficult and less comfortable. Was it true things had gone so far the politicians were seeking to reduce teachers to the level of operatives? There came into his head, with all the unnerving, exaggerated clarity of a dream, the vision of a school in which a core of qualified specialists plan and provide lessons for a body of para-teachers who deliver them to the letter. Mary, looking at his distracted expression, felt terribly alone, in spite of his good natured support, for she knew she was part of something essentially evil which had found a way of passing itself off as good and improving, as all forms of evil must, even the very worst; in fact, it occurred to her, the more vicious an evil, the more elevated, pure and liberating must be its excuses, which was why the educational rhetoric was otiose with excessively sincere promises of betterment, of improving the lives of children, why it offered an unattainable educational never-never-land while daily the system ground on in its rusty, inadequate way serving the needs of politicians more than those of pupils. Painfully aware of the gulf between this dishonesty and her own essentially pragmatic view: a generous desire to educate every child and to see each one blossom and flourish tempered by a realistic appreciation of the imponderables, difficulties and perversities which hobble every system, she realised she'd become an outsider, her way of thinking and feeling was despised, there was in the air a manic belief in absolute success and permanent improvement and an attendant faith that any putative knowledge or accomplishment can be turned into a crude numerical measure, and what had been lost was the recognition that though a factory might turn out nuts and bolts of regulation identity, a school turns out nothing, produces nothing. Learning is a process and only the process matters for it gives rise to minds and minds resolutely resist reduction to measurement.

For six weeks she worked from seven till close to midnight in an effort to make sure everything demanded was fulfilled, but at the next review, although Milner admitted she'd improved significantly, they renewed informal support for a further eight weeks and imposed a new set of targets. She wept the following weekend away, then buckled down and spent a further eight weeks with virtually no life beyond school, two months of days so long and weary she knew she was working to little avail, nodding over marking at eleven at night, days without joy and worst of all, days when she began to resent the children she taught. Though she could reason they were in no way to blame, she found herself facing them and filling with tension. There were three pupils in particular, two boys and a girl, children she'd always liked and striven hard to help; statemented children so slow at every task that it was virtually certain they would fail any lesson objective set before them. She began to see this trio as the certain cause of her downfall.

"You know, Tom," she said, "I'm starting to hate the children."

"No, you're just overwrought."

"Seriously, I am. I hate them because they've become the source of my humiliation. I used to like them, even the little tykes, but now I can't see them as kids. They're grades, targets, levels, numbers in boxes, and somebody's coming for me if they're not up to scratch."

"You'll get over it. This stuff will pass. It's doomed. Try to get it in perspective. You'll be back to your old self before long."

"I don't think so. It's gone. The old relationships have been destroyed. Once, the school was a roof over your head where you got on with teaching. Now it represents a system. Schools are exam factories and we're having productivity deals imposed on us. When you're looking at children in that way, it's impossible to like them anymore. You don't have the freedom to like them."

"Take the freedom. Forget the targets and numbers in boxes and see the kids as kids."

"I think that's the point, Tom, they're only children in context. We're obliterating their childhoods. Everything they do is measured. I've suddenly realised how much I'm being changed by this."

"It's a stressful time, but you'll get through it. Once you've wound down a bit you'll see the children through different eyes."

"I wish I could believe that."

As the second review approached, a sense of dread came over her. She knew what she'd done wouldn't be good enough, as surely as a Calvinist knows her good works make no difference to god's *a priori* condemnation. She laughed to herself at the thought that she was caught in a warmed-over Calvinism, as if dormant in the collective mind for decades that vicious doctrine had been sparked alive by some social virus, everyone now fearful of condemnation, chasing their tails to prove an impossible worth, and she, who considered gradations of worth stupid and malicious, fighting for her survival.

There were four at the meeting. It was a bright day and the Head's office was full of light, as if to offset the tension, and it struck Mary how apparently normal the most extraordinary situations can be: the young Human Resources officer smart in a dark jacket and trousers with a crisp white blouse, diligently making notes, Milner's neat, little burgundy suit, her reddish hair beautifully brushed, the clever cut showing off her white throat and the expanse of her upper chest, for she was one of those women who like to show off their cleavage, especially if there are men around, and Mary had noticed how part of her repertoire of tricks to get the male staff to do as they were told, was to stand in front of them with a bold, little look of defiance on her face and the dark valley between her big, snowy breasts clearly visible; at times, she would even, in a small, unconscious but devastatingly effective gesture, run her fingers from her throat down to the swoop of her neckline which she'd adjust while looking her interlocutor in the eyes; June Egger, reading through the support plan from the previous meeting as if she had some real idea of how to be effective. An unwitting observer might have concluded this was an entirely rational and fair procedure, but for Mary it was a ritual humiliation and a demonstration of her impotence; the impotence of those who are subjected to rules they have no hand in making, judged by those against whom they have no redress, condemned for putative failings they have no means of disproving, though it seemed she did: her union representative was beside her, as if her objections wouldn't be politely listened to and swept aside, as if her pleas for more time wouldn't be received with stony faces.

They discussed progress. Milner raised her anxieties. They called for an adjournment. Mary and June withdrew to a little classroom and sat on the tiny chairs.

"So what do you think?" said June.

"I think they'll go for formal support."

"I think you're right."

"I'm not going through with it," said Mary.

"No?"

"I'll resign."

"I wouldn't do that."

"You're not in my position."

"We'll fight it for you."

"I know you will, June. You've been wonderful, but it's a juggernaut. You can't stop them. Not if they've made up their minds and I'm convinced they have. You know what, I believe if this school wasn't in Special Measures and facing falling rolls, this wouldn't be happening."

"I think you're right."

"I'm not going through with it."

"I'm not allowed to say this to you in my union role, but if I were you I'd go to your doctor. Look up the symptoms of stress. Get yourself some time off . Take it easy for a few weeks. Being more relaxed you'll think straight."

233

"I'd thought of that."

"Well, it's a way of buying time. The last thing you want is to be dragged in front of the GTC and have your licence to teach taken away."

Mary almost laughed, seeing in a sudden little flash of insight, the kind of little flash she'd had many more of since this process began, the emptiness of the pretence that the GTC was equivalent to the BMA or the Law Society, genuine professional closed-shops whose interest was to defend their profession against corruption or erosion and which were truly independent, founded and run by the professions themselves, while the GTC was a government sponsored sham whose essential function was, on the one hand, to help convince the public the teaching profession was being enhanced, on the other, to punish teachers.

"No, I wouldn't want that."

Summoned back, they faced the inevitable and as Mary looked through the new targets, laid out in exactly the same way as the first set, very neat and official, conscientiously produced, she almost began to believe she was in the wrong, that her planning and teaching were poor, that this nailing her down was justified.

"You know, you're right?" said Tom, " it's a productivity deal."

"I know."

" It's just like the things they imposed in factories back in the sixties. It's simply old-fashioned management, screwing all it can out of the workers. Look at the sickness policy she foisted on you and the nonsense about a code of conduct that means if you're drinking in the pub on a Friday and some parents come in you should leave!"

"Sure."

"In the early years of the twentieth century in America, the Ford Motor Co sent its inspectors into workers' homes. That's the mentality. They don't even understand their own system, Mary. They don't even get that all they're buying is your work."

"I suppose they think they're doing the best for the children."

"I don't think so. The best for the children would be to stop testing them and let them learn."

The formal meeting was more stringent, with Milner, her deputy acting as scribe, Scott Tyebard scrubbed like a rugby player straight from the bath, groomed like a teenager on her first date, sporting an expensive suit and watch and giving off the intermittently detectable odour of superior after-shave; Hilary Mitchell, school advisor who had never recovered from the severe bout of excessive egotism which accompanied her promotion and whose prim demeanour and marginally intrusive attitude were the outward signs of a moderately unhinged sense of self-esteem, on one side of the desk, Mary and June on the other. Milner began by reading aloud the review, an account of Mary's failures and studied refusal to mention even the slightest of her successes, after which June was permitted to put her case: she apologised for the unmarked work, she pointed up the eight satisfactory observations, she pleaded for more time, but it was as worthless as asking Stalin for tolerance; the meeting was a necessary show. There would be eight weeks of formal support.

Two days later Mary went to her doctor and complained of being unable to sleep or eat, suffering palpitations, being overcome by negative thoughts and in response to the young G.P.'s questions said no, she didn't smoke, drank no more than a few glasses of wine a week, got plenty of exercise, and finally, she was a teacher.

"Ah!" said the astute young practitioner, looking up from her notes, for she read the papers, "everything all right at work?"

"Hardly, I'm under a cloud and in danger of getting the sack."

She signed her off for two weeks and told her to come back if the symptoms persisted; two weeks became four and four six, enough time for Mary to begin to feel the grip of school release, so that one morning, taking an early walk through the park beneath a fine blue sky with the silver light filling the great open expanse, she experienced herself as unconnected, not responsible, and it occurred to her that Sycamore Primary and even the system it was part of, was a relatively small arena, that she'd allowed it to expand in her mind and assume a significance it didn't deserve, a negative significance which was oppressing her, setting her at odds with herself, making her question herself in destructive ways. The cynical thought occurred to her that, finally, it was just a job, a means to the end of an income, and recoiling from the brutality of such reduction and calculation she revived the idealism that had taken her into teaching, immediately falling into confusion which almost made her dizzy till she increased her pace, focusing on her stride rather than her moral conflict until she found her way back to the saving cynicism. Wasn't it the reverse of the banknote of her idealism? Weren't they both, the concrete cynicism and the soft soil idealism, ways of arriving at ends beyond question? Wasn't she lurching from one rigid certainty to another? All the same, her cynical calculation rescued her and like a shipwrecked sailor who, clinging to driftwood, washes up on the shore of a barren rock of an island without an edible plant or attractive flower and must live for years alone on a diet of fish and insects, hiding in his cave from the fierce winds of winter and the relentless sun of summer, regretting the civilisation he will never see again, his soft bed, the sweet flesh of his lover, the timid storms of the worst months and the caressive warmth of summer, she found this unattractive asylum, in all its ugliness and unwelcoming harshness, a relief, a place of safety, and she understood the conditions that had given rise to her idealism were gone and though she might regret them, they could never be retrieved.

Once begun, she pushed this way of thinking to its conclusion: she had to think selfishly, to calculate her advantage in all things; she'd already had herself signed off on the basis of exaggerated symptoms though she'd not had a day off ill in years, why not then continue and get all she could from the mess she'd found herself in? This way of thinking taking over, she began to feel better: she was no longer facing insuperable forces, she regained a bit of control, and most of all, she wanted her revenge and took pleasure in the idea of the school finding it difficult to cope in her absence, word having come that the supply teacher looking after her class wasn't doing well, a revelation which gave her satisfaction and simultaneously made her reflect on the stupidity of a system which browbeats a teacher into taking time off with stress, on the grounds that she's inadequate, only to employ an inadequate teacher to temporarily take her place, an absurdity which, however, was perfectly in keeping with the current management of the system, whose engagement with reality seemed as shaky as a drunken lunatic's.

"I'm going to stay on the sick as long as I can," she said to Tom.

"Don't you get six months on full pay?"

"Only if you're half dead. They'll come after me quickly and want to know if and when."

"Will you go back?"

"Oh, I might. I was reading something interesting in the paper today about a woman who had depression and her employer didn't make reasonable adjustments so she went for constructive unfair dismissal and won."

"Not your situation though."

"Well, it could be. If I got an independent psychological report, all it would need to say is I'm suffering a mental health problem, then they'd have to make adjustments and if they didn't, I'd resign and go to tribunal."

"You crafty bugger!"

"Why should the devil have all the good ruses?"

Tom laughed in that unleashed way people do when humour has undermined some fixed idea or established convention and, though he was shocked at the straightforward cynicism of his wife's attitude, having always relied on her to put her principles first, it was a welcome cynicism because it lifted the pall of self-accusation, defeat and depression which had oppressed her since the business began and brought back the hopeful, positive, easy-going woman of the early days of their marriage. How strange that a negative sentiment could produce such positive results!

"Tess Turley's husband, isn't he something big in psychology?"

"Yeah, he has some position in the British Psychological Association, or whatever it's called."

"Invite them round," said Tom, "ply 'em with drink and get the bugger to write you a report."

So they did, and the eminent psychologist was delighted to be asked to help, convinced as he was of something close to a witch hunt of teachers. All the same, he had to stick to his professional code and Mary would have to undergo proper assessment and be registered as a client. Still, he waxed about the foolishness of punishment as a means of motivation and elaborated his version of the theory of positive reinforcement, arguing that no matter how poor a teacher's, or anyone else's work, the only sensible place to begin in helping them to improve is with what they're getting right.

"After all," he said, "isn't that what they say about the pupils, and quite rightly? Who would learn or improve if they were condemned for every mistake and never praised for what they do well? No, the

237

government has a not-very-hidden agenda to blame teachers for every ill in the system so the politicians are off the hook. I fear for the future of education if this goes on. Only parents who can afford to pay will get a decent schooling for the children."

The irony of his remark wasn't lost on Mary and Tom as his own children had been educated privately, gone to prestigious universities and were earning heavily in their fine careers. All the same, armed with the report, for which they had to pay the eyes in their head, Mary returned to work and requested the reasonable adjustments to which she was entitled.

"What adjustments do you think you'll need, Mary?" said Milner who combined the soft-spoken, friendly, personal manner of a beneficent doctor with the ruthlessness requisite in Headteachers when she was a little unsure of her ground.

"Oh, the support will have to be withdrawn, at least. That's the source of the stress and anxiety."

"But the support is there to help you."

"Yes, rather like apartheid was supposed to help the blacks."

"That's an inappropriate remark, Mary."

"I must say, I've somewhat lost my sense of what is and isn't appropriate recently."

"We can help you, but we can't withdraw support. The authority wouldn't allow it."

Mary, heartened by those words, knew Milner could have no idea how glad she was to hear them just as she could hardly have been aware of how Mary felt, at last, that she had swung things to her advantage sufficiently so she couldn't lose: if they agreed and withdrew support she would get on with her job, if they refused, she'd resign and go to tribunal.

"She played right into my hands," she said to Tom.

"Owzat!"

"Now I get the union to put on pressure and if they still won't move, I bang in my notice."

The NUT's Regional Officer took up the cause, but fearing a withdrawal would signal an easy means of wriggling out of support, the authority stuck to its position and Mary sat down to write her letter of resignation. If she'd thought about it six months earlier, had worked through the humiliation of having to leave the job she loved, she would have been crushed and tearful, but now she took her pen with a sense of freedom and delight: skulking behind the flimsy excuse of doing the best for the children, they'd tried to destroy her ; their motivation was vicious because, even if it were true there were failings in her work, and she admitted to herself her planning wasn't always all it could be, her room was sometimes untidy, she didn't always stick to the success criteria, it would have been easy for them to bolster her confidence with praise for her qualities while at the same time giving her little digs in the ribs over her shortcomings. It could all have been done pleasantly and with a sense of humour, but behind it was a stiff, nasty, preening, narcissistic bureaucratic mentality; a narrow-minded conformism, lack of imagination and want of simple *joie de vivre*; the mentality of the prissy careerist for whom the world is a mirror and who is constantly inwardly assessing herself, taking her temperature, measuring her success by comparison to others and for whom the slightest deviation from the externally imposed norms to which she is chained as irrevocably as an addict to his fix, sparks a fierce anxiety which makes her all the more obedient, dutiful, mentally myopic and blindly conscientious. She realised, as she paused in her writing, that she too had nearly embraced that mentality. Had she been promoted, had she been a little more bullet-headed and uncompromising, might she too have participated in the cruel, stupid and self-defeating obsession with standards and targets and league tables, all the wicked paraphernalia of measurement purporting to scientific objectivity but which was truly nothing more than a creeps' charter, a paradise for arse-lickers? But if she'd been one of those far-gone time-servers, lacking in autonomy, timid of resistance, complaisant to all authority however misguided, she wouldn't have fallen foul of their pusillanimity, she would have followed the strictures to the letter, always been looking over her shoulder; her fault, in the system's eyes, was her virtue: she used her intelligence and her judgement and behaved independently and what she considered senseless, she ignored.

She kept the letter beautifully brief and to the point.

The legal process was long and slow, but at every step the barrister reassured her: the employer was required to make reasonable adjustments; in the view of the psychologist, the support was inducing depression and anxiety; the only reasonable course, in the short term, was to suspend it. All the same, when the day of the tribunal arrived, her confidence drained away like oil from an opened sump and all she could imagine was that officialdom, that deadly and sly combination of jack-in-office interests, would close ranks against her, the isolated individual, would see through her ruse, dismiss her out of hand and leave her jobless, shamed, diminished and possibly facing costs if, as the lawyer put it, the claim was judged to be wholly without merit.

"I submit this document as evidence in chief," said the barrister.

She was called first to the box, to be cross-examined by the authority's barrister, a young woman with a slightly squeaky voice and a very precise manner who reminded her of a nervous vicar delivering a sermon in which he believed but with no confidence he had any right to persuade anyone else to have faith in it.

"Ms Birtwistle, it seems your attack of anxiety and depression has arrived quite conveniently. Have you ever suffered from such symptoms before."

"Never."

" Isn't it a little suspicious that you began to complain of these things only when you were asked to improve professionally?"

"I wasn't asked to improve professionally, I was browbeaten, given an impossible workload, pursued for trivialities and undermined. As you know, Mr Abingdon's report is clear in identifying the so-called support as the source of my problems. That's why they came out of nowhere and disappeared once I was no longer working. Context is everything."

"Would you say you're a strong person, Ms Birtwistle?"

"Physically?"

"Excuse me. Emotionally, psychologically. Teaching is demanding in these respects isn't it?"

"I never had any difficulty until I was put on support."

"Perhaps that's because you weren't doing your job properly."

"Then why were there no complaints?"

"Well, there were complaints, once your Headteacher caught up with you."

"Which happened to coincide with Special Measures and falling rolls."

" Did Ms Milner offer to make reasonable adjustments when you returned to work?"

" Yes."

"Then why did you resign?"

"Because the only adjustment I needed was to be allowed to get on with my job."

"But your employer has a right to ensure you're doing your job properly, surely."

"Of course, but this isn't about teachers doing their jobs properly. You have to do your job properly but I bet you make mistakes and have bad days. Teachers are the whipping boys in an attempt to lift all responsibility for failure from the politicians. I have eight Special Needs pupils in my class, out of fifteen children."

"We're not here to discuss those matters, Ms Birtwistle. The question is, did the school offer to make appropriate reasonable adjustments. Tell the tribunal, what adjustments would you have accepted?"

"The only one which would have made any difference would have been the suspension of support."

Mary refused to soften before the insistent questions, standing solidly on her little island of withdrawal of support being the only reasonable action, and when her lawyer got the chance to cross-examine, he hammered away at the fact that the psychologist's report was plain, that a temporary suspension would have been easily feasible, but the authority insisted, over and over, on its right to intervene to ensure competence, and behind this defence, a *droit de seigneur* of the employer, was concealed that urge to power and control which infests the human mind like maggots a dead bird, an urge born of weakness, of the indefeasibly temporary, shifting nature of identity, of fear of life itself whose forces work through us, granting us as individuals and as a species a brief span of wonder on the tiny, teeming oasis that is the earth. Sure the tribunal would find against her, casting glances at the expressionless chair who peered over her glasses, made sudden notes and seemed so razor-blade efficient Mary couldn't imagine any sympathy coming from her, she was as stunned

241

as relieved when, after the adjournment, the panel found in her favour.

It was when she was alone, after the celebratory meal and drinks with Tom, walking to the corner shop for a an evening paper that the sense of victory came over her: they hadn't driven her out, they hadn't found her incompetent, they couldn't drag her before the GTC and take away her licence to teach. They'd been found to be in the wrong. She was vindicated. She could apply for other jobs, if she felt like it. And she would, she'd start again, but this time she'd be careful. She wouldn't take a job in a school serving poor children, she'd be picky, wouldn't go anywhere that didn't having a glowing OFSTED report, would find out how the staff got along with the Head. That's what she'd do. She'd look after herself. And though she felt a tug of regret at having to make such cynical calculations, at the loss of that generous and open feeling she'd had when she started, that idealistic impulse of wanting to help children at the bottom end, she felt much, much better knowing she'd never again allow herself to fall into a trap. At the same time, she doubted herself. Was she less than competent? Now she was safe, she could admit her failings to herself. It was true she didn't plan tightly enough and her marking wasn't always up to date. But she rebelled against her own self-accusation. This system would find Beethoven incompetent to teach music! It was too rigid, too prescriptive, too lacking in imagination. It truly was a paradise for sycophants, time-servers and arse-lickers. In such a jungle, she concluded, what could she do but look out for herself?

BEYOND THE RUBICON

With dread Joe Mendel turned the pages of the *Times Educational Supplement*. Those little ads under the *English* rubric, might have been invitations to a long prison sentence. Why did the thought of employment weigh on him? This was supposed to be exciting! The first job, the beginning of the slow climb up the very greasy pole, the anticipation of long years of diligent arse-licking to arrive at the magnificent designation of Head Of Department, or Deputy Head, or Head of Year, or even, if things went really badly, Headteacher. Why did he feel so cynical about it He couldn't raise an ounce of enthusiasm. It felt like the closing in of slow death, as if a megalith were being lowered millimetre by millimetre until it would make him bend, crawl and finally crush him into the earth. He looked up. In the public library was the usual sad assortment of misfits, tragic cases, idlers, scholars and borderline lunatics. Maybe that was it. Perhaps he was just a borderline madman. Should he tear off his clothes and run screaming through the library, his scruffy genitals swinging and making the female staff and the young girls swotting over their O Level History scream. They'd throw him in the looney bin and give him thee meals a day. Maybe he could find a quiet corner and just read Chaucer and Cervantes from dawn till midnight. But they'd treat him with electric shocks and cut out his frontal lobes. No matter what you tried, the bastards would cut you down to their size. He thought of his contemporaries. Were they overcome by the same sense of horror or did they really relish the beginning of this decade's long entrapment in employment. He brought to mind his mates from college: Tom Edge, Jill Hudspith, Owen Egger, Sue Beamish, Steve Szczsciak. Seeing them in his mind's eye it struck him they had the same reluctance, the same dread, but they bit their lips because that's what you had to do. And then, they hadn't done what he'd done. They hadn't pressed on and changed their mentalities. They'd stayed, sensibly, this side of what was socially acceptable while he, fool, had taken hold of the ideas that had meant something to him and had driven them on and on. Somehow, he'd thought that he'd be able to come back: having crossed the Rubicon he'd wade back and stand on the shared, solid ground of something like convention. But it wasn't possible: once Galileo had looked through his telescope he couldn't chat with the priests about how God had put the earth at the centre of the universe. Once you've torn to shreds the fabric of which convention is made, you stand naked and alone. He was twenty-three and he didn't believe a word of his society's official excuses. Free enterprise was just *carte blanche* for the rich to screw the rest, democracy was a scam in which pusillanimous careerists stole the votes of millions to pump up their egos and line their pockets, peacekeeping was disinfected war-mongering, schools were exam factories which promoted those born with brains and ritually humiliated those without, the free press meant the right of bigoted editors in the service of millionaire owners to distort every fact, to twist every truth, to withhold inconvenient information and to hysterically exaggerate whatever served their interests, the church preached poverty, tolerance and humility and practised greed, arrogance and manipulation, and the family, bedrock of this great civilization was a petty battleground of egotism, tyranny, recrimination, control and heartbreak.

Maybe he just needed a drink.

Mendel was no good at daytime drinking. Even a meagre half made him sleepy, sent him to the sofa for a nap and left him feeling fuzzy-headed and disoriented. What he did like though was coffee. A good strong coffee and a hearty piece of carrot cake was just the remedy. Close by the library, in the corner of the Victorian arcade, someone had just opened a café called *Picasso's*. The blue sign was the flourish of the Spaniard's signature. Mendel turned up his collar against the mizzle that had kept going all morning, trotted across the street and in through the cream-painted door. Upstairs was a curvaceous counter, as if in homage to the old ram's appetite for women, and a couple of tables squeezed by the wall.

"Can I go down" said Mendel to the young woman behind the counter.

"Of course!" and her smile dissolved his ruminative gloom making him think that he'd been taking things too far, again.

The lower floor was much roomier. The tables were white-painted, florid cast-iron with circular glass tops, the chairs had little floral-covered cushions and back-rests and on the wall were cheap prints by the prolific little fanatic of the brush and palette. There was another young woman on duty down here who came to take Mendel's order. She was about eighteen, he thought, very petite and dainty but nicely filled out, with blonde hair pinned up in a bun from which charming little wisps escaped. Here she was, making a tiny living from serving in a café. Or maybe she was a student just pulling in a bit of pocket-money. He would have liked to have asked her. In fact, he'd have liked to know everything about her. He would have liked to have taken off her clothes and discovered just what kind of little cries of pleasure she emitted. It was funny that, how they were all as different as fingerprints, yet, in essence, all the same, like fingerprints.

"Are you ready to order?"

What did she think he was going to have, a five courser and a bottle of Bollinger, the *terrine maison* and *pain grillé*, the *consommé de chou-fleur*, the steak tartare medium rare with sauté potatoes and asparagus in butter, the…..

"Can I have a coffee and a piece of carrot cake, please?"

"Fine. Is that everything?"

"Yes, that's all."

In his pocket was a copy of *Revolutionary Road*. A friend who'd spent a year in America had brought it back for him and he was reading it for the second time. In a café, he had to do one of two things, talk or read. Conversation and reading were indispensable. Otherwise, a café was merely a place to eat and drink and they were essentially dull activities if you carried them out alone. A café existed to be a public arena , a place to exchange ideas and the eating and drinking were elevated from simple satisfactions of physical needs, to subtle cultural activities by the addition of newspapers, books and chat. Mendel opened the novel and took up where he'd left off the night before. He was horrified by Frank Wheeler. What was so terrifying was his ordinariness. Was America full of men like this ? Was this what it meant to be a man in modern America? Wheeler, Mendel thought, was a modern Babbitt, dogged by the same heartrending superficiality. He'd read Sinclair Lewis when he was eighteen or so and the story of the pathetic little man, his sordid adultery, his lunatic boosterism, was one of his favourites. But it was truly frightening. Imagine Babbitts and Wheelers in millions. Imagine they were typical of America. And wasn't that what Lewis and Yates were getting at?

"Joe! What are you doing here? This isn't your neck of the woods."

The voice made him wince inwardly and simultaneously sparked up an aggression he had to work hard to fight down.

"All right."

"Mind if I join you?" said Westerman sitting down.

He spoke as if he were holding a loud-hailer and addressing a crowd. Mendel cringed but tried to conceal it. His instinct was to return Westerman's rudeness, but he pulled back. Somehow, Westerman got away with this boorishness because everyone compensated for it.

"Not at all."

"What are you reading?"

"Richard Yates."

"Never heard of him!" declared Westerman dismissively.

"Well," said Mendel, "I'm sure he'll be dismayed."

"What?"

"So, shopping"

"Yep, bought some new shoes."

He took the box out of the bag and the shoes out of the box: a pair of brown suede *Hush Puppies*.

"Class, eh?"

"Very nice," said Mendel.

"Guess how much"

"No idea."

"No, guess. Remember, they're a classy shoe."

"Fiver," said Mendel.

"Fiver! Fifteen quid. Fiver! Were you tryin' to be funny" and Westerman leaned over in his usual over-intimate way.

Thankfully, the waitress arrived.

"Carrot cake and a coffee"

"Thanks."

"Yummy," said Westerman, "that looks nice. Can I see the menu, please?"

"Not found a job yet!" he said, picking up Mendel's copy of the

TES.

"No," said Mendel, his mouth full of carrot cake.

"Let me give you a tip," said Westerman, leaning in close again, as if he was going to kiss Mendel full on the mouth, "Hurst Park Grammar."

"What?" said Mendel, chewing.

"I've heard they're stuck for an English teacher. Vic Culshaw has had a heart attack."

"Who's he"

"English teacher. Been there donkey's years. Writes poetry. Bit of an arty-farty type."

"Are they going to advertise"

"They'll have to, but at this time of the year. Ring 'em. You might have a chance."

"Yeah. Thanks," and Mendel sipped his coffee feeling his blood turn to water.

As soon as he'd finished he made his excuses:

"Got to go, dentist's in half an hour."

"You were going to the dentist's last time I met you," said Westerman accusingly.

"Yeah, lot o'work. Terrible teeth. Crowns. All that stuff. See you, anyway."

He caught the bus back to his mother's in the sleepy suburbs and went and lay on his bed. It was really unmanly to be dependent at the age of twenty-three. Five years ago, he'd've been horrified at the thought. But life, as always, hadn't turned out as he'd expected. His mother, a widow whose husband had drunk himself to death, had endured decades of his reckless passion for alcohol. Standing in the middle of the avenue at two in the morning, turning to the neighbours woken by his raucuous singing and peeking round the curtains, he would cry:

"Yes, Mrs Hothersall, it's me, I'm 'ere and I'm pissed! Goodnight to you, Madam. Get back into bed and look after your husband, as I shall now take care of my wife!"

Mendel knew he couldn't go on sponging. His mother was very kind and never muttered a word of complaint. She did her little job typing for an accountant in town, kept the house neat, made nourishing and delicious meals, washed his clothes and tidied his room. It was terrible. He was twenty-three! At his age his father had established the bespoke tailoring business that would bring in the money even when he was too destroyed by booze to sew a button. But he, Joe Mendel, was a grown man living like a teenager. It was shameful and demeaning. He should be married. He should be a father. He should have responsibilities. Yet the thought of a dull job, and a quarter-century mortgage, and these sniffy suburbs where life went on between limits so narrow it took the discipline of a monk to tolerate it, made his mood sink. All the same, he owed it to his mother to go after the job at Hurst Park. She would be proud if he got it. He imagined her meeting the neighbours out shopping:

"Joe? Oh yes, he's doing fine. He's teaching English at Hurst Park. Such a good school. He's very happy there. And there are opportunities."

It was a gloomy prospect but what else could he do. He went downstairs and stood by the little telephone table in the hallway. The green two-tone phone perched like a smug frog and seemed to accuse him of cowardice. He took hold of the directory, looked up Hurst Park's number, dropped the book on the carpet and dialled. When a brisk secretarial voice answered he said:

"Could I speak to the Headmaster, please"

"Who's calling?" the question was sung with a cheery rising intonation which sapped his confidence. It called to mind the perfunctory "good morning!" of the workplace, the false bonhomie, the deadly reality of the petty struggle for money and place and the mean-minded back-biting and sick-making one-upmanship. He hesitated a second.

"I'm ringing about the English post. I heard you need someone for September."

"What's the name, please?"

"Mendel."

"One moment Mr Mendel!"

He had a few seconds in which to put down the receiver.

"Hello?"

"Hello!" Mendel became aware of the shaky, false enthusiasm in his intonation. He felt very disappointed in himself. "I was ringing about the English post."

"Are you qualified?"

"Yes, of course."

"Where did you get your degree?" the voice was moody, arrogant, brusque.

"Manchester."

"Can you come for an interview tomorrow?"

Mendel wanted to say: "Can I buggery you ignorant bastard."

"Yes, of course. No problem."

"Be here at ten. Do you know where we are?"

"Yes, I know the school well."

"Ten."

The line went dead.

Mendel climbed the stairs and lay once more across his bed. This little bedroom had been his through his happy childhood days and the terrifying years of adolescence. He'd packed his bags here before leaving for university, thinking he'd return only for the odd weekend and holiday. Somehow, he'd never thought much about earning a living. Lawrence's line about a man being lovely if he earns his life came back to him. It seemed utterly out-of-place in the suburbs where *everything* depended on earning a living, and a good one. Life itself here revolved around petty distinctions of salary and status and people would sell their souls for a promotion and a pension. It made long-term employment too terrible to contemplate. He jumped up, went out and walked nowhere in particular. Just the act of walking calmed him. He would have liked to set off walking and never stop. Anything to be free of this clammy, constricting life of the middle-class suburbs.

The next day, at nine-thirty, in the grey suit he'd worn only at his sister's wedding, he set off for Hurst Park. He walked. When he arrived, he stuck his head in front of the little, glass, louvred, office *guichet*.

"Mr Mendel. I'm here for interview at ten."

"Yes, Mr Mendel. Can you follow me, please?"

The receptionist, a woman of about forty, very trim and mincing with the figure of an eighteen year old, led him down a short corridor and into a room where there was a table, low armchairs tucked neatly side by side around the walls and a painting of a rural scene with horses and haymaking.

"Can you fill in this form, please? Mr Bracken will be with you in a few minutes."

Mendel filled in the details in black pen. His handwriting was hateful. The letters were small and ill-formed. Looking at his own script sapped his confidence. It was scruffy and incompetent and tight, not like the illegible, florid swirl of some of his university teachers. He finished and stood up to look out of the window. He had his back to the door when Bracken came in. He turned to see a thick-set man of nearly sixty with dense, wavy, greying hair brushed steeply back from his forehead. He wore a tweed jacket and dark trousers and behind his heavy glasses his eyes were fixed and angry. His head on his short neck was pulled down into his collar and his shoulders pushed forward a little as if he was about to launch himself at Mendel and tackle him to the ground. For a few seconds he stood still, glaring, and said nothing. Mendel, in his limber, slightly insolent way, stood looking back at him unable to stiffen at the older man's obvious and inexplicable disapproval.

"Have you filled in the form, Mr Mendel?"

"Yes, it's here."

Mendel picked it up and offered it. Bracken turned his back.

"Follow me," he said.

Bracken's office was the most comfortable, welcoming place in the school. It was about half the size of the staff-room where fifty teachers had to crowd at breaks and lunchtimes. The wooden desk was ancient and heavy and seemed to occupy its space as permanently as Sirius shines in the heavens. There were tall bookcases whose upper shelves were filled with lever arch files occupying an entire wall. The carpet was deep pile and the wallpaper heavily embossed. Amidst the customary racket of a school of nine hundred boys, this was a chapel of quiet and calm. Everything was utterly neat. It was hard to believe a man worked all day in this place. It had the pristine feel of a consulting-room or an antechamber where no real work gets done. The window looked out onto a circle of neatly mown grass in the middle of which grew a slightly crooked flowering cherry.

"Well, Mr Mendel," said Bracken, settled in his chair, "what makes you think you want to work at Hurst Park?"

Mendel wanted to say, in keeping with the direct nature of his thinking: "I don't want to work here, I just need the money."

"It's a school with a good reputation…."

"Of course, it has a good reputation. It's an ex-Grammar school. You don't have to explain the reputation of the place to me, you have to convince me you want to work here."

"Well, I'm keen to teach A level and I understand you have good numbers taking English and going on to university…"

"I see you've spent two years doing an M.A., Mr Mendel."

"Yes."

"What was that about, then?"

"I'm writing a thesis on American fiction. Sinclair Lewis as a matter of fact."

"Don't you think you'd be better finding a job in academia?"

"No," said Mendel, "I've decided against that."

"Why?"

"I don't want to retreat to the ivory tower."

"And you went to Kingsway Secondary Modern?"

"Yes."

"Missed out on the 11 plus, eh?"

"Yes."

Bracken looked up from the application form, a distinct, ugly little sneer on his lips. Mendel sat in the low chair and looked back , like the proverbial cat at a king. He had a natural insolence about him that came from early years in the back streets, before his father had come by the inheritance which allowed him to establish his business. Mendel was marked by his mean origins as surely as the child of an aristocrat absorbs a sense of superiority with its milk. His demeanour had the limber cockiness of a kid who spent his infancy kicking around the back alleys of a poor, working-class part of the old industrial town and he displayed the impeccable, egalitarian manners of the northern working-class. His very way of sitting in the chair lacked deference and he could see Bracken didn't like him. But he couldn't be other than he was. He saw no reason to adopt the manners of his supposed social superiors, to adjust his movements or facial expressions. He didn't want to be become a ridiculous phoney, trying to be something he wasn't for the sake of social advancement.

"Well, Mr Mendel," said Bracken, "I suppose I haven't anyone else in mind."

Mendel was inclined to scoff at the insult. He looked at Bracken whose ugly expression hadn't changed.

"Does that mean you're offering me the job?"

"I suppose so, unless you're one of these union chappies."

Mendel could have laughed out loud.

"Do you accept" said Bracken.

"Yes," said Mendel.

There were bits of administration to sort out in the office after which Mendel walked back home and collapsed once more across his bed. At least he wouldn't be dependent on his mother any more, but the thought of being sucked into the petty-minded routines of that stuffy place almost made him get up and up and run for his life. He comforted himself with the thought he would stay for only a year. No matter what, he must move on. But he was overcome by the sense of having been delivered to this outcome? In what way had he chosen it He'd been lifted by a wave, forming before he was even born, and cast onto this strange and lonely shore where he had no desire to live.

During the first half-term of his teaching at Hurst Park, he was persuaded to stand as a Labour candidate in a no-hope ward in the council elections. He'd joined the party because he favoured socialism, but also with an eye to its social opportunities: the milieu of the labour movement was where he might meet fellow-spirits. He hadn't been disappointed. Susie Spillard was the neglected wife of one of only four labour members on the council. Frank Spillard wanted to be mayor. He wanted to wear the chains. He wanted his tiny place in local history. Susie was dragged along in his egocentric flurry like a rowing boat that bobs on a liner's wake. She went to the ward meetings. She stuffed envelopes. She knocked on doors. She spent nights at home in front of the television while her teenage children went off to do whatever it was they did around the avenues with their mates. When Mendel turned up at the ward one Tuesday night, politics became suddenly attractive to her once more. He had about him that look of bachelor loneliness that sets a hungry woman's mind racing. Within a fortnight, she was in bed with him at home in her dormer bungalow while Frank made a verbose speech in front of drowsy members in pursuit of his petty glory. That day, Mendel had taken in a set of fourth year books and found one of them covered in outraged, reactionary graffiti. It belonged to Hilton Galgate, a pale, timid boy with a 1950s brilliantined quiff and ideas as rigid as a poker.

"He was obviously very angry," he said to Susie who had kicked off the duvet and had her knees crooked and opening and closing like an alligator's jaws.

"Really" she said, trying to sound interested.

"Yeah. *Down with communism*! *Long live the monarchy*! *Michael Foot is a Stalinist*! *Tories for freedom*! His book is just covered in the stuff!"

"Oh, teenagers," she said. "Don't fret about it."

"I'm stunned. Doesn't he understand what democracy means?"

"He's just a child. Never mind him."

One day, as his fourth years were drifting out of the room and he was trying to put some order into the chaos of his desk, he became aware of a boy lingering. He looked up. It was Galgate.

"Everything all right, Hilton"

"Yes."

"Is there something you want?"

Mendel pulled himself upright. He was four inches taller than the pupil and seemed to tower over him. He became aware that it might be intimidating so he sat down. The boy was very still and quiet, as if he were about to vomit or break down. Mendel smiled.

"Well"

"I saw you coming out of Mrs Spillard's house."

Mendel suddenly felt small and was about to stand up, but felt it would betray his emotion.

"What ?" he said, leaning forward.

"You've been having an affair with her."

"That's a very serious accusation, Hilton."

"It's not an accusation, it's the truth."

"Even if it were, what business is it of yours?"

"Mr Spillard is a governor."

"Is he?" said Mendel, as if it didn't matter.

"If I tell him, you'll get sacked."

Mendel rocked back in his chair and laughed.

"Hilton, you're just a child. These are adult matters."

He was aware of his mind working automatically and he was speaking before he had time to think.

"Anyway, Aaron Spillard told me."

"What?"

"He sneaked in one night when you were doing it with his mum."

"This is ridiculous."

"And you're a communist."

"Am I?"

"I don't want to be taught by socialists."

"You don't have any choice," snapped Mendel. "This is democracy. I'm a qualified teacher and I can teach in any school willing to employ me."

"I'm going to get you sacked."

Mendel looked up at the pale little boy. There was something of a corpse about him. He didn't move. His face was a mask. Could it really be true that this specimen was about to scupper his career?

"Well, go ahead, Hilton. Just go ahead and try."

Mendel picked up his mark-book and strode out.

The next day Bracken passed him in the corridor without a glance. In the staff-room at break he imagined he caught two colleagues look-ing askance at him. That evening his phone rang and when he picked it up it went dead. Day by day he grew more and more touchy. Final-ly he was called in by Bracken.

"We've had a parental complaint."

"Oh."

"Hilton Galgate."

Mendel resolved to tell the truth.

"I see," he said.

"Do you?"

"Well, Hilton seems to have taken a dislike to me."

"Has he?"

"His book is covered in graffiti."

"Of what kind?"

"Political."

"Why do you think that is, Mr Mendel?"

"Well, he has very fixed views."

"So do you, according to his parents."

"Sorry?"

"They're saying you're indoctrinating your classes with socialism."

"What?"

"You've been teaching them George Orwell and introducing Marx-ism."

Bracken's face was twisted into that ugly sneer which appeared whenever he encountered anything which didn't sit comfortably with his preconceptions.

"*1984* is a set book."

"Karl Marx isn't."

"I haven't been teaching them Marx."

"I should hope not, Mr Mendel. This is a Church of England school. It's right of centre and always has been."

"I had to explain totalitarianism."

"Did you"

"It's what the book's about."

"So what did you explain?"

"About fascism and the Soviet Union and the absence of democracy."

"And did you have to teach them Marxism to do that?"

"I had to mention Marx."

"Why"

"Because the Bolsheviks hid behind his ideas."

"So you were negative about them?"

"No. I was neutral."

"Do you think it's possible to be neutral about something so misguided?"

"I don't think we should be afraid of ideas."

"Do you think I'm afraid of half-baked socialists, Mr Mendel?"

"No. I just mean as teachers we should be free to discuss ideas without fear."

"These are fifteen-year-old boys, Mr Mendel. Their minds are half-formed. We have to be careful about introducing them to perverse views of human life."

"I wouldn't say anything I put in front of them was perverse."

"I'd say Karl Marx is perverse, wouldn't you?"

"No."

"You're not a Marxist are you, Mr Mendel?"

"My political views are my own business."

"Not if you start foisting them on my pupils."

Bracken gave Mendel a written warning. Mendel went to the union. The union told him to be careful.

That evening, he wrote out his resignation but sitting with a glass of red thinking of what he would do next, he screwed it up. He didn't want to stay at Hurst Park. He'd find another job. At the end of the year he'd move on. He got up the next morning and dressed in his jacket, trousers, shirt and tie. Looking at himself in the mirror he wondered why he went through this charade. Who was that man in the mirror? Who were all the other men looking at themselves dressed for shirt-and-tie jobs? If it'd been just the shirt and tie, he could have accepted it, but it was the whole dumb show. Was this life. Or was he mad to think there must be some more honest form of existence. Didn't everyone just have to conform. Wasn't that how life worked. Then it struck him that it was the *form* of conformity that was at fault. Yes, everyone lived in the context of their time like fish in water, but the context could be just or unjust, sane or mad, honest or dishonest. And he realised that this wasn't a mere general matter but that he was what he was in and through specific circum-stances. In a different time and place he would have thought, felt and behaved quite differently. Even in a very slightly different time and place. And he knew it was the consciousness of this that troubled him. Other people seemed to live as if they were what they were in-trinsically. But that was laughable! It was King Lear's mistake. This rush of ideas lifted his mood, but he had to go to work. He had to carry on with all the empty stupidities of the current arrangements as if he believed in them. As he strode off, his briefcase containing nothing but his lunch swinging in his hand, he realised he was in a trap. This life was a lousy trap and there was truly no way out.

Day by day he lived in expectation of another summons from Brack-en. In the classroom, he checked himself. When they studied Auden he deliberately didn't mention he'd been a public-school fellow trav-eller. The more he censored himself, the more it seemed someone else was speaking through his mouth. His own ideas and their articu-lation had to be put aside and the effort not to say what he thought made him struggle to express himself. Much of what he said seemed so circumlocutory as to be incomprehensible. His enthusiasm, which was all which rendered teaching thrilling, sank.

He scoured the *TES* for jobs. Before he found one he ed, Bracken called him in.

"Would you say you're happy here, Mr Mendel?"

"Perfectly."

"It strikes me this might not be the ideal school for a man like your-self."

"No school is ideal."

"Perhaps it'd be better both for you and the school if we parted company."

"Well, I'm looking for another job, actually."

"In teaching?"

"Of course."

"What if you don't find one?"

"Well, I will. In the long run."

"The long run is a bit too long, Mr Mendel."

"I'm sure I'll……"

"I'd like your resignation."

"Sorry?"

"I'd like you to resign and leave at the end of the term."

"I see."

"I think that'll be for the best, don't you?"

"If you say so."

Mendel went to the union. They said they didn't interfere over appointments and promotions. He said he wasn't being appointed or promoted, he was effectively being asked to sack himself. They said he should think carefully before resigning. He said he paid his subs, couldn't they do better than that? They said they didn't intervene over appointments and promotions.

He went for a long walk.

After a few days during which he wrote out his resignation several times, he decided he would sit tight. If Bracken decided to sack him, then he could take action, but he wasn't going to connive in his own ignominious departure. He expected to be called in and, in preparation, rehearsed his defiant little speech. But nothing happened. He passed Bracken in the corridor. He didn't meet his eyes or speak. The uncertainty unnerved him. He sat down and began his letter of resignation once more, but after the first line his pride rebelled. It enraged him that a petty jack-in-office could undermine him and make doubt and misery his daily companions.

One day after school he drove into town and went into *Picasso's*. He didn't know why, but something about the place drew him. It was welcoming. He ordered coffee and carrot cake and opened his book, *Tender Is The Night*. The friendly atmosphere, the strong smell of coffee, the moist cake, whose familiar taste was as reassuring as friendship, and Fitzgerald's beautiful prose relaxed him. After five minutes all thought of school had gone. Then he heard the voice:

"Joe! You again! `We always seem to meet in here!"

Mendel looked up at the ugly face that was craning towards him. Westerman had a habit of forcing himself physically on others. His big nose and his slightly obscene, flabby lips were so close to Mendel's face he might have been about to kiss him. The ugliness of Westerman's features, which bore the imprint of his boorish intrusiveness, was intensified by the unpleasantness of his behaviour. Mendel had to fight down an impulse to insult him or to physically push him away.

"Why don't you sit down" he said.

"Eh" said Westerman. "Sit down? I'm just saying hello, is there something wrong with that?"

"Not at all. But there's no need to stand over me."

"I'm not standing over you. You're being too sensitive."

"Why don't you just sit down?"

Westerman lowered his long ungainliness into the chair.

"What are you doing here, anyway" he said. "I heard you got that job at Hurst Park."

"That's right. But it's half past four. The school day's over."

"That was good advice I gave you, eh? You've me to thank for that job. Without me you'd still be looking through the TES."

"Well, maybe."

"No maybe about it. Going well "

"As a matter of fact, I'm leaving."

"Leaving? Already"

"Yeah. That's as I intended. I only wanted the job as a stop-gap."

"Where you going?"

"Don't know. I'll find something."

"Eh? Find something. That's no career plan. You should follow my example. I'm looking for head of department jobs already."

"Good luck."

"You don't need luck when you've got my ability. Eh?"

Mendel had had enough. In one of those moments when the entire meaning of our life seems to be revealed like a diamond sparkling among coal and we realise we are held in the grip of circumstances we haven't chosen and all our hopes, dreams and choices are mere illusions, his feeling flattened and like a man alone in a desert, lost and surrounded by limiting horizons he felt impotent to find his way.

"Got to go," he said.

"Go? You haven't even finished your cake."

"No. You have it. I've got to dash I'm in a meeting at seven."

"What meeting's that?"

"You wouldn't want to know."

"Eh?"

Mendel pulled on his coat, trotted up the stairs and out into the dusk. The town was just at that mongrel moment between its working day and the desertion of early evening. There were people, cars, buses, activity but he knew in an hour and a half or so the place would be quiet, the shops shut, everyone gone to their estates or suburbs and the town would be sad and heavy. He wanted to relish this time of bustle because the coming and going of the town heartened him like the autumn wind in the woods or the rush of a stream over little stones. What was he going to do? He wanted to hand in his notice, but he didn't. He wanted to leave Hurst Park but he didn't want to go to another school. He didn't want to work in the system as it was. What part had he played in establishing it? What had it do to with him? He felt once more that lack of freedom which made him stagger. What was all this talk of freedom? He felt processed. He wanted to be able to choose according to his nature. To live in keeping with his feelings, so long as he harmed no-one. But what was expected of him was out of tune with what he wanted to be. It was strange. To be here in the town. To be amongst the hurry he loved. To be here between the earth and the sky and to be in love with life yet out of sorts with his own. What could he do? He turned up his collar and walked. He had no idea what he was going to do. There was nothing for it but to stay true to his feelings and to push on. What he knew to be real at that moment was the entrapment of circumstance. What then was freedom except to see the circumstances without illusion and to try to change his own to suit his nature? Yet he knew he was up against that terrifying public opinion whose ignorance he'd encountered in his pathetic little foray into politics. But this was life, in all its difficulty and disappointment and frustration and confusion. This had to be faced and grappled with or there was nothing but resignation, nothing but the death of destiny. It was terrible, truly terrible.

He walked on easily, in his limber way to where he'd parked his car.

ANY OLD AFTERNOON

It was any old afternoon when an unexpected knock came at the door. Mrs Spacroft knew who was likely to arrive: the window-cleaner wasn't due, the vicar had called yesterday, and anyway, he always telephoned first. She wiped her hands as she left the kitchen. It bothered her that she couldn't picture who it would be, but not so much as discovering who it was.

Eleven years earlier she'd started teaching English. Miller College suited her fine. She worked two and half days, so could organize things around her two young children. Her mother and Colin's parents stepped in. They didn't have enough money because Colin wouldn't work full-time. She'd been attracted to him when they were students together in the sixth-form not only because he was clever and obviously going to have a lucrative career, but also because of his caution. Like her, he was afraid of life. In her case, the disappearance of her father when she was a girl of five and the later lurid stories from her mother of his unpleasant shenanigans, had filled her with a sense of dread: as if something of his badness lurked within her and would one day find its way into the light. And her mother rebelled against her own foolish choice and her abandonment. She turned into one of those women who cherish their resentment. Wronged and righteous, she inflicted on Marianne and her sister her sense of hurt and unhappiness and they grew with a little knot of funk in the solar plexus. In Joyce's case, it turned into teenage recklessness: she was in bed with her first boyfriend at fourteen, went through six or seven others by the time she was nineteen, found herself with herpes after fellatio with a one-night stand and pregnant by an unemployed van driver six years her senior at twenty. They made a brief and hopeless attempt at co-habitation in a flat over a butcher's shop. He twisted her arm up her back when she tried to slap him across the face and she came back to her mother's with the baby. The mess and shame made Marianne's heart shrink and she drew closer to Colin who was as likely to make her pregnant as the Pope. Though he went to university in London and she was in Bristol, they remained faithful. Weeks would go by when they wouldn't see one another and she would drink her coffee and chat to her friends and now and again see a good-looking boy and wonder. But though there was something missing with Colin, she had no idea what. If there'd been some other boy, if she'd met someone and fallen in love, she would have known what to do. It would have been easy. A woman in love is justified in everything. She would have written frankly to Colin:

I'm sorry to tell you, Colin, but I'm in love with someone else. It's the real thing and I know I have to follow my heart. I'm terribly sorry, but you and I....

What a relief to write such a letter. The trouble was she wasn't in love with anyone else and if what she felt for Colin was love, it was a disappointment. She tried over and over to convince herself the feeling was right, but the doubt persisted. Before she knew where she was, she'd been his girlfriend for five years. What would she do if she finished with him? Wasn't she being ungrateful? Didn't he come from a good background?

Colin's parents were traditional. His father, who worked in maintenance on the railways, had been brought up strictly, punished with a belt if he strayed, and was convinced the lashes across his hands and backside had made him the man he was: a devout Methodist and staunch Labour voter. He'd never touched alcohol, wouldn't buy a raffle ticket, and refused to go shopping on Sundays. When his sons were born he feared they'd turn out badly if the narrowest limits weren't placed on them. Both boys were clever which gave him the chance to enforce a regime of hard study from their early years;

"It's a gift from God," he'd say. "You must use it for the good of your fellow man. Work hard. Learn well. But remember, the world is full of clever devils."

The boys thrived intellectually under this regime, like Beethoven whipped to the piano. They were top of the class and tipped for great accomplishments. But the crisis came when they wanted to go out, to visit the youth club, to hang around with their pals and get back late. Their parents envisaged sexual debauchery, drink, crime…They were allowed out only under the tightest constraints. Colin came out of the youth club at dead on nine on a Sunday to find his dad waiting for him.

"Let me come home on my own, dad."

"I've seen some of the roughnecks that come to that place. You don't want to get beaten up do you?"

"I can look after myself."

His father walked in silence beside him. He was thinking how naïve his son was. Look after himself? He was nothing but eight stone of skin and bone. Decades of hard physical work, shifting sleepers, wielding spanners his son would be hard pushed to raise with one hand, had made him strong and tough. Broad, barrel-chested and thick-thighed, he knew he was a match for most men. But Colin was like his mother. He had the hands of a ballerina. He was as skinny as a lath. His future was in a university. He needed to be kept away from the rough lads.

"I'll come home with Steve and Pete. We'll be okay. They're rugby players."

His father relented. But if he came through the door later than ten past nine, he was in the hallway with the belt.

Marianne was sure all the discipline had been good for Colin, and there was no doubt he lived by his principles. He never drank. He got up at six. He worked hard. She couldn't have hoped for a more relia-ble man. But she dreamed of one less reliable. A man she would have to win and keep would have brought her to life. Colin was a pushover but having pushed him over she found he bounced back as a dictator. The strictures imposed by his dad had become strictures he imposed on himself and as his inner life was ruled by the need for tight rules, he expected Marianne's life to be ruled the same way. Before they started having sex it wasn't too bad: he'd object to her going out with her friends during the week but she would laugh it off and go anyway; he'd sulk if she arrived five minutes late for a ren-dezvous; if they went to a party, she wasn't allowed to talk to other men if he wasn't beside her but she'd flop on the sofa next to some half-way attractive bloke, throw back her head to show her strong white throat and dismiss his moaning on the way home. Once they'd done it things changed. It was in her house. Her mother and sister were out. She was tired of the tame kissing and lay on the rug with her legs apart. Colin got very agitated. The crutch of her knickers was on display and he'd never seen that before.

"Oh, I'd just like to take my clothes off now," she said.

"Would you?"

"Mmm. To be naked on this nice warm rug in front of the fire. Wouldn't you like to take your clothes off?"

"You mean have sex?" he said.

"I suppose it might lead to that," she said.

"Yes."

"Shall I take off my bra?"

He sat on the sofa unable to reply. She slipped off her cotton blouse, unfastened the bra and let her huge breasts fall. Colin looked as if he was about to be horse-whipped.

"What do you think?" she said.

"Very nice."

"Are they big enough for you?"

"They're big."

"Don't stay over there. Come and kiss me."

He took her breasts in his big hands like he was grabbing a fleeing animal. Once they were both naked and he stood in front of her with his erect cock pointing to his belly button she realised she'd always imagined it would be like the rest of him, long and thin; in fact it was quite fat and stubby. It amused her. His big balls amused her too. She wanted to get her hands on his cock to see how hard it felt. But he was standing like a dumbstruck child, unable to act.

"What's the matter?"

"I don't have a condom."

"Don't worry. Joyce will have some."

She skipped up the stairs to her sister's room while he perched on the sofa. He looked down at his erection as though it didn't belong to him. In a way it didn't. Had he been able to decide, he wouldn't have had an erection. He would have told Marianne they needed to wait a while; but the thing just sprang up as soon as he saw her knickers. Her white thighs seemed like expanses of magnetic temptation. The soft flesh of their insides and the little bulge in the cotton knickers were like a force acting at a distance. His physics came back to him. Sex was like gravity. It was irresistible. Life was founded on sex like the universe was controlled by gravity. All the lessons of control he'd learnt from his father and the church melted like chocolate in the sun. His cock was throbbing rhythmically. He counted the beats. The little jogging movement it produced was beyond his control.

Marianne came back in. She was completely naked and crossed the rug to stand in front of him, holding out the little foil packet. He looked at the vast territory of her flat white belly. She lay down on the rug and swung her thighs apart. His eyes couldn't move from the thick black triangle and the tiny glimpse of pink.

"Come on."

He stood up, but the excitement he'd managed to contain while holding himself tense on the sofa flooded through him, his cock jigged three or four times and blobs of spunk shot out and landed on the maroon rug next to Marianne.

"Oh dear," she said.

Colin looked down at his throbbing erection. In spite of his ejaculation it had lost hardly any tension. Marianne got up quickly and came back from the kitchen with a damp cloth. She rubbed at the rug while he stood behind her looking at her arse. As she moved he could see her cunt and his cock seemed harder than ever. There she was a vulnerable, white, beautiful, live, animal thing, her waist slim, her haunches wide, her back and shoulders strong. Her thick, brown hair fell across her face as she rubbed away. This was Marianne. But it wasn't. It was some curious revelation, some creature which existed within the everyday, clothed Marianne and had a power to close down all his usual thoughts. She stood up with the cloth in her hand.

"I hope that does it. If there's a mark, I'll say I spilt some yoghurt."

He stood looking into her eyes. Then he stared at her breast and crutch. She cast the rag towards the door.

"Can you still do it?"

She lay down again on the rug and opened her legs. He tore at the foil but it wouldn't rip. He turned the packet round, tugged again. It wouldn't tear.

"Give it me."

He handed it to her and she used her nail as a blade. When she gave it back he pulled out the johnny and struggled to roll it over. He lay on top of her and began to kiss her mouth frantically. She took hold of his cock and found it as hard as a bone. Amazing. She guided it and he slipped it in and at once let out a little cry. She felt the pulse and spurt. He lay there, a great weight on her, inert, finished. Ah, well, at least she knew how a hard cock felt and what it was like to have it inside her. It wasn't painful as she'd thought it might be and the hot fullness of it was thrilling. But would it always be like this? She patted his back and stroked his hair.

"You okay?" she said.

He raised himself on his arms and she realised: he hadn't bothered to take his glasses off.

After that they did it as often as they could and Colin could keep going for five minutes or so once he'd come and got erect again. In the long run, maybe she'd have an orgasm with him inside her but he could never approach her with a contained passion. Somehow the excitement exceeded him. She only had to stroke the tip of his cock a few times and he spurted like a whale. But now they were lovers, his expectations of her were multiplied. The helpless lover, this great vulnerable, naked, at-a-loss victim whose cock sprang up like a jack-in-a-box at the sight of her taut nipples and who shot over her belly before she had time to slip on the sheath, was as vigilant as the staff of a nuclear power station. She'd imagined that sex might change things. She'd thought he might become more relaxed and easy-going and that the intimacy would reassure him and he wouldn't need to hold onto her so fiercely. But the terrible realization came to her that what he was like was what he was like: sex had no transforming power. Why had she imagined it would? It was as if she had a gap in her mind. Somehow, the idea had got there, had been put there, that sex was a liberation, a force to overthrow what people are like in their everyday selves; but she knew now it wasn't true. People were in bed what they were at work, on the bus, in the pub, in the street. She let her mind dwell on the notion. Colin's parents. Their sex life must have been as tightly ruled as everything else. Those vulgar men with fat bellies she saw coming out of the pub, unsteady and raucous must have been the same in the bedroom. It was a terrible disappointment. Not that Colin was disappointing, though his over-excitement, rush, and early ejaculation didn't fill her with delight. No, it was sex itself. It was a big fraud. She let her mind accept the fact of the raw physicality of the act. And that was the truth: it was like pigs rutting in mud. There was no necessity of a transforming elevation, no inevitable finer feeling, no exquisite transport to a realm of gentleness and sweetness. Somehow, she'd always thought things would be different between herself and Colin once the Rubicon had been crossed. She'd thought her reservations about him, the patience she had to exert not to be exasperated by his excessive caution, would be consumed in the fire of passion; he would become the imperturbable man she dreamed of, indulgent of her whims, careless of her heedless flirting, sure of himself because at the end of the evening she would be stripping off and opening herself to him. And she would be able to live without a care, because he could accept everything she was and the two of them would sink into an enduring bliss which would colour all their activity and make the grey, everyday world recede so that the burdens of work and domestic responsibility would be gathered up into the clear sky of mutual joy.

"I wasn't flirting with him," she protested at one of Colin's accusations.

"You were. You were leaning forward so he could look down your blouse."

She let out a laugh of derision.

"My blouse. Honestly."

"I saw him. I was watching his eyes. He kept looking at your cleavage."

Her mood suddenly darkened.

" What's wrong with it anyway?"

"I'm not having it."

" Expect me to dress like a nun?"

"You can wear something that doesn't let other men ogle your breasts."

" I'm comfortable in a blouse with the top buttons undone. And it doesn't trouble me at all that Stu or some other man wants to admire me."

" Troubles me."

"Why should it?"

"I'm your boyfriend. No-one else should be looking at your breasts."

"I can't hide myself away because you're my boyfriend. And anyway, it's you I go to bed with so what's to worry about?"

"One thing leads to another."

"I didn't even notice Stuart looking at my tits. And if I had it doesn't mean I'd be wanting to get into bed with him."

"He might want to get into bed with you."

"Lots of men might."

"That's the point."

"What's the point?"

"It's provocative."

"What's provocative?"

"Letting other men see your tits."

"Bit of cleavage. Grown up men aren't going to get excited over that."

" They are."

"The Taliban."

"I know what men are like."

"So do I."

"Take a hint."

"Not hinting."

"They think so."

Though she went on *à contre coeur*, she could see no way of ending the relationship; as a matter of fact she didn't want to end it. The thought of Colin not being there filled her with fear: she would be alone and where would she find another man of such incontestable dependability? Once more, she found herself perversely wishing for a man who might let her down. Colin would never be unfaithful. She knew that if a beautiful young woman made herself available he'd turn her down. But might it be better if she had a man who strayed or at least was capable of straying. If she knew Colin was faithful in spite of strong attraction to other women and many opportunities, she might feel less oppressed. Yet she wasn't oppressed. He supported her. He was always there. He was just nervous and over-cautious. It was unreasonable of her to feel so negatively. All the same, she would like to appeal to some independent third party. She would like to have her case heard and responded to. But what was her case? It was hard to pin down; a background sense of dissatisfaction; the

269

feeling of going through the motions but never arriving at reality; she was unreal and unrealised. Yet what would reality and realization be? She dropped heavily on the sofa. It was curious this ponderous sense of not living, of never having lived, of wanting life to begin. But the days went by and inevitably she married Colin. It was as if a hand had pushed her. It wasn't her own volition. She'd never excitedly wanted to be married to him or to be married at all. Yet she'd been drawn into it like a stranger pulled to some intriguing quarter of a foreign city who finds herself suddenly amidst danger. The danger she faced was having to feign love. She had two children in quick succession. Outwardly they were a model family. She tried hard to see it this way. They had a good income, a nice house in a quiet lane, two lovely children. All the same, there were days when she could have walked out never to return and she knew she wouldn't miss it. Terrible. She looked into herself and asked if she was to blame. Did she lack some fundamental feeling? It was true, she wouldn't miss Colin if she never saw him again. Her son and daughter she clung to. Nevertheless, she could think about living without them and it didn't trouble her. The mystery of it defeated her and she carried on doing what was expected , what she expected of herself, ignoring as much as she could the void at the heart of it all.

Now Anton Bellis was at the door.

She threw back her head and laughed as she always did when things were too much for her.

"Hope you don't mind," he said.

"Not at all. Just washing up. What am I like? Come in."

It was ten yards from the front door to the kitchen and as she crossed that short distance with Bellis behind her, the whole of her life fell away.

"Cup o' tea?"

She'd rather have asked if he'd like to ravish her. She'd met him when she began at Miller. At first she simply noticed his better-than-average looks and flirted a little like she always did with men who might be attractive to women; but then she found herself thinking if anything happened to Colin....The thought surprised her, as did her conviction she'd marry Bellis, especially as he was already married. All the same, the notion seized her mind with the ferociousness of a hawk's claws on a chick. Yet she daren't act on it. When Bellis said:

"Fancy a drink?"

After an interminable parents' evening in a frozen January, she zipped up her blouson, smiled and gave a little shake of her head.

"Not allowed."

"Who says?"

" In enough trouble already."

There were other little occasions and each time her heart surged, her mind filled with excited images of a new life and she said no. She felt almost as virtuous as Emma Bovary in her religious phase. But desire was stronger than virtue. It was all well and good to elaborate a view of herself as the dutiful wife and mother, but she'd only to look at Colin for her heart to beat heavily with regret. At every opportunity she flirted with Bellis, but if he moved a millimetre towards taking what she offered, she shrank like a snail before salt.

They went into the lounge. The great bay window let the light flood in. She sat on the sofa, illuminated. The warm sun played on her auburn hair and she knew its shades would attract him. When he looked away for a moment she shook her mane free so it hung in abandon. She let her decorated slipper dangle from her toes and drew attention to her dainty feet. Inevitably, she threw back her head because she knew how lovely was her slender neck and her vigorous white throat. All the same, when he came over to her, she wanted to push him away, to run from the room shouting:

"But I'm a married woman."

She wanted to bat her eyelids and wave her marriage certificate.

There was a second when she might have refused and he'd have pulled back in humiliation, but somehow she let it pass and he took the opportunity to lift her thin cotton skirt, pull down her thong and kiss her. So on any old afternoon Mrs Spacroft became an adulteress. At last she had Bellis where she wanted him. Potentially, this was the start of a new life. Physically it wasn't vastly better than sex with Colin. Bellis was better looking and that enhanced the pleasure. Yet it wasn't her physical arousal which was transforming, it was her sense of emotional rightness. Bellis didn't have a possessive or controlling atom in his cells. If she'd told him while they were still naked she was nipping next door for sex with her neighbour, he'd have remained calm and pleasant. It was the escape from Colin's anxious control which made her happy.

"Going back tomorrow?"

"Have to."

"Up again?"

"Do my best."

"Things to sort out I suppose."

Bellis's father had died. The cremation had been the previous day.

"Sister'll look after it."

"Not be here often then?"

"Not for that."

"Job'll keep you busy."

"If I still have one."

Bellis had moved to a school in South London, a very different place from middle-class Melling College where the results were always good. Grosvenor Business and Enterprise Academy which had been a secondary modern till 1978 was full of kids from poor homes and struggled to hit the national targets. Its academy sponsor was ex-Eton Eddie Dowling who set up a car phone company when the trend was obvious with twenty thousand borrowed from his dad and was now the multi-millionaire owner of Phones Galore. Bellis led the campaign against the change.

"Keep your nose clean."

"Pretty impossible."

Marianne experienced a little shudder. His recklessness was exciting but scary.

"I was in favour at first," she said.

"Nothing to be in favour of."

"No."

She wasn't at all sure Bellis was right. Why not just let it happen? It seemed to be the natural flow of things. That's how life seemed to her. She thought of social events like she thought of the weather. A tsunami or a hurricane was terrible but there was nothing to be done. Things happened. As the Americans fatalistically said *shit happens*. It might be sad. It might be wrong. But it was life. Bellis wasn't like

272

that at all. He resisted. He seemed to resist the present and it puzzled her. It seemed like resisting rain. Why was he so opposed to Academies? She couldn't bring it into focus. The arguments about changes to teachers' conditions swayed her. She wouldn't like to be forced to work longer hours and the protection of national conditions reassured her. But what if Academies really were better for children? What if they were the cure for failing schools? She really didn't know. Why was Bellis so sure?

"If they sack me they sack me."

"Can they?"

"Sack anyone. Claim incompetence."

"But they'd have to prove it."

"Nothing simpler."

"You're not incompetent."

"They say you are you are. Stalin says you're a traitor you're a traitor."

It couldn't be true. Her mind swam. She thought of Caroline Nightingale who'd had to leave Melling because of competency procedures. Surely she was incompetent? Then she remembered how people had whispered about her being fifty-seven and the school needing to trim its budget. Thirty-five years work and no serious problems. Was it true? Did they invent incompetence to force people out? She couldn't believe it. It was too awful.

"Not as bad as that," and she threw back her head and laughed.

"Know what it's about Marianne?" he looked at her in that calm way which seemed so full of affection. She let her slipper dangle again and her dressing gown fall away from her knee.

"Not really. Politics baffles me."

" Threat to the rich is the public sector. The more we expand it, the less territory there is for them. Last thirty years wealth has moved upwards. At the bottom an underclass is being created. People like us are the target now. Failure is the smoke screen. Improvement is the big lie. Modernisation. Reform. Liars words. How can they tell the truth: we want the rich to profit from your schools and hospitals; we want to cut your pensions and move the wealth to the bankers, the CEOs, the celebs? It's a fight between the market and democracy.

The public sector was built by democracy. So the threat to the rich is democracy. That's what it's about. Take schools out of local democratic oversight. Make each one a free floating, quasi-private affair paid for by the taxpayer. Undermine democracy. That's the fight: democracy or property. Whose side are you on?"

She rocked her white leg and the little slipper waved and threatened to fall.

"Yours," she said.

He came over to her and unfastened the cord of her gown. Opening it up he smiled at the sight of her breasts, her belly, her pubic hair and parting her legs tugged off his t-shirt and jeans. His cock was tight and throbbing. He stroked her wet cunt and let his finger penetrate.

"Why not come on the London demo on the 26th? There'll be half a million of us."

"I will," she said with a little gasp.

A RESCUE

"The best leader Italy ever had was Mussolini and they hung him from a lamppost," said Tommy.

He was sitting on the edge of the narrow boat as it slowed before the lock. His pot belly hampered him as he stood up to give his stepson advice about steering. He had a thin moustache which he was very proud of and trimmed carefully every morning. His wavy brown hair which was still thick was brushed back from his low forehead. He wore brown trousers a blue shirt and a thin red cardigan, unbuttoned because the day was warm. No-one responded to his provocative remark but his son-in-law who was sitting in a folding chair reading a paperback Complete Plays of Joe Orton, looked up at him, squinting because of the sun.

"Slower, slower!" called Tommy. "Bring her to your left. That's better."

His wife was making lunch having just finished clearing up the breakfast things. She was always making lunch, or dinner, or tea or breakfast or a snack. She shuffled about in the narrow little galley. Her hips were stiff. She was waiting for replacement surgery. A little, overweight woman of fifty, she'd married Tommy sixteen years earlier when she found herself pregnant. Having been a widow for seven years, when he showed an interest in her, she couldn't resist. She was so keen to have a man in her life, she let him bully her children. He cuffed her sons round the ear if they annoyed him. As for her daughter, the mother was blithely unaware of what was going on. She gave birth to a third son six months after the wedding. Tommy went along with it because he read the *Daily Mail* and knew the meaning of respectability, but he resented her. He'd always seen women as fair game. All women. He wasn't fussy. If he could get a woman in bed, why shouldn't he? Beryl was just another conquest though he found her neither attractive nor congenial. Her twelve year-old-daughter though, svelte, shy, her little breasts starting to show beneath her blouses and t-shirts, he found very appealing.

The son-in-law put down his book and went to the bow where his wife was nestled in a corner smoking a joint.

"Where's mum?" she said.

"Cooking. Where else? Your step-father is lecturing on Mussolini."

Lynn drew on the spliff and narrowed her eyes to look at him. She was slender, blonde and looked much younger than nearly thirty. Something girlish remained about her and when she moved she still had awkward, adolescent self-consciousness in her limbs.

"We could have sex here," she said and let her knees fall apart so her leather skirt rode up nearly to her waist.

"Your mother will be sounding the gong in a minute."

"Well?"

She lifted her backside and pulled down her knickers, kicking them off her feet and over the side. She giggled as she drew in more smoke and stroked herself between the legs.

"Come on."

Tony, hearing something, looked to the stern.

"It's Malc."

Lynn tugged down her skirt and crossed her legs. Her brother arrived, smiling, big, full of false confidence.

"Dad's sacked me. He's doing the steering."

"Are we going to moor and have a walk to a pub?" said Lynn.

"Yeah, we've just got to get through this lock."

Malcolm heard his mother call him.

"What now?" he smiled again and went gingerly along the side.

Lynn finished the joint, threw the stub in the water, hitched up her skirt and lay down in her little corner.

"Quick, before we have to eat."

Tony stood looking down at the beauty of her slim hips, her long legs, the exposed sex whose lips she was pulling apart.

Then there was a loud splash and a cry. He went as quickly as he could to the stern and as he put his feet carefully on the narrow board, the image came into his head of Tommy falling backwards, his great, ungainly bulk thrashing in the water and he slowed down. He was first to the rudder. The older man, who couldn't swim, was slapping with his arms and kicking madly to stay afloat, but his head kept bobbing under the black, dirty, cold water.

276

"Hang on!" called Tony. "I'll get the lifebelt."

He jumped up onto the roof where the belt was fixed. It didn't come easily from its hooks and he took his time. Malc had rushed up from below.

"Quick, Tony," he called. "He's going under."

"Here!"

Tony threw the belt to Malc who dropped it, picked it up, tossed it to Tommy, hanging onto the rope. But the drowning man reached for it and missed. The belt began to drift. Malc pulled it in and threw it again but Tommy was in such an exhausted panic he couldn't grab it. Malc launched himself feet first into the canal, grabbed the life-saver and forced one of his step-father's arms through it. Beryl was now on deck with her youngest son, Peter, who looked on dismayed and helpless.

"Oh, my god!" she shouted and began to weep.

"We'll need an ambulance," shouted Malc.

They couldn't lift the sixteen stone, fully dressed soaking man from the water and had to wait for the firemen. By the time they arrived he'd passed out. They put him on a stretcher wrapped in blankets and hurried to the ambulance parked on the crest of a little bridge. Beryl and Peter went with him. Lynn returned to her sunny, private corner in the bow and rolled another joint. When the call came through, Tony went to her.

"He's had a heart attack. It's touch and go."

"Really?" she said. She drew on the cigarette. "Oh, it's so nice here. And I've still got no knickers on. Look." And she hitched up her skirt and opened her legs and smiled.

A SOUND INVESTMENT

The next day she began clearing his room. From the narrow wardrobe which she'd known since childhood, she took the brown and
navy, tobacco-reeking suits and the tan shoes whose soles he mended
over and over on his iron last. The dark chest of drawers was emptied of shirts and underwear; in the top left-hand drawer she found
his papers. His will was in a simple, rectangular, unsealed manila
envelope on which he'd written in his looping hand: Last Will and
Testament. Bert Dallas.   What shocked her was the building society
book: £10,573 16s and 9d. She sat down in his armchair. How long
had it taken? At once she wondered if Alice, Henry and Alf would
get their share. She pulled out the will and tried to read without
glasses. Getting up hurriedly she brought them from the neighbouring room. Even so, the language defeated her. She read through it
once and had to begin again. Finally, she came to the clause: "All
accumulated monies….to my daughter, Patience Derwent." Her excitement was followed quickly by guilt. She ran up to her bedroom,
put the documents in her dressing table and continued her work.

When everything was settled, she decorated the living-room. Hanging paper she found too difficult, so she emulsioned. She paid for a
fitted green carpet with a beautiful gold and brown floral motif and
bought a three piece suite to match; when she sat in the armchair,
alone, with a cup of tea and the evening paper, she had the feeling
that at last life had done her a kindness. Her son came home from his
hated office job. She heard him in the hallway, hanging up his coat
and taking off his shoes. The familiar click and he popped his head
inside:

"Our Billy in?"

"No," she replied without shifting her eyes from the paper.

He closed the door and she listened to his quick feet on the stairs.
Once, the sound of him around the house had been her joy; now he
was a stranger. She went to the kitchen to make his meal. He ate in
the same room, at a square, dark-stained table pushed against the
wall because the back room he used for his music. Sometimes she
lay in bed and thought that he had more space in the house than her
and her irritation made her resent him; but she had indulged him and
now found it impossible to retreat. He ate the corned beef hash ea-

278

gerly, pouring brown sauce and mashing with his fork; he lifted little heaps of the stew onto his folded bread and bit into it lavishly. When he'd finished, she took away his plate and brought him his mug of tea, as he liked it, almost black, with the merest drop of milk and no sugar. He turned on the television and sat on the sofa as she read through the death notices for the third time. After an hour, he went into the back room and began on the guitar; she plumped a cushion, spread out on the sofa and, with the television still on, drifted into sleep.

There were repairs to be carried out and proud of her practicality and providence, she had the rotting window frames replaced and painted brown and cream, the cracked slates removed and the pointing done. In a fit of excess, she bought a new gas cooker, though the old was serviceable, and each time she used it, experienced a little thrill of extravagance. Billy, who at eleven had never had a new bike, she treated to a blue racer with ten gears. Yet when she'd paid for everything, there was still £8,800 . She wondered if she was now rich. She considered putting it in the Post Office because it was responsible and secure. One day she saw an advert for private investments in the paper and her heart skipped; her mind filled with pictures of Stock Exchange dealers, bankers in dark blue Savile Row suits, black Rolls Royces in the Mall and other parts of the capital she had visited only once as a child. She considered giving it to a charity or the church but the parable of the widow's mite came back to her and she felt ashamed that perhaps she was trying to buy grace. Sometimes she woke in the early hours, her head full of odd, frightening dreams of exorbitant wealth, eternal damnation, speculation and ruin. For months she left it in the building society and tried not to think about it. Nevertheless, when she opened her brown wage packet on a Thursday and saw that for her wearying forty hours in the canteen she'd earned £9 17s 3d, she thought of her little fortune and wondered if she couldn't give up work.

After tea, when Billy was out on the park with his pals and Paul not yet home from work, she sat down with a pencil and paper. She was fifty-two. At five hundred a year her windfall wouldn't be exhausted by pension age. But how much was the pension? Would she manage? And what if the roof needing replacing or the gutters collapsed? Then if she spent it all there would be nothing to leave for the boys; and how long would she live? If she went on to seventy or seventy-five or even eighty, might she need the money? She put the paper aside with a sense of defeat. The responsible thing was to go on for another eight years and let the money grow; but the thought of work was barbed wire round her heart. She served meals to the men from the shop floor, wiped the tables, cleaned the floors, filled the salt cellars and vinegar shakers. She was a dogsbody. Terrified of making a mistake, of being reprimanded or sacked, she was extravagantly conscientious; but no-one noticed. The effort left her weary, the fear drained her, the daily humiliation robbed her of worth.

She'd thought marriage would save her. When the war ended and Stan was demobbed, they lived first of all with her parents in their two-up, two-down. But he had a go-getting spirit and though she disapproved, she was glad when he landed a job as manager of a shoe shop and they could afford to rent. After two years they'd saved enough to buy and the modest self-sufficiency pleased her. The house was decent and big enough for a family. There was even a good-sized yard where they could grow fuchsias and begonias in pots. But Stan pushed ahead, always ingratiating himself with the big-wigs; he moved to a regional position. They bought a three-bedroomed in the suburbs. He got a black Wolseley with the job. She disliked his impatience to climb and his desire for more and better, but all the same, she had a good home for her children. She didn't need to work. The area was stable, secure, the schools were good and there was a Congregational Church close by.

Then one Monday, putting the clothes in the tub, she found red lip-stick on his shirt.

She took it to living-room and sat down with it in her hands. For an hour she reviewed carefully the time they'd spent together over the past week. She hadn't kissed him and in any case, she didn't have the shade. She saw the house sold, she and the boys going back to her mother's, the poverty of her childhood returned. She would have to work. What could she do? She had no skill or qualification. Her children's lives would be ruined. Their father was on the side of the devil. She wept and wanted to hide away. When she confronted him he denied it but later, half contrite and half couldn't-care-less, he confessed. It had happened only once. She was young and had thrown herself at him day after day. Finally, he'd given in. It meant nothing. Her mind filled with images of hordes of young women with neat waists. She responded with the absolutism of her faith. There were moments when she calmed down and it seemed forgivable, but at once she summoned her adherence to the Ten Commandments; he was expelled; the settlement gave her the house and he was free of further support. She lived in poverty in the affluent suburb and a terrible gloom descended on the home; no visitors ever came; the boys weren't allowed to let their friends over the threshold; she worked, cooked, cleaned and slept; she had no friends; another husband was out of the question.

When her mother died, her father moved in because he was incapable of keeping house. His little terrace in the mean streets sold for £1,600. He offered it her but she told him to bank it. Though they barely spoke, she was reassured by his presence; the boys loved him because he was quiet and kind, took them to watch football and gave them pocket money.

She had lived without a man since the age of thirty-seven and though at times the lack of intimacy troubled her, what caused her pain was the shame. She was the only woman she knew who had divorced, the only woman therefore, she assumed, whose husband had betrayed her. Frequently before the boys, she let fly:

"If your father had been a proper husband...." or "If your father hadn't gone the way of the devil...."

If only her husband had been more like her own father.

Her nephew, the son of her elder sister who sent her a card at Christmas, had become successful as a painter. There was to be an exhibition locally and some of his canvases would be on show. She thought of him as a baby, when she'd looked after him so his mother could work; a mischievous, cheeky little boy she'd loved him as her own and in her trance of retrospection she heard his sweet, soft voice: Aunty Patty! Aunty Patty! Though she had no interest in the arts, she went along to show support. She would send Jimmy a card:

Dear Jimmy,

I went to see your paintings at the gallery. I thought they were very good. You always were good at drawing. I hope this finds you well.

Love,

Aunty Patience.

When she visited the exhibition, however, she was shocked to find the canvases were for sale. There were two by Jimmy, one for £300 and another for £200, but some of the others were £500, £800, £1,000. She went outside and sat on a bench to eat the cheese sandwich she'd made. There was a weak sun which warmed her mildly through her good grey coat. People were coming and going. How nice life was if you didn't have to work. But she rebelled at the thought of her own laziness until a thought calmed her: working hard she didn't mind, but being employed brought her pain. She thought of her work in the canteen and of her £9 a week and was stunned to think people could earn so much for a painting. When she went back in, she stood before each work for a long while. Most of them she disdained; she couldn't understand a painting which didn't show a nice scene; but a portrait held her attention because the face was full of kindness and she said to herself that was real painting because you felt you knew the person. She wrote to Jimmy:

Dear Jimmy,

I've been to see the exhibition and I think your paintings are very good. I don't understand them but I suppose they aren't for simple people like me. I would like to buy them and also the picture of the man with the blue eyes and the white shirt. Can you tell me how I should go about it? I hope this finds you well.

Love,

Aunty Patience.

Jimmy came to see her. He still had his crooked little smile and the creasing around his eyes before he laughed. She explained she'd been left a little money by his grandfather and the paintings had made her think. Would they be a good investment? He told her he was a very minor artist and his work would never be worth much, but Patrick Wardman, who did the portrait, was up-and-coming. All the same, a thousand pounds was a lot of money; did she want to risk it? She clasped her fingers as she asked if it might lose value.

"Oh no," he said. "It won't lose value, not in long run. Keep it ten or fifteen years and it'll be worth a lot more."

Her mind dissolved at the thought of a lot more, but she felt she'd been sensible: buying Jimmy's work was an act of kindness, the other she hoped would help her a little in retirement.

The two abstracts hung in the hallway where the light never made them noticeable, but the portrait she put in an alcove of the living-room; when she was alone in the evening she would study the face and attribute a life to the subject. Such a man could have been her husband; she knew from the look in his eyes he would be incapable of cruelty.

She worked on to retirement and they had a collection which raised enough to buy her a pair of candlesticks: she wanted something that would last and candles reminded her of her infant days, before the gaslights. Everyone signed a card, which she thought very kind, and sometimes, grateful for the friendly words and the compliments on how well she'd done her job, she almost missed the menial tasks. Her little horde, though it accumulated interest slowly, was nibbled at: Paul decided to give up his job and go to college to improve himself, so she supported him; there was a school trip to Rome which Billy wouldn't have been able to go on if she hadn't dipped into her savings, nor could she deny him his trips to away matches or the records she thought nothing but noise. Nevertheless, on her sixty-fifth birthday she still had six thousand so to the newly-married Billy and the second-time father Paul she gave a thousand each. As for herself, she lived carefully within her pension, never went out except to church, had no holidays, shopped wisely and thought herself perfectly comfortable.

Her one anxiety was the house.

There had been no major expenses, but the little things that went wrong made her worry. Would four thousand pay for a new roof? Hadn't Mrs Griffin had to pay five when they found dry rot? It made her heart beat fast and she dreamed of a tidy bungalow, just big enough for herself and cheap to maintain. But where? She mentioned it to her sons and they came back with suggestions, but she didn't want to leave the area: she knew people and church was close at hand. Finally, they found, half a mile away, a two-bedroomed place in a cul-de-sac; the garden was small enough for her to potter in; it had been well-maintained. She knew she must move but leaving her big, old house where she'd raised her boys, even though it had been the arena of much unhappiness, saddened her. It was valued at £26,000 and the bungalow was selling for nineteen. Seven thousand added to the four she already had: it seemed a huge fortune. To be done with the matter quickly, she told the estate agent to drop the price to twenty-four; he suggested twenty-four and a half and at that price potential buyers arrived every day. She considered herself very lucky, and when a young couple with a baby looked round, felt mean to be asking so much.

It was in the midst of all this that Jimmy turned up. He was losing his hair but in his face she could still see the little boy who laid his head on her shoulder to sleep and she got out her best teapot and cake-stand. He told her, as he chewed her home-made fruit cake, that the paintings of his she'd bought would now sell at £700 or £800 pounds each. It didn't seem right to her that simply for hanging on her wall they could have gained so much value.

"Wait till I tell you about the Wardman," he said.

The artist was now considered one of the best in the country. His big canvases sold for nearly a million. She put down her cup and saucer. The portrait would be worth at least £150,000. She felt as though she'd done something terrible. That night she dreamed the police came to question her. How had she come into so much money? She pointed to the painting. They put on the handcuffs.

She asked Jimmy to say nothing to Paul and Billy, but she changed her mind about moving.

Every day she put on her glasses and studied the portrait. She'd grown fond of the face. Something in its expression reminded her of her father. She wondered, over and over, how he had managed to save so much. When she thought about selling the painting, which Jimmy had offered to handle for her, the idea of £150,000 in the building society filled her with dread. She would truly then be rich and wasn't it harder for a rich man, or woman, to enter the Kingdom of Heaven than for a camel to pass through the eye of a needle? She wasn't sure how it could be that God condemned the rich yet still permitted them to make money, but she didn't want to gain the world and lose her soul. It occurred to her she could sell it for £10,000 or 15 or 20, and that would be easily enough to keep her going; but she thought of her sons and grandchildren and what might lie in the future for them. The dreadful idea came to her that one of them, like her, might have to earn a living in a shameful way. Not that she was ashamed of the simple tasks. She took pride in them. No-one could wipe down a table as thoroughly, nor ensure the condiments were as quickly replenished; but to be ignored, invisible, to come and go day after day without acknowledgement, to work year after year and to leave no mark. She wished she could have millions. Not for herself, but to protect her children and most of all her grandchildren. How sweet life would be if they could have enough to get by and live simply without suffering the indignity of mean work and poor pay. But she was ashamed of her wish for wealth; it was vulgar and selfish. She looked at the face. If a gentle look like that could have greeted her every day she would have been happy. Wasn't she happy once? But life had hit her like a sudden storm and she'd run for shelter as best she could. Life wasn't happiness, it was keeping going in spite of everything.

She put the thought of what to do with the painting at the back of her mind and, now she was no longer working and didn't need to worry about time, the days, weeks and months passed. She went to church, listened to the radio, watched documentaries, Coronation St and adaptations of Dickens who she'd loved at school. When she thought hard about it, having such a valuable item in the house made her fret terribly. Yet every time she went to stand in front of it, she seemed to see something new. In her dreams, the face appeared and talked to her in her father's voice. She wished it had no value at all. She'd grown so fond of it, she wanted to keep it till she died. It had become as dear to her as the photographs of her children and grandchildren. She couldn't reconcile her affection for the face and her admiration for the artist's skill with the huge sum of money.

Then a terrible realization came to her.

She'd paid £1,000 and now it was worth £150,000, maybe more. When did Jimmy tell her? She struggled to recall how long ago. She'd had it how many years? She'd worked for eight, or was it nine? She couldn't hold the dates in her mind as she tried to think. In any case, it was a short time. If she lived another ten years, how much might it be worth? She took up a pencil and paper and divided 150,000 by 1,000 in the way she'd been taught as a girl. The she multiplied 150,000 by 150. The number was so big she couldn't say it. She flushed with embarrassment. Was it possible? She decided she should sell it at once before she became too rich. She lay awake wondering by what mysterious process a painting could gain so much value. But just when she'd resolved she would write to Jimmy and ask him to sell the painting for her, she was struck by illness. One evening, after tea, she began to feel sick. She wondered if it was something she'd eaten. Then she began to sweat and a vicious hand gripped her chest. She went to the bathroom and vomited, thinking it would pass when her stomach was empty. She lay on the bed but the pain in her chest grew worse and spread down her arm. Slowly, the notion began to form it might be her heart. She got up and in spite of the horrible agony and sweating and turning cold, rang Paul. When the ambulance arrived, she was on the floor by the phone.

After three days in intensive care she died.

The afternoon of the funeral, Paul and Billy began clearing the house. Jimmy advised them to auction the portrait: an original Wardman was really something. It brought £2,500,000. They gave Jimmy £100,000 for his trouble. Patience bequeathed a third of her estate to her grandchildren so the four of them got nearly £250,000 each. Paul and Billy bought big houses and lived lavishly; they drove Bentleys and Porsches, took long cruises, stayed in the best hotels and ate at the best restaurants. Billy established an estate agency which flourished across the county till he drew on the profits for an ocean-going yacht, his managing director walked out in protest and it collapsed for want of hard work and careful regulation. Paul indulged his habit for the horses, which had once taken him to the bookmakers twice a week, by attending all the major meetings and losing money faster than his investments could produce it. When she passed her test at seventeen, his daughter Lynn bought herself a red Ferrari, took her friends to London to celebrate, and driving back to the hotel on an unfamiliar, wet road in the early hours, lost control at high speed hit a lamppost and, in spite of the seat belt, died of head injuries before reaching hospital.

Patience Derwent was cremated. In the crematorium grounds is a small, insignificant stone on which is carved: Patience Derwent 1920 - 1998.

ALL YOU NEED IS LOVE

Sap Capstick got most of such education as he had in the Victorian town library where the oak fiction shelves were six feet high and stacked with complete sets of every author since Richardson. On his fortieth birthday, lugubriously surveying the thin set of biographies of celebrities, the single, small shelf of poetry and the drama section without a single play by Jonson, he was beset by a dragging sense of failure and futility: over twenty expectant years devoted to books and writing but no more than a pamphlet of two dozen poems which had been praised by faint damning in three small magazines, sold two hundred copies and sunk into deep oblivion. His definition of himself as a writer was hard to maintain. An embarrassing little panic at his pretension made him flush and wince. He had to write something that would find an audience! Surely biography couldn't be too difficult. And he began to sift his poor brains for someone he could write about. It must be someone leftish to match his own views. Someone whose life was yet unwritten. As he slid his spoon beneath the froth of his cappuccino, the idea came to him: Barry Noonan! The popular leftist poet who'd pranced across stages from Inverness to The Isle of Dogs, risen on the wave of sixties pop culture and ridden it ever since: the perfect subject. He was about to turn sixty. What better way to celebrate than a life?

As soon as Capstick arrived home he sat at his computer and wrote:

Dear Barry Noonan,

Twenty years ago I attended a reading of yours: Barry Noonan at forty. I've been a fan of your work since *Straight Talking* and wondered if you'd be interested in a biography or even just an article about your life and work?

Yours,

He included his phone number and less than a week later Noonan rang him.

"Hi, Sap! Barry Noonan!"

"Oh, hello."

"Got your letter. Great. Why don't you come down and see us?"

"Yes, sure."

Capstick told his wife.

"Barry Noonan! He's really famous isn't he?"

"Quite famous," said Capstick not meeting her eyes.

The following gloomy Saturday he was on an early train to London. He felt very serious and literary among frivolous shoppers, football supporters, lap-topped businessmen. His trips to London had been few and short. He'd never met any of the capital's literati. There'd been a time when he'd hung around notorious bohemian pubs in the hope of running into someone worth knowing. Didn't friendships spark up that way? Once he bought B.S.Johnson a drink but when he tried to stimulate conversation Johnson said:

"Who the fuck are you anyway?"

Finally, he was gaining entry to the world he loved but from which he'd been excluded: writers, books, novels, collections, plays, directors, actors, reviews, biographies! And Noonan knew just about everyone.

At Euston he followed the anonymous crowd up the black platform. Everyone was hurrying. They all had their pressing little business. And he had his: an appointment to begin work on the book which might presently be on the shelves of every library. To be lifted from obscurity at last. To correspond with writers. To meet them in pubs, restaurants, their homes. It was as if concrete blocks had been lifted from his shoulders. He took the rocking tube to NW3 and emerging pulled out the scribbled directions Noonan gave him over the phone. The day was overcast and greyness seeped from every surface. Hampstead, home of intellectuals, politicians, actors celebrities; but it seemed impossibly ordinary. The pavements were cracked and uneven, the tarmac as worn and weathered as at home, the trimmed hedges were mostly conventionally trimmed but the ed sprouted waving stems of privet just as they did where he came from. The place failed to meet his vague expectations.

He reconnoitred Noonan's avenue and seeing a woman heading away from him with baguettes in her arms, wondered if it was Noonan's wife out buying the titbits for lunch. But he was early and disappointed: he would have liked to arrive in a rush like a man with much to do, to have had the confidence to time his appearance to the minute; but the petty anxiety he might not easily find his way made him cautious as a sparrow. He stood on the lonely corner wondering how to kill the eternal hour and a half. Was there a café? He wandered, but not too far , and coming across an estate agency, paused to consider the prices. A one-bedroomed flat on the fourth floor was thirty thousand more than his family semi. A place with four bedrooms cost more than he would earn in his entire teaching career. Walking on he passed a few shoppers, well-dressed, middle-aged, middle-class men and women with confident expressions and purposeful demeanours. He tried to look as if he knew where he was and where he was going. At length he came across a second-hand bookshop and ducking into its gloom felt more at home. He hoped he might find something, but the prices were high. Even foxed paperbacks were marked at what he'd pay for a hardback in the little backstreet shop at home. Then looking up from the rows of orange and blue spines on the packed table in front of him, he met the eyes of a face he recognised. For a few seconds, they stared into his own before the man moved to the biography shelves. Who was it? It took an instant for his fuddled brain to find the answer: Joseph Brodsky. He looked round in time to see him leaving. Should he go after him? What would he say? "Excuse me! Joseph Brodsky? Pleased to meet you. I'm a great admirer of your work. I'm just on my way to Barry Noonan's. Yes, I'm working on his biography. Maybe we could grab a quick coffee?" But lacking the courage, his mind at once sprang to correction. Was he the kind of pathetic hanger-on who would do such a thing? All the same, the disturbing idea arose of mentioning it to Noonan: "Oh, I was in the bookshop round the corner and bumped into Joseph Brodsky." The ambiguous suggestion of acquaintanceship pleased him. But the truth was he found Brodsky's work boring.

He left the shop after what seemed a long hour only to find he still had forty-five minutes to waste. He mooched, looked in another estate agency window, read the headlines in a cramped paper shop before very slowly making his way to Noonan's . Tall on its mound with three worn stone steps up to its racing green, brass-knockered door it immediately set Capstick thinking about prices. Three storeys and a mansard. This alone made the famous socialist a millionaire. But perhaps he was mortgaged to his marrow. All the same, he'd need a fine income to pay it. He was trying to put these thoughts out of his mind and force himself into an easy mood when Noonan opened the door just wide enough to poke his head round as he struggled to restrain a barking, eager sheepdog whose muzzle was forced desperately through the narrow gap. Capstick looked down at the pointed snout, the unfriendly eyes and bared teeth.

"She's friendly, honestly. Never bites. Won't bite. She's a guard dog, that's all. We need a guard dog here. Quiet, Norma. It's a friend. A friend, Norma. Quiet. She won't bite, honestly. Just a second."

The door closed on ferocious yelping, the scratching of nails against polished wood and the sound of Noonan's insistent voice:

"Quiet, Norma. Quiet. It's a friend, Norma."

When he opened for the second time he had his thick fingers curled round the dog's black leather collar and as she lurched for Capstick, yanked her back so her paws lifted from the floor and her yelp rose nearly an octave.

"Come in, Sap. Come in. Quiet, Norma. It's a friend, Norma."

Noonan dragged the animal down the long hallway as Capstick closed the door behind him, trying to ingratiate himself with soppy baby talk, but the barking became only more fierce and Noonan's struggle more strenuous. Capstick stood still. He became aware of the size of the place. The ceiling was at least twice his height. Ahead, broad stairs carpeted in burgundy went up to a little landing and doubled back.

"Look, I'd better put her in the kitchen for a minute till she calms down. She'll be used to you in no time. Come on, Norma. It's a friend. Come on."

He tugged the sliding dog away down the hallway that narrowed to the left of the stairs leaving Capstick, who'd hoped for a smiling, handshaking welcome, looking around trying to understand why Noonan had brought the dog to the door and wondering if her obvious instinctive aversion to him was shared by her master.

"She'll be all right now. Just not used to you. Never seen you before. She's a friendly dog. Never bites, never bitten anybody. Come on through."

"Thanks."

The room they entered was divided in two, the rear part lower by two steps and in the front a great, bare wooden farmhouse table dominated, sitting in the half circle of the tall, lace-curtained bay window which, even on this dull day, shed a heartening dose of light.

"Good to meet you, anyway," said Noonan extending his broad hand.

"Did you have a good journey? I'll just go and get Alison."

He disappeared again and Capstick was about to sit down but restrained himself. He liked the room. It had the right kind of artistic feel. The chairs around the table didn't match and in the lower half were two huge sofas and an armchair. There was no carpet but fringed, exotic rugs on the varnished boards and plenty of books and papers in the kind of disorder which spoke of a mind preoccupied with important things.

"This is Sap. Alison."

Noonan circled the continent of the table, looked out of the window.

"Nice day. Good day."

"Pleased to meet you," said Capstick shaking the hand of the little woman whose creased and ageing face still showed the strong, handsome qualities that had served her well on stage.

"Hi, do sit down."

"Let's have some coffee!" said Noonan.

"Yes," said Alison. "What about you, Sap? Coffee okay?"

"Fine, fine."

"Are you hungry?"

"No, no. I grabbed a sandwich on the train."

Noonan bounced off to the kitchen.

"So, how was your journey?"

"Oh, okay. No delays."

"No. How long does it take from….?"

"Three hours. Just a bit more."

Alison's legs were stretched out and crossed at the ankles. Her hands lay with the fingers intertwined in her lap. She wore jeans and a big, heavy, sloppy, burgundy sweater that reminded Capstick of his student days: the dressing down, the hippy hangover, the general derision, at least in his circle, for slick consumerism. The emollient, gentle, controlled tone of her voice made him wonder if she was acting. Behind the small talk he detected her desire to get to the heart of him and it made him wary. Conscious of his nervousness, he realised his oikish accent and manners gave him away. Here was a woman, well-

291

spoken, educated who had worked in the British theatre for years and, since her marriage , had rubbed shoulders with some of the most lauded writers in the country, and here was he, a teacher from a nondescript northern town who knew no-one, had no profile and spoke like a joiner or bus driver.

"So what do you do up there in......?"

"Teach."

"English?"

"Yes."

"What kind of school?"

"Comprehensive."

"That must be hard work, I guess?"

"Well, quite. Not made any easier by the government's lunatic policies."

"I know. Our children went to comprehensives. They did okay, though Jessica had a troubled time. I was privately educated, like Brian, so what I know of comps is all second hand. Is yours in the centre of......?"

"No, it's in the suburbs. Middle-class place as a matter of fact."

"Oh, you've got it easy then!"

"Easier than some but it's not easy anywhere these days."

"But the children will be biddable, won't they? Is it mixed?"

"No, boys to sixteen, then co-ed in the sixth-form."

"A sixth-form. That must be better."

"Yeah. It's a relief from the younger ones."

"Well, you've got it quite cushy! How long have you been teaching?"

"Thirteen years."

"Are you Head of Department?"

"No, I haven't managed to get promoted."

"And do you come from.......?

"Born and bred."

"Ah, never had itchy feet?"

"Oh yeah. Never thought I'd go back. But you know how it is, things happen you've no control over. My father was ill so I went home. Needed a job. Took this one. Got married. The kids came along and moving on became more difficult."

"Kids haven't stopped us! We've been all over the place. America, Australia, Kent, Cornwall, Yorkshire, Scotland, North Wales, East Anglia. We haven't lived in a house for more than eighteen months."

"Really."

"Yes. In fact I tell a lie. We've been here, what, twenty months I think. That's the record."

"So, do you still act?"

"God, no. I gave that up when Billy was born. I run a little business. Theatrical agency. My contacts were useful. It ticks over nicely and supplements what Brian can bring in."

"Oh, that's good," said Capstick, but he was thinking about their income. It hadn't occurred to him that he'd be visiting the rich. Noonan was known, after all, for his excoriation of privilege and inequality.

"So, is your wife a teacher?"

"No, she works in Boots, in the opticians."

"She's an optician herself then ."

"No, no, she's just an assistant. Does the booking and the preliminary tests and so on."

"I see."

Capstick thought he detected a little collapse of interest in Alison's tone.

"She's got a degree. Fine art. But she didn't want to teach and finding a job using her skills where we live…"

"Yes, pity. She's wasted."

"She is."

"And how old are your children?"

"Six and four. Boy and a girl."

"God, six and four. Long time since mine were that age. Do they get on?"

"Yes, pretty well. They have their moments but in general…"

"And you're a writer! I'm surprised you find the time."

"Well, I try to do a bit. The holidays are useful of course."

"Yes, I can imagine. What have you published, then?"

"Poetry."

"Did it sell?"

"No, small print run. Usual independent press thing. Few hundred copies. Got some nice reviews though."

"Oh, that helps. Brian always manages to get his books reviewed where it matters. Knowing a few people is invaluable. Who publishes your books?"

"Only one actually. It was done by Bluestream press. They're based in Rotherham. It's a one-man outfit. John Weights. He's a writer himself and he does a good job."

"I see. What was your book called?"

"Oranges and Lemons."

"A children's book!"

"No, not at all. The title's from one of the poems which is about singing nursery rhymes to my kids."

"Oh. Oranges and Lemons. I don't remember hearing about it, and Brian didn't mention it. Will he have a copy?"

"I don't know. I didn't send him one."

"You must. Let us have a copy. I'd love to read it. Yes. So, is there a thriving poetry scene in……?"

"No. Nothing happens. A few of us used to meet in a pub once a fortnight and read our stuff to one another, do the odd performance and that kind of thing. But there's no vibrant literary culture in the town. Not that kind of place. It lacks imagination and with a small population you just don't get sufficient numbers of interested folk."

"That's a shame. Brian is very friendly with the Liverpool poets, of course. But I suppose Liverpool's a different kettle of fish. Do you get there much?"

"No, hardly ever. I go to Manchester more. But the Liverpool scene was very much of the sixties. The pop music and all that."

"Oh, yes. Brian's a great fan . He's got all the records."

"Coffee!" called Noonan balancing a wooden tray on which the cafe-tiere slid dangerously.

"Sap's children are six and four, Brian. Remember those days?"

"Six and four. Yep. Great times when kids are little. Great times."

There were three small, thick white cups decorated with a frieze of vines and little matching saucers, a bowl of brown sugar, three spoons and a generous plate of digestives nestling alongside irregular fingers of fruit cake. They had to wait for the coffee to brew.

"Have you got a copy of Sap's book, Brian? Oranges and Lemons."

" Er, don't think I have, no. Who published it?"

"Bluestream," said Sap hoping Noonan would know the name.

"John Weights! I didn't know he was still going."

"Yeah, he does quite a lot. Still gets money from Yorkshire Arts."

"He did some of Ted Byron's stuff. Great. Great poet, Ted. Read with him in Liverpool. Know him?"

Capstick was at once struck by the idea that being northern Noonan assumed he knew everyone who wrote poetry from Birmingham to The Borders; as if that mythical place The North was an homogenous destination where geographical, intellectual, moral and psychological distances were magically dissolved.

"No, I've never met him. I know his stuff of course, but our paths haven't crossed."

"Does he live in..........?" asked Alison.

"No, I think he lives in Manchester these days."

Noonan pressed the plunger and poured the steaming coffee. They drank and ate, Capstick accepting a tapering column of the moist, brandy-rich fruit cake. The desultory conversation spluttered along, the Noonan's at moments talking about matters which excluded the visitor who at once felt he'd failed to engage their interest.

"We'll eat about two shall we, Brian?"

"Two, fine. That's great."

"Is there anything you particularly don't like, Sap?"

"No, I'm pretty omnivorous."

"Right," said Noonan, "let's go to my refuge!"

He led the way along the book-lined hall, through a couple of small rooms cluttered with odd bits of furniture and full of volumes at all angles, out to the garden and down the winding little crazy-paving path to a pitch-roofed shed the size of a four-berth caravan. It was served by the central system and was warm with that soporific stifle of small, over-heated places. There was a long desk which faced the stretching, oblong window out onto the garden, plenty more books and further inside, beyond the window's extent, two armchairs, a coffee table, a television and a cooker. What Sap noticed first, however, was a little model of *The Beatles* sitting on the back wall shelf, complete with collarless jackets, forward-combed hair, replica guitars and a tiny drum kit behind which a beaky Ringo sat, the drumsticks in his bejewelled fists, his head tilted and thrown back in concentrated effort. Noonan noticing his glance turned to the maquette.

"I had it made," he said, "after I first interviewed them. I was the first journalist in Britain to publish an interview. Fantastic. My proudest moment was reading on Paul's world tour."

Capstick nodded, smiled and pretended to be admiring the figures. He'd been a Beatles fan himself. At twelve he queued outside Hindley's Record Shop to buy *She Loves You*, handing over the shillings he earned delivering papers, and from then on bought every single, E.P. and L.P., listening to them endlessly in his bedroom or with friends in their living-rooms when their parents were out, the stylus arm rocking as it followed the groove, the thin sound emanating from the single speaker of the second-hand Dansette. It had been a delirious five years of identification with fabulous wealth and fame, a fantastic whirl of expectation that life would forever be as simple and undemanding as a Lennon-McCartney song; a mad confusion of realms in which the slick marketing of entertainment had been conflated with Harold Wilson's promise of white-hot progress and cherry-sweet equality; and it had all come crashing humiliatingly down when at seventeen Capstick began to listen seriously to Mozart, Beethoven, Haydn, Stravinsky and Shostakovich and to read George Orwell, D.H.Lawrence, Walt Whitman and R.H.Tawney. He was deeply embarrassed to find himself duped, sold his pop records at once and in one of those revolts against a stupidity of our own which we can never expunge from our minds, swung to virulent dismissal of pop culture and castigated *The Beatles* as musical idiots with three-minute minds.

He hadn't expected Noonan to be as adulatory towards them as a thirteen-year-old knicker-wetter, those screaming girls whose factitious emotionalism put him off getting tickets for concerts. The image he'd evolved was of a serious man (and the house, after all, was full of weighty books); a thinking leftie, furrowed and with that dark tone to his character typical of minds that climb to the lofty and perilous branches of objectivity. Didn't even the playful and childlike Einstein evince it? Capstick had long ago concluded that all entertainment was debased art and the reverse side of the economy's compulsive work ethic. His instinct was to mock the childish little model and to say tush to admiration of pop music. But he was Noonan's guest. In another man's house, you behaved well. He'd been brought up in those strict ways of the northern working-class. He had no right. At the same time, he felt he was being tested. There was an inauthentic exaggeration in Noonan's attitude. Was he trying to provoke him? Was he striking a pose as a man of the people, a thoroughgoing populist and daring Capstick to challenge him? He smiled and nodded as Noonan sat at his desk.

"I asked John Lennon why they'd chosen the name, and he said because a man appeared from a flaming pie and said…"

But Capstick wasn't listening. Desperately trying to conceal his discomfort, he was running his gaze over the books. Fighting the thought he'd made a bad mistake, he was striving to adjust his thinking, already composing the sentences carefully expressing Noonan's charming spontaneity in responding to *Helter Skelter* or *Mary Had A Little Lamb*. Noonan talked at length about his time as a journalist, how thrilled he was to get to know the Fab Four, his instrumentality in getting the first charts published in the British press, but little by little the conversation turned towards his own early life. They moved to the armchairs and Noonan sat with one heavy thigh over the other, the childlike little smile in which Capstick imagined he detected something forced often on his eyes and lips.

"Yeah, my dad was an economist. Worked for The Bank of England!" and the little smile flickered. "Don't know what he did. Helped come up with some theory about money supply, something like that I think. He was a quiet man. When people came to the house he went out among his roses. He was a great rose-grower."

"What was he like as a father?"

"Yeah. Er, he was kind. But my mother ruled the roost. My mother was all energy. She was a whirlwind."

Capstick listened, threw in the occasional predictable question, nodded smiled and laughed as Noonan's recollections oozed and spread like spilt paint. Capstick was surprised at how much his subject liked talking about himself but at the same time struck by the odd sense of it all pouring involuntarily, as if some part of Noonan's mind needed to unburden itself of what he knew about himself, as if there was a pursuit of blankness, of some atavistic purity, some state prior to experience. When he came to his first marriage, Capstick felt almost intrusive. He'd met Pam on a blind date organised by his great friend Doug Payne, now married to a best-selling popular novelist; they fell into a mad affair and went to Ealing Register Office after seventeen weeks; two children were born in the first two years and when the second developed a high fever and red rash at the age of three months, Pam refused to let Noonan take him to the hospital or a doctor. She belonged to a sect which believed all illness was sent from outer space; medical knowledge was powerless against it. Noonan took the child to his GP and he was admitted to hospital with measles. Pam threatened to kill him and in days he'd walked out.

Something in Noonan's tone gave Capstick the feeling he was talking about someone else's experience. As if it had all pened without him being able to intervene to prevent it. And at times a curious glance appeared in Noonan's eye, leftward and shifty which made Capstick's heart quicken with unease. But the shape and tenor of Noonan's life was coming together in his mind, in the way a crossword grid fills with letters. The outline he'd created from the poems, articles and interviews was twisted into a new form. Noonan, he realised, was hardly anything like he'd imagined.

The lunch was delightfully simple: baguettes, salad, tuna, sardines; the kind of thing Capstick might have hurled together for himself in his usual impatience with preparing food, but here, carefully combined and presented, as straightforward but attractive as Alison's clothes. For dessert there were raspberries and ice-cream. The big tub of vanilla sat beside the steep white dish which gleamed starkly against the red juice of the marinating fruit and when Capstick wanted a second helping he hesitated to use the spoon he'd already eaten from. But as there was no communal cutlery, he wondered if the

298

Noonans were unfussy. Perhaps the best thing was to do without. But then he thought that might appear churlish. To eat heartily was a compliment. So he sank his spoon in the soft yellow just as Noonan turned from the table, skipped down the steps and disappeared. In seconds he was back with a serving spoon, but seeing Capstick's heaped dish, tried to conceal his motivation by tapping it against his palm before discreetly slipping it onto the table. Capstick felt the heat in his cheeks but what could he do except continue to lift the melting, sweet stuff to his mouth?

The little mortification of the table stayed with him all afternoon as they sat in the cabin, Noonan elaborating enthusiastically more details of his life.

"I've written a short autobiog. Up to eighteen. I like childhood. Publisher offered me ten thousand but I'm sticking out for twenty."

Capstick nodded but he wanted to exclaim: "You turned down ten grand! I have to work a year to bring that home!"

And as the one-sided conversation rattled along, Capstick became more and more conscious of the gulf between his socialist subject and his own experience as an easy-going oik. He couldn't expel from his mind the thought that Noonan was very much a product of his upper-middle-class, public-school, Oxford background.

"I had to leave the *Courier*. Changed the office. I was put in this place with no windows. I couldn't stand it. Gave me nightmares. So I walked out. Mortgage, kids, mmm. Rang Johnny Ovenden, he was editing *The Mirror*. Went down to see him and he gave me a weekly column and that let us move to London."

"How did you know him?"

"He was at Oxford with me."

Capstick ran the story through his mind: a change in working conditions; gives up his job; rings an old friend who finds him another and better; and comparing this to his own working life, the keeping going day after day whatever the conditions, which was most people's fate, he felt flat and out-of-place. Noonan's was the old-boy-network world, closed, self-flattering and hypocritical. How could that be squared with socialism? It barely even tallied with Tory meritocracy. It was essentially a nexus of inherited privilege. He was inured by the time Noonan told about the play on Richmal Crompton he'd written and sold for ten thousand to his old friend Sir Michael Horne at the National, even though it was never performed.

By the time Capstick had to leave to catch his train, he was beginning to feel a weight of negativity bearing down on his mind. Perhaps it would be better to give up the idea? But when, as he was pulling on his shapeless coat, Noonan said:

"Well, maybe the article then?"

Capstick insisted:

"No, no. I'd like to have a go at the book."

The phone rang. Alison answered. It was Noonan's eldest son. There was some problem so Capstick gently withdrew and waited outside while they talked. On the way to the station, Noonan said:

"My son Colin's manic-depressive. Thirteen years this has been going on."

Capstick looked at him, his eyes on the pavement, his face curiously intense but bewildered. He felt atrociously sorry for him and grateful for his hospitality and the kindness of walking him to the tube; but at the same time he felt an uncomfortable sense of revolt against the assumptions of his culture.

It wasn't uncomfortable enough, however, to make Capstick change his mind; or rather, he persisted in a perverse defiance of a better impulse. The first draft of the first chapter went off to Noonan. Pages of questions were responded to by tapes of Noonan's halting baritone. Capstick typed away, banged off letters. Wrote and rewrote and the manuscript was touching fifty thousand words. His wife excitedly told all their friends about the project. Capstick began to try to interest publishers and agents. He wrote to Henry Judge, the famous poet who'd been at Oxford with Noonan, but he refused to answer any questions until the manuscript had been placed. Then he needed to contact William Broughton who Noonan had worked with on a translation of Ovid.

"Do you have a current address for Bill Broughton?" he wrote.

Two days later came the brief reply:

Dear Sap,

How dare you call my good friend Bill? It's William Broughton, even to those closest to him, among whom I'm proud to count myself.

Capstick was flabbergasted . This little jab in the sternum from a man who proclaimed himself an enemy of all pomposity, who identified with all-boundaries-down pop culture, who claimed to be an avid supporter of Liverpool F.C., seemed like simple snobbery, a public school rebuke to a vertical-invading oik. To lift himself from his humiliation, Capstick wanted to write back:

Don't be such a snooty toffee-nosed cissy. Do you think the working folk you claim to support go around calling one another, James, Kenneth, Joseph, Andrew, Stanley and Edward all day long?

But he was restrained by fear of Noonan's withdrawal. It occurred to him that the response was perhaps a way of putting him off. Maybe Noonan just didn't have confidence in him, was fed up with the project but too polite to say. The more it nagged, the more he wondered if Noonan was right: maybe it was intrusive and impertinent of him to use a diminutive about his friend; maybe the easy-going ways of the back-street culture Capstick was raised in were sentimental; perhaps the more formal manners of Noonan's upper-middle-class culture really were superior. The thought that the fault was with him made him writhe and worry. But he soon rebelled and felt like giving up. He'd chosen Noonan because of his public image as a subversive, a mischievous imp, always willing to spike inherited privilege, inequality, the power of money. Now he found himself put down for a trivial lapse.

He thought better of renunciation, however, imagining his book on the shelves of *Waterstones* in every town from Exeter to Inverness. It was worth playing down Noonan's brittle petulance for the prize of publication. It happened that Noonan was on tour. Once a year his agent organized a thirty venue sprint, he pulled in a thousand quid a night, and retired to his cabin for months. He was reading in York so Capstick said he'd get over, and bring his wife. Noonan promised to arrange free tickets and the generosity was a balm. The throbbing sore of Capstick's injured pride which made his heart skip and his mouth go dry calmed. The Saturday arrived. They drove over early, ate in a gentle vegetarian, mooched in the busy, narrow streets. Capstick browsed a couple of well-stocked, dusty second-hands. At seven they turned up at the venue and, leaning on the tall, pale walnut counter he asked the little dark woman in glasses and a purple blouse unbuttoned to her cleavage:

"Is there a pair of tickets for Capstick?"

"Capstick?"

She foraged. Her long white fingers whose nails were painted black flicked through the tickets in a long, narrow wooden box.

"No, sorry. When did you ring?"

"Oh, I didn't ring. Brian Noonan was supposed to be organizing it."

"I see. I'll just check."

She clicked and twitched her mouse, her little dark eyes scanning the screen.

"No, there's no message. Just hang on a minute."

She disappeared through a rear door. Capstick turned to his wife who raised her brows and tilted her head. He shook his. She turned away and idly surveyed a poster. He drummed his fingers, tried to assume an untroubled demeanour.

"No, he hasn't left anything, but if you'd like to go through those doors at the end John South will have a word with you. He's the arts officer."

"Thanks very much."

Capstick gestured to his wife who followed him as he strode. His confidence rallied. He'd come across South in writing workshops, at readings and their poems had appeared in the same little magazines. The couple passed through the swing doors and found the bearded little man spreading books and leaflets over a large table. He turned and looked at them over his round, gold-framed glasses, went back to his work and made them wait a few seconds.

"What's the problem?" he said coming towards them.

He was dressed in clean, neatly-ironed jeans and a fawn crew-neck sweater which met the thick hair of his neck. It was obvious he wasn't going to acknowledge Capstick.

"There should be a couple of tickets for us. Brian Noonan was organizing them."

South shook his head and turned down his mouth. His fixed gaze was an accusation. Capstick felt a little rage rising.

"I'm working on a biography of him you see. He promised he'd set the tickets aside."

302

South went on shaking his head in the same way and his look was all disdain for a cheap trick.

"There's nothing here," he said. "Brian didn't mention it."

"Has he arrived?" said Capstick.

"Yeah."

"Can I speak to him?"

Capstick's confidence was now at a critical point: if he got to speak to Noonan, he would make South look silly. The poet would admit his neglect, tell South to sort out the complimentaries. Capstick would be vindicated and take his seat serenely. But South shook his head again.

"No chance."

Capstick, standing no more than a metre away fixed him. South looked back, baldly confident. In those two seconds, Capstick had to decide: either there would be a row or he would have to withdraw, but he knew that if he started to raise the temperature he'd lose his *sang-froid* and in seconds he'd be saying things he'd regret.

"Okay."

He walked out calmly, his wife beside him. When they were through the doors she said:

"Officious little man!"

"Not his fault."

"What shall we do?"

Capstick would have gladly left, gone to the cinema, found a pub, but the sense of duty the biography had turned into weighed on him. At the counter he handed over his card and as he waited for the quick little woman to process and deliver the tickets, the awful sense came over him that she thought he was a charlatan.

"That's thirty pounds," she said and once in his seat Capstick couldn't keep himself from a quick headcount: three hundred. What was Noonan pulling in. A grand? Two? And then the book signings.

The lights went down. He galloped on stage, somewhat awkward and overweight and went through the routine he'd perfected over the decades: the early stuff first, the old favourites like *Magna Carta Milk Shake* , then the newer stuff, interspersed with songs and piano accompaniment. When it was over there were queues for signatures. Capstick caught Noonan's eye as he was sitting down, but he quickly put on his glasses and picked up his pen.

In the car on the way home Capstick's wife said:

"He's a bit babyish, isn't he?"

"How do you mean?"

"Well, the way he skipped on stage, like a lamb in spring. It just struck me as sort of, infantile."

"Maybe."

A few days later Capstick got a reply from Victor Brown, an old Oxford friend of Noonan's, a poet who was close to Kingsley Amis and John Wain, and married to the biographer Sally Brown who had written lives of Enid Blyton, Agatha Christie and Marie Corelli:

Get back to me when you've done some proper work.

His wife had appended a little hand-written note:

I suppose it's too early yet to go into details about the breakdown of the first marriage, all that heartache…

Capstick, who disliked Brown's collar-and-tie poetry, screwed up the letter and dropped it in the bin. Some proper work! It was true the manuscript was still first draft, but he was teaching full-time, looking after a young family and writing in the gaps. Brown, manufacturing marathon reviews for the Sundays, could get up in the morning and sit at his screen all day. Capstick was all but ready to give up, but though the work he'd done was only preparatory, it amounted to hundreds of hours. If he could interest a publisher, the effort wouldn't have been wasted. He switched his attention. For weeks he did nothing in his spare time but bang out letters and sample chapters to publishers and agents. After seventy-five rejections, he decided they'd made his mind up for him.

He let time go by without adding a word or making contact with Noonan. At length, he got a note. He replied that he'd tried hard to raise interest, but no-one wanted the book. In the circumstances, he didn't feel it worth carrying on. Noonan graciously thanked him for what he'd done, expressed regret that there was so little response and asked if he'd keep the material, just in case someone else came along.

Capstick packed it all in a cardboard box and put it in the attic. Eighteen months later a flyer arrived from the local theatre: Brian Noonan was on tour. He dropped it in the bin and didn't mention it to his wife.

BLUE CARPET

Mike Braun bounded up the narrow stairs past the Head of Sixth Form's office. As he arrived, Hiscock appeared. He seemed surprised, pulled himself to his full height. Braun paused.

"All right, Dave?"

Hiscock nodded and peered through his glasses. The two men hesitated. Hiscock straightened his jacket and went quickly down. Odd? What's the matter with him? Braun loitered for a minute or two in the classroom beyond. The office door opened. Aye, aye! A female head peeped out.

"Oh, hello, Mike. Have you seen Dave?"

"No," said Braun, "not at all."

Mrs Twinklekeys emerged holding her note-pad and pen.

"I'm supposed to be doing shorthand."

"Ah, shorthand."

"I'd better go and find him."

"Yeah. I haven't seen him. Maybe he's in the staffroom."

"He's never where he's supposed to be."

"No. So it seems."

She trotted nimbly down and Braun noticed little bits of blue carpet fabric stuck to her back. She was gone in a flash. She was trim and quick all right for a woman beyond forty.

Two minutes later, Braun was in the P.E. office.

"Hey, hey, hey! Guess what I've just seen?"

The two young P.E. teachers stopped what they were doing.

"Tina Twinklekeys coming out of Dave Hiscock's office with bits of carpet stuck to her back!"

"He's been shagging the arse off her for ages!" said one of the others with a hint of disdain.

"You knew?"

"Everybody knows."

"How did you find out?"

306

"I bumped into him in town, going the wrong way down Butler St."

"With her?"

"No. Going. She lives that way. Since her marriage broke up. One of those ancient terraced places on Old Mill St. So I says to him 'Where you off, Dave? Not your neck of the woods.' And he says 'For a drink.' 'A drink,' I says. 'Down here!' 'Yes,' he says, defiant, you know. And then shuts up. 'Well, watch yourself,' I says. 'Crack a tenner in *The Rosebud* and they'll mug you on the doorstep.' And off he goes. Well, I knew all right. Nine o'clock. He's been dipping his wick for years."

"Well, he's doing it in school hours now. He's getting paid for it!"

"Forty quid an hour. Nice work if you can get it!"

"His wife'll find out sooner or later."

"Bet she knows already."

"She's blind if she doesn't."

The three of them went back to their work.

That week Eric Brain, Headteacher of Chipping Grammar, was checking the accounts. He'd done the calculations seven times, like a writer dissatisfied with a simile. Always the same result. A thousand short. He summoned the bursar.

"There's a discrepancy. See what you find."

She was away for two hours.

"A thousand down."

The office staff had to be questioned. One by one he called them in. Tina Twinklekeys, sixteen years in the school, devoted Anglican, Guide mistress, diligent to a fault, secretary to both Brain and Hiscock, was above suspicion. He called her last. No sooner had he mentioned the sum than she broke down. She was sorry; she'd only borrowed it; she was going to pay it back; she'd got into trouble with her credit cards; she meant no harm; she'd resign immediately; being a single parent was hard.

Brain sat impassive as the dapper little woman dabbed her eyes and blew her nose. He was a Christian and what was a Christian's duty in such circumstances? Wasn't his faith being tested? Wasn't this an opportunity? He felt that sense of superiority which floods the minds

307

of the religious when they defend their belief against sceptics or offer forgiveness to sinners. He heard God speaking to him. God's ways were so mysterious he could even turn secretaries into thieves so the wonder of Christian charity might be revealed. Nothing happened on earth, after all, without God wishing it to be so: not Nazi gas chambers, nor Hiroshima, nor Stalin's mass murders. No. Hard though it was for non-believers to understand, these were the ways God permitted his goodness to be manifest.

"Calm down, Mrs Twinklekeys," he said in his thin, mousey voice. "I understand your predicament. What you've done is wrong. No doubt about that. It's a crime. A moral lapse. You do appreciate that?"

"Yes. I'm sorry. I don't know what came over me."

"Temptation," Mrs Twinklekeys. "The devil goes round like a roaring lion."

She looked up, startled.

"I'm going to forgive you, Mrs Twinklekeys."

He felt himself rise. He was a mile nearer heaven. He imagined paradise as the Home Counties, without rain. Everything was orderly and moderate. Moderate was one of Brain's favourite words. It excluded all he despised: socialists, the working class, argument, modern music, cities. He conceived the afterlife as Sunday afternoon in an upper middle-class home on the Sussex Downs: replete, quiet, contented, superior. He saw himself as God's right-hand man. His place was secure. And all his enemies would be consigned to the flames of hell! Heaven had to be a very exclusive venue.

Tina Twinklekeys felt awkward. She stopped crying, sniffed a few times and looked Brain in the eye. She wasn't sure she enjoyed being forgiven.

"You must repay the money in full."

"Of course."

"How much can you afford per month?"

"Would a hundred be okay?"

"Ten months. That seems fair. But there must be no lapses. I'm afraid a repetition and I'd have to ask for your resignation."

"No. I won't miss a payment. Thank you very much Mr Brain."

"That's all right, Tina."

She stiffened a little at his use of her first name: he was such a formal, buttoned-up character. She felt humiliated. She was glad she was to keep her job but she disliked his attitude. In a way, she wished he'd told her to hand in her notice. At least that was straight. The business of being forgiven pulled her mouth down at the corners. She left.

Later that day, collecting his mail from the tray in the office, Brain found a small white envelope marked *Mr E.Brain, Private and Confidential*. The handwriting was familiar but he couldn't pin it down. Inside was a note:

Mr Brain,

I think you should know that David Hiscock and Tina Twinklekeys have been having sexual relations on school premises during the school day.

Brain sat back in horror. The image came into his head of Hiscock on top of Twinkelkeys, her legs around him, his buttocks thrusting away with the regularity of an ink-jet printer, his trousers round his ankles, and she trying to suppress her little squeals of pleasure. Where! Where on these premises were they engaging in this foulness? He paced his office. He wanted to confront her. He wanted to thrust the letter into Hiscock's hand. He sat down. He was full of rage and disgust. This was his school! A Christian school! He had just forgiven Twinklekeys! But he couldn't forgive her this! Sex during the school day! On the premises!

He was so beside himself he had forgotten that in his drawer was Hiscock's letter of application for the post of Assistant Headteacher. When it occurred to him he almost fell to his knees to thank God. Wasn't this too coincidental? Didn't it point to divine intervention? Hadn't he been intending to give Hiscock an interview? He had always known, of course, that the two of them were closer than they should be but he'd never imagined it had gone so far. But he had the perfect means to discomfit Hiscock. He scribbled a note:

Dear David,

Thank you for your application for the post of Assistant Headteacher. I'm afraid I'm unable...

He stopped. He went over to the window and looked at the weeping willow and the lawn. Wasn't this a little corner of paradise? A pupil walked by on some errand. An innocent boy of twelve or thirteen. He stood for a long time. Someone knocked at the door and he ignored it. The phone rang and he refused to pick it up. He sat down. He was resolved. He screwed up the note and dropped it in his bin.

Two days later, Hiscock walked into the staffroom and saw a new notice pinned to the Headteacher's notice board. He knew at once what it was and rushed to read it. The interviews were to take place next Thursday. There was a timetable and a list of names. He read it. He read it again. He read it over and over. It was as if he had been physically attacked. He felt under threat and in need of fighting back. He wanted to walk out. Someone approached and asked him a question. He looked her in the eye but didn't answer. He turned on his heels, marched out and went and shut himself in his office. But the day went on. He had matters to attend to. People came looking for him. A student knocked on his door and getting no answer poked his head round:

"Get out! How dare you!"

Hiscock leapt from his chair and went after the lad. He stood inches from him.

"I'll wipe the smile off your face, sunshine!"

But the nettle had to be grasped. He postponed as long as he could, but at two thirty he knocked on Brain's door.

"Come in!" trilled the thin little voice.

Hiscock closed the door behind him.

"Hello David. Do have a seat."

Hiscock sat down without a word. He was too angry to dare to speak. He sat upright in the low chair. He was a big man with broad shoulders and heavy thighs. He seemed too large for the seat. Little beads of sweat appeared on his forehead. He looked at Brain who lay back in his swivel chair in his favourite executive pose. He wore a grey suit and one of those odd-coloured cotton shirts he favoured, a sort of greeny grey, indeterminate and dull. His hair was perfectly neat and trimmed as ever. At fifty-two his face still had something of a little boy. It was the face of an obedient choirboy or boy scout but the jowls were beginning to droop.

"What can I do for you, David?"

"I think you know."

Hiscock felt his pulse race. He would have liked to have punched Brain in the nose. He would have relished a playground scrap. He was bigger, fitter, younger. He would have laid him out and left him bloodied and defeated.

"I'm sorry?"

"Oh for God's sake!"

Brain sat forward and adopted a serious expression.

"Could you restrain your language, please. This is a Christian school."

"I've read the notice about the interviews. I'd like to know why I'm not being considered."

"Well, why should you know?" said Brain in a tone of absolute reasonableness.

"It's customary."

Hiscock was holding back as best he could.

"But if you'd applied for the post of Assistant Head in another school, you wouldn't expect to be sitting with the Head discussing why you'd been turned down, would you?"

"That's different."

"Why so?"

"Because the Head of another school wouldn't be writing a reference for me for any future job I applied for."

"Oh, are you thinking of leaving us?"

Hiscock paused. He looked Brain in the eye. The other man looked back at him undaunted, secure behind his status. Hiscock realised how much he hated him, a violent and destructive hatred. He would have gladly murdered him and felt no remorse.

"If I applied for an Assistant Headship elsewhere, would you support me?"

Brain entwined his fingers, cat's cradle style. He swivelled in his chair to face the window. For thirty seconds he held the posture. Turning back he said:

"You'd have to come to see me and we'd build your platform."

311

"And what might be wrong with my platform?"

Brain looked down at the blotting pad on his desk. He used it only to dry his signature. He was fond of his signature. He'd spent many hours refining it. It was a symbol of his status.

"I don't trust you." he said looking up, and before Hiscock could respond he added, "By the way, did you get that message from Mrs Twinklekeys this morning?"

He looked hard into Hiscock's eyes. Knowing what was going on, the other man felt suddenly subordinate. His mind raced. How had he found out? Maybe he didn't know at all. Maybe it was bluff. Maybe he merely suspected. Perhaps he should defend himself. He was on the point of saying: "Are you conniving at a relationship between me and Mrs Twinklekeys?" when he realised how dangerous it might be. He would have to see it through. He would have to deny everything. What if they'd been spotted together? What if someone knew about the sex in his office? Suddenly he remembered Mike Braun. The image sprang into his head like a vole from a riverbank . Had he suspected? Tina had still been in there. Had he seen her? He was swamped by confusion.

"Well?" said Brain.

"Yes," said Hiscock.

"Is there anything else?"

Hiscock got up and left. He seethed with anger, hatred and humiliation. He was ready to murder. His face had taken on that ugly sneer that meant he wasn't getting his own way. He experienced his impotence as a terrible threat. His very existence was in danger. He went straight to Mrs Twinklekeys.

"Can you come and take some dictation in my office, please."

The two other clerks looked knowingly at one another as she took up her pad and pencil.

" Did Mike Braun see you coming out of my office?"

"What?"

"Think for fuck's sake, Tina! This is important. One day I met Braun at the top of the stairs. You were still in here. Did he see you?"

"Yes. He was hanging around when I came out."

"Shit a brick!"

"What?"

"Why didn't you stay in here till the coast was clear?"

"How did I know?"

"Use your fucking brain woman! You do have a brain don't you?"

"Don't talk to me like that!"

"How are you going to stop me? I'm your boss. Remember?"

"You may be my boss, David, but you've had me on this carpet. I've sucked your cock while you sat in that chair. Mind how you talk to me!"

"Are you threatening me, Tina?"

"I'm telling you to watch your tongue!"

"You can't do a fucking thing, Tina! You've stolen from the school. You've no power. You'll do what I fucking-well tell you."

"No I won't, Dave. You listen to me. I'll tell Brain you seduced me. I'll say you used your position to screw me. I'll tell him you fucked me in this office while the kids were in the classrooms. He can sack me if he wants. But he'll sack you too. I can get another job on thirteen grand a year tomorrow, but where are you going to get one on fifty. Just back off, Dave, or I'll finish you!"

Hiscock sank into his chair.

"Get out of here."

Mrs Twinklekeys hesitated. She played the pencil between her fingers.

"You've had me for the last time. But just remember, treat me well or I'll tell him everything."

She was gone.

The interviews took place and a devout Christian was appointed. A'woman ten years Hiscock's junior. He shook her hand and congratulated her. That evening he went to town alone. He told his wife he was going out with colleagues. He visited some dives. The drinkers were mostly rough and ready men but there were some raucous, boozy, smoking, tarted-up women. He looked at them and wished he could fuck one of them in a doorway.

At school, he kept an eye on Mike Braun. One day, he missed a break duty. Hiscock went straight to the new Assistant Head:

"He needs speaking to. It's not the first time."

Then, out for a curry with some of the blokes, he heard the story of Braun having had sex with a sixth-form girl. How hadn't he known? He was Head of Sixth-Form after all. How had he kept it quiet? He wanted chapter and verse but pretended to be blasé.
"Who was it?"

Someone came up with a name.

"Was she eighteen?"

There was a silence.

"No," someone said after a few seconds. "She was Year 12. Seventeen at the most. Probably only sixteen when he started."

"Christ! Was Mike married at the time?"

"No, no! It was when he was still single. You know what he was like then. Anything in knickers."

The next day Hiscock ransacked the files stored in the old boiler room. He found what he wanted. From her picture he recalled her. She'd been excellent at sport. No doubt that was how Braun got his chance. But he would need more than hearsay. Discreetly he spoke to staff.

"Hey, did you know about Mike Braun?"

"What's that?"

And he would tell conspiratorially what he knew hoping for some detail in return, but nothing emerged. His colleagues were cagey. Finally, he went to the new Assistant Head.

"But this is years ago!" she said.

"Does that matter when the good name of the school is at stake?"

"I'll speak to Eric."

"No! Talk to Braun first. Get some evidence. Don't go to the Head till you've a real case."

He waited but nothing happened. Should he go back to her? He didn't want to seem too eager. Weeks went by. He began to lose hope. Then came just what he wanted. A pupil accused Braun of having hit him. Everyone knew it was malicious but Hiscock volunteered to investigate. The Assistant Head, run off her feet and thinking it trivial, let him get on with it. He talked to all the boys who had witnessed the exchange:

"What did you see?"

"Mr Braun was shouting at him, sir."

"Just shouting?"

"Yes, sir."

"Was he close to him?"

"Quite close, sir."

"How close?"

"I couldn't say, sir."

"This close?"

"Not as close at that, sir."

"Did he raise his hand?"

"Kind of, sir."

"What do you mean, kind of?"

"He sort of went like that, sir."

The boy jabbed his finger.

"So he poked Lygoe with his finger?"

"I don't know, sir."

"Well think. Did he touch him? That's what matters. Did he make contact with him?"

"He might have done, sir."

Hiscock went to the Assistant Head. He had the evidence. A boy had seen Braun jab Lygoe with his finger.

"Let's play it down," she said.

"The parents have a right to know. Their son has been assaulted."

"Assaulted is an exaggeration."

"Would you say so if it was your child?"

"Above all we have to make sure there's no publicity. You know what happens if the local rag gets hold of this kind of thing."

"Sure. We have to keep it quiet. But he needs to be dealt with. Take it from me, he's a loose cannon."

She looked at him. He knew the school much better than she did. Was he telling the truth? Hiscock stared at her. A little smile crossed his lips. He felt things were moving his way. He could feel his advantage growing greater. He would fuck that Braun good and proper. He would have the bastard sacked.

Everything had to be handled very formally. The letter to Lygoe's parents was typed by Mrs Twinklekeys. She kept a copy for herself. At lunchtime she went out alone and had a sandwich in *The Dog and Gun*. She took the letter from her handbag. It was to be signed by Brain, but she knew who'd composed it. She'd also typed the letters inviting the interviewees and the offer letter to the new Assistant Head. She knew how devastated Hiscock was and she knew too the ugly side of his character. She folded the letter and put it away. In the afternoon she spoke to Mike Braun:

"How are things, Mike?"

"Fine. How are you?"

"Oh, okay. Except for that moody bugger, Hiscock."

"Is he on your case?"

"He's on everybody's case!"

"Yeah?"

"He's been impossible since he didn't get an interview."

"Well, that's understandable."

"I don't get why they didn't invite him. He's been here so long. And he's Head of Sixth Form. Somebody must know something."

"You think so?"

"You know what Dave's like. He gets on the wrong side of people. I can easily imagine someone wanting revenge."

Braun had had several run-ins with Hiscock. Once he had said to him, in the staff-room, in front of other staff: "Your name is mud, Mr Braun!"

The Lygoes came into school. He had to account for himself. Hiscock was in the meeting. He pushed the issue of the jabbing finger.

"No," insisted Braun. "I waved a stiff finger at him but I didn't touch him."

Hiscock looked down his nose.

"In any case," continued Braun, "the lad's story is that I hit him with my right hand. That's impossible."

"Why?" asked Hiscock.

"My right arm was in a sling that week. I sprained my wrist lifting a weight."

The Lygoes looked at one another. Hiscock studied his papers. Braun was found not to have touched the boy.

One afternoon he was bounding up the stairs to Hiscock's office. They met at the top. Hiscock refused to stand aside. Braun waited a second and eased round him. The big man went rapidly down the stairs. A few seconds later, Tina Twinklekeys appeared from the office.

"Hi Mike!" she called.

She tripped down, nimble and athletic . He turned to watch but there was no sign of carpet fabric on her back.

ANN LEAKEY'S ROLLS-ROYCE

Students were arriving by car, bus and train, lugging heavy suitcases, wheeling trunks on battered, tilting, squeaking trolleys ; there were rucksacks, holdalls, shoulder bags, carrier bags, Gladstones, clydes. The campus swarmed. Concerned parents followed their offspring across the square and into halls: brick-built, three-storey blocks, mostly, where ten students shared a floor. Mrs Treanor was following her son who was six inches taller and whose stride was long and swift. She'd expected him to go to Oxbridge, or at least Durham . Being married to a minor diplomat, her children were educated in private schools at the expense of the taxpayer, an arrangement she thought excellent. That the children of the working-class were educated at university by the same means, she thought of as Bolshevism. Still, here they were, in Lancaster. It was a university, apparently. As she entered her son's college, she crossed paths with a startlingly good-looking girl. At once it struck her that her son might soon be in bed with such a young woman. Or even that very one! This was 1972 after all. The sexual revolution had happened. He was no longer in the exclusive atmosphere of a public school. And this was the north! He might mix with all kinds of riff-raff.

The riff-raff in question was Ann Leakey and John Treanor did end up in bed with her.

They were both studying French and Russian. Ann was the outstanding beauty of her year. Slim and dark with wide blue eyes she looked lovely in the downbeat clothes she usually wore. She was also stunningly intelligent and whipped through Proust as if it were the *Daily Mail*, while her fellow students struggled, looking up every tenth word. Boys were after her, as they'd been for years. Most of them bored her. She was looking for something different, though she didn't know what. She just had a sense, like someone who has grown bored of a repetitive diet, that something unusual was necessary. John had noticed her on the first day. When she'd appeared in the lecture theatre for the talk on Charles Péguy, his heart quickened. He got to know girls on her floor. He was in their kitchen with a bottle of Sauternes when she came in. She was unobtrusive but unmissable. She went to her cupboard and took out her mug.

"I was hoping my father would get posted to Paris," he said loudly.

318

"I'd love to live in Paris. Madrid is fine, of course, but I adore Paris."

Ann quietly made a cup of coffee. One of the girls asked her what she was up to and she said she was translating.

"Oh, I love translating!" said John. "I was always the best in my class. But I agree with Voltaire about translations, don't you?"

Ann disappeared. As she went down the corridor, she could hear John's loud, annoying voice. He was tall and strong and intelligent looking. But his loud, intrusive arrogance made her wince.

A few days later she was buying a TLS when someone hissed. She turned round. It was him. He stood over her with a big smile, as if he were posing for a camera.

"What are you buying?"

She looked at the paper.

"TLS."

"That's very intellectual."

"That's an exaggeration."

He laughed loudly and nervously.

"Are you going to the disco tonight?" he asked.

"Maybe. Or maybe I'll finish *L'existentialisme est un humanisme.*"

He laughed loudly again.

"I think I prefer a disco to Sartre!"

"Do you? I'm still trying to decide."

"Are you walking back?"

"When I've paid for this. I'm not shoplifting."

"No!" he guffawed. "I'll wait outside."

Ann joined the queue. She wished one of her friends would appear. She'd met two or three girls she got on with brilliantly. Like her, they were from unpretentious families and had a homely ease to them. If only one of them would arrive now and they could walk back together.

"By the way," said John as she came out of the shop, "you wouldn't have a clothes brush I could borrow would you?"

"A clothes brush?" she put her change in her purse wondering if she should lie.

"Yes, my jacket got amazingly dusty in the bar last night. Things got a bit hectic and my jacket fell off the chair and everyone walked over it. It's a real mess!"

She glanced up at him. He was one of those fine specimens the English public schools turn out: tall, clean, smooth and lacking in character like a newly-built Wimpey house. Without knowing it, she dropped her guard a little. She found herself thinking he was a buffoon, but harmless, and her natural generosity took hold. She was like a boy who ventures out onto a frozen pond , and has no idea how it might feel to be in the chill water, beneath the ice.

"As a matter of fact, I have. But it'll cost you."

"Oh, don't worry about that," he said loudly, "I'm loaded."

She made him wait outside while she searched. He tried to peep through the door left ajar. She remained inside and held the brush out to him. The electric light caught her eyes and made them shine bright blue. He stared at her.

"Here. I hope it does the trick."

"Thanks."

He took it from her and stood awkwardly.

"Do you fancy the disco tonight?"

He had the big smile again and his eyes were wide. She looked up at him and blenched a little as she might from a garish neon sign.

"As a matter of fact, I fancy Jean-Paul Sartre. He's gorgeous."

John looked bewildered.

"Good luck with the jacket."

All the same, she turned up. She was with the girls she'd got to know. The disco was in a college bar and the place was packed, noisy, drunken and reeked of alcohol. John had drunk a bottle of Sauternes and was loud and staggering. He watched Ann as she danced with her friends. A boy moved in and tried to talk to her as he jigged to the repetitive beat. When the song ended, she walked away. He lost sight of her and pushed through the crowd to find her.

"I see that Ann Leakey's here!" one of his mates shouted into his ear.

"Yes!"

"I wouldn't climb over her to get to you!"

John rocked with laughter. Where was she? He tried to keep her in his view and to summon up courage. Each time he caught sight of her his heart raced. She seemed different from minute to minute. He couldn't look at her enough. Her beauty defeated looking. At last, he approached her.

"I thought you were reading Sartre!" he shouted.

"I'm a fast reader!"

He rocked with laughter again.

"Do you want to dance?"

"No, I want to elaborate my own project."

"What?"

"Never mind."

"I'm pissed. I've drunk a whole bottle of Sauternes."

"You obviously have refined tastes."

"What are you drinking?"

"Dandelion and burdock."

He walked her back. Outside her room he tried to kiss her. She allowed him a peck on the cheek and disappeared. He knocked on her door.

"No home to go to?"

"Can I come in?"

"Of course not. I've got Jean-Paul Sartre naked in here."

Before going to bed, Ann decided to keep her distance. He was handsome enough, but empty, and something about his behaviour disturbed her, like an alarm heard faintly which keeps sounding through the night. She turned out the lamp and was quickly asleep.

In spite of her resolution, he seemed more present than ever. He was always in the kitchen, talking loudly and laughing in his embarrassing, raucous way. The more time she spent in his company, the more her original irritation and defensiveness waned. Like a bad smell which strikes you when you enter a room but which fades as you get used to it, his intrusive, insensitive manner became less noticeable.

And he pursued her. The phone rang: it was John wanting to know if she'd done the Russian assignment. There was a knock at her door: could she help him translate a difficult sentence into French? In her easy-going way, at first she thought these requests were genuine. When she realised their ulterior motive she pulled up short with a little shock. The lads she'd known at home were more plain-dealing.

"My mother has just got a new Mercedes for going shopping," John said.

He was sitting at the table by the kitchen window, his long legs outstretched.

"My mum goes on the bus," said Ann, " it's too difficult to park the Rolls near the market."

"Why don't you come and visit us in the vacation? You'd like Godalming."

"Mmmm. But Godalming might not like me."

"Why not?"

She looked at him. He really was a buffoon. His mind was as flat and clear as the Antarctic wastes. The blind whiteness of snow stretched endlessly and the certainties were thrown off harshly. It made her wince, that public-school assumption and arrogance, that psychological and emotional tundra so typical of the English upper classes. She was used to the relaxed warmth of a working-class home. Her people had no opportunity to think of themselves as superior. They got by as they could and valued closeness and friendship. And as insult usually drew a sharp response and unpleasant consequences, they avoided it. Her father was a common northern joiner, but his manners were impeccable.

"People fit their circumstances and my circumstances don't fit with Godalming."

"Why not?"

"We're all socialists where I come from."

"You should talk to my father . He'd straighten you out. He says five million on the dole would teach the unions a thing or two."

" He should patent that theory. He could make a fortune."

"The thing is," he intoned, "only the Conservatives can run the economy. You see, they're the people who understand about money."

"Oh, they understand that all right."

"Without the rich, no-one would work. They organise things, you see. They're the movers and shakers. It's just ingratitude that makes the workers bolshie. And envy."

"What an original mind you have," she said.

Did he really think she could envy him? Did he imagine he was remotely the man her father and brother were? She looked at him as if he were an exotic creature, some anthropological discovery.

"Have you started *Germinal*? she asked.

"No. Have you?"

"I've finished it. You'll love it. It's all about the movers and shakers."

She went.

After that, she decided to have nothing to do with him. They came from different planets. But he stuck. She came out of a lecture on Stendhal and he was waiting.

"Hi, Ann! Fancy a coffee?"

"Are you paying?"

Why did she accept? They sat in the crowded college bar. She loved the activity and the people. She was at home with the coming and going of crowds. As a child she'd watched the men streaming from the factory round the corner at five. It was life. People together, working or enjoying themselves. John talked loudly about himself. But he couldn't reduce her mood. What a fool he was! What a harmless, purblind fool. In this mood, her fondness and generosity overcame her.

The days and weeks went by and John was always there. He bought her coffee and beer. She explained the origins of the French Revolution. They went to the cinema together to see *Last Tango In Paris*. During the sex scenes he froze.

"Bit raunchy," she said as they left.

Then one evening when she'd had too much to drink and he walked her back from a disco, she found herself kissing him. In spite of herself, she enjoyed the closeness. He was heavy on top of her. His kissing was clumsy but she hadn't kissed for months. When he tried to unhook her bra she said:

"Would you like me to do that?"

For her, the warmth of intimacy swept away superficial differences. As their love-making continued, she grew more relaxed. She laughed at his blundering ways and his blimpish opinions. She was enjoying herself in that untroubled way she'd learned in the streets, the back-alleys and the woods across the river, when parents were far away and freedom seemed endless.

Then one evening he was supposed to arrive at seven and didn't turn up. She fretted. At ten she went to see if the light was on in his room.

"Lost your watch?" she said when he opened the door.

"What?"

" A la recherche du temps perdu. About three hours in fact."

"I forgot."

Her eyes hardened.

"You should see a psychologist about that complaint."

"I forgot!"

"Aren't you going to let me in?"

"I'm busy."

"What's her name?"

"What?"

"I could murder a cup of coffee," and she pushed the door quickly and slid past him.

The pages of a hand-written letter lay on his desk. He gathered them hurriedly and pushed them in his drawer.

"Writing to mother?"

"Let's go and sit in the kitchen."

"Oh, let's not. It's much nicer here. I'll wait while you brew."

He took the pages from the drawer, folded them into an envelope and sealed it.

"Come in the kitchen while I make the coffee."

"I'm comfy now. I'll stay here. Off you go."

He went stiffly, with sullen obedience.

She looked around the neat room. On the bookshelf was a row of swimming trophies. She imagined him diving like a gannet, powering the lengths. She saw the smirk of self-satisfaction on his lips when the cup was handed to him. There was a framed picture of his class. All the boys had that air of assumption public-school pupils can never shake off. She got up and took the envelope out of the drawer, turning it in her hands, feeling its small weight as enormously significant. She almost felt she had the right to open it. Her heart raced and she wanted to go. She put it back, closed the drawer and sat down. John appeared with two steaming mugs.

"Does absent-mindedness run in your family?" she said.

"I just forgot. Okay."

He had his back to her, looking out over the quad.

"Do you think it's genetic or a product of your upbringing?"

"Can't we let it drop?"

He turned to her and she saw the shadow of an ugly expression in his eyes and on his mouth.

"Sure. Letting it drop sounds a good idea to me."

She put the mug on the floor, got up and went.

She closed the door of her room behind her in a rage of self-accusation. Still, that was that. The fact that it was over meant she could pull herself up from the humiliation. But each time she thought of it, she was angry and ashamed. How could she have been such a fool? All the same, there was no doubt she'd revelled in the intimacy. She couldn't sleep and curled in her armchair with *Le Neveu de Rameau*. Every time her thoughts began to drift, she forced her attention back to the book and the good intellectual effort calmed her down.

The rapping on her door woke her up. For a few seconds she was disoriented. Where was she? What day was it? Who was knocking? Then all at once her full consciousness returned, she got up throwing the blanket she'd had round her shoulders on the bed, put the book on her desk, and quickly straightening her hair in mirror, opened the door.

"Can I come in?"

"I'm surprised you can remember where I live."

"Have you prepared for the seminar on Rimbaud?"

"The real seminar is elsewhere."

"What?"

"Finished your letter writing?"

"That was nothing."

She sat in the chair and he perched on the bed.

"Of course. Who was it to?"

"No-one."

"Wow! Writing nothing to no-one. You could be the next Samuel Beckett."

"Okay. It was to my ex-girlfriend."

"Who is no-one, of course. What's no-one's name?"

"She's at Oxford."

"That's quite a name."

"I thought we could keep it going but it's no good."

"Thanks for telling me."

At once she felt a twinge of regret. Why was she asking him to be considerate? He made an apology of sorts and came over to her. She went stiff and cold enough to keep him at a distance. He sat on the bed again and they talked till two. He was restrained and quiet but she wouldn't relent. When he left, she went to bed resolved to keep him at a distance.

 The next week he came striding up as she was leaving a lecture on *Les Contemplations*. He was full of that intrusive, toothy cheeriness which made her cringe and laugh at the same time.

"Hi, Ann!" he called. "I haven't seen you for ages!"

"You saw me on Tuesday."

"Did I?"

"Yes."

"Where?"

" Do you suffer from juvenile dementia?"

" Oh yes, I remember. We talked in the library didn't we."

"We did. Libraries being ideal places for conversation."

"Fancy a coffee?"

"You should try a variation on that line?"

"What?"

"Actually, I'm just going to meet a couple of girls in Bowland bar."

"Mind if I tag along?"

She stared at him. He stood tall and a little gangly, his big white teeth on display. There was something too present about him. In fact, everything he did was an exaggeration. He couldn't lift a cup without looking as if he was acting out, as if he'd just read a book entitled *How To Lift A Cup In Polite Society So As To Reveal Your Class Origins And Intrinsic Superiority.* She was amazed.

"By all means."

They sat in the far corner of the busy bar, their cheap white mugs and saucers on the low table. The girls chatted away inconsequentially with that female genius for emotional communication which leaves men bemused.

"I haven't even learnt all my lines yet!" said one of them who was playing Martha in *Who's Afraid Of Virginia Woolf.*

"I played Hamlet in the sixth-form," John interrupted. "I was pretty good, actually. I learnt the lines in bed."

"I suppose it whiles away the time when you've nothing better to do there," said Ann.

"Actually, I thought I might try my luck on the boards once over."

The girls tried to imagine him on stage. All they could see was a wooden, amateur-dramatics ham. They smiled indulgently but he didn't get it.

"What's it about anyway, this play you're in?"

"Well," began the girl, "it's not easy to say…"

"The poisonous centre of the sugary delicacy known as The American Dream," said Ann.

"The problem with America, of course, is its lack of tradition," said John.

"Or its lack of socialists," said Ann.

"It's a great country, but they need to learn how to be less vulgar," said John.

"It's hard not be vulgar when your existence revolves around making money," said Ann.

"People of real class have money without making a fuss about it," said John. "It's only the nouveaux riches who need to be ostentatious."

"Oh, I don't know," said Ann, "Buckingham Palace is hardly a paradigm of modesty."

John waxed on about the responsibilities of wealth and how the country would go to the dogs if people who didn't understand the value of money were allowed to have influence. The girls ignored him and drifted back to their light-hearted chatter, so seemingly trivial, so actually vital. They ignored him and he sat aside trying now and again to find a foothold in the conversation but failing because he didn't grasp that conversation isn't a philosophy seminar.

Ann was pleased he'd been discomfited. In her room she sat at her little portable Remington to bash out an essay on portraiture from David to Delacroix. She enjoyed work. The research could be tedious but the challenge of writing she relished. It was a great feeling to get to the end of a five thousand word essay, re-read it, re-work it and hand it in. So she liked these hours alone with words and she disliked being disturbed.

As soon as she heard the knock, she knew it was him.

"I'm not disturbing you am I?"

"Yes."

"I just wanted to talk."

"I'm writing an essay."

"On what?"

"Paper. Come in."

She was mildly irritated at herself for giving way, but he looked so pathetic, like a boy who's lost his mummy at the fairground, and in truth she was ready for a break, having hammered away for two hours or so. She made coffee and sat on the bed propped by her pillows while he sat in the chair.

"I wanted to say sorry," he said.

"For what?"

"I've been a bit of a cad."

She almost laughed out loud. A what? He talked as if he was straight from the pages of *Billy Bunter*! His ridiculousness made him un-threatening and she felt herself relax. She was trusting and easy-going because it was the way among her people. The old cliché was true, in the street where she grew up people did leave their front doors unlocked. Kids were always out skipping, playing hopscotch or *Queenie-o-coco*. Adults were always keeping an eye. Everyone watched out for everyone.

"Don't worry, we know how to cope with cads in the north."

"I was hoping we could have another go."

"Another go?"

"You know, start again."

He was so preposterous she wanted to bustle him out of the door. But she let him stay and the time ran on. They went out to eat in the refectory, bought a bottle of Bordeaux on the way back and tired, tipsy, full of her native generosity, she let him into her bed.

Then things ran along quite well for a few weeks. Gradually, she was teaching him how to be in less of a panicky hurry in bed, though he couldn't yet satisfy her. He would roll off, blow a great phew from his pursed lips and say:

"That was fantastic, wasn't it?"

"It wasn't too bad," she'd say.

She didn't really know where this was going, but for the moment she didn't worry. She felt she had the measure of him and without being fully aware of it, she believed she could chip away at his ludicrous upper-middle-class assumptions and postures and make a straight-forward human being of him.

Then the Easter holidays came round.

"I'll give you a ring," she said

"No, don't do that."

They were sitting in the bar that was already sparse. It was the last day of term and those who could had escaped early. She looked at him. He was staring blankly ahead.

"Why not?"

"I might not be at home."

"What is it, emergency surgery?"

"I just might not be at home, that's all."

His petulance and distance disturbed her. Like a lone yachtsman who senses a dangerous change in the wind and tacks for the shore, she should have made for safe ground; but she was too at ease. She dismissed her fretfulness.

"You can write to me though," he said.

"Okay."

All through the Easter holiday she was on edge. She took a job in a café and had a great laugh with the other waitresses. The work was tedious - serving, wiping, collecting, - but they joked their way through the days making quiet fun of the customers. There was a man who came in every day, bought a small coffee and sat at the same corner table to read the paper for an hour. They invented an elaborate, mysterious, sinister or romantic life for him.

"Small coffee?" one of the girls would say as he came to the counter and the others would hide their suppressed giggles by bowing their heads and looking busy.

But when she was alone her doubts gnawed away at her until she sat down and wrote a brief note. She didn't like him being incommunicado. What did he have to hide? In any case, they belonged in different worlds. Forget it. A reply came by return:

Ann, you bugger. Nothing's going on. I'll see you back on campus....

She felt suddenly unfair and silly. Too willing to give others the benefit of the doubt, she left herself exposed and accused herself of hurt to others when she was merely engaged in justified defence of her own feelings. In her relief, she expanded into wild affection. She was desperate for the start of term.

On the first day, she was delighted to meet all her friends and to chat away. But where was John? She knocked on his door. She went to the bar. Then on her way to the library she spotted him striding across Alexandra Square. She smiled at his ludicrous purposiveness. He walked as if he was on his way into battle to save the world from aliens. She went towards him but as he spotted her he veered away and then walked straight past her as if she didn't exist. She stopped and turned, watching him stride on, amongst the students milling in their appalling ordinariness. She went to the library and sat down with *Les Illusions Perdues* but the surging of her emotion, the pounding of her heart, the humiliating image of him powering past her as if a complete stranger, melted her concentration. She sat and stared. Then she jumped up, stuffed the book in her bag and in a white, eyeless rage went straight to his room. His door was open. She heard voices and laughter. He was playing cards with a trio of his rugby pals.

"Pontoon?"

"Poker. All right, Ann?"

"Fine. You'll need a straight face not to be fleeced with a hand like that," she said to John, standing behind him.

"Play poker, Ann?"

"Oh, I'm an expert. Bluff and counter bluff. I can take John to the cleaners any time I like."

"Join in!"

"No, I've got more important games to play. So, how was your holiday, John?"

The three mates exchanged looks.

"Excellent. How was yours?"

"Wonderful. I was just wondering about the deterioration in your psychological condition."

"Come on, play!" said John.

"Yes, come on, play. There's a game on here all right and someone's going to lose their shirt! You should get to the medical centre as soon as you can, John. I mean it's only four weeks and you've completely lost any memory of me whatsoever. A degenerative loss like that at your age! You need acute psychiatry."

The game stopped. One of the lads put down his cards.

"I'd better be off. I've to see my tutor about missed essays."

331

"That's a problem," said Ann, "but it's nothing compared to John's deficiency. He could be utterly gaga in a fortnight."

The other two lads stood up.

"We'd better make tracks too, mate."

"There's no need to go," said John.

"No need at all," said Ann. "Take a ringside seat. Seconds out."

They left.

"You've no right…" he began.

"Don't walk past me as if I'm a piece of furniture and then start talking about rights."

He got up and turned away from her, making as if he needed to tidy.

"So where did you spend your holiday? On top of She's-at-Oxford?"

"None of your business."

"It is my business when I write to you telling you things are over and you reply like lover-boy of the century!"

"Can you get out of my room."

"Can you get out of my life."

He swung round suddenly and grabbed her by the wrist. She was stunned by his cowardice. His face was contorted into an ugly sneer. Behind the guffawing, socially gauche public schoolboy was this vicious, spoilt, violent little boy who must have his own way in all things.

"Stop poking your nose into my affairs," he said his gleaming teeth clenched.

She yanked her arm away and strode out. There were red marks on her wrist. She rubbed them as if they were poison. In her room she closed the curtains, slumped in her chair and sobbed.

Three weeks later, on a Wednesday, at six in the evening, she walked into the porter's lodge.

"Sorry to bother you, Bob, but I've left my file in my boyfriend's room and I need to get on with an essay. I don't suppose there's any chance you could come and open his door for me?"

"No, I can't leave the lodge, luv. If you can wait till eight Tom'll be here to start his shift and I can go with you then."

"Damn! I just need to get stuck into this work."

Bob was very fond of Ann. She was down-to-earth and often made him a brew on nights when he was on patrol duty. He'd sit in the kitchen with her and she'd ask him about his family and his hobbies and had a way of listening that cheered him up.

"You couldn't…Look, it's my boyfriend's room. I'm in there all the time. God knows where he's gone. If I could just have the key…"

"I can't, luv. I'm not allowed."

"'Course not. But am I going to tell? It's B53. I'll be there and back in less then a minute. I wouldn't ask, but I just have to get this work done and there's my file, I can picture it, sitting on the desk, with all my beautifully written notes…"

She tilted her head like an inquisitive pigeon and smiled.

"If anyone asks you….."

Bob reached behind him and took the key from the hook.

"You're a luv, Bob, I'll remember you in my will."

She sprinted across the quad to B block and panted up the stairs. Pulling open the right-hand drawer of his desk, she saw the little stack of envelopes. She took hold of the first one and pulled out its two-page contents. It was a conventional love-letter signed Marie-Eve. She memorised the address, shoved it back and rifled through the rest. She found one that contained the lines: and now you say you're drifting away from me, John. And for who, for a bitch of a student, a working-class slut…..A sudden calm came over her and a clear resolution. She put everything away, closed the door behind her, scooted to her room to pick up her file and ran back to the porter's lodge.

"Got it Bob! You've saved my life, again! No-one spotted me. Your secret goes to the grave with my corpse."

"You're too young to think about such things!"

Back in her room she sat quietly at her desk. She had a fountain pen and a pad of good quality note-paper which she kept for official letters. She wrote her address and the date in the top corner. Then she began: Dear Marie-Eve, and paused. There were so many things she could say, but she wanted one sentence that could say everything. Finally she put down: I'm enclosing a letter John Treanor sent me during the Easter holidays. I thought you might find it of interest. She put the two letters in the little blue envelope, sealed it and wrote on the front the address she'd had no difficulty remembering.

The next morning she took it to the post-office and then went to the library where she read Balzac intently for four hours.

It was almost a week before the knock came on her door. She opened and stood back. He was in the corridor with the envelope and letters in his hand. She looked into his eyes and saw the anguish. He was about to cry.

"How did you get her address?"

"It was in your drawer, John. All her letters are in your drawer."

"How did you get into my room?"

"You let me in. Don't you remember? We beguiled a few vagrant hours in bed together. You were clumsy but you can't be blamed for that. A public school education is a poor start in life."

"She wants to finish with me now!" he roared.

He lurched into the room and threw himself down in her chair.

"You bitch! She wants to finish with me!"

His mouth pulled down at the corners and she saw his bottom lip quiver.

"Write to her, John. Say something like, Marie-Eve, you bugger..."

He leapt from the chair and grabbed the mug from the edge of her desk raising his long, swimmer's arm in the same action and swinging it down to try to smash into her head. She dropped onto the bed and the mug crashed onto her bedside table leaving him holding the handle in his fingers.

"You'd better get out of here before I call the police," she said.

He was standing over her, the tears squeezing from his eyes, his mouth like a distressed baby's, his chest starting to heave, the letters in one hand, the little china handle in the other. Slowly he turned and dragged out, slumped like a man whose entire life is bereft. She closed the door behind him.

"Buffoon!" she said to herself. " Complete buffoon!"

CORNED BEEF HASH

Every morning a packet of six tomato sandwiches sat on the corner of the table wrapped in greaseproof paper waiting for Tony to grab them . This morning it was cold so he stuffed them into the pocket of his navy blue overcoat, pulled up the collar and called:

"I'm off, mum! See you later."

She coughed and shouted from the kitchen:

"Ta-ta!"

Usually she'd left the house before him to do her job as a school cleaner. She was back by half past eight to take his younger sister to school. His elder sister left later as she worked in town and caught only one bus. But today his mother had stayed at home because she was ill and was going to the doctor. He wished she didn't have to work. He wished somehow he could make enough money to say to her:

"Here, look. I'll pay for everything. Put your feet up. Enjoy life."

But his mother was one of those women for whom life was more suffering than enjoyment. It troubled him. Since he was a little boy he'd done all he could to help her. For her birthday he always went to great trouble, looking round the gift shops, carefully choosing something that might make her happy. But it never did. He couldn't give her anything that would make her happy, not even love, and the thought of it made his heart beat unpleasantly.

The morning walk to the bus stop was the best part of his day. At seven thirty things were beginning to stir but there remained some of the quiet of the night. When he was at school, he did a morning paper round during the holidays and Sundays all year. To be out of the house at six and scooting round the avenues and groves on his bike while all the curtains were closed, the garage doors locked, the roads silent and the odour of breaking day in the air was a great pleasure. Now he had this little walk each day, past the big houses, down little Princes Road where there was no tarmac and only residents could take their cars, out by Priory Lane onto Liverpool Rd, where the traffic was beginning to hum, to join the queue opposite the little library where he'd first failed to get a taste for books. As he passed St Teresa's, he dragged the parcel of white bread, margarine and tomatoes

335

from his pocket, and launched it over the high hedge into the lilacs. Today he would be going to the pub with the lads but to tell his mother her sandwiches weren't wanted would have been too offensive.

He walked quickly but without hurry. Walking was ease. The two miles into town he did on foot often. Walking was time for thinking and even this short five minutes to the bus, his left hand in the now empty pocket, his right tight against the copy of *Sons and Lovers*, was a welcome respite. The queue was all people he recognised. John Kennington was rolling a cigarette.

"All right, John?"

"Hi. Nippy."

"What's new?"

They knew one another from the pubs, clubs and dances. They'd both left school at sixteen and were doing stupid jobs and they both had a passion. Kennington was an artist who vaguely hoped he'd find a way to make a living from painting. Every April he left the northern town and went to St Ives where he would spend the summer sleeping on people's floors and drawing portraits on the beach at two and six a time. During the winter he took what work he could and enjoyed himself with the other would-be bohemians of *Brucciani's*, *The Exchange* and *The Warehouse*. So the two of them met on the morning bus or in the crush of the Friday night pub. They were alike in their easy-going ways. Neither had sharp elbows. Both preferred a good time to the big time. As they were talking, an articulated lorry slowed and pulled into the bus-stop. On its towering side was an advert for Blue Band margarine.

"See you, John."

Tony reached for high handle of the passenger door, tugged and hauled himself up the steps into the elevated cab.

"Thanks!"

"All right, lad."

The driver was a neat, slim, dark-haired little Liverpudlian in his mid-forties. Like Tony he didn't have much small-talk so the journey passed mostly in silence. He was a stately, careful driver, as gentle in his braking and accelerating as a royal chauffeur so they glided through the town and out past the big council estates of Ribbleton onto the Longridge Rd heading for the open spaces to the north. The depot lay on the corner of an industrial estate, an uninspiring little semi-circle of functional buildings in a no-man's-land five miles out of town. They drew into the half-darkened warehouse and the meticulous driver backed onto the loading bay. When he heard the unceremonious clang of the bridge being laid he switched off the engine.

"Thanks," said Tony. "Very kind of you."

"Any time, lad," said the little man with a nod.

Upstairs the stock-clerks were settling into their desks. Neville Myers, the office manager was standing behind his in a crisp white shirt, his hair beautifully brushed, his heavy beard closely shaven, singing as he opened the mail and surveying the girls wondering which one he would go to bed with next. Facing the opposite way, already seated, the smoke from his cigarette curling over the black hair of his big, round head, Martin Birley was rolling up the sleeves of his crumpled, grubby, also white shirt. Tony sat beside him on the swivel chair.

"Right, Martin?"

"Mornin' Tone."

Birley was five years older and had taken the youngster under his wing, intending to initiate him into the ways of smoking, drinking, gambling and chasing women. But he was a poor pupil. He didn't smoke, drank moderately, had a flutter on the National and fell in love like blackbirds peck for worms. Birley wore an engagement ring. Being Catholic, his fiancé was a virgin, but he liked to pursue the office girls, to grope drunkenly at the Christmas party, to be constantly on the *qui vive* for a furtive encounter though he too was uninitiated. The two of them were the Traffic Department. Mornings were a rush of dockets, arithmetic and thick wads bulldog clipped and balanced on the desk's edge for the girls to collect. Tony enjoyed the activity and sociability but the serious business, the moneymaking, the efficient pursuit of greater profit meant nothing to him. Nor did thoughts of advancement. He was one of those young men so happy in their skins they can't be constrained to the ugly struggle for place and reward. He was lucky enough to find the world interesting, so he didn't think of his lowly position, his modest pay and the need to improve his prospects . He was delighted by the mundane and infuriated his managers.

Since the age of eleven he'd lived with his mother, two sisters and grandfather. His father was kicked out for what Tony later found Shakespeare called the rebellion of a codpiece. There was none of that relaxed acceptance of the facts of human desire in his mother's household and after his father went, once she'd come through her hysteric breakdown when she lived on tranquillisers and wandered the house like a revenant, she occupied all the space. While they'd been together, Tony lived under their resentment and recriminations like an earwig under a stone. Only when the light of their break-up flooded in did the sheltering dark of his ignorance and innocence disperse and leave him blinded and scurrying for cover. Now his mother talked endlessly of his father:

"Your dad was no use. I had it all to do. Cleared the table he thought he'd done summat….

And when she was in her vilest mood and wanted to undermine what she saw as tendencies in her son which she'd hated in her husband:

"You're just like your father!"

There was nothing he could say. He went out on his bike, or called for his mates, took off to the woods to light fires and carve the bark of oaks, played cricket or football on the park and came home to her sullen silence and his tea put before him on the table as if she was performing a *corvée*.

Then there were the moods when she became loose and silly, laughing exaggeratedly at some jejune sitcom or comedy show and repeating over and over the mindless joke that made her limp with unconvincing amusement. Perhaps worst of all was her fierce hatred of learning. Raised in strict Methodism, she took the Bible literally, believed the Devil a roaring lion and all truth revealed.

"You can't get it from books!" she would say whenever Tony read and her disapproval of his intelligence was expressed most poignantly when she put aside the good reports he brought home term after term and never offered a word of praise.

In this unhealthy atmosphere he'd had to find a way to get by. Luckily, in the years before the separation he'd lived blissfully, doted on by his elder sister, an untroubled little boy free to enjoy the unending charming newness of childhood. So he'd established resources to call on and tending to his little sister, only two when his father disappeared, turned him away from his mother's bitter spite and destructive hatred. All the same, he was shy and unformed, expected the world to respond to his innocence and had little sense of how vicious in both public and personal life is the struggle for power. So he came every day to work in excited anticipation of a laugh with Martin, chats with the stock clerks, a pleasant hour in the afternoon in the cold store office at the far end of the depot where the manager seldom arrived, listening to the tales of Winston Browne, the mixed-race supervisor, who leaned back in his chair, puffed on his cigar and explained why the pakis should be sent home. Tony thought Winston's ideas nonsense, but all the same he liked him and for the prize of his company was willing simply to laugh at his loopy schemes for repatriation.

Then there was reception.

Two girls worked here: Bernadette Milne and Marie Singleton, both Catholics. Bernadette was the manager's secretary and after her affair with Neville Myers which she hoped would get her a pay rise but didn't, she'd moved on to the boss, earned well and did what she liked. She was brisk and pert, full of cheery good mornings and equally upbeat goodnights, wore impossibly short mini-skirts and expressed opinions culled from the *Daily Express* as if they were hard-won intellectual truths. Marie at sixteen was three years younger, small, well-formed, a good athlete, with blonde hair down to her thighs, teeth as big as a horse and a cold superior manner until you got to know her when she revealed herself giddy, flippant and conformist. Where she differed from Bernie, who she liked well enough, was in saving herself for the right man. Bernie was having sex in the back of Neville's car before her seventeenth birthday and from her Catholic upbringing had derived an instrumental attitude to sex: the Church taught, after all, that it should be used only for reproduction. What was the difference then in using it to get on a bit in life? The point, it seemed to her, was that god had given women sex precisely so they could use it. Women had it and men wanted it. Well then, let them pay. And in that way she felt curiously guiltless, as if her sex didn't really belong to her at all. Of course, there was respectability to think of. She didn't want to be known as the local bike. She knew the vulgar things men said: more pricks than a second-hand dartboard or a revolving door on her bedroom. So she had a fiancé and they were saving for a house. She liked to believe her affairs were secret, though the whole depot and beyond knew about them. She

339

could keep up appearances like the next woman, but she was doing well: two men to make love to her and her boss in her pocket. And not yet twenty.

Marie and Tony knew one another outside work. They lived in the same suburb and turned up in the same pubs and at the same youth club where teenagers crammed into a semi-darkened room filled with deafening pop music to shout in one another's ears and sip coca-cola from plastic cups; and many years earlier they'd met as little children at the socials held by the Commerical Travellers' Association because Tony's dad sold motor oil and Marie's beer and spirits. He remembered her from those few occasions. Even then she'd seemed unreachable. Little by little Tony had become fascinated by her; that stiff superiority seemed to conceal something worth discovering, and in the curious process by which we project our most fervent desires and hopes onto others on the flimsiest of grounds, he found in her complexion, her large, pale lips, the high curve of her dark brows, the sudden opening of her smile, the perfect formation of her thighs, the press of her round breasts against her tight dress, the careful shaping and painting of her fingernails, a promise of happiness, togetherness, of a shared life which is what all men dream of while they imagine what they want is sex. Having become this promise, she was as fragile as its basis and his attitude to her as careful as that of a man handling precious porcelain which the slightest shock might shatter. He was unable to talk to her naturally. All the stored disappointment of his failed love for his mother and the long tiptoeing of a tightrope between erotic idealism and cynicism made him taut with expectation and the slightest sign of interest from her set his imagination running full tilt till negotiating the territory between them became impossible.

"He fancies you like mad!" said Bernie.

"Not my type."

"Oh, I don't know," said the older girl slipping more notepaper into her typewriter, "he's good-looking and he has something about him. I bet he's good in bed."

Marie typed a little faster and wriggled on her chair.

"Too quiet," she said.

"Oh, the quiet ones are the best. The blokes who brag about sex all the time are usually a disappointment."

340

Marie hammered away at the keys. She almost wanted to turn and say:

"Have you been to bed with every man in the county!"

She finished the letter, whipped it from the roller, tossed it into the tray and loaded another two sheets divided by carbon paper.

"You might as well make the best of it while he's completely besotted…"

"Got to nip to the loo," said Marie sliding from her chair.

She clunked up the open-tread stairs in her Scholl's sandals and at the top as she headed off right to the ladies, encountered Tony coming from the main office. He gave her a nice smile so she forced her lips over her big white teeth and quickly turned away. For the rest of the day Tony wondered if he'd done something to offend her. But that was just girls: they could be as affectionate as a Labrador one minute and aloof as a cat the next. Then the idea came to him that her abruptness might be the reverse side of her interest. He'd seen it before: girls who feigned complete indifference as a defence against seeming too keen. Perhaps this was the moment to make his play.

By ten past twelve he and Martin had finished their work. Martin slipped the paper under his jacket and went to study form for twenty minutes in the gents. At half past they piled into Jack Glynn's Volvo estate and drove the mile to the *Wheatsheaf*. Jack Glynn was a dapper sales rep, a florid, smiling man of forty who treated everyone as if they were about to set up an account with him. Neville Myers and two other blokes from accounts came along, one a surly, bulldog of a man Tony had surprised on top of Nadia Wasilewski in the filing room at the Christmas party. His trousers were round his knees and as Tony pushed open the door the first thing he saw was a hairy backside, then the angry face as he twisted his neck and called "Fuck off out of here!" Tony just had time to glimpse the reddened cheeks of the girl, her fringe stuck to her sweaty forehead, her knees in the air. He couldn't resist laughing as he pulled the door closed, but at the same time he was shocked: Nadia was so sweet and pleasant. What was she doing having sordid sex with that fat, ugly fool?

The landlord of the *Wheatsheaf* was a pot-bellied local Tory councillor and magistrate. Seeing Martin come first through the door he said:

341

"Pint of the best as usual?" and eased the black handle of the pump.

"You've a memory like an elephant, Wilf," said Martin.

"Aye, but I need a hide like a rhino to put up with you lot."

Spotting Tony he said:

"Lemonade for the kiddie?"

The men laughed in a collective roar which made Tony shrink and blush.

"He'll have a pint," said Martin.

"You'll have me up before the beak!" replied Wilf.

"Well, if you appear before yourself you can excuse yourself on the grounds that you're just an honest bloke trying to make a simple living in a hard world," said the ugly character from accounts.

They ordered sandwiches and went through to the side room where there was a dartboard.

"Twice round and two tops?" said Martin who already had the arrows in his hand and whose father was a reputed pub player, taking money from gullible drunkards who overestimated their skill and underestimated their intoxication.

It was a great male moment, the clear, brown beer in the straight glasses on the little round tables with their planished copper tops and the bulls eye the centre of attention as Martin launched the fleet darts which landed with a clean thud in their appropriate cheeses: one, two, three.

"Good arrows!"

They picked up their pints as Neville Myers stepped forward. He was one of those men who laugh easily at their own shortcomings as a way of drawing attention to their strengths and as his shots went drunkenly awry, his high, tight, near-giggle excused him. He plucked the darts from the dry board and passed them to Tony. One Friday a gaggle of the office girls had come with them and joined in the game. The men treated them with condescending indulgence until Marie won the first round.

"Best of three!" Martin had called

But when she won the next, hurt and anxiety could be discerned beneath their laughter and banter.

"Do you practise in your bedroom?"

"Can I practise with you?"

"Best of five then."

She won the third. Tony thought of her as he stepped up to the line. He recalled her poise and slow preparation, the absolute concentration on her features and the sureness of the missile leaving her fingers. He tried to imitate her. By thinking of her it seemed to him something of her skill passed into him. His first and second darts hit their targets and the third bounced off the wire.

"Not bad arrows, Tone."

Martin won of course. The sandwiches arrived and the men sat to eat. As usual the conversation turned to women.

"The boss still shaggin' Bernadette Milne?" asked the accounts clerk.

"Shaggin' the arse off her," said Martin.

"I'd go after the other one myself," replied accounts.

"Yes, I'm working on it," said Myers, at which they all laughed. "Didn't you get anywhere with her at Christmas, Martin?"

Tony concentrated on his beef sandwich.

"Snoggin' session. Wouldn't let me get my hand up her skirt."

"Maybe the lad should initiate her," said accounts.

"Aye," said Martin, "I believe she favours virgins."

And the men roared again as Tony blushed and chewed and tried to look as if he didn't care.

"Nice little arse she has though," said Myers.

"Get your dick up there," said accounts, "you wouldn't pull it out for a fortnight."

In the afternoon, Tony wandered to the cold-store office. The planning was all done in the hectic morning and the afternoons were reserved for whatever cropped up: a lorry breakdown or an urgent delivery, and the compilation of depot statistics, filing and other bits of housekeeping. But the management hadn't worked out how the time was used and had little idea of what Martin and Tony did after lunch, so when there was nothing pressing to attend to, they made the best of it. Winston had his feet on his desk and a cigar in his mouth.

"All right skids?" he said.

"All right, Winston."

Tony sat opposite him. He wanted someone to talk to. He needed to relieve a horrible sense of loneliness.

"You're a bright lad," said Winston picking up his paper, "what do you think this is?" He slipped his glasses on. "Fond of company, ten letters, g something, something g, a,r,something, something, something, s."

"Gregarious," said Tony.

"Greg what?"

Tony spelled it out.

"Now how would you know a word like that?" said Winston taking off his glasses.

"I read it in a poem: Fleeing the herd he came to a graveyard on a hill, and felt the mound proclaim the bone gregarious still."

The older man cast a hard glance at the lad.

"And you read that sort of thing, do you?"

"Yeah."

"Why," and he puffed hard on his cigar.

"Because it's interesting."

Winston stroked his chin, and looked out of the office window to where the refrigerated vans were waiting to be loaded with fish fingers, arctic roll and beefburgers.

"If I was a bright lad like you," he said, "I wouldn't waste my time in this place."

Tony looked at him and could see a fatherly concern in his eyes. The supervisor turned away and stubbed his cigar in a little, green metal ashtray.

"I'd get myself an education."

"I'd rather get myself a girlfriend," said Tony without knowing where the words came from.

344

Winston threw back his head, laughed and ran his hand through his sparse hair.

"You don't want to worry about that, lad. You'll be fine. I've been married twenty-three years and I'm an ugly old bugger."

Tony laughed to show his appreciation.

"It's the one thing I regret," said the other, "that I didn't get an education. I'm ignorant. That's the truth. All I know is how to do this bloody job. I left school at fifteen. Education, that's the thing. If I'd had an education I might have made something of myself. Engineering. That's what I'd like to have done. Something that uses the brain. A monkey could do this job." He put his hands under his armpits and made monkey noises.

He got up and switched on the kettle.

"Taken a fancy to one of the girls here, have you?" he asked, his back to the youngster.

"Oh, I don't know."

"Tarts. Most of 'em. No better than tarts. Take that Bernadette. You know what's going on with her and the boss?"

"Yeah."

"No better than a tart. Find a lass with something about her. You're together a long time if you marry."

"Yes," said Tony accepting the mug of tea.

"You could have a good future, lad, if you got an education. There's nothing worth having in this place. And the boss is a bastard. You could go abroad. They've ruined this country, and you know how? Socialism and immigration…."

That evening Tony had to work late. The dockets for frozen food deliveries were printed off during the afternoon and quickly sorted into loads, but if the flexi-room had a breakdown, they had to wait for the machines to be repaired. Tonight was Tony's turn.

"Hope it's not too late," said Martin as he grabbed his coat and left at five.

Tony hung around in the empty office as the technician traced wires and checked diagrams, but by twenty past five the ribbon of perforated paper was curling on the floor and the machines printing the little square, grey, carbonated dockets. At ten to six he'd finished. The bundled dockets were in the cold store office. He headed for the door, the bus and home. But passing reception, found Marie still typing. He closed the door quietly behind him.

"Still at it?"

He saw her bridle a little.

"Yeah."

"Not like you."

"No. The boss wants some letters done and Bernie had to go."

"Ah. Much to do?"

He saw her twitch slightly again. He looked at her thighs in her light tan tights. Her short skirt left them visible. His heart thumped.

"Naw. Nearly finished."

"Fancy a drink?"

The words were out before he could think

"No, can't. I'm busy." There was a tiny pause. "I have to tidy my room."

On the bus which followed the darkened road towards the town he kept thinking of Martin and the Christmas snogging session. Was Winston right? Was she just another tart? But he couldn't believe that. Over and over he heard the tone of her rejection: the cold closure of the most trite of excuses delivered with that superciliousness which shrank his heart. The little bus station was quiet. He decided to go for a drink alone and enjoying the warmth of the little pub and the gentle comfort of the beer, finished three pints. He had no idea what time it was when he left.

In front of his mother's house was a low privet and at the other side a little lawn in the shape of a capital D, its straight side parallel to the hedge. As usual he scissor jumped it landing on the bald patch. As he was hanging up his coat she came from the living-room.

"Where've you been till this time?"

"Working."

She paused and stared at him.

"You stink of beer."

She went to the kitchen and he knew he had to sit at the table. His younger sister was already in bed and his elder out with her fiancé. The minutes till she appeared seemed a year. Finally, he heard the slap of her slippers. She banged the plate down in front of him and slammed the door.

It was Wednesday, so corned beef hash.

CASTILLOS EN ESPAÑA

Mrs Bremner was thrilled when she was called for interview at Whitechapel Grammar. Its reputation was severe. She would belong to the educational elite; its results were the best in the county, outside the private schools, and though she would've preferred to work in one of those, Whitechapel was next best. There were four interviewees. What swung it for Mrs Bremner was her pedigree. She'd been sent to private school herself. True, she got her degree from Portsmouth Poly, but her compliant demeanour and obvious bending before the centuries-old cachet was appreciated. She was determined to make the best of her good luck. She knew how to ingratiate herself. And her boss found her extraordinarily attractive.

David Scurfield knew how to ingratiate himself too. He was one of those public-school educated men, sensitised early to minute differences of status, who throw themselves at the world, like a baby onto a bed, in pursuit of full acceptance. Born as the Second World War ended, he was inevitably influenced by the new atmosphere. At the age when he began to think politically, the NHS was in place, rail, coal and steel were nationalised, trade union leaders on the television every day and *The Beatles* about to become a best-selling commodity. The old order seemed to be crumbling. When Alec Douglas-Home was defeated by a grammar-school boy from Huddersfield who'd made common cause with an energetic orator from the Welsh coalfields, Scurfield felt his private-school background might soon become a symbol of dishonour. Had the Tories remained in power, he would've looked for a job in a private school. Instead, he applied to grammars. He wouldn't've contemplated a secondary modern, but not wanting to look antediluvian if the social mind changed utterly, he became a firm supporter of comprehensive schools. He voted Labour because he believed social democracy was the best defence against socialism.

The day Caroline Bremner was interviewed, he decided he'd have an affair with her. She was young, ambitious and ready to please. He was sixteen years older, experienced, cynical and sure of success.

Twenty years later he still hadn't got her into bed and comprehensivisation had done its work. The local ex-secondary modern, which had trailed badly when Bremner was appointed, now rivalled White-

348

chapel for results. The laurels on which the place had rested for years were withered. She was forty-two. Scurfield was inches from retirement, but his campaign didn't falter. Tantalised but kept on a stiff leash, he rode the rising and crashing of his anticipation and disappointment without ever telling himself the truth. All he needed was the right moment to wrap his arms around her waist from behind or to press his palms on the breasts so diligently displayed beneath her tight, open-necked blouses. Like a boy who clings into adulthood to the illusion of a footballing career, he saw himself successful where in fact there was no possibility. By astute manipulation, by hitching up her skirt and mentioning her wedding anniversary, she'd kept him keen and got herself promoted, but she would have arced at the suggestion. She believed herself thoroughly professional and her advancement the proper reward for hard work. All the same, eighteen more years! She wished she'd taken a job in the private sector.

"I can't go on for all that time!" she complained to her husband. "There must be a better life. The discipline is atrocious. Eighteen years! There's got to be a way out."

Charlie Bremner was retired. He was twenty years older, had worked in education too, lecturing for a time and then finding his way into administration, which meant having an office of his own and pretending to take important decisions. He was old enough for the sense of age's reductions to play keenly on his mind. He saw himself at eighty, slow and stiff, unable any longer to adequately tend the garden or walk in the hills, and though his own pension was enough, Caroline's career would provide the compensatory material ease. He'd encouraged her to push, hoped she'd make it to Headteacher and filled the backs of dozens of envelopes with spatchcock sums. As she'd complained more and more about declining behaviour, increasing management intrusion and the long wait to maybe put on a dead man's suit, disappointment dragged at his nerves. There must be some means to turn all this descent to advantage.

"Spain!" he said.

"Are you serious?"

"Why not? There are loads of opportunities in private schools. You can teach the cream. And we can get away from the rain and the milky skies."

He believed Spain was relatively backward educationally. A well-qualified, experienced woman like Caroline could take a school by storm. There was easy money to be made from the monied looking for qualifications for their children. And wasn't Britain still regarded world-wide as the best source of certificates? In the long run, they might own their own school; only the rich would get through the door; the fees would exceed the average income; they would pay the staff modestly and make them work for every penny. He imagined a white hill-top villa looking towards Africa. He would sit by the pool dozing or reading something light beneath a sky of taut, uninterrupted blue. The days would blend into one another and the hours would pass in untroubled delight. His old age would be warmed by gentle winds. He would decline slowly towards death as Caroline kept money cascading into the bank. With no children because she found them noisy and importunate and thus denied the delight of grandparenting, the money, the light, the food, the wine, the villa would comfort him.

They began their research on the web. There were plenty of schools looking for English teachers. She got herself on an EFL course. They took the car on the ferry to Bilbao and spent four weeks of the summer touring.

"It's a wonderful country," she said to her colleagues in September. "The south is where I fancy. Malaga. You should see the skies down there."

"Oh, lucky you!"

"Yes, I can't wait."

They sold their big house in the suburbs for three hundred thousand and moved into cramped rented accommodation. All their furniture was in storage. It was simply a matter of hitting on the right school. She applied to one in Badajoz but they turned her down at interview. She'd gone alone and sitting at a café table in the early evening she tried to convince herself the alienation she felt was a passing phenomenon. Her Home Counties posture, her Marks and Spencer's dress sense, her fixed little smile of tolerant condescension marked her as unflinchingly English and resolutely middle-class. She would always be an outsider. Some people were able, after a time in a foreign place, to modify their habits by imperceptible stages so they became, at least superficially, indistinguishable from the born and bred; but she could never be like these dark-skinned Spaniards who

walked with a sensuous sway and seemed to inhabit a realm of time-
lessness. Mañana. She was familiar with the cliché but there was
something more than just putting things off: even the men with brief-
cases, no doubt involved in serious business, looked as if they cared
about nothing more than the next glass of red. She ate an olive, gingerly skewing it on her pick. She noticed a man at another table tar-
geting her with fanatical dark eyes. Walking back to her hotel in the
stifling heat she was convinced he was behind her, but when she
turned to look there was just a shuffling old woman in a black dress
down to her ankles and a boy on a bike.

"The place wasn't for me," she said to Charlie. "Very unfriendly."

She tried another in Madrid. Nothing. She kept sending her CV and
carefully phrased letter. The weeks and months went by; she began
to think it wasn't going to be so easy after all.

"Nothing to worry about," said Charles. "There are bound to be
hordes of applicants. Everyone wants to work there. The life is amazing. For three hundred grand we'll be able to afford a huge villa with
acres of land. We'll grow grapes, olives and oranges. Think of it,
Caroline, stepping out in the morning and picking oranges off your
own trees. Who wouldn't want that? You'll get something in the
long run."

And wasn't Charles proven right? She was invited to attend at the
Amanda De Rome Academy on the outskirts of Malaga! Could it
have been more perfect? She considered she handled the jealousy of
her colleagues with great aplomb. It was a shame for them. They
were staying in the rainy north in the grim atmosphere of schools
under threat from Ofsted, league tables, unreasonable parents and
children who learned their manners from television chefs. She was
on her way to a sunny, easy-going country, a school where the pupils
had to pay to be taught, were kicked out if they didn't behave, teachers were respected and the plentiful private tuition guaranteed to
double her income.

There was a sentimental farewell at Whitechapel. The customary
collection raised £187.56. When Laura Mountcastle, subject leader
for Modern Languages, left, they bought her a kayak and a life jacket. How much would that come to? She'd been in the school almost
as long. Her position wasn't as elevated, but all the same her title
was senior tutor without departmental responsibility. Jealousy, she

reasoned, must have held her colleagues back. She made a smiling little speech in which she fulsomely expressed how much she'd miss everyone and what a wonderful place Whitechapel was. Scurfield kissed her on the cheek and held her too long and too close. A month and half later, she and Charlie moved into their rent-free apartment. Concrete, flat-roofed, one-bedroomed, when the temperature fell that night they piled jumpers and dressing-gowns on the bed. The shower didn't work, they found cockroaches in the kitchen cupboards and the rings on the gas cooker burned with such feeble intensity warming a pan of beans took half an hour.

She complained. They'd been promised proper quarters. They were used to comfortable circumstances. They must be found something else.

"There is nothing else," said Ms De Rome. "This is the only temporary accommodation we have."

"We expected a decent flat. The place is freezing at night and there's no heating."

"But it's only temporary. You will find a house soon."

Having to make do, they ate out every night, went back as late as possible, wore thick t-shirts in bed and left little trails of white, insecticide around the kitchen. They started looking for houses but the prices were far higher than they'd imagined and some of them were tucked away in the hills, ten or fifteen miles from the school.

"That's for the long-term," said Charlie philosophically, as if they could live as they were for a decade.

Eager to begin teaching, Caroline believed that once she was underway, the teething problems would resolve themselves; but her timetable was so heavy she barely had a minute to herself; she was expected to work on Saturdays (was that in the contract?); the pupils were spoiled and arrogant and at the end of September, her pay failed to appear in her bank account.

"It sometimes happens," said Ms De Rome as if a tap had started dripping. "I will speak to accounts."

By the end of October, not a euro had appeared.

"How are we supposed to live!" protested Caroline.

"Oh, two months. You must have brought enough to live for a little

352

while."

Caroline said nothing to the other staff, wanting to maintain a positive front, but it turned out no-one had been paid. Those who'd been there a few years began to talk apocalyptically. Two teachers disappeared overnight.

"What's going on in this place?" said Caroline to one of the English teachers.

"De Rome's a crook, that's what's going on?"

"What?"

"Have you seen where she lives? The police'll be here any day I bet."

Ms De Rome was taken away in handcuffs before the amused and scandalised boys and girls. The school was locked. Caroline and Charlie were told they had to leave the flat, piled their belongings in the car, booked into a hotel and sat facing one another and their future over an indifferent paella.

"I've worked for two months for nothing!"

"I know."

"Suppose I don't find a job."

"There's always supply."

"Supply!" and she clanked her fork down on the table.

"For the time being. In the right places."

"I am not doing supply anywhere under any circumstances" she uttered.

On the day they arrived back in England there was a couldn't-careless wind and lashing rain which grew ever more resolute and fierce as they moved north. Their sad belongings were shipped home and put in storage and they moved in with Charlie's reluctant brother and wife, an alcoholic barrister whose career had been ruined by the bottle and who lounged around the house in revealing nightwear from breakfast-time to the early hours. They stayed two nights, decamped to a roomy flat over a bank, discovered the car park was the haunt of the local youths who rode tiny bikes recklessly with their dark hoods pulled over their shaven heads, threw empty lager cans at their bedroom window, screamed and shouted raucously and left their used condoms on their back doorstep. Adept at dissolving into the night before the police cars arrived they terrified them by their lawlessness, though in fact they were merely bored youngsters showing off. Desperate to leave, they found a beautiful old house in an exclusive area, exchanged contracts and moved in within a month. Caroline had made sure the cul-de-sac was child-free, but a fortnight after their arrival, the house opposite welcomed a new family of five. The children were aged from two to thirteen.

"We can't stay here!" she whined. "Imagine the noise."

"It's a good area. They'll have to be kept in check."

But the mere thought of the children kept her awake. They put the house on the market for twenty thousand more than they'd paid; people trooped through, smiled, made approving little noises and disappeared.

"Nothing, again!" sighed Caroline, setting the *Times Educational Supplement* on the coffee table.

"Don't worry. Something'll come along."

"There are jobs I could apply for in London."

Charlie made no response.

"Perhaps we should think of going south."

"London? Think of the house prices. We'd be living in a box in Fulham."

She turned away to look at the honeysuckle whose leaves were brushing the broad, sash window. It was true. They could live well here, were high on the ladder of property and wealth; but they were eating into their savings week by week (she'd even begun to think weekly rather than monthly). Charlie had advertised and found a few private pupils, but the pressure was on her. She wished she hadn't left Whitechapel but at the same time her nerves grew tight at the thought of what she'd had to put up with. If only a job would come up at one of the exclusive private schools. Still, the dashing of her expectations in Spain had left a residue. She couldn't envisage a better life without at the same time fearing she would be let down, and caught in this snare, she felt as if the air was thickening and it was getting harder for her to breathe.

People she'd kept in touch with at Whitechapel spread word of her return. One day, she ran into an ex-colleague in town. He was a scrawny little man, full of an energy which seemed too much for him and he talked excessively quickly, laughing at his own observations though she found nothing funny in them. She wanted to get away quickly but he quizzed her about Spain and the more she revealed, the more ashamed she felt. She was on the wrong side of a dream of happiness and it was shredding her heart.

But two days later, Scurfield rang her: her replacement had thrown in her hand. They hadn't seen him for a fortnight and he wasn't answering the phone. Was she interested?

It was fate. She couldn't resist the thought some higher power was looking after her and her mind raced: she would go back to take the low-level English job, but surely they would promote her? She would have to be complaisant of course, exhibit humility, work diligently, stay on the right side of David; but she believed this was her opportunity. It was too unlikely to be mere coincidence. It was meant to be. She would have to tolerate rude, ignorant youngsters with their I-know-my-rights arrogance, but only for a year or so. She saw herself elevated, given her own office, making decisions along with the other half dozen members of the *SLT* , and though she would still sit in the staffroom some lunchtimes, would chat amiably with her lower-level colleagues, she would rise above them, impose on them, become impervious to their complaints and behind the closed doors of elite meetings, exchange knowing glances and derogatory remarks about their fecklessness, laziness and general inadequacy. She would assume the burden of superior responsibility. She would be superior.

David Scurfield too felt providence was acting on his behalf. Like a lion sniffing out weak prey, he knew Caroline was injured. She'd confided to him her exorbitant hopes for her future in Spain and her prim-and-proper middle-class mentality predisposed her to believe life must deliver pleasantness. Cruel blows, she believed, must be reserved for those who deserved them: principally the lower orders. The working-classes, of course, weren't so sensitive. It was in the order of things their lives should be hit by disappointment and failure. They were untrustworthy, selfish, indulgent, uncultured. But her own kind were made for success, advancement, reward, belonging. Wasn't that the meaning of meritocracy? And as a thoroughgoing meritocrat she voted consistently for the party in the middle, not because she thought at all deeply about politics, but to distance herself from unseemly passion. When she saw Arthur Scargill on the television, her blood ran cold, but it wasn't his arguments which offended her. In the mouth of a cool and measured Cambridge professor, she'd have found them the very model of reason. It was Scargill's demeanour, his accent, his gestures. He was so obviously a cocky little working bloke, had he passionately defended the rotation of the planets she would have been impelled to disagree. He was the kind of man who drank pints in a working mans' club on a Saturday night, whose wife went to bingo and whose scruffy children played noisy games in the street. He wore a suit and a collar and tie, but they looked awkward. She saw a picture of him in *The Guardian,* coming up from the pit, a young miner in his dirt, his upper chest and arms on show in his singlet. That was the real Scargill and that was where he belonged: underground, in the dark, getting on with the work ordained by his betters. So it had been a bitter lesson to her, the failure in Spain. She had to convince herself and others it was no fault of her own. Over and over her mind came back to her hopes and to their shattering and over and over she had to fight against the defeating idea that she'd made a bad judgement.

Scurfield knew the injury now at the heart of her. He would be kind, he would let her know at once he was on her side, would do all he could to push her on; she could use him to climb. But of course, he would extract his pound of flesh and the thought of her naked, that stiff correctness violated by his urgent thrusting, made him run around madly, as if night and day themselves depended on him. He had little time, but he was sure she would succumb. If her promotion depended on it. If he were as insistent as toothache.

So Caroline returned to her familiar classroom and explained to the importunate pupils how things hadn't quite worked out in Spain.

"Did they sack, you Miss?"

"Did the food give you the shits, Miss? My dad always gets the runs when we go to Tenerife."

"The school ran into financial problems," she said. "Quite beyond my control."

All she'd wanted to escape was once again part of her every day routine. Some pupils came to her lessons without a pen or book. Others simply refused to do any work. The boundaries were constantly challenged and on the *qui vive* every minute, she went home exhausted.

But she compensated by remembering it was Whitechapel, whose reputation, though fraying at the edges, was still intact, and there were excellent pupils and some good classes. She had a job. Scurfield had even swung it so she was paid on her former scale so £2,200 went into her account every month. The days and weeks went by and it was as if she'd never left.

"The problem is," Scurfield said to her, "the authority insists on posts being advertised nationally."

"Oh, well."

"Of course, there's nothing I want more than you doing the job."

"Yes."

"I'd give it you right now, if I could."

"Thanks."

"I'll have to try to find some way round it."

"Is there a way?"

"Oh, a man can always find a way, if the motivation's strong enough."

"What about the Head?"

"He'll want to do things by the book, but he'll leave it to me if I speak to him."

"I see."

"Even if we advertise and interview, I can probably ensure you get it. But you never know, a good young candidate who's cheap…"

"The Head would go for that."

"I'd go for that, let's face it. That's the game these days. I'm doing you a favour, Caroline."

"I appreciate it."

He approached the Chair of governors and explained how much the school valued Caroline's work, then he went to the Head with the governors' agreement that the post didn't need to be advertised externally and the Head informed the authority that on this one occasion, in this particular circumstance, they were waiving the rules and advertising internally. A tiny notice in eight point appeared in a top corner of the cluttered staffroom board:

Colleagues are invited to submit applications for the post of Teacher of English. Apply by letter to the Headteacher by the last day of the month.

Caroline wrote of her achievements, her commitment, her loyalty, her admiration for Whitechapel. She explained how she felt fate had returned her to the school where she belonged and she expressed her ambition to take on a leading role. She was sure Whitechapel was where she would stay for the rest of her career. She was now ready to assume serious responsibility. She gave the letter to Scurfield, who didn't bother to show it to the Head.

She was re-appointed.

"I won't be here much longer of course," he said as she sat in his office to receive the good news.

"How much longer?"

"I haven't decided. It depends. There are things I still want to do."

"You're very committed."

"I'm still energetic."

"Oh, yes."

"I can outperform a lot of men ten or fifteen years younger."

"That's obvious."

"I could line you up for my job."

"I'd be grateful."

"We'll need to talk a few things over."

"I'm available."

"After school."

"I've no pressing engagements."

"We keep this between ourselves."

"Naturally."

"There'll be jealousies."

"Human nature."

"It's yours if you want it."

"I want it."

He groomed her, fed her information and kept potential rivals in the dark, let the Head know how much she was helping him, what a fine colleague she was; but though she smiled and tilted her head so her blond hair fell sweetly onto the shoulder of her smart, navy-blue suit, though she laughed at his weary stories and limp jokes, though she stayed till six or seven alone with him in his quiet little office, he never found just the right moment to slip his arm round her waist or to kiss her long neck.

Two years passed quickly. Every day he hoped his opportunity would come. On many, he went home to his wife in a dismal mood. He was abrupt and sank into the sofa with the newspaper. When the time came to resign, he told himself he'd failed; he would never kiss her, take off her clothes, draw the duvet around them. Yet hope sprang up in him at the thought he'd stay in contact and, no longer employed, perhaps he'd feel less constrained. He was still robust. He played golf three times a week. He still had a physique. All that was necessary was that perfect instant in which he would know she was saying yes.

His post was advertised internally, in keeping with the regulations. There were four applicants. The other three knew full well Caroline was favoured, but they imagined they could come across well enough in interview to overtake her. Such are the illusions by which injustice maintains its rule. On the day before the interview, she was modesty itself.

"I'll be lucky if I get it. There are three very good candidates against me."

But driving home she mentally prepared how she would conduct herself after her appointment: she would feign surprise, she would claim she interviewed badly, she would express anxiety about her ability.

The other three were no-hopers.

The collection for Scurfield raised £563.48. They bought him a plasma tv as he was a keen fan of sports transmissions. He made a heartfelt speech about how much the place meant to him, how he would miss everyone, how he would treasure the values of honesty and integrity on which the school was founded. There was a tear in his eye when they presented his gift. He laid on a lavish leaving party at the Masonic Hall. From one end of the room to the other an unbroken line of trestle tables supported whole dressed salmon, sides of beef that would have defeated Henry VIII, hams waiting to be sliced, canyon deep bowls of salad, coleslaw, rice; enormous oval plates spilling triangular tuna, egg, ham, beef, prawn, salmon, cheese, and cheese and tomato sandwiches; castles of succulent pork pies, sausage rolls as warm as bed on Sunday morning; fruit salad in which apples, grapes, kiwi fruit, oranges, mandarins, pears, pineapples luxuriated in alcohol-laced juice; cheesecakes, gateaux of lemon, strawberry and chocolate and a cheeseboard big enough to satisfy a medieval king and his entourage.

There was a disco.

The beer, wine and spirits flowed like the Severn in spate, gurgled like mountain streams over little rocks.. Scurfield got very drunk. He watched Caroline dancing with her husband who was three inches shorter and, grey-haired and pot-bellied, might have passed for her father or a seldom seen uncle. She weaved her way through the jigging bodies and he thought she must be going to the ladies, but then her saw her veer to the right and realised she was heading outside. With all the discretion of a man whose speech is slurring badly and whose legs seem to be controlled from outer space, he lurched across the floor. Outside, the night was still and inviting, the clear sky had a bluish hue and the stars, which he noticed with a child's surprise and delight, seemed to dance. She was alone leaning on the balustrade overlooking the bowling green and at once the idea seized him that she'd come out here to give him his chance. He approached her and as she heard the click of his Italian shoes she turned and smiled.

"Oh, hi Dave!"

He grabbed her by the waist which, to his astonishment had a little roll of fat, and pressed his mouth against hers. At once she began to struggle but his strength restrained her. It was true, he was still fit and strong. She was making little squealing noises and pushing hard against his shoulders and something filtered through to his consciousness to say this wasn't quite right, but he was so sure she wanted him he went on kissing her warm mouth with all the passion he could muster till he felt strong hands on his biceps and was unceremoniously yanked back. Two of his colleagues, a burly P.E. teacher and martial arts I.T. man held him tight.

"Leave her alone, Dave."

She wiped the back of her hand compulsively across her mouth.

People had spilled out of the building and their uninhibited drunken chat and laughter was carried on the motionless air. Charlie Bremner came across the gravel, his rubber soles making a soft crunching sound. He asked his wife what was going on; she shook her head and set off back to the hall. Scurfield's arms had been set free. His glasses were awry. He took them off and staring towards the source of the party-noise made out indistinct shapes in a swaying fog, till he slipped them back in place and saw Caroline's angry back and her podgy husband at her side, climbing the steps in a stiff-kneed way. The P.E. teacher slapped him on the shoulder and said:

"Don't worry, Dave. We didn't see anything."

Scurfield nodded.

His rescuers put their arms round each other's shoulders and, singing raucously, pulling and pushing one another like carefree adolescents, crossed awkwardly the expanse of white stones. He was alone. In a few days he would no longer be a Senior Leader at Whitechapel. In September Caroline would assume the responsibilities which had made him feel competent, superior, almost indispensable. Finally, he'd taken his chance and she'd rebuffed him like a sow her runt. As he dragged slowly back to the gathering, careless of what anyone might know or think, what seized his mind was the image of Caroline in his office, addressing the school, talking to parents, writing references, interviewing applicants for jobs. That she was second-rate went without saying but what upset him wasn't her advancement exceeding her competence but that he no longer had any power, she no longer needed to be nice to him; he'd lifted her to ascendancy and felt himself falling, falling forever through an endless emptiness of shame and regret.

There was nothing he could do but find his wife.

MUMMY'S NEW BOYFRIEND

Every April in the late 1960s a group of easy-going teenagers from a little, industrial Lancashire town took off for St Ives, found jobs and rooms and stayed till the end of September. During the winter they hunkered down in the northern cold and damp, lived with their parents, worked in shops, offices, factories, on building sites and met up a few times a week to reminisce and plan. Most of them were run-of-the mill youngsters, but two were out of the ordinary: Meg Park who could sing like a diva and Jem Illingworth who drew beautifully and fluently. Meg sang outside The Sloop, on packed Porthmeor Beach, in busy Fore St, among the holiday crowds, accompanied by one half-competent guitar player or another and Jem drew swift portraits which he sold to the subjects for half a crown. They were the only two who didn't need to work and the others who did split shifts in hotels, bars, restaurants and cafes admired and envied their talent and income. They were all trying to be bohemians, but serving greasy egg and chips on rainy lunchtimes or changing beds smelling of booze and intimacy in a little guesthouse were serious dampers on the sense of living beyond the customary routines and values. Of course, there were the eternal beach parties, the little fires lit at balmy midnights, the plentiful cannabis and the sex. The idea of free love was in the background like a tiny cooling breeze on a sultry day, but they paired off and felt reassured by faithfulness. It was only three or four summers. Jobs and marriage broke the group up. But it was something to look back on, something not to have missed.

Meg Park married a fireman and sang in pubs until her daughter was born and Jem Illingworth went to art college only to find there was no work afterwards but teaching. Teaching art in schools he couldn't think of: he was too gentle to discipline children and his own schooldays had been marked by resentment of teachers who threw their weight around, shouted and taught their subject as if everyone was as skilled at it as them. He couldn't see why school shouldn't be voluntary, which made him an outsider. He freelanced a bit as a teacher of drawing and then uncomfortable with squatting in his parents' house took a job as a draughtsman for an engineering firm so he could afford his own flat. He disliked the routine and found his colleagues frosty. He liked them as people and tried to get on with them, but as employees they were wary of him. His attitude wasn't right: they were trying to make careers and he was trying to enjoy life. One of the other draughtsmen said to him:

"We'll never make the big time working here."

"Big time is dead time," said Jem.

The restless months went by. He drew and painted in the free-spirited evenings and at breathlessly short weekends; he met up with the old crowd and relived for a few hours the atmosphere of heedless enjoyment and anticipation of a different world. But Monday morning came round as regularly as the milkman. He was at the bus stop at seven thirty. He'd come to rely on the salary. The months became years and somehow it seemed life had slipped away from him.

He was twenty-seven when he met Louise.

She wasn't arty, rebellious or restless; she worked at the stolid Town Hall in administration. She'd started there at sixteen and being intelligent, diligent and ambitious had risen to a senior post. But Jem didn't think about that. She was pretty and charming and after years of come-day-go-day relationships it was a delight to have someone he could feel committed to. She complained his flat was messy and she didn't like him spending long, intent hours drawing but she was so touchingly slim and shapely and they spent such carefree evenings and weekends together, he shut out all thought of anything negative and let himself enjoy the ecstasy of new love. She was twenty-seven too and eager to start a family, so within a year they married and bought a little house in the quiet suburb where Jem's parents lived. When she became pregnant Jem was thrilled and uplifted; watching his little daughter come into the world, seeing the woman he loved sweat and strain and grunt and tear to deliver this wrinkled little package of joy was the best and most transforming experience of his life. That everyone on earth had come into the world in the same way meant nothing to him; it was newness. He was a father. He was lifted out of himself and Holly became the centre of his being.

When dark clouds began to assemble in the sky of his happiness he ignored them. All his life he'd ignored unpleasantness: violence, greed, exploitation; they weren't part of his sensibility. Oh, they were real enough, but he had one life and couldn't change the world, so he made a small enclave of generosity, friendliness and tolerance and felt that was the best he could do.

"It's too small," Louise began to say.

"It's fine for three of us."

"But what if we have another? Or two more?"

"We've got three bedrooms."

"Look at the size of them."

"Who needs a big bedroom? All you do there is sleep."

She threw the comment back at him and they didn't have sex. His sweet, joyous satisfaction turned into dismal misery and on the long walks he took alone by the river to calm his frustration, he realised how he'd let his happiness depend fundamentally on their intimacy, her generous opening to him, and for that he'd been willing to treat her materialist conformism as a midge in summer. He agreed to moving house and increasing the mortgage. She wanted him to push for promotion. They needed two cars. Her friends all had more than one holiday abroad . She wanted a new bathroom and then a new kitchen.

"What does all this stuff matter?" he said flopping onto the sofa and opening a book about Goya.

"It matters more than those books you're always reading."

Had it not been for Holly, he'd have cleared out, gone back to a little one- bedroomed flat and pseudo-bohemian relaxation although there was no bohemia in this little place . He realised they'd been trying to do the impossible when they sneaked off to St Ives in their tatty jeans with a packet of Rizla in the back pocket. The conditions that sustained alternative communities were being wiped out. He'd been sucked into a system he despised. What kept him going was his love for his daughter. That outweighed the irritations of conventional marriage by far. Louise, he realised, wasn't relating to him. He was a husband. He took on, in her Catholic mind, the characteristics a husband must have. She spent more and more time at her mother's. They went shopping every Saturday. They came home and talked about what needed to be done around the house. Louise made a list of things he should be getting on with: the bathroom tiles, painting the kitchen…..He found a quiet corner and read about Chagall.

But the hours he spent with Holly were bliss. At home together he read to her for as long as she liked. He drew for her and showed her the rudiments. By the time she was six she could sketch impressive cats, tigers, rabbits, robins, daffodils, trees. He smiled to think she might have his talent. He took her to the best parks, the library, the nice old Italian café which served home-made ice-cream. She held his hand as they walked through town and he imagined everyone must look at them and be charmed by the bloom of their simple mutual love. And the child did love her father. She climbed on his lap and snuggled to sleep and then none of the cares of his life counted for a fig.

Shortly after Holly's seventh birthday Louise announced she was going back to her mother's and taking the child with her. He remonstrated and pleaded the girl's well-being but she insisted she couldn't live with him: they were incompatible; the marriage was a mistake; she didn't share his values; she wanted to find someone like herself and be happy again. She went. The house was sold. He got his portion and moved into a little flat where he could do what he liked. He saw Holly every Tuesday and Thursday evening and every second weekend she came to stay. He tried to make things just like they'd always been. But little by little he noticed changes in her he couldn't fathom. She was less affectionate and responded indifferently to his suggestions for fun. The hours went by so fast he'd hardly time to start getting on the old footing than she was away. One Saturday she said to him:

"Mummy's got a new boyfriend."

"That's nice," he said. "What's his name?"

"Colin."

"Is he good fun?"

"Mummy says we're moving."

"Does she? Where to?"

"Spain."

He put the plate he was wiping in the drainer and turned to the window. His heart was thudding to break his ribs.

"I don't want to go to Spain, daddy," the child said and started to cry.

"It's okay, sweetie," he said, picking her up. "You don't have to go. You can stay with me. We'll have great fun, eh?"

When Louise came to collect her he said:

"What's this about Spain?"

"You'll find out. All in good time."

"Holly doesn't want to go."

"She's a child. She doesn't know what she wants."

But when they were alone he lost his temper:

"For fuck's sake, Louise. I'm her father."

"So?"

"So she needs her fucking father. Children need fathers."

"Do they?"

"I think so."

"Are you sure it's not you who needs a daughter?"

"Well of course I need her. She's my fucking daughter. It's my place to bring her up."

"She'll be fine. She'll have everything she needs."

"Except me. Don't you think she needs to keep her relationship to me?"

"No, I don't, Jem. Frankly I think you're bad for her. She's a bright girl and she needs to be pushed. She can get on in life. All she learns from you is how to sit around reading and drawing."

"Picasso spent his life sitting around drawing."

"At least he made some money from it. You don't make a penny. It's a waste of time. I don't want her to grow up like you. I want her to get on."

"You should want her to be happy."

"Oh, happiness. You don't live in the real world, Jem. Everybody manipulates everybody to get what they want. Don't you understand that?"

He couldn't answer. His nerves were badly shocked. This pretty, apparently charming woman he'd loved was a monster. He was bereft of means to make contact with her.

He discovered Colin owned a language school in Madrid, employed young linguists with TEFL certificates and made a fortune. He went to a solicitor to see if he could stop Louise; it cost him thousands to lose the case. The arrangement was he would fly out to see Holly once a month. She would stay with him for a few days at Christmas and for a week during the summer. He comforted himself with the thought of his monthly visit. He booked no frills, stayed in a cheap hotel, explored Madrid with her. But a visit was cancelled because they were going to Malaga and another because she was to stay with Colin's sister, then he was ill, he didn't have the money. Three months went by and he didn't see her.

His little flat was full of pictures of her. He sent her sketches of birds, flowers, trees, odd people he saw on the street or in the library. He recorded messages on tape telling her all he'd done and everything that was happening and asked her to do the same for him, but nothing arrived. He wrote to Louise to protest she was turning the child against him. She didn't reply. One wet, windy October evening he followed the swollen, swirling river to the old, wooden tram bridge. Through the gaps in the boards he could see the mad water smashing its head against the pillars and the white crests rising up defiantly, falling back to join the next surge. He jumped up onto the barrier, stood still for a second then launched himself headfirst. He was swept fiercely away and his body jammed against a pillar of the next bridge.

They resuscitated him but knew he had brain damage. He was unconscious for three weeks. When he came round, the doctor was surprised he could speak. She asked him what year it was. He had no idea. Who was Prime Minister? He said Harold Wilson. What was his phone number? He didn't know he had a phone. His physical recovery was relatively rapid. He was able to walk around the grounds, his appetite was good; but when he was taken back to his flat he didn't recognise it. A clinical psychologist worked with him for months and little by little he pieced together a picture of who he'd been.

"Who is this child?" he asked holding a picture of Holly.

"Your daughter."

He shook his head.

Going back to his job was impossible. He'd accumulated a little pension and with benefits had enough to exist. Every day he went for a long walk by the river and once, coming back through the town, someone he didn't recognize stopped him on the street.

"Jem! How are you?"

He smiled and shook the proffered hand.

"Remember me?"

"I'm sorry."

"Vic. Vic Toulmin. We used to go to St Ives together. I played guitar for Meg Park. Remember. We shared a room one year."

Jem looked into the man's face and into his head there came a series of images: a beach, breakers rolling in beneath a blue sky; a fire at night; a girl on the street singing; a young man with long hair in torn jeans and a t-shirt sketching holidaymakers; a pretty girl with a slim waist; a birthing room and a baby's head stretching the lips impossibly to force its way into the world.

"Vic?" he said. "No, I'm sorry. I don't remember."

He let go of the hand and walked on.

DEFEATING FINNEY

More than one premiership footballer lived within walking distance of John Little. He was proud to be amongst some of the richest people in the country. But when one of them was humiliated in the press for his antics with prostitutes, it wasn't pleasant. Little wasn't rich and hadn't come by money easily. In his early days as a teacher, with a mortgage and one child, he used to play raucous guitar in a sweaty rock band three nights a week around the back street pubs. The money paid a bill or two. His promotions had come relatively quickly and once he'd decided he was going to climb, there was no turning back: he had to do what had to be done. He was twenty when Thatcher was elected. Harold Wilson's two victories in 1974 made him think the tide of policy was going to continue what the previous thirty years had established: a steady closing of the wealth gap, the acceptance of a large, strong public sector, and the permanent power of organised labour. Coming from modest circumstances in Cheetham Hill he voted Labour like he spoke with a Mancunian accent but he wasn't deeply political. He didn't think about the struggle for power every day. He was simply moderately well-disposed to the Labour party and the idea of greater equality, democracy and openness. What preoccupied him was God. His parents, also reflex Labour voters, were devout Anglicans. Steady in their adherence to democratic equality, the secular couldn't rouse them to passion. It was the glory of salvation which animated them. John and his sister grew in this atmosphere of fervent belief. There was always, therefore, a sense that life hadn't really begun. This was mere preparation. Only when the burdens of the flesh were cast off could the spirit soar and the burdens seemed to weigh heavily on his mother and father. His dad began his working life in the Co-op, educated himself at night school and became office manager for a regional transport firm. His mother worked part-time in a florists. Neither had any enthusiasm for what they did. They bore the weight and routine of it like an ass loaded with a pack it knows nothing of. There was a grim tenacity about his father on work days. He moved as if an evil spirit he didn't dare disturb squatted on his shoulders. His tweed jacket became for John a symbol of some mysterious compulsion. What was this curious thing work which made people go about like zombies? His father's face was pale. His mother exhibited a nervous busyness and became ill-tempered. Yet it was instilled into him that he must work hard at school to secure a good job. What was a good job? It was obviously to do with money. His father earned enough to move them to a modest semi in Didsbury. School and his family conveyed the same message, sometimes explicitly, sometimes tacitly: education was the means to a better job and a better job was what everyone wanted.

So John worked very hard and did moderately well. He was privately tutored for the 11-plus and spent hours working through books where shapes had to be imagined turning through ninety degrees, or sequences of numbers completed and definitions chosen for words. It struck him as a bit strange and unconnected. He liked to read, especially about the universe. Reading was exciting if it was something you wanted to know about. But why was it important to be able to choose the best definition out of three for *competent?* He found it boring but he accepted it because his parents and teachers said it must be done and was the way to good results and a better job. He passed and went to the Grammar school where he turned out to be quick and accurate at maths and good enough to hold his own in English, though having to write essays on Richard III left him staring out of the window at the little garden wondering if there were any birds' nest in the hedges. Latin and French though made him want to cry. He was put in the C stream because he couldn't master them.

"Remember," said his father, "you're in the top twenty per cent by being in the Grammar. Even in the C stream you'll get eight O Levels and be able to do A Levels. But if you try really hard you might get moved to B."

His elder sister, who produced Latin at the tea table to get on his nerves, was recruited to help him.

"Pecunia viro atque puellae dabitur quod puer aeger est!" she would say irritably as she back-combed her hair. "It's the dative you nitwit! To the girl. Get it? The money will be given to the girl?"

He didn't get it. He didn't get French either. Why was it *le crayon* but *la règle?* It didn't make any sense. The teacher said to forget male and female, it was just a way of distinguishing words within the language but it didn't make it any clearer. He could never remember which was le or la but worse, he didn't know why they were needed. When he had to learn verb forms his brain swam with confusion. It was always a great relief to have an equation in front of him or to be looking through his logs to work out an angle.

He failed Latin and French at O Level, but passed seven others. Because he was only average in the sciences, he decided to take Maths, Further Maths and Economics for A Level. He liked Economics because he could do the maths easily and it started to make clear to him why it was important to get on. It was a set of rules. He came to it as he came to religion, willingly and unquestioningly. He responded warmly to the graphs and he loved the push-pull aspect of it: if you do x to interest rates y will happen to inflation. It was like a machine! The idea appealed to him. The economy was just a big machine which needed to be kept running: the right amount of oil here, the input of fuel there, a tweak of this screw, a tightening of that bolt and it chugged along like a steam engine. He began to understand why his mother and father approached work as they did: what were they but parts in the machine? Everyone had to perform their function. It was greatly reassuring. He began to think of his own role. He would have to find a place in the machine, he would have to be a whirring cog which did its job perfectly. He wanted to be amongst the few who made the decisions. That was how it had to be. A piston didn't question why it moved up and down in a cylinder and people shouldn't question what they had to do at work. Behind it all was God. The universe ran according to laws God had created so the same must be true of the economy. His text-book didn't mention God but it did talk of the invisible hand. Wasn't it more or less the same? It couldn't simply be that all these people working like ants gave rise to an over-arching scheme. The scheme must come from outside, it must be imposed. God made the economy work just as he made the planets move. But in the economy there had to be people in charge. That was obvious. There had to be people who imposed what was necessary. That was what was meant by a good job.

He didn't make a single decision to become a teacher: the idea formed in his head slowly. By the time he did his O Levels teachers had received a big pay award. His dad said they were doing very nicely. He could teach in Church of England schools. Teaching tallied with his inclination to Labour. So when he'd finished his degree in Economics he stayed on to do the PGCE and it was during that year he met Ruth. His girl-friends had been just that: there'd been no passion, none of the delirium that was supposed to accompany being in love. They'd gone to the cinema, held hands, kissed like statues and after a few weeks or at best a few months it'd become too much of an effort. But Ruth ignited something in him. She was sullen and uncommunicative. He had to flit around her attending to her needs. She had no interests or enthusiasms and worked doggedly at her Biology and educational theory as if she had no choice. It appealed to him greatly. That same mulish application to work, which became an attitude to life for his parents, was replicated in Ruth. It was as if her inner life were stilled. She might be under a spell. Some malevolent force had enchanted her and dictated she should go through life like a spectre. He jigged about excitedly over one thing or another: the new rock band he was playing in, the good marks he was getting for his essays, while she remained rock-like; a pale presence, somehow not there yet inordinately demanding. They went to church together. They went for walks by the river when the weather was good. They kissed with the passion of refrigerators.

They were virgins when they married which though it may have pleased god rendered the wedding night somewhat hasty and inadequate.

It was decided early but without any explicit discussion that John's career would take precedence. The first child was born after two years and Ruth took the full maternity leave. There was the necessary scrimping and scraping and John felt quite grown up having to worry about the bills and the mortgage and getting enough together for a holiday; but his parents bought the cot and the pram and drawerfuls of baby clothes and every now and again a cheque for a hundred pounds would arrive. He was in his first job. He made it clear to the Head he was looking for promotion:

"I want to take on responsibility," he said.

"Of course," replied the Head sitting upright and dapper behind his desk. "We'll do what we can. Of course, Economics is a small department…."

John began to panic.

"I think I should retrain," he said to Ruth.

"What as?"

"A Maths teacher. Every school teaches Maths. All pupils have to do it. My opportunities are limited in Economics."

So he took a two-year, part-time course and once he'd got the certifi-

cate applied immediately for a Head of Maths post. He was interviewed but didn't make it. The fact he'd been teaching Economics
went against him. His panic began to mount: what if he couldn't
make the switch? What if he had to remain an Economics teacher
and the openings were few? What if he couldn't get on and climb to
Deputy Head or Head? He had a horrible vision of himself at fifty-
five, grey, tired, thirty-odd years in the classroom behind him and
still having to face classes every day; but much worse than the humiliation of not having power was the thought of a modest salary. If
he was to be the main breadwinner (the word made him think of his
parents, of the atmosphere of his early years, of the sense of oppres-
sion which seemed to seep from the very wallpaper) how would they
be living if he had no more than a classroom teacher's salary? He
saw the unprepossessing semi in a reasonable suburb, the small garden in front with a neat little lawn and flower beds where lily-of-the-
valley would nod in January; the ugly sectional garage at the end of
the little drive and the back garden surrounded by privets where they
would sit out in summer drinking home-made lemonade at a little
picnic table bought second hand from an ad in the local paper; he
imagined the comfortable but small living-room, the dining-room
used only for special occasions because the oak table and six chairs
were far too dear for everyday wear; the little kitchen with a functional table where they usually ate, the bedrooms, one a fair size, the
second cramped and the third no more than an expanded cupboard
and the bathroom rendered as pleasant as possible and lined with big
tiles to make it seem roomier. They would be middle-class, or at
least lower middle-class. There might be a solicitor next door or
across the road. But perhaps a bricklayer too. Maybe a lorry driver
who worked all hours. Perhaps a taxi driver. A mechanic. What
would the schools be like? Might immigrants start moving in? John
rejected racism utterly, but he worried. An area could get a bad
name. House prices could fall. You had to look after yourself.

This prospect of himself thirty years on depressed him badly and
gave him a restlessness and impatience which disturbed him. One
evening he visited the Deputy Head's home. They weren't friendly
but his son was starting to play guitar and John was invited round to
give him some tips. It was a detached place on a quiet avenue close
to St Mary's, the old Anglican church perched on a hill overlooking
the river two miles outside town. Twenty yards back from the road, it

was tall and assured. In the front garden was a maple, an oak, a sycamore. The windows were leaded lights. Inside, a huge hallway with a polished parquet floor let him pause to look up the broad staircase. The living-room ceiling was eleven feet high with a beautiful old rose from which hung a chandelier of six lights. They wandered through to the kitchen. It was as big as his living-room and dining-room combined. The cupboards were hand-made. The appliances expensive. Through the window he saw the garden stretching thirty yards to a row of tall poplars. As he drove home he felt sick. Was that going to be denied him? Had he made a terrible mistake by choosing Economics? The disturbing thought came to him that he was being punished. Was it God's will he should be a failure? In the great machine of the economy should he be a small part? Would he spend his life wishing for a bigger house, a newer car, more affluent neighbours?

He gritted his teeth and applied for every Head of Maths post he could find.

"But I don't want to move to Bletchley," said Ruth.

"We have no choice," he said. "The economy doesn't give us that much flexibility. If I'm going to get a Headship, I have to make my way quickly. We'll just have to accept that if a promotion comes up which I can get, I'll have to take it. The prize will be a big house in the best area. You want that, don't you?"

She wanted it but she wanted also to be able to choose where to live. When he was appointed in a school in Yorkshire she was almost in despair.

"What kind of place is Huddersfield?"

"It's just an ordinary, working-class Yorkshire town like any other. We won't be there long," he reassured her. "I'll be going for Deputy Headships after two years."

So they moved to a bigger house and they had more to spend on furniture and holidays and a better car but Ruth complained.

"I don't know anyone and I don't like the town."

"Well, don't go into town. I don't."

They'd chosen a village where he wouldn't encounter pupils . He was very anxious about running into them outside school where his authority no longer applied. He'd known colleagues who'd had eggs thrown at their windows, their cars scratched, found kids climbing on their garage roof or ripping up the flowers in their garden. He wanted a strict division. He never went near the areas the school drew its intake from. His dread of meeting pupils on the street turned him pale and cold. Many of them were polite enough of course and understood social context sufficiently not to be troublesome; but there were the few who felt a teacher in public was fair game. He'd heard the tales of the insults shouted across the street in a crowded town centre on a Saturday afternoon, of the boys who followed a teacher and his wife around for hours, evening loitering outside the pub where they sought asylum. Within the bounds of the school he had a range of powers: he could suspend, call in parents, even begin the process of exclusion; but on the street he was vulnerable and the pupils all potential enemies.

The effect of his promotion surprised him. He was filled with a sense of election. He was Head of Maths. Along with English it was the biggest department. He was, therefore, together with the Head of English, the most senior departmental Head. After the Head, the two deputies and the Heads of year, he was the most senior member of staff. That made him the ninth most senior person in the school. He found himself pulling away from his inferiors a little. Towards the eight more senior colleagues, however, and especially the Head, he was as complaisant as possible. He nestled. He liked to find himself with two or three of them especially when they fell to talking about the shortcomings of the rest of the staff. He had a problem with one of the women in his department who began an affair with a younger teacher.

"Between you and me, John," the Head said, "she's as mad as a box of frogs."

The remark delighted him. It seemed to open up at once a chasm between him and the junior staff. He was taken into the Head's confidence. How many other teachers did the Head disdain? He liked being part of a judging elite. Yet the old anxiety crept up on him. What if this was as far as he got? What if he were never to have the power of the Head? What if he could never close his office door, sit at his desk and think about which staff he favoured and which he would like to be rid of? What if he should be an underling till retirement? But he wasn't really an underling. He was part of the hierarchy. Yes, but it was petty. How many secondary schools were there? How many Heads of Department per school? Tens of thousands. To be one among tens of thousands, what good was that? Again the idea of money made his guts churn. The gulf between his salary and the Head's was big. Why shouldn't he have that money? He was being tested and he had to prove himself.

If there was a course in school management, he enrolled. He ingratiated himself with advisers. In front of the Head he was a performing poodle. He filled in application forms every week. He was turned down and turned down. It made him want to cry. Internally he was weeping. He would have liked to tear out his own heart. They were killing him. It was murder. Those polite letters of rejection were daggers which slid between his ribs. His warm blood ran from him. His scarlet shirt stuck to his flesh. He did his job. He made love to Ruth. He looked after his children. But he was being savaged. Society was a rabid pit-bull and its teeth tore at the flesh of his exposed chest. Every time he posted an application he was holding out his beating heart in his cupped hands and every time he opened a rejecting letter it was seized by a neglectful hand and thrown in the nearest bin. He wanted to cry out loud. It was unjust. It was cruel. He had a dream in which he dug and climbed into his own grave. When he looked at Ruth he saw a stranger. His children were a burden. They sucked money from him. They ate into his time. He would have liked to be rid of them. He wanted to live alone. To close the door on the world. To blacken the windows. He wanted no more contact with vicious humanity.

Then he was called for interview.

It was an ex-secondary which served a poor catchment. The exam results were awful.

"Do you want to be associated with failure?" said Ruth.

"It's my chance. If can prove myself I could be a Head within five years."

There was an emergency during his interview: boys were smashing windows in the sports hall. The Head was called away. Everyone looked at the floor. He was appointed.

They moved again, this time to a sweet little town forty miles from the school. It was well worth driving eighty miles a day to be sure he wouldn't meet a pupil or parent in the newsagent. These were people at the bottom end. He was wary of them. They were ignorant, feckless, violent. The drug sub-culture was rife. It was his Christian and professional duty to try to educate them, but personally he wanted nothing to do with them. He wanted his children to be kept away from them. The idea they might become part of his private life made his muscles shrink. They were awful. He despised them. But professional help was a clinical matter. A teacher no more needed to like the children he taught than a doctor the patient whose appendix he removed. Behind his professionalism he was safe. He intervened therapeutically. That's what he was paid for, to try to cure the problems of these people through education. But in truth he knew it was hopeless. What he could do was advance his career. John Major had just been elected. John had hoped Kinnock would win. But he adjusted. Ofsted was established. He saw the way ahead clearly: everything would be measured; those found wanting would be sacrificed; henceforth, what mattered was how things appeared; the public had to be convinced schools were getting better and better; it was all smoke and mirrors but if he wanted a Headship he had to play the game. He realised the dream of every child attending the nearest school because all schools were good was dead. Had it ever been realistic? It was too big a question and he feared it. Why should he trouble himself with tormenting ideas? His role was to serve. Other people disposed. He'd made it to Deputy Head but in a poor school. He wasn't going to stay long. This was his moment. One last leap and he would be among an elite. How many secondary Heads were there? A few thousand. That was something. To be one of only a few thousand in a population of sixty million. That was election. It was God's will. He must make it happen.

The staff's constant complaint was that the pupils' behaviour was awful. He knew it was true, but it was no longer politic to say so. Pupils were customers. If they behaved badly, it was because the lessons weren't interesting. But he still had to do some teaching himself and he had one truly impossible class. Because maths was such a vital subject, because all pupils needed it to be able to go on to college or into decent jobs, by and large they worked hard. It wasn't like languages. They were mocked like an Arab in a synagogue. By Year 9, most pupils had decided not to carry on with French or German. They were hard. To get a good grade you really had to work. Why do that when Media Studies or IT were much easier? Released from the pressure to succeed, pupils ran wild in French and German lessons. The management turned a blind eye, until the inspectors arrived. Then the linguists had to perform. John knew how hellish it could be for the French and German teachers, but when they came to him in desperation, he put up the defences: it was just the way the pupils presented; a good teacher had to deal with it; the school couldn't sanction sloppy classroom management. Yet his own little Year 9 Maths class was out of control. There were seven of them. They were very weak. Some of them still couldn't grasp a simple concept like a third. But their intellectual limitations weren't the problem: at the centre of the disruption was Henry Driver. A tall, gangly lad whose big, raw hands stuck out of the sleeves of his too small jacket like weeds sprouting between bricks, he could never find room for his long heavy legs and constantly had to sweep his thick, curly, black hair which hung onto his shoulders from his eyes. He never brought books. He never had a pen. He couldn't stay still for more than twenty seconds. He must be the centre of attention. His needs were importunate. He lashed out at the slightest provocation. He cursed liberally. Born to a seventeen year-old mother who had two younger children from different fathers, he lived with them in his grandmother's house where she presided. A brittle, high-handed little woman she accepted criticism from no-one. Her husband who had dropped dead of a heart attack in the pub, was a great admirer of Franco. They went on package holidays to Mallorca or the Costa del Sol. He thought Spain a great country thanks to Franco. What Britain needed was the same kind of strong leadership. He despised communists and socialists and liberals of all kinds. He hated niggers. It was a good thing they put a bullet through that Martin Luther King because he'd gone to Memphis to support a strike. He was a communist. Mrs Dyer was very proud of her husband. She thought him a real man. She shared his opinions. She imposed them on her children. If they misbehaved, which meant doing something to annoy her, she gave them a slap. That was what children needed to teach them the difference between right and wrong. When her daughter became pregnant by a seventeen-year-old without a job or qualifications who made money selling dope on the estate and had a swastika tattooed on his forehead, she kicked her out. They baby was born. The boy turned violent and the daughter came home.

"If you live under my roof, I'm in charge!" declared Mrs Dyer.

She resented the presence of the baby. She was forty. Her first child was born when she was nineteen. He was now in prison for drug dealing and grievous bodily harm. Her second son, born a year later, went wild at the age of fourteen and was diagnosed bi-polar. He turned to drink, sank into alcoholism, now worked as a gardener for the council and lived alone in a flat above a betting shop. Kirsty was her third. She was a timid baby and Mrs Dyer tried to put some fire in her. She shouted at her and slapped her in the hope it would make her more assertive, but the child became withdrawn and weepy. Mrs Dyer concluded she was hopeless and paid her as little attention as possible. Now she had this baby. He woke up at four in the morning:

"Shut that fucking baby up!" she cried. "I've to be at work at half past eight."

But Kirsty couldn't cope and she had to drag herself out of bed.

"Here! Give the little bastard to me! Are you gonna shut up you little bugger! Shut up! Stop that fucking noise!"

And she held the baby tight in her hands, up in the air and growled into his face as he screamed and the mother stood aside in her faded nightdress, yawning and scratching.

As the boy grew, so did his grandmother's bitterness. She wanted some time to herself. She wanted to bring men home. She still had something to offer. She could open her legs as well as the next woman. She might find a nice man. Someone with a bit of money. Someone who could buy her a big white, leather sofa and a huge plasma television, take her on three cruises a year, keep her well stocked with gin. Her life wasn't over. But with the kid in the house it was a nightmare. If she brought a man home there were toys all over the floor. He'd be bumping away at her when the baby would start screaming. Kirsty would knock on the bedroom door.

"Can't I even have a shag in peace!" Mrs Dyer would hurl.

The child cried all the time. She shut him the garden. He hammered at the back door:

"Let me in! Let me in, grandma!"

"Stay out there till you learn to shut up!"

From the first, Henry was in trouble at school.

John Little attempted to cajole him. He had a long talk with him in his study. The boy sat opposite him and fidgeted. He looked out of the window. He pushed his great, ponderous lock of hair from his eyes.

"I mean, don't you want to be here, Henry?"

"No," said the boy with an idiotic smile.

"Where do you want to be?"

"Smoking dope in my bedroom."

In the classroom, his size gave him a presence which intimidated, and his behaviour was so utterly remote from all social sense, the other pupils were amazed. He climbed on the desks. He took off his shirt and ripped it up. He scrawled:

Mr Little is a cunt

in huge letters in indelible pen across the whiteboard. He took his cock out in the lesson and said to the boy next to him:

"D'you wanna suck it?"

He was suspended for three days, five days, ten days. When he came back he was worse. Mrs Dyer was called into school:

"Why can't the teachers control him?" she said.

"Mrs Dyer," said John patiently, "we are getting close to permanent exclusion."

"Just try it. I've got all the evidence I need against this school. I've already been to a solicitor."

"What for?"

"Assault."

"Assault?"

"Mr Wilmer hit him. I've got witnesses."

"That's already been investigated. There was no case against Mr Wilmer."

"You try and exclude my grandson and you'll find different. Make the teachers do their job properly. It's what they're paid for."

John couldn't ever get the lesson started. The pupils learned nothing. There were two other boys who imitated everything Henry did. The rest treated it as spectator sport. If he got through the hour without a serious incident John thought he'd succeeded. For the Ofsted inspection he ensured Henry and the other two were not in the room.

And after two years he applied for every Headship available.

He was well thought of by the County. He knew how to toe the line and deliver. He understood that was the important matter: delivery. Above him was the Head, above whom were the Advisers, above whom was the Director of Education, above whom was the Chief Executive, above whom were the junior ministers, above whom were the cabinet ministers, above whom was the Prime Minister who was supposed to do the people's will. Whose will was being done? God's. John had no doubt about that. But in the Great Chain of Being stretching from the lowliest teaching assistant to the PM, who was making the decisions? Often, the feeling came over him that no-one was deciding but everyone was behaving as if someone was. He dismissed this disturbing idea. He had to focus on getting on. There were no second chances and the losers got it in the neck. The adviser for his school tipped him off about a rich promotion. An ex-grammar in a well-heeled catchment thirty miles away was about to advertise for a Head. He applied, was interviewed, they didn't appoint. The adviser told him to apply again. He did. He was interviewed and appointed.

It wasn't a big school so his salary was £65,000 which disappointed him. He began to worry: he was forty-four, he might be in this school till retirement, he'd be one of the lowest paid Heads in the County. He had the compensation that Blackwell Grammar produced consistently excellent results. All the same, he didn't like it when he went to area Heads meetings and talked to colleagues he knew were earning £15,000 or £20,000 a year more. Were they looking down on him? He drove a new Toyota but some of them turned up in Mercedes, BMWs, Jaguars. It nagged away at him that though he'd made it to Head, he still had a sense of inferiority and dissatisfaction. His governing body though had the discretion to award more pay for recruitment and retention or special contribution. He put together a case, discussed it with the Chair. A sub-committee was set up which made the decision. The full body was asked to rubber stamp. His salary was increased to £75,000.

John began to think, as soon as he was appointed, that this could be a nice stepping stone to something better. Maybe senior adviser.

Maybe Head of a very big school, or a high-profile Academy. Perhaps he'd be in line for an MBE. Perhaps even a Knighthood. Sir John Little. He liked the sound of it. He liked the idea of being addressed as Sir John. But first he had to ensure Blackwell was classed outstanding in the next inspection. The problem was the staff. He'd always viewed his colleagues with suspicion. They were rivals for limited promotions. He'd kept an eye on them, tried to ingratiate himself with power, constantly compared himself to teachers he thought of as lazier, less dutiful, more likely to question. Now he was in charge, his staff seemed to him nothing but a burden and a problem. They arrived too late, left too early, spent too much time talking or reading the paper in the staff-room, expected to have a lunch-hour, didn't like staying for meetings, and worst of all, taught boring lessons. The culture dictated: if pupils did badly or misbehaved, it was the teachers' fault. Pupils could no longer be required to behave. To insist they work hard was passé. They were consumers. They must be pleased. School must become as attractive to them as McDonalds or an amusement arcade. He stood in front of his staff and said:

"We are here to entertain them."

He established a Teaching and Learning Group which met after school every Wednesday. Attendance was voluntary but anyone who refused wouldn't pass through the Threshold or get promotion. He stood at the gate in the morning. Any member of staff not on the premises by 8.35 was sent a warning letter. The weather turned icy. It snowed. Mrs Hoque was two minutes late. She came to his office with the letter in her hands:

"I had to clear the snow from my drive. Then the traffic was at a standstill. I set off half an hour earlier than usual."

"Set off an hour earlier tomorrow."

"This is unfair. I've never been late in seven years! A warning letter!"

"I can't accept people turning up late. A rule is a rule."

He had cameras fitted at all points of entrance or exit. His excuse was security but he briefed his secretary whose computer received the images:

"If any member of staff leaves the premises during the school day tell me immediately."

Helen Hicks was spotted getting into her car at 3.16. He called her in.

"Did you leave the premises early yesterday, Helen?"

"I don't think so."

"You did. School ends at 3.20."

"That's when I left."

"No. 3.16."

"Oh yes, I may have been a minute or two early, but I was putting books in my car…"

"We don't leave a minute or two early, Helen. No-one leaves before 3.20."

When word came that the GTC was tightening up on teachers' conduct outside school, he spoke to his staff.

"If you were on holiday, on the beach, and some of our pupils were there, I would expect you to leave."

There was a moment's silence, as if a universe was about to be born.

"Why?"

"It wouldn't be appropriate. Female members of staff perhaps in bikinis, or men in trunks. It's not the right setting."

"But," said an older member of staff, "we have a right to be on holiday. If pupils happen to be in the same place, that's too bad."

"Well, we have a responsibility to behave properly. I wouldn't expect you to stay in a restaurant for example, if you were there, eating and drinking and some of our pupils came in with their parents."

"You'd expect us to leave?"

"Yes."

"Even if we hadn't finished our meal?"

"Yes."

"Look," said a younger teacher, "I go around the clubs. I often run into our sixth-formers. What do you expect me to do if I happen to be in the same place at three in the morning?"

"Go home."

John didn't like the older staff. They knew the previous culture. They disliked the way things were going. They raised their voices. As far as he could he appointed and promoted young teachers. One of the neighbouring Heads said to him:

"They're cheap, compliant and this is all they know."

John thought it sound advice. By the time Ofsted was due he felt everything was in place.

"It's all in the self-evaluation," he said to the little SLT he'd established to protect him . "Even if the staff let us down, we'll come through."

His anxiety was that he'd get a good or good and improving. But that was what his predecessor had managed. To be no better than that would be a humiliation and if he wanted to move up...... It was crucial lessons should be at least good. He ran through his staff list. Who could he rely on? Who would let him down? A worrying number of people had been classed satisfactory during his observations. He set aside the list when he came to Kevin Finney. Fifty-seven, a lefty of the unreconstructed sort: John despised him. If there was anyone who'd take the inspection nonchalantly it was him. Not that he was a bad teacher. John had observed him and the lesson was fine. Delivered by a favoured teacher, he'd have given it good. But he needed to diminish Finney. He rated it satisfactory but divided the category into a, b, and c giving Finney the lowest rank. Word came back: there was no need to use Ofsted gradings for in-school observations. That was government advice. Finney rejected the grading. John paced his office. He was Head. Staff should know their place. If only he could find a way of getting rid of Finney. He almost wished the inspectors would find against him.

The school was deemed outstanding. The only negative was one lesson considered unsatisfactory. Unfortunately, it wasn't Finney's.

Helena Main had been in the school only two years. She'd resigned from her previous school because of bad behaviour and worked as supply. John took her on when a Maths teacher suffered a stroke, first part-time and temporary, but in her second year permanent and full-time. The lesson scaled unsatisfactory was with a small Year 9 class. Two of the girls had police records. One had been found unconscious and marinated in booze behind a supermarket after her parents reported her missing. The other assaulted a pensioner for her purse. One of the boys had been suspended for setting fire to a science teacher's hair. Then there was Kirsty Slinger. She refused to wear uniform, arrived in tiny skirts and tottering heels, unbuttoned her blouse as low as she dared, wore thick make-up, false nails, chewed gum and responded to all attempts to make her work with the same:

"Too fuckin' borin'!"

She was known to have offered boys blow-jobs for money. She caused uproar in a History class by blurting:

"Eh, I'm skint, sir. Fancy a fuck?"

One of five sisters, all with names beginning H, her mother left home when she was seven. Her father drove lorries, was often away, and depended on his ageing mother, who cooked bacon and eggs or chips and fish fingers, then settled down in front of the television. A wiry, energetic little man, he'd shaved his head and had it tattooed with the names of the Manchester United first team. His chest was a shrine to Elvis Presley and his back to Sylvester Stallone. He came into school in a T-shirt which read:

Made to be laid.

"I don't know what I can say, like. I can do nowt wi 'er. She's a good lass, in her way. But she's wild. 'Er mother's same."

John felt sorry for him. The girl exhausted three final warnings. When the inspection was due, Helena Main came to see him.

"Can we get Kirsty Slinger out of my lesson during the inspection?"

"We have to educate everyone, Helena."

"Yes, but just for one lesson. She's beyond control."

"No child is beyond control. It's just the way they present."

"I know lots of them just play up, but she's disturbed."

"Even disturbed children deserve an education."

"Of course, but I can't control her. If I'm seen for that lesson, it will be unsatisfactory."

"Not if you make it interesting, Helena."

She looked at him over her heavy glasses for a second, then fell silent.

"If I say yes to you, I'd have to say yes to everyone. You know what I mean?"

She nodded.

One unsatisfactory lesson. Perhaps he could let it pass. But the annoyance of it wouldn't leave him alone. He had to take action. He made drop-in visits to several of Helena's lessons and decided two of them were unsatisfactory. She was told she was being placed on informal support; there was the inevitable grisly meeting with John, her union representative and the HR woman from County. She was given the usual programme for improvement. Six weeks later came the predictable review and she was ineluctably moved to formal support.

John told himself that if she improved, he would back off; but he hoped she wouldn't and knew it was unlikely. It would send the right message to the staff if he got rid of her. There were to be no unsatisfactory lessons in his school. They would watch their backs a little more. He liked the idea of his staff being ill-at-ease, even anxious. Wasn't that, after all, how he'd got on? Hadn't he always worried about what his bosses were thinking of him and hadn't that been the spur? Or perhaps the spur was money and he'd been careful of his bosses as a way to get it? He read in the paper that only 4% of the population earned as much as him or more. The thought of tens of millions of people who were worse off than him was very comforting. He deserved his success. He had special talents. He'd worked hard. He'd made a contribution to society. But when he read of the incomes of the top 1% he felt a dim pulse of resentment. His £75,000 seemed paltry, feeble and insulting . How could anyone be worth that much? £2,000,000 a year! £3,000,000! He did the arithmetic quickly. £250,000 a month gross. How much net? Who could spend that kind of money? It was outrageous. And he'd worked as a classroom teacher for no more than £30,000 a year. The thought of his widowed mother surviving on £15,000 came to him. It was wrong! There was no need for such gross disparities. What rational economic or social purpose could they serve? But against this tide of indignation came the eddy of ideology: surely the market must decide. It was subjective preference. If folk wanted to reward the best people this way, who could argue against it? And if that argument was permitted, who knows, it might be decided he was earning too much. It was horrible to be denied access to the highest wealth, it belittled him. Were those bankers any better than him? He understood economics just as well, he could work just as hard, he could be ruthless. Why had he chosen teaching? He realised his background had been against him. The modesty of his circumstances had made him think a Headteacher's salary generous. What a fool! He should have aimed higher. Imagine being one of those untouchables. You could simply pull away from the mass. There would be no need to rub shoulders with them. Everything about your life could become exclusive. You could move in a circle of wealth, fame and power. It was heartbreaking to realize he would never make it. Yes, he lived on a gated estate. Yes, he was well away from the chavs, the plebs, the low-lifes. But the super-rich were well away from him. No doubt they looked down on him. £75,000! They would scoff. And he had to work hard, day in day out, for that. It brought an ugly feeling. He strained on the leash of his salary like a status dog on its chain. Yet it had to be tolerated. Once intervene armed with ideas of fairness and justice, once cross that Rubicon and where was the line to be drawn? If we decided to cap the incomes of the rich, why not of the not so rich? If we judged they received too much, why not that others received too little? And what agency could do anything about it but the State? And what mechanisms did the State possess but taxes, benefits and enforced limits? No! It was better to accept the free- for- all of the market and a huge gap between rich and poor, even if it meant his own mother was pinched. Yet his economist's brain told him the market was rigged. Every event in the economy flowed from decisions made in boardrooms, by managers, by investors. He was no economic innocent. He knew the theory of markets was as full of holes as a tramp's underwear. He knew decision was behind all activity. The question was: should decision be left to the few, the rich, the powerful? What was the alternative? Economic democracy? The idea made his mind melt. Imagine it! Imagine a school being run democratically. No. Democracy must be driven to the periphery and at the centre must lie the decisions of the worthy. And democracy itself must do no more than provide people the illusion of power. Let the masses vote by all means, but let their votes elect an elite. Yes. It was terrible. He hated it. But it was the way it must be if he wasn't going to lose his advantage. So he was right. His staff must be made to feel uncomfortable. That was the nature of work. It wasn't supposed to be enjoyable. It was a struggle for place. Everyone had to understand they were being tested and those found wanting would be sacrificed. As God cast his judgement on sinners so the economy judged those who didn't perform. His mind began to recover its poise. He was in the top four per cent after all. The majority were his inferiors. It was something never to forget.

Helena Main's union representative argued it was one bad class that was ruining her. John countered that there are no bad classes. The union man produced evidence of the detentions and suspensions the pupils had been given. John said the children can't be blamed. The union man had chapter and verse on Kirsty Slinger. John said a competent teacher must be able to manage any child.

She was given a compromise deal: £8,000 and a good reference. There would be no more unsatisfactory lessons.

It was shortly after this Finney came to see John. He was tall and hefty, and had never tried to expunge his lower-class origins from his demeanour or accent. He had big, strong hands like a plumber or bricklayer. He looked odd in a suit, as if it constrained his power, as if he wanted to cast it off, throw away his tie and roll up his sleeves. He spoke with the heavy accent of his small, down-at-heel town. John recoiled from him. He still had an indelible trace of Manchester in his own speech but tried to sound neutral. Above all, he tried to look as though power came naturally. Finney would have been at home eating a hot meat pie on a football terrace or among the noisy throng of tipsy travellers on the rollicking last bus home at midnight on Friday. Yet he was intelligent and well-read. John saw him as one of those men who have thrown away their chances. He spoke bluntly his opposition to policy. He refused to comply with the school's systems if he thought them stupid. He asked awkward questions in meetings. He left school at three twenty every day eating an apple and caught the bus with the pupils.

He had a letter in his hand.

"I've come by a copy of this," he said, " about the County wanting to avoid redundancies and the possibility of bumping."

"That letter was for Headteachers," said John, slightly shocked.

"Aye, but I've got a copy. I'm interested. If it could be bumped. I'd go. Are you willing to look into it?"

John found the request insolent. He'd deliberately kept the letter from his staff. How had Finney got a copy? He wanted to say no. He wanted to deny him. He would have liked to have said: "That letter is nothing to do with you. It's not for your eyes. It's for those of us who make decisions. Give it to me!"

"Yes," he said, "I'll look into it."

"Good," said Finney. "I'll come back in a week or two."

"Yes," said John.

He had no intention. There were serious job losses pending in a school at the other end of the County. Heads had been asked to do what they could to avoid people being forced out. But John wasn't going to accept someone onto his staff just because they were surplus elsewhere. He wanted to select carefully. And why should he help? If some teacher was made redundant in a school thirty miles away, what was it to do with him? As for Finney, he wouldn't yawn to help him. He wanted him out, but not at the cost of appointing someone he might have doubts about. No. He wouldn't do a thing. But he had to be careful because the County was working hard to avoid compulsory losses.

Two days later another teacher in his late fifties appeared in his office with the letter in his hand.

"Kevin Finney gave me this," he said.

"That letter was for Headteachers."

"Well, Kevin Finney gave it to me. I was wondering…my health isn't good. I've got my back problem and high blood pressure and this might be a way out…"

"But you're only fifty-three," said John.

He was furious with Finney. What was the point of being a Head if your authority could be challenged by someone like him? Of course, he knew he ought to have told his staff about the letter. He was paid by the Authority after all. He insisted his staff do everything by the book but that wasn't reasonable for himself. He'd spoken to a couple of local Heads who'd said they'd keep the letter quiet. It was perfectly easy except for a troublemaker like Finney. He'd've got the letter from the union. Driving home John reflected on his impotence . He couldn't discipline Finney. What could he do? He'd promised Finney and was worried he might kick up a fuss if he just did nothing. But he'd call his bluff. He could always claim he'd investigated. How would Finney know?

Two weeks to the day, Finney came back.

"Did you get anywhere with the bump redundancy?" he asked.

"No."

"You did look into it?"

"Yes."

"That's not what I've been told."

"Sorry?"

"I e-mailed Tom Newman. He told me it could go ahead. It just depended on you, but he hadn't heard from you."

John would have liked to thump the table and order Finney out of his office. His raised his eyebrows and picked up his pen.

"I made a few enquiries," he said.

"But you didn't speak to Tom Newman."

"I didn't need to."

"How can you not need to speak to the man responsible?"

"I asked a few questions and decided it wasn't right for this school."

"But if you didn't speak to Tom you couldn't know the details. They'd found a Physics teacher willing to come here. You just needed to interview him."

"I know that."

"How could you if you didn't speak to Tom Newman?"

"I made enquiries."

"There isn't anyone else to make enquiries of. I've exchanged e-mails with him. He told me you hadn't been in touch so you didn't know what was going on."

"That's not true."

"Well, are you willing to interview this bloke?"

"No."

"Why not?"

"As I say, it's not right for this school."

"But County are trying to stop people being forced out and if you won't say yes, this guy is going to lose his job and I lose about ten grand in redundancy pay. Why not just interview him? If he's no good you can turn him down."

"I've told you my decision. It isn't right for this school."

Why did a low-level nobody like Finney think he had the right to e-mail the County's Head of HR? Did he know him personally? John seethed for days. This wouldn't do him any good in the eyes of the County. Suppose Finney told Newman what he'd said. Would there be repercussions? It gave him a very poisoned feeling as if he inhabited a sewer and must get used to the stench. He'd always done everything demanded of him to please his superiors. Of course, what his superiors didn't know wouldn't hurt them. In any case, the final decision was with the Head, so what did it matter. He'd simply made an early final decision.

Within a week Finney was in his office again.

"I've decided to go. I'm taking the reduced pension. I think you need this."

He handed over the completed form.

"Fine. Yes. I'll see to that."

"Not getting the redundancy costs me ten grand. I'll lose two a year on the reduction so another six on the lump sum. If I live twenty years that's forty thousand down on the annual pension. About fifty-six grand in total. At least."

Finney sat, his huge hands on his thighs, staring straight at him.

"Well," said John, "the reduced benefits scheme is good. You'll have a decent pension."

"Thirteen thousand three hundred. How would you like that?"

John laughed. Finney got up heavily and left.

John arrived home that evening in a very good mood. He hardly thought about Finney but months later when he had to draft the advert for his replacement he paused. £13,300. It wasn't much. What would he expect? He'd bought added years. By the time he retired he should be earning a good £90,000. He wouldn't expect a pension of less than £45,000. The lump sum of £135,000 he'd invest. People like Finney just had to get by. That was the way of things. Nothing could be done about it. His pension was liveable. He could take part-time work . What did his wife do? John had no idea. It was none of his business. In fact, whether Finney managed or sank into poverty was none of his business. He was an employee soon to become an ex-employee. It wasn't an employer's business to worry about the personal finances of employees. Employees were there to do the job. They got the market rate. That was the end of an employer's responsibility. He went back to the advert. He'd defeated Finney. He felt very pleased with himself. He was a manager. A good manager. He knew how to keep staff in their place. His decision had been right: he'd forced Finney out. He could replace him with someone young, cheap and compliant. That was good management.

It was a few months later the papers were full of the football scandal. The tabloids ran pictures of the prostitute who'd sold her story. It was a sordid, cynical business and it bothered John. When he walked to the patissierie on Saturday to buy a *tarte aux fruits* for Ruth, or to the newsagents to pick up a paper, he passed the huge house behind electronic gates where the Craig Dawson lived. He'd bought an old, six-bedroomed Georgian place, had it demolished and replaced by a vast, thirty-roomed edifice with a swimming-pool, stables and garaging for seven cars. Though John thought it vulgar, he liked being close to such obvious signs of success. When his children were younger, he'd enjoyed pointing places out and saying, such-and such lives here, he's worth millions. The association with low-life was troubling. When he passed the house now he looked resolutely at the pavement. And he hoped they would soon move. If the marriage cracked up, surely they would? The waters would close over the affair. The house would sell for £3,000,000 or so to someone who deserved to be admired. John hoped it would happen quickly.

DEMOBBED

When Freddie Cunliffe was demobbed in 1946 he had nowhere to go but his fiancé's house. It was an end terrace right next to the wood-yard where the rats were big enough to scare the cats; but an end terrace brought status: it was one step from semi-detached. There were four rooms and six people: Mary, her mother and father, her brother Henry and his wife Ethel and Freddie. The bigger bedroom was for the mother and father, Henry and Ethel had the smaller, Mary slept on the couch in the front room and Freddie on the floor in the kitchen. There was a terrible draught from under the back door. He fitted an excluder but the wind still made its way in. He pulled the itchy blankets over his head and smiled to himself. After six years in Egypt and Italy even a draughty kitchen floor was a relief, and he was used to miserable conditions: his mother, who had him at nineteen, left him with her grandparents when she found a husband. He was three. His grandparents were diligent drinkers. His grandfather earned decent money as a brass turner, but he was in the pub every night. His mother didn't work, so she could drink all day. The house was filthy and stank. He stank. When he was left alone at night, he amused himself by banging the fire surround with his clog and chasing the cockroaches across the flagged floor.

But the world had changed. Clem Attlee had won and there was no going back to unemployment and poverty. There were opportunities for young men willing to do what was necessary. Freddie had no manual skills. He could write; he'd always done well at composition; but he'd left school at fourteen. He'd have been a journalist if he'd known how. You needed qualifications and he hadn't time to get those. He needed work fast. One thing they'd taught him in the forces was to drive, so he applied for a job as a commercial traveller and was the first person in the street to have a car parked outside the house. He sold wallpaper, but it didn't matter. He'd've sold anything. He had no interest in wallpaper or interior décor. What he was interested in was selling. The knack of it was to sell yourself: a timid or self-effacing salesman couldn't sell the best wallpaper in the world; but a confident salesman, well-dressed, slick, with a thoroughly rehearsed patter could sell a lousy product to the most discerning shopkeeper. He invested in three smart suits.

"How much!" said Mary.

"It's a tool of the trade," he said. "Henry has a bagful of plumbing tools. Well me, I need smart suits."

He bought the most expensive Loake shoes, Real Brook shirts, gold cufflinks and cravats. He considered the cravat a coup: the other commercial travellers he knew wore ties. They were smart enough, but a cravat was classy. He accumulated fifteen.

"You can only wear one at a time," said Mary.

His confidence was justified: his boss was delighted; he increased sales by more than a half. He was given a rise. He celebrated by buying an overcoat.

"We're supposed to be saving up!" said Mary.

When they got married, he was still sleeping on the kitchen floor. He kept his clothes in a cardboard box. But he no longer stank. He washed conscientiously at the kitchen sink each day and took no chances: he had a good stock of after-shave, talcum powder and the eau-de-cologne he'd seen advertised in the Sunday paper. The crisis arrived, though, when Mary and Ethel became pregnant within a month of one another. Freddie went in search of a rented house but mostly they were in poor condition, over-priced, damp, infested or in the very worst parts of the town. Henry did the same. His boss owned a few small terrace houses and because Henry was a good worker, strong, skilled and fast, he offered him one at low rent. It was a tumbledown place with dry rot in the floorboards and a roof the rain dripped through with the sly insistence of a naughty child raiding the biscuit tin. Henry asked if he could do the work. His boss paid for the materials and by the time their baby was due, the couple moved into a cosy, clean, dry home with a bathroom and inside toilet.

"If they can do it why can't we?" said Mary.

"I'm not a plumber!"

"But you earn more than Henry."

"I can't afford to pay a tradesman to do the kind of work he did."

"You can afford fancy clothes and jazz records."

Freddie had bought a little player and was accumulating a collection of 78s by Louis Armstrong, Buddy Bolden and The Original Dixieland Jazz Band. Mary, who had no feel for music other than the hymns of Charles Wesley, thought it a foolish extravagance. All the same, when Henry and Ethel moved out, Freddie and Mary got the front room. They bought a put-u-up sofa which folded out on squeaky springs and stiff metal joints to make an uncomfortable bed with a great malicious ridge across the middle which made Freddie wake with an aching back each morning; and a van arrived with a wardrobe he'd ordered. He hung his suits and shirts. His cravats were folded in a drawer. His seven pairs of shoes sat beneath his clothes.

"Why did you need something so big?" said Mary.

"It'll last a lifetime," he said.

Shortly after the birth of his daughter, Freddie took his courage in both hands, borrowed thousands from the bank and opened a wallpaper shop in the town centre.

"We should be getting our own house," said Mary. "And what if it fails?"

But it didn't. Freddie was a brilliant salesman. He smiled obligingly at his customers. Nothing was too much trouble. He was always smart in his expensive suits and silk cravats. It was, he knew, the women who made the decisions, and they liked him. In fact, he knew they liked him more than the wallpaper. He took out a mortgage on a three-bedroomed house in the suburbs, bought a new Hillman Minx and could hardly believe he'd once lived in a slum.

He employed three female assistants. Two were married but the youngest, Elspeth, was nineteen and seemed free and easy. She was cross-eyed and not noticeably pretty, but her body was firm and curvaceous. She leaned over the counter and he was transfixed by her behind. In summer she wore blouses which revealed her gorgeous cleavage.

"What d'you think of this pattern?" Freddie asked her the great heavy book of wallpaper samples open in front of him.

"I like it. Too expensive for me though."

"Is it?"

"You need a posh house to put up embossed paper like that."

"I have it in my house."

"Very nice, Mr Cunliffe."

"Freddie. No need to stand on ceremony."

"You must have a nice house."

"Like to see it?"

"I wouldn't mind."

"I'll take you there one day."

From that instant he was spying his opportunity. The problem was, Mary was such a stay-at-home. He encouraged her to go out in the evening: June Rathbone ran amateur dramatics at the church. She could go along and enjoy herself.

"I've too much to do," Mary would say.

"Of an evening?"

"And I'm tired. I've looked after Barbara all day."

"It'll perk you up. A good laugh, a bit of fun and a cup of tea and a natter. You'll feel much better."

"What you always trying to push me out the door for?"

"I'm just thinking you need to get out. You spend too much time in these four walls."

"I like my home."

"So you should, but you ought to enjoy yourself a bit."

It was useless. Mary was no more likely to go out in the evening than the Pope to smile on homosexuality. He wondered if there were somewhere else he could take Elspeth. He thought of booking a hotel on half-day closing, but he feared she'd blench from the suggestion. Maybe he could get her to take him to her house; but he knew her grandmother lived with them and being almost bed-bound was sure to be in. No, he needed to be able to bring the girl to his house. In any case, he wanted to show off. It might be a modest little semi but it was in a good area. Round the corner were houses which sold for ten or fifteen thousand. And they'd made it nice. Mary protested at the expense but he insisted on Axminster, Stag and Shand Kydd. A girl like Elspeth from the backstreets, used to the cramped, make-do little houses of the working-class with their tiny yards, alleys and chilly outside toilets would be softened by the aura of luxury. He'd offer her the bathroom. She could luxuriate in the water or take a quick shower. And what he wouldn't do to her in the big double bed. If only he could pinch a couple of hours when Mary wasn't there.

Then fate smiled on him.

Mary's aunty, a big, overweight woman who walked once a fortnight the two miles form the rabbit-hutch two-up-two-down where she lived with her daughter and family to visit for an afternoon, sitting on a straight-backed chair taking one custard cream or chocolate digestive after another from the floral cake stand, slurping milky, sweet tea and treating Mary to the details of a life as eventful as a night in a nunnery, had to go into hospital to have her gall stones removed. Mary went visiting and took Barbara with her.

"I'll close the shop for an hour this afternoon and show you my house," said Freddie to Elspeth.

"Close the shop?"

"Only for an hour or so. Tuesdays are quiet anyway."

"Won't your wife mind?"

"She's out. Hospital visiting."

Elspeth's expression turned serious and somewhat wary.

"Nothing serious," said Freddie with a smile. "Her aunty's gall-stones. She'll take her a bunch of grapes and a *Woman's Own*."

Elspeth didn't so much consent as go along with her boss's plan. She was one of those young women who'd been brought up to believe employers were quasi-gods. Though her parents, being hard-up, were Labour voters, they weren't subversives: bosses must be shown respect and opportunities made the best of. Dipped in this varnish of Labour conformism, Elspeth had a stiff carapace of obedience even to a petty shopkeeper like Freddie. Not that she didn't see through him. He was vain and preening and fancied himself and she thought him a laughable peacock; but he was her boss and she mustn't offend him. She knew well enough what he might be about and was determined to keep him at bay.

"What d'you think?" he said, showing her into the bathroom.

"Very nice."

She surveyed the pale blue tiles, the white bath with the black panel and the plastic shower curtain on which athletic salmon leaped arching like living springs, the superior lino and the big airing cupboard in the corner.

"Take a bath if you like."

"No thanks," and she edged out of the room

When he took her into his bedroom he told her how much the furniture had cost. In his mind was the notion that the mention of money would somehow make her more willing, but when he slipped his arm round her waist, she quickly extricated herself and went trippingly downstairs on her stilettos. He felt he had to say something, so in the car as they stopped at traffic lights he said:

"Look I'm sorry if I offended you, Ellie."

"That's all right," she said.

His pulse quickened.

"You're a very attractive girl."

"Thank you."

"I don't mind telling you I'm very fond of you."

"That's nice."

"But I don't want to be intrusive."

"Don't worry. I'm okay."

"Good," he said, "good," and he patted her knee with his left hand.

He felt it politic to desist for a while, but when Mary's aunty came out of hospital, she needed looking after at home and Mary went back and forth everyday to give a hand to her daughter who was lame in her right leg. Day after day the house was empty for a few hours, the big bed was silently waiting, the pillows nicely fluffed, the mattress firm, the eiderdown ready to cover their eager, naked forms.

"You didn't get to see the garden," he said to her.

"No."

"Would you like to?"

"I wouldn't mind. I'm fond of flowers, especially primroses."

"I'll close up at lunchtime."

"People might wonder why."

"I'll say it's stocktaking."

"At lunchtime?"

But at twelve thirty they were in his Minx crossing the river and climbing the hill to the pleasant suburb. They went straight to the back garden and he let her loiter a little on her own while he went inside to make coffee. She sat on the sofa, the light from the bay bathing her and making her sensuous form seem all the more radiant. Her legs were crossed and his eyes kept focussing on her strong thighs. Oh yes, she was a splendid young girl all right. Such strength in the way she walked and her movements were all graceful and controlled. He noticed how long her fingers were and the nails perfectly manicured and painted pink made him think of her scratching his back in the throes of her pleasure.

"Another biscuit?" and he offered her the plate.

"No thanks. I'll ruin my dinner."

He sat beside her. She pulled a little towards the arm of the sofa. He finished his coffee, put the cup and saucer on the floor and turned towards her.

"Ellie?"

"Careful, you'll spill my coffee."

He put his hand on her knee.

"I'm not sure you should do that, Mr Cunliffe."

"Freddie."

She removed his hand.

"Your wife might be back any time."

"No," he said, putting his arm round her shoulders, "she'll be away for hours."

"I'm not sure…"

He ran his left hand up her skirt and pulled her towards him.

"Freddie!"

The cup and saucer in her hand, balanced like a bird on a wire, made her hold still. Freddie felt the flesh of her thigh beyond her stocking top and forced his fingers between her squeezed legs. The cup tilted, wobbled and fell to the carpet.

"Oh!"

"Never mind."

He began to kiss her mouth while she held the saucer out in front of her like a priest proffering the host. In spite of his probing fingers, she wouldn't uncross her legs. He thought this mere girlish bashfulness. He was the man and needed to show her the way.

"Let's go upstairs," he said.

"Upstairs?"

He took her hand and pulled her from the sofa. She tottered on her heels. She still had the saucer in her hand when they got to the bedroom. He began undoing the buttons her blouse as if he was going to find the answer to the mystery of creation in her bra.

"Are you sure you should be doing that?"

"I love you, Ellie," he blurted like a child lying about having eaten her chocolate before Easter.

"I'm not sure we should."

But his hands were in her blouse and when he'd released her hooks and her great breasts fell free, white and warm and ponderous as the udders of cows going slowly into the milking parlour, he sucked on one nipple and then the other, supporting her in his ravenous fingers. He pulled off all her clothes and spread her legs. He was almost aghast at the thick, black triangle. Her belly was flat and soft and white. Her thighs were as heavy as sides of beef. He pushed her into the middle of the bed and threw the eiderdown around her. He fumbled with his buttons in his rush to get his clothes off and standing naked with his throbbing little erection pointing to his belly-button like a road sign to Blackpool, he expected her to show some indication of being impressed, but she turned her head away as if someone had just offered her a plate of soggy dumplings.

"What a woman you are," he said, climbing on top of her; and remembering his reading of *Lady Chatterley's Lover* (in a pirated edition in Italy), which seemed appropriate on this occasion of his first adultery, he thought he ought to be crude and raw like Mellors, as if he was as much at home in nature and as direct in the pursuit of his pleasures as Arthur Lawrence. "That's a lovely cunt you have, Ellie," he said slipping his finger in.

"Oh, don't call it that," she said.

"Why not?"

"It's not a nice word, Mr Cunliffe."

"Freddie," he said trying to kiss her mouth. "Do you want me to fuck your lovely cunt?"

"I'm not sure we should. This is your wife's bed."

"It's your bed now, you mucky little hussy," he said directly in her ear.

"I'm not mucky," she protested.

"You want a good fucking don't you, Ellie? Eh? A good fucking in your gorgeous cunt."

"I don't like these words, Freddie. It's not what I'm used to."

"What are you used to? Taking it up the arse?"

"What!" she tried to push him away.

"Or a knee trembler. I bet you've had it in a few shop doorways in your time."

"I'm not that kind of girl, Mr Cunliffe."

He was kissing her neck as if she were as consenting and aroused as a girl at her first communion, but when he pulled his finger out and tried to get into position her thighs closed like lock gates against the mounting waters of his urgency.

"Let the dog see the rabbit," he said.

"I might get pregnant," she said.

"It's a risk I'm prepared to take."

"Well, I'm not."

She pushed with all her might against his thin shoulders and he fell to her side. The eiderdown slipped off him and he was exposed, his erection as urgent as a final demand from the gas board. She swung her strong, white legs off the bed and stood up.

"I don't now what you think I am," she said, picking up her pink cotton knickers.

"What are you doing?" he asked, a note of pain and panic in his voice.

"It's time to get back to work, Mr Cunliffe."

She cast a disdainful glance at his cock, as if she were looking at blocked drain.

"Get back into bed," he said cajolingly, "you can't leave me like this."

"You don't even bother taking precautions," she said, fastening her bra. "It's not responsible."

The sight of clothes starting to conceal the beautiful young flesh which a few moments before had been his, made him want to cry and shout. He pulled the eiderdown over his lower half.

"Ellie," he pleaded. "I'm sorry if I've offended you. Don't get dressed. Come on. Get back into bed. I'm sorry."

"I don't want to. I might have done it if you'd taken precautions but now I've changed my mind. Anyway, I'm a virgin and I want my first time to be special."

"A virgin?"

"Don't sound so surprised."

"I'm not."

"You spoke to me like I was common."

"No I didn't."

"You did. All those common words. That's not what I want for my first time."

"That's just love talk, Ellie. Men and women use it all the time."

"Well I don't. It's not love talk, it's dirty. I don't like it. I want a man to respect me."

"I do respect you."

"Why didn't you take precautions then?"

She was pulling on her skirt. The horrible thought occurred to him that never again would he see her naked, that the territory of her enticing soft whiteness, the great, full planets of her breasts would be forever forbidden to his hands and worst of all he'd never slip inside her, never know what the tight, warm softness of her young cunt felt like against his cock.

"You're right. It wasn't responsible. I've got some in the bedside table."

"Too late now," she said like a landlady shutting the door on an unruly guest.

"We've plenty of time."

"That's not what I mean."

"But I love you, Ellie," he said in desperation, yet not even this final, outrageous recourse of male manipulation could soften her. She was fully dressed. She was the Elspeth of the shop, demure and efficient. What he paid her for five and half days a week he wanted her to cast off; he wished her a rampant, sex-fuelled, bed-wrecker; he wanted to hear her glass-smashing cries of pleasure, he wanted to pat her backside as he squeezed past her in the store-room and say: "You're a lovely bit of cunt, Ellie."

"I'll wait for you downstairs," she said.

Getting dressed was a lonely, terrible business. She'd seen his hard cock yet she'd no more wanted to get her hands on it and to guide it inside her than to visit Barnsley and shake hands with the President of the Yorkshire Miners. Now, forever, she would have the edge over him. Whenever he met her eyes he'd know she could see him as he was on the bed and it made him ridiculous. Her body drew him like the sniff of blood a hungry shark. He was completely at a loss. The only naked woman he'd seen was Mary and her body was as familiar as fish and chips. When he was ready for his tea, fish and chips was very welcome, but it was hardly cordon bleu. Ellie, on the other hand was caviar, venison soup, rump steak, strawberries and cream, aromatic coffee and a brandy for digestif. But his body was as easy to resist for Ellie as a greasy spoon full of lorry drivers on a wet Thursday afternoon. What could he do to bring her round? He thought he'd offer her a pay-rise but he'd have to wait. If he did it right away she might take it the wrong way. All the same, he would have paid her three times what she earned if she'd agreed to go to bed with him twice a week.

On the journey back neither spoke. Freddie thought it best to carry on as normal, not mention the failed love-making and wait his chance. The afternoon was interminable. There were four customers. Only one bought anything. At half past four he said:

"You can go early, Elspeth. I'll finish off."

"Are you sure?"

"Of course. Go and enjoy your evening."

That night, as he was fastening the cord of his pyjama trousers Mary said:

"This bed smells."

"What?"

She put her nose to the sheets and sniffed.

"Perfume."

She stood up and faced him, her expression as stern as Abraham Lincoln.

"Must be you," he said finishing his bow.

"Don't be stupid. I know my own perfume."

She sniffed again and he cursed himself for not having changed the sheets. He'd thought it wouldn't matter, as nothing had happened.

"A woman's been in this bed."

She looked at him like a judge at a defendant who has just perjured himself.

"Let me smell," he said.

He nuzzled the sheet like a dog after a bitch on heat. It was the smell of Ellie right enough.

"I can't smell a thing," he said standing up and facing her. "Get into bed and stop fussing."

"You've had a woman in my bed," she said.

He threw back his head and laughed like he did at Ken Dodd on the pier in summer.

"Chance'd be a fine thing. It must be Barbara. She'll've been playing in here."

"Who is it? That young baggage who works in the shop?"

He could have wagged his finger at her for calling Ellie a baggage.

"Elspeth? She's a devout Catholic. She goes to Mass twice a day."

"I've known plenty of Catholics who are no better than they should be. Go and sleep in the box room."

"The box room. For God's sake, Mary!"

But she had a woman's instinct for a lying man and the dogged will to confirm her suspicions of a vigilant busybody. She spoke to the neighbours.

"You may have seen her come to the house with Freddie. She's a nice young woman. Works very hard in the shop."

One after another they showed no hint of recognition until Mrs Totty said:

"Oh, that'd be the lass I saw him with one afternoon. Very smart girl."

Mary questioned apparently nonchalantly.

"You damn fool," she said to Freddie. "Did you imagine no-one would spot you?"

"Spot me doing what?"

"Veronica Totty saw you. She even described the shoes she was wearing."

"Ttittle-tattle," he said.

But he had to leave. He took a dingy flat not far from the shop. He wouldn't let Barbara visit. There was damp in the corner of the bed-room, it was impossible to keep warm. He invited Elspeth round for tea but she refused. He tried to make contact with old mates but they were all married now and no-one was up for his suggestions of nights out or card schools on a Friday evening. Day in day out he was tormented by Elspeth's irresistible physicality. Her breasts seemed ever bigger, her haunches more rounded. He had lost his family because of her. It seemed utterly unjust that he had no access to her, that he couldn't slip his finger once more into that welcoming cleft whose attraction had made him risk everything. One day, in the store-room, she was atop a little set of steps. He went close to her and caught the odour of her cheap perfume. She knew he was there. She reached for something high and her right foot lifted from the step. He took his chance and ran his hand up her skirt. She squealed, climbed down and slapped him hard across his left cheek. The next day she handed in her notice. The winter closed in. He sat before his electric fire wrapped in a blanket. The damp patch grew bigger and when it rained hard, a metronome drip hit the floorboards, and one night, getting up for a glass of water, he found a cockroach scuttling across the kitchen lino.